THE HIDDEN EMPIRE

THE HIDDEN EMPIRE

Howard Lawson and Ron Speers

www.ivyhousebooks.com

Aircraft photos are official U.S. Navy photographs,
courtesy of The Tailhook Association.

PUBLISHED BY IVY HOUSE PUBLISHING GROUP
5122 Bur Oak Circle, Raleigh, North Carolina 27612
United States of America
919-782-0281
www.ivyhousebooks.com

ISBN 1-57197-356-7
Library of Congress Control Number: 2002113544

Printed in the United States of America

DEDICATION

CAST OF CHARACTERS

THE AMERICANS

CDR Deke Mallory, USN	Skipper of a Navy Fighter Squadron
Luisa	Mallory's Spanish wife
David	The Mallorys' college-age son
Nathan Foxlee	President of the United States
Terry Truman	Head of CIA clandestine operations; Advisor to the President
RADM Conrad Frazier	Head of the Navy's Joint Strike Fighter Evaluation Team
Bill Burton	Head of CIA operations in Latin America
Wade Holloway	CIA Station Chief in Costa Verde
Gretchen Reese	A veteran CIA analyst
J. Frederick Cathcart II	U.S. Ambassador to Costa Verde
LCDR Ruth Tanaka, USN	Naval Attache in Costa Verde
Smith	A mercenary fighter pilot

THE COSTA VERDEANS

Ignacio (Nacho) Peralta	The son of Costa Verde's ousted president
Elena Peralta	Peralta's widowed sister

THE COSTA VERDEANS cont.

GEN Francisco Mora	Military advisor to the Peraltas
Diego	Peralta's bodyguard
Carlos	Leader of the Peraltista guerillas
Arturo	A leader of the student underground
Ernesto Subueso	Bishop of Pacifico Provence
Enrique Maldonado	A Peraltista pilot
The Generalissimo	Leader of the military junta
COL Hector Benes	A member of the junta

THE KOHORTE

Werner Tolt	Reichsfuhrer (no U.S. equivalent)
Fritz-Julius Karpf	Obergruppenfuhrer (General), Intelligence Director; formerly of the Stasi (East German State Police)
Karl Kreeber	Gruppenfuhrer (Major General), Finance Director
Heinrich Kaalten	Brigadefuhrer (Brigadier General), Operations Director
Ludwig Staib	Sturmbannfuhrer (Major), assassin
Gerhardt Hesse	A Kohorte operative

THE VATICAN

Antonio Cardinal Guilianni	The Vatican Secretary of State
Monsignor Siegfried Albert	Cardinal Guilianni's aide

ONE

STRALSUND, COMMUNIST EAST GERMANY
1989

The seaman emerged from Der Hafen Hund, a dingy bierhaus below street level near the Volksmarine dry docks on the Baltic. He found his two-wheel pushcart where he'd left it on the sidewalk with one of its bicycle tires wedged among the ornamental iron wickets guarding a nearby tree. He quickly rolled it away from the establishment's dimly lit entrance and up the street where the sounds from inside the bierhaus faded into silence. He paused to retrieve a knitted stocking cap from his short seaman's coat and pull it onto his head and over his ears before proceeding.

The dew point had changed and the cobblestones were slippery. He hesitated at the bridge to the Old City to get his bearings, then crossed and entered the blackness of a medieval street on the far side of a canal. Single dim bulbs lit a few of the intersections, but their faint yellow glow dissipated before reaching the pavement and offered little help in finding his way.

"Our patriotic precaution against air attack," the defiant posters proclaimed, but everybody knew it was to conserve the Deutsche Demokratische Republik's meager energy reserves.

He shook his head and drew a deep breath. The chill of the Baltic air was bracing.

Minutes later, a small, high-arched bridge came into view. It spanned another canal guarded by a dark parliament of weeping willows. He went across, stopping once in the middle to glance about and fix the way in his mind. Not so much as a window candle or crack of light shone among the ancient shops and family quarters. *Good,* he thought. Finally, he found the little iron foot bridge that crossed over an older, narrow canal, and pushed the cart up, over, and down to the other side.

The church was across the street, its front door slightly ajar. *A good sign,* he thought as he entered the nave by the side door. A rack beneath a picture of the Virgin held a mere sprinkling of votive candles. Perhaps a good showing, though, in the Volks Republik, where religion had become more or less a clandestine business. They were close to flickering out in their red glass cups. It was miserably damp in the church, and the cold stilled the characteristic odor he had noticed during his first visit. *Something could be wrong,* he thought, suddenly aware of the utter stillness in the place.

My God, he isn't here tonight?

He felt his way in near darkness toward the confessional, entered it, and drew the curtain.

Minutes passed.

"Aren't you here?" he whispered. "God help me . . . please."

His speech was slurred.

The plea was followed by footsteps on the stone floor and the sound of creaking wood as the priest seated himself and slid the panel open.

"It's me, Father. Zimmermann, remember? The seaman. I came at midnight, as agreed, so you needn't answer to the state."

"You've been drinking?"

"Father, please help my poor confession."

The priest exhaled noisily. "Answer me," he said.

"Some beer is all. I'm all right now."

"Proceed."

"Father, bless me, for I have sinned. Pray God, please . . . to understand."

"Peace! The Lord's peace be with you."

"I have sinned. I'm not acceptable to the Church, not to God in heaven."

"Tell me everything, my son. God is aware."

"I killed three men. I am sure of it. More? I don't know. God knows."

"How could such a thing happen?"

"On our first patrol in the strait. More like sea trials, really. The day was warm, perfect. The sky, sea . . . were bright and soft. Just like happy pictures in a child's book.

"We apprehended a small fishing boat, from Fehmarn, in the Federal Republic. They were definitely within our territorial waters.

"I manned the forward gun," he continued, "a 15 mm. They turned and fled. The captain ordered me to fire when they didn't heed the order to stop."

He swallowed, clearing his throat.

"Father?"

"I'm here."

"I killed these men. I . . ."

"My son, you must . . ."

He bolted from the booth into the shadows across the foyer and hunched there with his forehead pressed against the ancient stone wall. Tremors rippled his body as he sobbed softly.

He was aware of steps on the stone floor coming toward him and soon felt the priest's strong hands grasp him by the shoulders and turn him half around.

"Come back to the confessional, my son. At times like this, it's best—"

The garrote did its work in seconds.

Unbelievably, the young priest offered little resistance once he realized what was happening. His hands dropped to his chest and he crossed himself. Finally, his body twisted to face the altar before slipping to the musty carpet runner. There wasn't any blood.

The killer listened awhile but heard nothing but water lapping in the canal and an old rowboat fretting against the stone quay where it was tied. He took the knitted cap from his pocket and pulled it on. Then he stripped and removed all identification from the body and tugged at the priest's signet ring until it came off.

He poked the ring and the priest's silver crucifix into his pocket, with those of his previous victims.

TWO

USS *KITTY HAWK* OPERATING IN THE NORTH PACIFIC

The icy wind across the pitching flight deck tore at Commander Decatur "Deke" Mallory's craggy face as he fought to keep his balance. He grabbed hold of the boarding ladder on his F/A-18 Hornet and handed his helmet and oxygen mask to his plane captain, Airman Second Class Kosky. Climbing up the port side of the gull-gray Hornet, the lanky skipper of Navy Fighter Squadron VF-263 thought about how many times he had mounted up for a launch—over 800, according to his log book. *Nothing new here except this damn squall.*

In spite of the angry February weather, he still believed carrier duty to be just about the most satisfying thing a man could do. He loved the sea and he loved flying, but the combination of the two for months at a time away from his family had grown stale. He had missed a lot of anniversaries, birthday parties, graduations, soccer games and bedtime stories, and maybe it was time to turn the page on a new chapter. The old thrill was gone, like the head on a flat beer, but you can't just jump ship in the middle of a cruise because you'd like to spend more time with your family. He reminded himself that this was, after all, the life he had chosen, but that didn't make it any easier to live with.

He had achieved the dream of every Naval Aviator, three stripes and squadron command, and it had all seemed to be a foreordained part of The Mallory Legacy. His father, a destroyer XO in World War Two, had named him after Stephen Decatur, the swashbuckling hero of the Shores of Tripoli. His grandfather had been a Naval Academy grad, and a Naval Aviator, and it all seemed to make sense.

Until now.

Legacy be damned, he thought, as he lowered his six foot two inch frame cautiously down into the cockpit, squirming his butt around to achieve a reasonably comfortable relationship with the seat that housed the parachute pack. After all these years at sea he had plenty of salt in his braid, and maybe after this cruise he'd apply for a tour of choice shore duty, perhaps something at the Pentagon or the Naval War College, maybe R & D of some sort. And there was always the option of just retiring and picking up a prime job with a defense contractor. The pay was good and officers of his experience were in high demand.

Yes, he would have to think about that.

As for the Navy, he knew his fitness reports would show him to be a first rate officer and squadron commander. He was also one hell of a fighter pilot. He had no doubts about that. He had earned his stripes and had the medals and TOPGUN credentials to prove it: a Silver Star, two Distinguished Flying Crosses and a flock of Air Medals.

The Silver Star had been awarded for a daring mission in which he had saved his wingman from certain torture at the hands of the Iraqi Republican Guard. Deployed in *Ranger* in the Persian Gulf during Desert Storm, he had flown Combat Air Patrol to cover an EA-6B Prowler on a mission to take out radar stations deep in Iraqi territory. On this sortie his wingman, LT Brian Fiske, took hits from ground fire and had to punch out. In the clear moonlit night the downed American became a prime target for the Republican Guard troops swarming on the desert below, eager to capture one of The Great Satan's pilots.

Mallory had called for the rescue helo as Iraqi troops, supported by two tanks, were advancing toward Fiske. He was carrying two air-to-ground Maverick missiles and he put them to good use in taking out the two tanks.

He relied on his 20 mm cannon to discourage the Republican Guards from getting any closer to his downed wingman. As he fired the last of his 20 mm his radio crackled with information that the helo was due in about five minutes, but he could see that the Iraqis were beginning to close in on Fiske's position. He was out of ammo but the Iraqis didn't know it yet. He swung in for another run and the troops scattered as he went by almost on the deck. He made another low pass, in burner this time, hoping the deafening noise might shake them up. It did, but not for long. Mallory was past Bingo fuel and he hauled ass for the tanker as soon as the rescue helo and more air cover arrived. All had ended well—he had tanked from an Air Force KC-135 and made it back to the boat—but he was met with the ambiguity of a chewing out for going beyond Bingo fuel and a hearty "Well Done" for saving his wingman. Fiske was returned in one piece by the helo and would be buying Mallory drinks for a long time to come.

All good stuff in a fighter pilot's record, especially when nearing the promotion zone for captain.

Kosky climbed up the ladder and helped him strap into the parachute, seat belt, and shoulder harness, making sure that nothing would become entangled during ejection if such a rapid exodus was necessary. Kosky pulled the red-tagged pin from the ejection seat behind Mallory's head and handed it to Mallory, who stowed it in the cockpit. He took his helmet from Kosky, put it on, and plugged the oxygen and communications equipment into the proper fittings. No words were exchanged. Kosky knew better than to say anything when his usually upbeat skipper was in one of his recent foul moods. He retreated down to the deck, secured the boarding ladder, and flipped Mallory a salute.

The only problem with my career, Mallory thought, was that little matter of the Syrian MiG he had encountered flying a routine patrol from the *Eisenhower* on an earlier tour. Fed up with being tracked by Syrian missile batteries while flying boring patrols, like a stupid duck flying past a duck blind to show the flag, something in his "push-the-enve-lope" DNA had taken over and he had provoked a conflict by darting just a bit too close to the Syrian frontier—just for the hell of it—and that had led to an engagement in which a less than TOPGUN caliber MiG pilot had attacked him, only to be promptly flamed into the Mediterranean. Since it wasn't clear just who had violated the other's air space, the matter received the "regrettable incident" tag, but Mallory knew he had pushed the envelope too far. So perhaps his dream of the four stripes of a captain wasn't in the cards after all. He knew as well as anyone that the Navy doesn't promote loose cannons.

The blurry grayness of the early afternoon sun slouching above the angry storm clouds building on the horizon seemed to match his mood, as did the angry seas that were rising by the minute.

He was given the signal to start engines. The two GE 400 turbofans roared to life and gradually settled to idle as he checked his systems. The yellowshirt deck crewman motioned him forward and passed him on to the Flight Deck Officer for positioning on the catapult.

The Grumman E-2C Hawkeye, the "Eyes of the Fleet," with its huge 24-foot, frisbee-like radome, had been launched fifteen minutes earlier to scope out the operating area preparatory to coordinating the intercepts. The Lockheed S-3 Viking tanker was already airborne, as was the Combat Air Patrol of two divisions of F-14 Tomcats, and another S-3 to check on the presence of any Russian submarines in the area. Mallory's flight of four F/A-18 Hornets would be next off the deck, followed by a second division of Hornets. They would join Mallory's division for today's mission, an Air Defense Exercise with Air Force B-52s and F-15s from Elmendorf AFB near Anchorage, Alaska.

Spotted on the starboard bow catapult, he let off his brakes as the nose gear was attached to the shuttle. In his rearview mirror, he could see the ten-foot-high "barn door" jet blast deflector rise from the deck behind his Hornet. As *Kitty Hawk* rose up and plunged from crest to trough through the rough seas, he felt like a kid riding backwards on a 1,000 foot long steel teeter-totter. As the bow rose, he was painfully aware of the ominous, charcoal gray clouds that would soon engulf them. As the bow fell he faced the roiling angry waves spewing white foam over a dark green sea. *Welcome to the notorious "Bering Sea Weather Factory,"* he thought, as he realized that his division was about to be initiated into its mysteries.

The Catapult Officer called for a run-up to full power and waited for Mallory's acceptance of the launch. Scanning his instruments and satisfied he had a flyable bird, he wrapped his throttle hand around the catapult grip, saluted the Cat Officer, and returned his right hand to the control stick. With two fingers pointed toward the bow, the Cat Officer dropped his arm like a karate chop and dropped to the deck to clear the left wing. Seconds later, Mallory crossed the bow at 160 knots and, a few seconds later, his stomach rejoined him in the cockpit.

It takes a while for the human body to catch up with the aircraft on a cat shot.

The weather in the ops area to the east was better, but the final phase of the exercises was cut short due to worsening weather in the recovery area where the carrier was operating. As *Kitty Hawk* recovered her Air Wing, the E-2C Hawkeye picked up a Russian Tu-144 Bear reconnaissance bomber as it flew south from the Bering Sea. Mallory's division was topped off by the tanker and ordered north for intercept, lest the Russians think they could get within striking distance of an American Battle Group unchallenged. Yes, the Cold War was winding down and the wall might come down, but the Russians were still out there, and they weren't on a goodwill cruise.

Four hundred fifty miles south of Adak Island, Mallory peered through the windscreen into the growing darkness and surveyed the bleak expanse stretching north beyond the chain of the Aleutians into the Bering Sea. At 51 degrees north latitude the sun was retiring early, even though it was still mid-afternoon. At 30,000 feet, the sky above was near black and shaded through cobalt blue to lighter blues on the horizon. Beneath the dark cloud layer below them, 50-knot winds were churning the sea into a frenzy. *Kitty Hawk* was almost 600 miles to the south now, encountering even worse weather.

The other three Hornets of his division were strung out to the left in a loose echelon, as he studied the "head-up" display on his windscreen giving the target's range, bearing, altitude, and airspeed. One hundred fifty-five miles to the Russian Bear. He glanced to the left at his flight. The three other pilots were closing up the formation to keep closer station on his navigation lights in the growing darkness.

His second section leader, LT Tom Brady, like Mallory, was a graduate of the Navy's Fighter Weapons School, TOPGUN, and an exceptionally competent pilot, as was his wingman, LTJG Sven Lindstrom. The weak link was Mallory's own wingman, LTJG Donald Egan, fresh from the training command, with a new set of wings and an attitude. Mallory tolerated cockiness in his pilots. It's a macho business that leaves little room for self-doubt, but smart-ass arrogance like Egan's was a different matter. His mother, Representative Margaret Whittle Egan, was a ranking member of the House Armed Services Committee, who could easily become Chairman if the House changed hands in the next election. Egan liked reminding his squadron mates she was Queen of the May in Washington. Observing Egan's lackluster performance during squadron work-ups, Mallory had placed him on his wing, hoping one-on-one tutoring would improve his flying skills.

As they bore through the darkening sky, Mallory's thoughts turned to his wife and kids. Thanks to sea duty he wouldn't be seeing them for months. Yes, he had been to sea many times before. And yes, Luisa had always been there for the kids while he was away, playing both parental roles. And yes, this was the career he chose for himself, but the thought of early retirement seemed to be tapping him on the shoulder like a persistent stag at a dance.

He had met Luisa, from a wealthy Barcelona family, at a diplomatic reception during his first tour of duty with the Sixth Fleet, and they were married the following year. And now Luisa, with fourteen-year-old Laura and twelve-year-old David, was in Central America visiting the family of Mallory's old friend Ignacio "Nacho" Peralta, whose father was the President of Costa Verde. Mallory had known Nacho since flight training days, when the irrepressible Costa Verden had won U.S. Navy Wings as an exchange student pilot while serving in the Costa Verde Air Force. Nacho, his sister Elena, and Elena's doctor husband all lived in the Peralta family compound in the capital city of San Marcos, but for this visit Nacho had promised Luisa and the kids a night or two in the Presidential Palace as guests of his father. Luisa had made sure Laura and David were bilingual, and this would be their opportunity to experience Latin American culture at the highest level of society.

Quite a contrast to my present situation, Mallory thought, as he looked down at the ominous gray overcast that covered a hostile, near freezing ocean. His grandfather had commanded a PBY Catalina squadron at aptly named Cold Bay in the Aleutians during the nine-month Japanese occupation of Attu and Kiska in 1942, and Mallory shuddered as he recalled the tales of duty there. The real enemy hadn't been the Japanese but miserable weather: wind in the face, snow on the ground, ice on control surfaces, and fog on the runway.

He returned to the present, quickly scanned his instruments, and keyed his mike. "Ninety miles to target. Stand by."

The huge, lumbering Russian bombers always shadowed elements of the American fleet when they were in range of Russian land bases, and there had developed a bawdy cultural exchange. At first, flipped digits and insulting hand-lettered signs were offered. Amateur photography flourished and eventually radio exchanges took place in English. At the moment the Bear was paralleling the Aleutians, headed west at its cruising speed of 460 miles per hour. Navy patrol doctrine was to fly alongside for a while, but instead of taking up formation on the bomber, Mallory had prepared some extra entertainment this time. Although his first CO had warned that "free enterprise is the forbidden fruit of military life," he had come to believe a mere nibble now and then was a refreshing tonic for the sometimes boring routine of sea duty. Coming in from behind the target in full afterburner, he planned to suddenly split his division, with two aircraft going on each side of the Russian. After passing close abeam at supersonic speed, they would pull straight up and fan out into a high, air-show-type looping maneuver, then loop back down again and pass across the Bear's flight path, going in opposite directions, with Mallory's section passing directly over the bomber and the other section passing underneath. Having properly introduced themselves as hot sticks and given Ivan cause to wet his flight suit, they would fly along with the Bear to make their mastery of the situation known loud and clear before returning to *Kitty Hawk*. At the preflight briefing they had dubbed the caper the "Busby Berkeley," after the choreographer of Hollywood's 1930s musical extravaganzas, but young Egan was uncomfortable at deviating from procedure. Someone suggested that when he had more salt in his braid he would have a better understanding of these things, but it hadn't registered with Egan.

Kitty Hawk's skipper peered through the windscreen of the bridge at the raging sea enveloping his ship in the gathering darkness. The wipers could barely handle the onslaught of water drenching the ship. "Dammit!" he growled. "What the hell good are weather satellites if Congress doesn't fund enough of them? Do they think we're a tea-cup Navy that never puts to sea?"

The navigator considered his remarks rhetorical and remained silent.

"It's bad enough to have ice on the flight deck," the skipper roared, "eighty-knot gusts with wind chill making the temperature minus forty. But, dammit, where the hell did this King Kong storm that's about to hit us come from anyway?"

The navigator knew he expected an answer this time. "Well, sir," he offered, "weatherwise, we're in kind of a dark hole right now. The last P-3 overflight of this position was five days ago, and we're well beyond reach of Japan's patrol planes or the Air Force at Elmendorf. I guess we discovered this weather all by ourselves."

Captain Conrad Frazier, the Air Wing Commander ("CAG," a designation left over from the days when air wings were known as Air Groups), stormed onto the bridge. "How bad is this crap we're headed into? I have four F-18s aloft, an hour out."

Kitty Hawk's skipper shook his head. "The voice of doom here," he glowered at the navigator, "says things are not good."

The navigator turned to Frazier, furrowed his brow, and tried to smile. "Well, CAG, there was the great typhoon of 1945 and, of course, the flood of Old Testament times." He hooked his arm around a stanchion as Frazier spread his feet against the rolling and pitching deck. "This may be a contender for third place, sir."

"I'm calling my Hornets home," Frazier barked. "They'll need all their fuel to come aboard in this shit."

A ninety-degree turn to the west would put Mallory's flight directly astern of the Bear. As he eased them into a gradual turn and came out on a westerly heading, the unmistakable, gravelly voice of CAG crackled in his headset.

"Three Zero One, this is CAG," Frazier said. "Return to force immediately. I say again. RETURN TO FORCE. Seas are high and the weather is rapidly deteriorating."

"Roger that, CAG," Mallory answered. "We're about to complete the intercept and head for the barn."

"Negative, Three Zero One. The Bear pilot knows you're there. I want your butts back on the deck ASAP. Do you read me?"

"Loud and clear, sir. Three Zero One out."

Mallory considered his change of orders for a moment as he followed the Bear's changing course on the head-up display, and then flashed his navigation lights twice, a signal for the other pilots to switch to a pre-set frequency for secure communication among themselves.

"We'll do the Busby Berkeley bit," Mallory said, "omit the photo-op, then head for the boat."

A "Roger that," sounded in his headphone, as did a "Sound's cool, Skipper," but Egan's uppity voice disagreed. "We've been given an RTF and—"

"That we have, Mister Egan," Mallory answered. "And we will indeed return to the force . . . after we terrify our friends up ahead. As you may have noticed, the target has dog-legged again, this time ninety degrees to the left, which puts him exactly on our way home. Now just slide under my right wing and stay glued to it," Mallory said, "so I can smile at the nice Russian man as we go by."

"But, sir—"

"Stow it, Mister Egan. It's showtime."

The Hornets spread apart for passage on either side of the Bear, following Mallory as he pushed the throttle into full afterburner. Overtaking the huge bomber at twice its speed, they broke into their own private air-show routine, similar to the Blue Angels' "Fleur-de-lis" maneuver. Pulling straight up and rolling to the right into a descending loop, Mallory was pleased to see Egan keeping a fairly close station on his wing. Moments later, after passing over the Bear, he pulled back out of afterburner to allow the second section to reverse course and catch up. They soon appeared off his left wing with their speed brakes out, swinging into a finger-four formation, as he corrected the heading back to the ship.

Scanning his instruments, Mallory contemplated the fuel remaining and scowled as a tinge of concern rose within him. Maybe hotdogging for the Russians wasn't such a good idea after all, since consumption in afterburner could rise by 300 percent. *Relax,* he told himself, if things get really hairy, *there's always the tanker to top us off,* but he couldn't help thinking about the ultimate test of their Naval Aviator's skill looming before them—coming aboard a carrier's pitching deck at night in foul weather.

THREE

STRALSUND, COMMUNIST EAST GERMANY

The handcart rolled easily with the weight of the priest's body centered above its axle. The killer encountered no one as he pushed it along the darkened streets of Stralsund. Passing the bierhaus again, now hidden in shadows, he continued toward the body of water leading to the Eastern Baltic Sea. Minutes later he paused at a traffic barrier consisting of a length of pipe suspended above the road. A sign warned, *IX Flotille / ENTTRITT VERBOTEN*. He slid the cart underneath the crossbar, being careful not to touch it, then ducked under. Electrified fencing on either side guarded the road to the Volksmarine base. From there, locally built Sperber class coastal defense boats sortied to prevent West German, Danish, or Swedish craft from entering East German waters. It was demanding duty, given that only forty miles of the Baltic Sea separated the four powers, and was heavily trafficked.

As he rolled the cart silently down the center of the road, a dimly lit two story concrete building appeared in the distance. It was set at the near end of a half-mile stone quay that served U-Boat training squadrons in both World Wars. Sentries with dogs patrolled the quay and the area where the main structure and its outbuildings stood. The weak perimeter lights, strung above a high chain link fence enclosing the structures, seemed to have reached an impasse with the night.

A sentry's hut suddenly loomed in the darker foreground.

"Gut Abend!" he called ahead in a friendly voice. "I've something here for your commander, *Kapitan-Leutnant* Buchholz."

He could make out a back-lit form, raising a bull-horn.

"Halten!" came the metallic voice.

He raised his hands, palms forward in surrender, and slowly stepped aside from the cart, just as he was caught in the beams of a pair of high-powered lanterns. A second sentry leveled a Russian submachine gun at him, while another approached with a dog.

"What's under the blanket?" the latter demanded, waving a drawn Luger at the cart.

"A dead body," he told him, arms still raised.

The sentry laughed, then stiffened.

"I'm going to blow a hole in you bigger than the dog's head," he warned, "unless you keep one hand in the air, where I can see it, and pull that blanket back slowly."

He did as he was told.

ABOVE THE NORTH PACIFIC

Mallory's headset crackled with the voice of the ship's Air Traffic Controller advising them of twenty-foot seas, violently shifting winds, and extreme pitching of the deck. Mallory bit his lip. Then came the shock; because of the weather, no tanker was airborne to refuel them.

Shit!

The news triggered a flashback to his first cruise when Mallory's division had returned from a mission to find the deck spotted for launch rather than recovery. In the days of straight-deck carriers, it was one or the other, so they had been ordered to orbit the ship until the captain gave the order to re-spot. They had been down to fumes when they were finally given a Charlie. Mallory's close friend had flamed out a mile aft of the ship and gone down with his aircraft. The others had barely made it aboard, with Mallory flaming out on the deck.

His mind snapped back into the present, as something like electricity tingled the back of his neck. With no tanker in the air, the same tragic scenario could easily be replayed right now if wave-offs consumed the last of their precious fuel.

He quickly rearranged the formation, putting Brady first in line to trap, with the least experienced Egan in the Number Two position. Lindstrom would take the Number Three slot, and Mallory would be Number Four. The second slot would give Egan more fuel reserve should he be waved off by the LSO, or have his hook fail to trap and "bolter" for a go-around. As Number Four, Mallory would burn the most fuel while the others were recovered, but as their "fearless leader" he could see no other course of action.

Minutes later they arrived at an invisible point in the sky called "marshal," twenty miles astern of *Kitty Hawk,* and held in a descending pattern until each was given a "Charlie Time" when he would be called down for approach. They plunged down into the angry storm clouds stacked to twenty thousand feet. Brady was given his Charlie Time and called down, flew an OK Pass, and successfully trapped. As Mallory monitored Egan's progress on the radio, he hoped the kid's arrogance would get him aboard in one piece, but a minute later he heard the LSO wave him off. Although the glide slope is gyroscopically stabilized, pilots have a tendency at night to pay more attention to the pitching deck than the Optical Landing System and the LSO's instructions. Egan was obviously "flying the deck," and came in high. Circling for another pass at twelve hundred feet, Egan intercepted the glide slope once again, guided by the LSO, but boltered this time when his hook bounced over the arresting cable. As he went around again, Lindstrom was brought down, flew a smooth pass, but was waved off as a violent gust of wind tossed him left of center. Mallory's stomach tightened with Egan now reporting less than a thousand pounds of fuel, barely enough to go around again if he didn't make it this time. Egan was probably scared shitless, but the LSO, with the calm, soothing voice of an ER nurse, carefully talked him down across the ramp for a successful trap, what would probably be a "fair pass" in the LSO's logbook. A minute later, Lindstrom reentered the approach pattern, flew an OK pass, trapped, and Mallory was called down.

Sweat dampened the insides of his gloves. There was a metallic taste in his mouth, and he could hear his own breathing in his headset. Level at twelve hundred feet, ten miles out, he dropped his gear, flaps and tail hook, and trimmed for landing. The TACAN gear, giving a constant bearing and distance to the ship, showed two miles out when he heard the controller's voice.

"Three Zero One," he said. "You're on glide path . . . slightly left of center . . . correcting . . . good . . . Call the ball."

Mallory corrected and continued peering through the windscreen, searching for the ship's Light Landing Device, port side amidships, a horizontal bar of green lights with the orange "meatball" in the center. The position of the ball with relation to the green bar would tell him whether he was high, low, or on the glide path. A line of droplights extending down over the fantail would indicate his position relative to centerline.

The ship should be there, right now, he thought, as his Hornet hung in the turbulent sky barely above stall speed. Squinting ahead, he strained to see something in the blackness and was about to call "Clara," meaning he couldn't see the ball, when it emerged in the heavy rain.

"Three Zero One," he called instead. "Hornet ball, point eight, REPEAT POINT EIGHT," telling the LSO who, what, and where he was, and how much fuel remained—eight hundred pounds, barely enough for a go-around if he boltered.

One roll of the dice, two at best. *Holy shit!*

But the LSO's response was comforting. "Roger ball. Looking good, Zero One."

Suddenly, the ship's centerline lights burst into view, and Mallory fought the urge to glance at the pitching deck and instead concentrated on the ball.

"Looking good," the LSO repeated.

With no red lights flashing around the ball indicating a mandatory wave-off, he applied full power as he crossed the ramp so he could be instantly airborne if his hook skipped a wire and he boltered. But he trapped number four wire, slamming onto a rising deck, and was thrown forward against his shoulder harness as the Hornet was yanked to a stop in under four hundred feet. He rolled backwards with the rebound of the cable, retracted the hook and was directed by a yellow-shirt to a parking space next to the island. As the plane's two GE turbines spooled down, he unstrapped, caught his breath, and opened the canopy, taking a stinging blast of sleet in his face.

———————

One of the perks of squadron command is a private cabin, however small, and the mixed blessing of a telephone. Mallory's was ringing as he lay in his bunk in a deep sleep.

"Deke, CAG here. You're wanted on the bridge ASAP."

"Sure, CAG." He switched on the bed light. Three-thirty in the morning. He slowly emerged from his bunk, splashed water on his face, dressed, and headed for the bridge in the pale red light aboard ship at night. With the ship still rolling and pitching through a violent quartering sea, he used his hands more than once to ward off bulkheads that seemed to be attacking him from the sides of the passageway. *Why the hell am I wanted on the bridge?* he wondered, preparing for the worst while timing his stride through watertight door openings whose thresholds several inches above the deck were rightly called "knee-knockers." A surreal scenario danced in his mind, and he figured he must have been dreaming when CAG called. The dream sequence involved a flurry of accusations and specifications for a special court-martial for disobeying orders to return to the ship, while throwing fuel management overboard so he could hotdog for the Russians—all of it involving serious goddammits and threats of keelhauling. Even in his half-awake state pulling on his clothes, he was assaulted by images of the Russians protesting his challenge to their right of peaceful passage, and the possibility that Egan might whine to his most Congressional mother.

A tense flag lieutenant met him at the entrance to the bridge and led him to the Captain's quarters where a rear admiral from the Pentagon, who had come aboard at Pearl Harbor, waited with CAG and the ship's skipper.

"I'm Admiral Archer, Commander. I'm afraid I have disturbing news for you. The Pentagon has informed us a civil war broke out in Costa Verde this morning. The worst of the fighting is near the Presidential Palace in San Marcos." The admiral shook his head. "Our embassy has been collecting Americans all morning . . . but they haven't as yet accounted for your wife and children."

Mallory sank back against the bulkhead, feeling like he had caught a flying sandbag in the stomach. An eerie feeling of detachment enveloped him as he realized their dream vacation may have become a death sentence, while he was trapped in the middle of the Pacific Ocean.

"You all right, Commander?" he heard the admiral ask.

"I'm okay, sir," he said quietly, straightening himself. His guts twisted as he realized there wasn't a thing he could do to help Luisa and the children—if they were still alive.

FOUR

STRASLAND, COMMUNIST EAST GERMANY

This is the brig for miscreants here at the Volksmarine base, the killer reasoned. It wasn't much larger than a closet, with a concrete floor, unpainted cinder block walls, and a low ceiling. A simple drain was the only feature of the unpainted floor. A powerful lamp drenched the room in uncomfortable light. He was grateful for the heat, if not its glare, as he sat naked on the sole furnishing, a straight-back steel chair. Obviously, this was a psychological ploy to dehumanize and soften him up, he decided. It didn't bother him; he'd endured worse in training. What did worry him was the awful prospect of facing summary execution should there be a snag in the plan and his rescuer not extract him in time.

There was no way of telling time. It was mid-afternoon the next day, he guessed. *Maybe so, maybe not,* he thought, testing his instincts. He decided to occupy himself making a game of it. Ten till four was his guess, when the scraping of a key in the lock jarred him. The door opened to reveal two men peering in.

"I have never seen him before!" The voice carried a tinge of irritation and belonged to Buchholz, the base commander. The denial was aimed at the petty officer with the keys, who seemed flustered.

The killer smiled. *"Gut Nachmittag, Kapitan-Leutnant,"* he said. "What time is it? Ten till four already?"

Buchholz glanced at his watch. *"Ja!* Almost."

"I thought so," he said, relieved at the officer's diffident manner.

Buchholz grunted and turned to the petty officer. "Scharff, get him some clothes," he ordered, "and don't let him out of your sight." Scharff drew his sidearm and motioned for the killer to precede him down the hall.

Sausages, soup, and beer, service for one, waited on the table. The killer entered and seated himself, taking the soup first. He was alone except for Scharff, who stood by the door. Presently, a tall, gaunt man in civilian clothes entered, trailed by Buchholz.

"I am General Karpf of State Security, in Berlin." A dueling scar rode his high cheekbone as he spoke.

"The *Stasi?"* The killer tried keep a level voice as his heart raced. *My God! What's happened to the rescue plan?*

Karpf's sneer said, yes, Stasi!

"You must excuse Kapitan-Leutnant Buchholz, here," he continued. "He is sorry for your treatment, but he believed you were one of a pair of deserters he's been warned about. He thought you brought in your shipmate's body."

Nice touch, the killer thought, careful to appear impassive as his spirits soared. He knew the plan called for him to be rescued from Volksmarine custody but never imagined that the notorious General Karpf was a *Kohorte* brother and would participate in the mission personally.

"My apologies, *Hauptmann* (Captain)," Buchholz said, "addressing the killer. "You carried no identity card, you see," he added nervously. It was clear he feared the Stasi.

"Leave us," Karpf hissed, and took a seat. When they were alone he leaned forward and squinted at his new charge. Tabling an identity card, without losing eye contact, he slid it toward the killer and withdrew an American cigarette from a slim silver case and touched it to his lip, where it adhered and bobbed up and down as he spoke.

"No doubt Reichsfuhrer Tolt will be pleased with your performance, at least so far, *Herr Sturmbannfuhrer* Staib."

Staib bobbed his head and examined the genuine Stasi identity card bearing his own picture and the name Walter Zimmermann, Hauptmann, Central Bureau, Berlin.

Karpf blew smoke toward the ceiling. "I think you will agree there is no safer way to exit the Volks Republik than aboard a Volksmarine patrol craft!"

"Agreed, Herr General. Did you invent the story about the deserters too?"

"Of course," Karpf grunted. "I had two sailors liquidated just to give it credence. More to the business at hand, however," he continued. "I'm working a further deception on Buchholz."

Staib raised an eyebrow and waited.

"I told him the corpse in question belongs to a traitorous politburo clerk whom you, Hauptmann Zimmermann, tracked down and eliminated. Buchholz is arranging an anonymous burial at sea," Karpf smiled, "as the politburo wants the sordid mess covered up immediately."

"Excellent!" Staib chirped as they stood.

"And now, Staib, are you ready for the remaining challenge of your mission?"

THE BALTIC SEA

The Volksmarine coastal defense boat *Fritz Engel* was headed into the area of maximum international traffic twenty miles at sea. Water washed rhythmically over her deck and rushed from her scuppers as she rose and fell in the greenish-brown deep. The waves ahead were capped with angry white water and contrasted with a dark layer above the horizon, signaling a looming storm at sea. Staib stationed himself behind Buchholz in the partially open wheelhouse, watching the helmsman keep a fairly even keel in the following sea.

"There," Buchholz announced, handing over his binoculars. Adjusting the lenses, Staib spotted a boat in the distance, flying the Swedish ensign and heading home. She appeared to be a commercial fisherman, about a thirty-footer, with a single-diesel stack aft of the pilothouse.

"Two or three man crew," Buchholz said. "Apparently without a radio, as you specified."

The *Fritz Engel* flashed an order to heave to, and the fishermen waved compliantly. As Buchholz prepared to board, Staib rechecked the contents of his briefcase. There was a Swedish passport with his picture, a quantity of Swedish kroner and U.S. dollars, and a loaded Walther PPK, with Schramm silencer and extra ammunition clip. He fondled a small velvet bag, knowing it contained the priests' crucifixes, finger rings, and eyeglasses. He counted four East German identity cards. All were authentic, not forgeries, suitably worn but without the photographs that would be added later when the effects were delivered to the eventual users. He tapped a notarial-type seal—Stasi hardware for crimping photos on identity cards—and ruffled the pages of the priests' Stasi files that Karpf furnished, then snapped the case shut.

Today Staib was Max Jacobson, a Swedish petroleum trader of German origin. Suitable to the part, he wore business attire and a three-quarter-length leather coat.

The sound of parting water merged with gurgling exhaust and the rhythmic popping of the *Fritz Engel*'s diesels, as the sea curled and lapped along her hull. The two craft were held together by boatswain's hooks while Buchholz examined the fishing boat and spoke politely to her crew. Sea birds circled at a distance, diving, rising, and squawking, observant but wary.

Buchholz saluted the boat's skipper and shouted for Staib to come aboard. The fishermen would gladly accept a countryman who was being expelled from East Germany.

––––––––––––

The owner talked incessantly as he manned the wheel. His son and an employee were below tending the ancient three-cylinder diesel. Staib perched behind him on a fold-down seat in the pilothouse and did his best to seem amiable. No, he wasn't related to Max Jacobson, the fishing magnate. Yes, he was of German birth but a Swedish citizen. Yes, the cost of diesel oil should rise, making this a good time to buy a reserve. He was relieved when the man lashed the wheel on course for port and went below.

The sun disappeared into a layer of weather on the western horizon and winked out, but a spreading corona of salmon brightened a few wispy high-altitude clouds and gave light for awhile longer. The wind dropped to a breeze, calming the sea, which now rolled pleasantly and seemed to boost the little boat on her shoulders and pass her forward. It would be easy to shoot the fishermen when tying up at Trelleborg. *No,* Staib decided, *better to do it outside the harbor and row ashore in the dinghy.* There was a limit to what could be planned when operating in the field. He would find a spot where he could land unnoticed after nightfall. *Some things should be left to instinct.*

He smiled as he considered his successful mission. The four priests he murdered were selected for physical resemblance to Werner Tolt, two of his lieutenants, and Staib himself. He personally disposed of three of the bodies and knew the police blotters would indicate they disappeared without a trace. The youngest, his alter ego, was buried at sea from the *Fritz Engel* an hour ago. He had the victims' personal effects, and when their bishops in East Germany received letters apologizing for their defections, the loose ends would come together.

"Here is good Swedish coffee," the fisherman said, returning to the wheel. Staib accepted the cup, sipping approvingly. The lights of

Trelleborg were beckoning as he reached into his briefcase for the Walther. *This won't take long,* he thought, as he attached the silencer.

STOCKHOLM

"My name is Jacobson, Max Jacobson," Staib told the desk clerk at the Hotel Sundsvall in Stockholm. He glanced about as the attendant retrieved a message slip and handed it to him. "You may use the courtesy telephones, sir."

He dialed a Mexico City number and a man answered.

"Jacobson here. I obtained the oil at your price."

"Excellent!" The accent was Bavarian. "How many million barrels?"

"Four," Staib replied, meaning priests.

"Excellent! Now you should visit our man in Rome."

"Agreed. I've booked a flight for this evening."

"Good evening, then, Mister Jacobson. May I recommend the Restaurant Scannia for a fine meal? You've earned it."

"Tack. God afton," he answered in Swedish.

He called the restaurant and made a reservation. Chaining his briefcase to his wrist, he paused at the curb to help a young mother and her brood exit a taxi and ordered the driver to take him to Scannia. He thought he would order sea trout with an expensive 1945 or 1947 Moselle. Then he'd reward himself with a costly bottle of Muscatel Chateau d'Yquem, with cheese, over which he would finally allow himself to unwind and savor details of the deaths of the four priests. He snickered at the theological implications of his victims being resurrected soon in another hemisphere. Recalling how efficiently he had dispatched them brought tingles of the old high he knew so well. It was raining as the cab swerved to the curb a minute later and he paid the fare.

"Valkommen," the maître d' greeted him, bowing gracefully. "I have a nice table for you," he said, leading the way to one near the hearth. "Sorry about the weather, but Stockholm's isn't the best this time of year." He straightened the table setting and stood back and smiled.

"Excellent," Staib replied. "It seems like a lifetime since I've had a fine meal." *Four lives, in fact,* he thought, rubbing his hands together and taking his seat. "But what's past is prologue, don't you think?"

"Yes, of course, Mister Jacobson," said the host, who wondered what the hell he was talking about.

Minutes later the sauterne was served. As Staib sipped the wine, his hand absently slipped into his jacket pocket and fondled the crucifixes.

The thought of further need of his services brought a crooked smile to his face, as the fire flickered pleasantly in the hearth before him.

FIVE

Monsignor Siegfried Albert stared into the small fireplace in his musty office in the Vatican. A quilted dressing gown with velvet lapels drooped from his aging frame as he poked at the dying coals and added wood. A cold rain pelted the courtyard two stories below, as it had all day. *Take this cup from me,* he prayed. *If possible,* he added, paraphrasing Christ. An elderly, trim six-footer with thin strands of hair slicked across his shiny pate, he was born to a stonemason and char lady employed at Cologne Cathedral, where he attended catechism class and sang in a boys' choir. So far as the Church knew, he escaped military service in Nazi Germany and fled to Rome in 1944, taking holy orders as soon as he could qualify academically and canonically. His gift for adminis-tration, and sound judgment in delicate matters of church craft, caught the eye of a then young Bishop Guilianni—now Antonio Cardinal Guilianni, the Vatican's powerful Secretary of State.

The diminutive Guilianni was known throughout the Church as the Little Pope, for good reason, since he exercised virtual autonomy over many departments within the Vatican, far more than Secretaries of State traditionally oversee. Albert served as the Cardinal's longtime personal assistant, and the two usually thought as one, sometimes speaking only the beginning of sentences to each other.

Oh, my God! Albert muttered, as he dropped into his swivel chair and spread his palms on the desk. *How could this evil have returned to torment me? After all these years!*

The scene was burned into his brain as if it happened yesterday, not decades before. In his mind's eye he was a twenty-two-year-old SS-trooper again, scrunched in the rear of a Fiesler Storch observation plane taking off from a road near the collapsing Western Front. He was an officer's orderly, and the man was sending him on a secret mission.

"Good luck, Corporal," the officer shouted through the Plexiglas canopy, as the pilot revved the engine. He wore the full-length black leather field coat favored by the SS, and cupped his hands to punch out his words over the roar: "This isn't the end. Our little Kohorte will rule the world one day. You will be reactivated."

As the plane taxied, Albert read his lips: "Excel at priest craft, Corporal!"

The plane flew south for hours and discharged him in a meadow in Northern Italy after dark. In Rome he used his real name and cathedral upbringing to gain admission to seminary. He buried the awful story of his SS career—they were veterans of the death squads—in the deep vaults of his subconscious. Over the years he as good as forgot his role of "sleeper" agent at the Vatican, and that the time might come when the Kohorte would activate him.

The Corporal Albert of old never imagined he would embrace God, but unaccountably, supernaturally, Christ became as real to him as the bricks and mortar of the seminary buildings themselves. Though unable to make a proper confession, he repented, or thought he had, supposing that somehow a gracious God could forgive and forget.

The evil was all behind him, in a different life.

Until now.

Well, the way out is obvious, he reasoned. *I'll obtain Vatican citizenship for the murdered priests, as the Kohorte demands. . . . Enabling a few aging former*

SS men to live out their lives in peace isn't such a bad thing . . . sinful, yes, but it's not like I'm going to deny Christ. . . . Besides, the truth would destroy the cardinal, even tarnish his Holiness the Pope's reign.

He suddenly realized what underlay his rationalization: he held a lifetime sinecure, rating quarters here at the Vatican, but God knows in what kind of hell he'd spend his remaining years if he were found out.

Monsignor Albert was a moral coward, and he knew it. The SS-Oath Unto Death was suddenly more real to him than his weak faith. Nothing to do now but comply with the demand whispered by the Kohorte agent who contacted him. His mind made up, he happened to glance at the window. The rain was heavier and the wind was picking up. A blowing leaf stuck to the glass momentarily, and then was gone. He winced as the symbolism struck him.

He tried to recall Staib's appearance. Short, stocky was all he could summon. Something about the man's eyes, though. Albert had seen lifeless eyes before, in the death squads. Staib had assassin's eyes.

He rose and moved to the hearth again, pausing with a short poker in his hand, confronting the unwilling fire. He had successfully stalled the Kohorte off for months now by pleading Vatican red tape, but he sensed that he could do it no longer. Known to the Cardinal's staff as "The Hammer" for the rapidity and force of his words, Albert was feeling anything but strong as he gazed vacantly at the flickering flame. "Forgive me," he whimpered, "for what I must do."

A moment later, he nudged the poker onto its hook in the nest of fire tools at his feet. His fire had just died.

He was suddenly aware of Guilianni hesitating in the doorway. "Are you well?" the cardinal asked.

"Why, yes," Albert managed. "Perhaps a little tired," he added as cheerfully as he could.

"What was it you wanted to see me about this morning," the Little Pope asked, "when I was summoned to the Holy Father's apartment? I thought perhaps it shouldn't wait."

"No, Eminence, it can wait, unless—"

31

"Very well," Guilianni offered, "let's dispose of it now, if we can."

"It's come to my attention, Eminence, that four priests have some-how managed to escape East Germany. They're in Mexico City now, living in squalor."

He motioned toward the electric teapot. Guilianni nodded yes, he'd take tea.

"They need to be placed," Albert continued, pouring and handing the Cardinal a cup. "And I think Vatican citizenship could be in order."

Guilianni frowned. "Vatican citizenship requires very unusual cir-cumstances, as we both know, especially for nonresidents. Were you thinking of moving them here?"

"Oh, no. Latin America," Albert said. "Their case for citizenship is a strong one, I think. Consider the repressive nature of the East German regime, their service to the poor in Mexico City and—"

The cardinal held up his hand. "I gather your mind's made up, old friend," he said. "But, let's face it, you're reaching for straws. You might as well cite Trotsky's case!"

For once Albert couldn't tell if he was serious or mildly sarcastic.

"Leon Trotsky," Guilianni continued, "Stalin's nemesis, murdered in Mexico City in 1940 by Kremlin agents, for the sin of having defect-ed, no doubt. The Church mustn't allow such a thing to happen again, so the argument might go."

Albert was nonplussed, a rare occurrence, Guilianni knew. The Little Pope stepped to the window, leaned his elbows on its broad sill and peered into the night.

"Empathy for your countrymen, I suppose," he sighed.

Albert nodded. "Eminence, I'll leave this to your prayerful consid-eration and unfailingly sound discretion."

Guilianni turned to face him, the relaxed slump of his shoulders telegraphing his accession to Albert's wishes.

"No. Prepare the necessary documents and I'll sign them immedi-ately. That should make quite a present," his eyes sparkled, "for our four German brothers."

"No, Eminence, you should follow the prescribed—"

Guilianni's small hand swept the air gracefully, like a conductor inviting his first violin to take a bow.

"Well then, in that case, you—"

Albert finished the sentence for him, "may commence an investigation concerning the possibility of Vatican citizenship. Yes, Eminence, I'll do it in the morning."

Guilianni nodded and returned his cup to the table, closed the heavy oak door to Albert's office with the merest click, and was gone. His light footsteps receded down the hallway and the room fell silent, except for the blowing rain pelting the tall leaded glazing.

Albert's spirits suddenly soared. He could put it about that the Little Pope was giving the matter his *placet*—"it pleases," Vaticanese for "approval." Lesser lights, though bound to diligent inquiry themselves, wouldn't challenge him by giving their *non-placet*.

As he was tidying up, Albert remembered that this was the week of Fuhrer Tag—Hitler's birthday—and that he had bent to the will of the man with assassin's eyes. He shuddered and sat down on his bed.

Well, he thought after a few moments, *he won't kill me as long as he thinks I'm making progress on obtaining the passports. Yes, that's it. I must show Staib a little progress here and there . . . while protracting the process as long as I possibly can. But what about afterward?*

He recalled Christ's saying that each day has enough trouble; not to worry about tomorrow, that tomorrow will take care of itself. He tried to take comfort from this, but he found that the dull fear remained in his heart.

SIX

THE PERALTA FAMILY COMPOUND
SAN MARCOS, COSTA VERDE

Luisa Mallory was flattened by the concussion from a round fired from the main gun of a tank. Knocked off her feet to the floor, she lay on her back in a bright apricot silk dressing gown, her eyes and ears filled with plaster dust and the acrid sting of cordite in her nostrils. Swirling dust and something like an electric field filled the room in the Peralta family compound in San Marcos, and it seemed to her a granary filled with grain dust exploded. The round blew out the room across the hall where her daughter Laura was sleeping barely moments before, when she darted into her mother's bed, wild-eyed and afraid.

"David!" Luisa screamed. "Where's David? Where's my son?" Her mouth was too dry to enunciate. She gathered herself, stumbled to her feet, and flew toward the maid, who also picked herself up but fled wild-eyed, without answering.

"Mom, I see six tanks! Six tanks right there, right there in the street out front!" came David's voice from behind the heavy drapery, in which he'd wrapped himself, as if not to be seen is the same as being safe.

Luisa grabbed David and yanked him and Laura into the bathroom and locked the door. She tried to rinse her mouth with tap water, but the flow stopped before she could.

"But, gee, Mom—"

"Quiet!" Luisa clamped her hand over David's mouth, her eyes flashing like a cornered animal sorting its remaining choices.

BLAMMMM! BLAMMMM! CRACK!

A panel of the door near the lock split open to reveal the stock, then the snout of a heavy automatic rifle. The gun barrel withdrew.

"No, God!" Luisa cried. "Oh, God!"

Soldiers kicked in the door and dragged the three of them back into the bedroom, forcing mother and children to lie on the bed face down while they talked excitedly among themselves. Minutes passed. Luisa's eyes flashing at her children kept them silent. No more firing. The soldiers broke out a bottle of rum and passed it among themselves. Eventually the breeze picked up, dispersing the smell of gunpowder but not the acrid scent of smoldering lumber from across the hall, or the odor of the soldiers' sweaty, rum-splashed battle fatigues.

Her mind turned to the fate of Czar Nicholas, his wife and their children, who were shot by their captors after a period of house arrest following the 1917 revolution in Russia.

Two or three hours passed, during which the soldiers were relieved by an officer wearing a freshly pressed uniform and sunglasses, who announced himself as a captain of the army of "Libertad" and permitted them to stretch themselves and sit on the bed instead of lying on it. He was accompanied by a muscular young soldier who stood by the door dangling an Uzi in one hand. Luisa's efforts to elicit information from the captain were fruitless. It was hard to tell his politics, if he had any, but one thing was sure: the Peraltas were being overthrown and he was with the overthrowers. And he and his superiors obviously thought she was a Peralta, if not by name then by some relationship of blood or marriage. Hers and the kids' Castilian Spanish, and their Latin appearance, cemented the impression in the captain's mind.

Three sharp reports, sounding like pistol shots, came from what Luisa assumed was the driveway outside. The captain went to the window and peered down.

"The fool shouldn't have tried to run," he observed to no one in particular and returned to his post by the door, where he sat in a chair to watch them again. Later, a higher-ranking officer poked his head into the room, looked them over, and said something to the captain. Luisa thought she heard "these can be moved tonight, with the others from the Palace." *Oh, God!* she thought. *They're going to kill us all.* She had no idea what happened to Elena Peralta and her husband, Roberto, but guessed they were in custody here or elsewhere. Nacho had left for Paris the day before the coup and was presumably safe, but the cause of President Peralta was precarious, if not lost, according to her captor and the voices she heard in the house.

As time passed, she heard a variety of sounds, from rifle and machine-gun fire in the distance to the crackle of a field radio right outside, presumably mounted in a tank or vehicle, and the shuffle of soldiers' boots on the tile floors of the halls. Once, a male voice laughed derisively from the direction of the room Laura had occupied. Luisa tried not to pay attention as she mentally reviewed what she could remember of the floor plan of this, the main house in the Peralta family compound.

She thought about the view from the bathroom here on the second floor. Two blocks away was the American Embassy and sanctuary. She had seen the flag flying there last night. The Embassy was American soil, guarded by U.S. Marines and backed by international law, as well as the resolve of a nation of people who didn't take to being pushed around by rogue states, great or small.

Occasionally, a helicopter thumped overhead or a flight of jets screamed nearby, headed somewhere.

Suddenly, she knew what she was going to do. They would flee over the rooftops at last light, and dart the two blocks through the bushes to the embassy. *Better to be killed fleeing than to be shot against a wall, like the Romanovs,* she decided. She prayed, and she asked God, and Deke, if it was the right thing to do.

L'Audace! Always *L'Audace!* she recalled Mallory telling another fighter pilot in some officers club somewhere, *Pax River, maybe,* she thought. Mallory had quoted George Patton quoting Frederick the Great about the need for audacity, she knew, but audacity was her husband's hallmark too.

L'Audace!

The sun settled over the western hills minutes later. The sky was turning a strange greenish purple in the gathering darkness.

"My daughter has to go to the bathroom," Luisa announced sweetly, as if considering nothing more important than filing her nails. "I'll take care of her there for a minute," she said. "Now David, you stay right here with the nice captain," she told him, in Spanish for their captors' benefit. "*Uno, dos, tres,* David," she added, with a preemptory wag of her finger, the way she might order a dog to "stay."

"*Sí,* Mama," David answered, as he suddenly brightened. The captain nodded and lit a cigarette. The soldier sighed and shifted his weight.

It was a game they played when Laura and David were little. *Uno, dos, tres* was the count that signaled a head start in their games of hide-and-seek. Only this time, David knew exactly where to find his mother and sister. A minute later, when she slipped the window open and lowered Laura a few feet to the tiles of the roof outside, Luisa cracked the broken door a few inches and poked her head into the bedroom. She smiled at their captors.

"We'll be just a minute more," she told them. "But, I'll need my purse, I'm afraid." Turning to David, she gestured toward the dresser. "Bring it here to me, son."

"*Sí,* Mama," David said, in the singsong voice of a dispirited but obedient child.

He found the purse and shuffled to the bathroom.

THE AMERICAN EMBASSY IN SAN MARCOS

Luisa ducked behind the ficus hedge fronting a palatial residence across the street from the embassy. It was a night of dancing shadows, with a bright moon sporadically breaking through a heavy cover of moving clouds, only to be blocked out again. She could see Laura and David inside the American compound, and it gave her heart peace and joy, despite her jeopardy at the moment. The bathroom ruse worked to perfection. She cranked out the large iron window frame and held Laura's wrist until her toes reached the tile roof below. From there Laura scampered barefoot along the ridge to a giant banyan-like tree and thence to the ground. David followed. Luisa told them to speak only Spanish, wave happily at the soldiers they saw, and make their way like they were kids from the neighborhood enjoying the excitement of the moment. Mercifully, David was mostly dressed and Luisa left a pair of her shorts and a top in the bathroom, which she was able to pin about Laura. Then she had taken off her apricot-colored silk gown, balled it around a bar of soap to weight it, and thrown it as far out onto the back lawn as she could manage. She watched from behind the shower curtain as her decoy worked.

Bursting into the bathroom, the captain saw the open window and her gown on the lawn and screamed for the soldier to follow, as he raced down the hall to the stairs.

She took the maids' stairs to the laundry, found an old raincoat hanging there, and crept into the night. Once outside the Peralta compound, she darted across lawns, crouched under bushes, and crawled through the thick ficus hedges predominating in the neighborhood, until reaching this vantage point so near but so far from ultimate safety. The sights and smells along the way shocked and traumatized her. She encountered at least a dozen bodies in the streets and on the lawns she traversed, some scorched, others full of holes, caked with blood, many of them civilians. She was startled at the sight of one in particular, a young woman dangling from the driver's door of a Mercedes that looked something like Elena's. She mumbled a prayer for Elena, wondering if she were even still alive. None of this was observable from the bathroom window, or she wouldn't have had the courage to launch her children on their way alone.

Luisa's heart leapt as some soldiers at the street corner a block away began firing their weapons, apparently into the air. Were they celebrating their victory or were they drunk? Her heart felt a stab as David came to the fence almost directly across the street from her, as if in response to the firing, and called out "MOM!" as his frightened eyes searched the night. Laura soon joined him, and they sat down on the damp grass to wait.

The huge compound behind her was reachable and was possibly an embassy too, Luisa thought, but she couldn't be sure in the faint moonlight. The only real light was provided by the headlights of army trucks rumbling by in twos and threes every few minutes, and a small bonfire the rebel soldiers built in the intersection a couple of hundred feet away. She quietly brushed a mosquito and began sorting her options. Enter the residence on the lawn where she was, in which case she could be refused asylum, or make a dash across the street, where she might be shot in front of her children, or wait, and wait. She let the next mosquito begin biting her and squashed it while it was busy. The oversweet smell of franjipani mixed with night-blooming jasmine was heavy in the air. A bright nylon American flag hung listlessly from a pole over the door of the embassy, illuminated by a couple of small spotlights. Within the American compound, surrounded by a high wrought-iron fence, she could see dozens of people, including children, milling about in the tropical night air, as if attending a cocktail party. Despite their good spirits, their impromptu get-ups said they were refugees who fled there without much warning. A woman in a white terry bathrobe, who was drinking coffee from a paper cup and talking animatedly, caught her eye, as did a man wearing a USC football jersey over pajama bottoms and wingtip shoes without socks. From the look of the crowd inside the fence, she had the impression that those who sought the sanctuary of American soil that day included some supporters of

President Peralta, perhaps even members of his government. She thought she recognized Finance Minister Tito Garza, who she met as a dinner guest of the Peraltas. Their presence in the American compound accounted for her immediate problem—a cordon of anti-Peralta soldiers, spaced twenty feet apart, standing at parade rest with their backs to her facing the embassy. They carried assault rifles. She could smell their sweaty bodies from her hiding place in the hedge.

Across the way, Marines in dress uniforms stood guard at the embassy gate. In an apparent gesture of peace, they weren't armed. She could see others, however, in battle gear on the roof. Laura and David huddled together and looked asleep now, as best she could see.

Soon, she thought, the revolutionary soldiers would certainly stand down or be replaced by others. Any moment they might spot her here in the shrubbery.

Her lips moved in silent prayer. *Tell me what to do now, O God. Please help me to know what to do!*

Moments later she struggled to her feet and rubbed a cramp that suddenly tore at one of her calves. She tightened the raincoat about herself and pushed through the chest-high hedge where she was crouching. There was no sidewalk, so she advanced to the concrete gutter where the macadam of the street met the lawn. She could almost touch the nearest soldier now. She heard him breathing. He stood just beyond reach to her left; another, fifteen or twenty feet to her right. She stood still a moment, a quiet poise settling onto her shoulders. No one saw her. Thank God the civilians who were there for excitement were milling around the bonfire down at the corner.

L'Audace! Yes, but what would it be in this situation? she wondered. What was the most unexpected thing she could possibly do? Suddenly, it came to mind; she knew what she would do now. She stepped between the sentries and strode to the middle of the street, moving easily, with the grace of a jungle cat. There she stopped and turned to face one of the startled soldiers. He was maybe nineteen, she guessed.

41

"Buenas Noches, mi hijo!" she called in a friendly voice, and advanced to plant a kiss on his cheek and hand him a sprig of jasmine. He lowered his rifle to accept it. The officer in command ran toward her but stopped short and yelled for his troops to hold their line. He glared at her with an expression that seemed to combine a frown with a tentative smile. Apparently, he was more than a little flustered and trying to decide what he should do next. She smiled brightly and blew him a kiss.

She began clapping her hands, slowly, rhythmically, until some people at the embassy heard and turned to look. Soon all eyes were on her. Turning her back on the rebel soldiers, she began to sing in a clear, melodious voice:

> "I'm a Yankee Doodle Dandy
> I'm a Yankee Doodle Girl
> A real live niece of my Uncle Sam
> Born on the Fourth of July"

People within the embassy compound began clapping. The man in the football jersey stirred them up, made them sing along. Moments later, Luisa strolled past the Marines and through the embassy gate to safety, where she was tackled by Laura and David on the wet lawn, and the three of them hugged and hugged and rolled over and over, squealing like five-year-olds.

SEVEN

NEW YORK CITY

Terence "Terry" Truman crouched on the edge of the rear seat of a taxi as it crawled slowly along West 87th Street in residential upper Manhattan late at night. He strained to see through the slapping windshield wipers as he searched the house numbers on the row of old brownstones. As if the chilly rain weren't enough, the street lights were out here in the middle of the block and contributed to the foreboding appearance of the deserted sidewalk and doorways.

"There!" he said, pointing at the number on one of the buildings. The cabbie braked hard, jamming Truman's ribs against the front seat. He got out and paid the fare just as a deluge soaked his shoes and cuffs. He held his hat down on his head, ducked into a doorway, and consulted his watch as he waited for the rain to abate. 12:10 A.M.

Truman was in his late fifties, a lithe six-footer who moved with the assurance of a man used to the corridors of power. The evening in New York with his wife tonight was more or less a bust. Their theater trip always had a way of defaulting to his career. This time she had the foresight to bring a novel, and she reached for it when the phone rang in their hotel room as they returned from the show.

The rain let up some and he crossed the street. He wasn't expecting shots in the dark or the *paparazzi,* but caution was indicated in his work. His card read "Central Intelligence Agency, Assistant Director, Department of Finance," and he worked at cultivating the image of a bureaucrat nearing retirement. It was cover: Truman was in charge of all clandestine operations and had been for years, though only four people knew it—the Director of Central Intelligence, the actual finance chief, the Senate Intelligence Committee Chairman, and the President—not counting the former Presidents.

He punched the bell and the door opened.

"Evening, Mister Truman," the man said, quickly identifying Truman's bushy eyebrows and trademark bow tie.

"I'm Harrison, sir. Remember me?"

"Of course, Bert. Been a while though."

Secret Service Agent Harrison had the duty tonight, and it showed in his swiveling eyes and catlike gait.

"He's in the kitchen, Mister Truman. Sorry about the hour. You know how he can lose his sense of the clock."

"Right." Truman followed him down the hall.

Richard Nixon stepped from behind the kitchen table with a scotch in his hand. He wore a navy silk Chinese gown, pajamas and leather slippers. He put his hand on Truman's shoulder and looked at him earnestly. The familiar physique had shrunk with age but Nixon looked fit. His brown eyes shone with curiosity as he studied Truman's face.

"Good to see ya, T-Square," he said, in the indelible Nixon voice, guiding Truman to a chair. "How about a chicken sandwich? Made it myself. There's cold beer. Want a scotch, instead? Harrison, I don't want anyone within earshot. Secure this end of the house and leave us awhile."

"Yes, sir,"

Truman took in his surroundings. The rumors were true. Nixon had taken up gourmet cooking. The kitchen befitted a *Cordon Bleu* chief, except the cookware was mostly Chinese. The former President was prone to inviting a half dozen notables, often ones he hadn't met, for intimate Chinese dinners he prepared himself, to pick their brains and so keep up with current views and information.

"I'm not hungry, but I would enjoy a drink with you, Mister President. It's been a long time."

Nixon's mobile face lit up, and he smiled.

"Scotch it is, then. Black Label on the rocks, as I recall?" he said, selecting the bottle for Truman's drink.

"There's no need to call me 'Mister President,' when I'm in the doghouse."

Truman had wondered what his feelings would be when encountering the ex-President the first time since he left the White House in disgrace. To his surprise, they were warm. The man was humbled and was paying his dues again, with dignity. It felt right to be drinking with him.

"A man who loves his country enough to resign when he ought to isn't in the doghouse, Mister President."

Nixon's eyes softened. "Thank you," he said quietly.

Truman tasted his drink and was going to express condolences for Pat's death when Nixon reached across the table and placed a hand on his arm.

"I'm worried about Edwardo Peralta, you know," he said. "Good friend of America, Peralta." His voice carried conviction, and his countenance was serious, like Truman remembered him in the Oval Office. "Damn fine man, Peralta is, a family man," Nixon continued. "And one helluva sports fisherman too, let me tell you." Nixon stared into middle distance. "Spent some of the most peaceful moments of my life aboard his yacht off, what's it called, Puerto—no, Bahia Pajaros. America needs to save him, any way we can."

"Too late," Truman told him. "The coup succeeded. Drago, the upstart army sergeant who led it, occupied the Presidential Palace in San Marcos as of a few hours ago. He's declared martial law and proclaimed himself Generalissimo. It's all but over down there."

"Damn!" Nixon muttered, holding up his hand as if it were a claw. "I was afraid of that. Just how bad is it?"

45

"About a hundred killed," Truman told him. "Most of the officer corps just stood aside, watching, while the corpulent former sergeant took over."

"Well, politics ain't bean bags," Nixon said. "I guess it goes doubly for coups."

"That's right," Truman agreed. "The brass taking a powder, though, tells me all I need to know about Drago's coup. Obviously, the skids were greased with payoff money."

Nixon seemed lost in thought. "It didn't make the press," he said, as if he were thinking out loud, "but Edwardo came here to see me just last year, after he visited the White House. Sat right in that chair you're sitting in now. Brought his son Nacho along, Edwardo did, just the two of them. He told me he considered me his friend, no matter about the Watergate thing. Invited me for fishing, and I was planning on doing it too, this year."

Truman waited as Nixon seemed to sort his memory.

"Young Nacho used to come to the White House, you know," Nixon continued, "when he was attached to their embassy. He'd call and then drop over when Pat would be asleep or out of town. I encouraged it too. I think he thought of me as another father. Not having a son of my own, I enjoyed his company and what he'd say from the perspective of youth. We'd have a drink or two, and then he'd be gone, so as not to impose. He always had some kind of a gift, usually some of their family's rum. Once he brought me a stuffed marlin I caught from Edwardo's boat.

"There was a young naval officer too, friend of Nacho's. They'd gone through flight training together. Let's see, what was his name? Maloney? No. Mallory, that's it. A Lieutenant Deke Mallory. He came a couple of times with Nacho. Seemed a little embarrassed to be drinking with his commander-in-chief, I guess, but I liked him. Impressive young man, Deke Mallory, and a damn fine counterweight to Nacho's party-animal side."

"Nacho Peralta," Truman told him, "is in Europe and wasn't caught up in the coup."

"Well that's good," Nixon said. He turned his palms up. "Well, can we at least get Edwardo out of the country?"

Truman checked his watch. "The plane carrying him and his wife should be on the ground in Madrid now," he said.

"Courtesy of Air America?" Nixon chuckled, meaning CIA's clandestine air ops.

"Right, sir. Actually, a chartered Grumman Gulfstream this time, with Air America pilots."

The ex-President sighed. "Good man though he is, Edwardo didn't keep his guard up, did he?" Nixon's jowls flopped as he moved his head side to side. "Got to keep your guard up in politics, like prize fighting, you know.

"T-Square? May I still call you that?"

"Of course."

Truman thought his tone of voice waxed conspiratorial. "I hate the goddamn CIA, T-Square."

"Okay," Truman parried.

"I suppose you know it, T-Square. And it isn't just the CIA, it's any of these goddammed intel smart-asses. I don't trust what they tell me. Don't trust their ability. Don't trust their motives. Never did. Not after they screwed Jack Kennedy that way over the Bay of Pigs, and still swore up and down they gave him good advice."

Nixon spread his hands on the table. "I never let the bastards do that to me, you know. But, I trust you, T-Square," he said. "Always trusted your wisdom, ability, lack of any improper motives. You served my administration well. I'm sorry I never bestowed the Medal of Freedom on you, while I was in office."

It was a nice compliment, though Truman had served as National Security Advisor to other Presidents and would probably get the medal anyway one day. Since it wouldn't do to acknowledge a spook in a

President's inner circle, he'd served anonymously, when the billet was supposedly vacant.

Nixon shifted on his wooden chair. "You're the only intel man I trust," he said. "That's why I had them call you tonight, when I found out you were right here in town at the Pierre. Good hotel, the Pierre. Lived there myself a couple of times." He topped off their glasses.

"CIA's gone right to hell in a hand basket, all over again, T-Square, though I don't expect you to comment, of course." Nixon swirled his scotch. "The President fired the acting Director last month," he continued. "Another scandal, a mole they didn't find before this *New York Times* guy breaks the story. Imagine that! Some smirking reporter's a better sleuth than our friggin' CIA Director.

"Congress wants to close down the whole operation," he growled. "The CIA, that is. That young Senator from California? What's his name, Foxfire? No, Foxlee! Why, hell, Foxlee's really got a burr under his tail about it this time. He thinks the CIA's become an unregulated government within the government. The little bastard's right, too. He's a comer, T-Square, you mark my words."

He tilted the bottle, but Truman declined. The bright kitchen lighting seemed to etch the furrows on Nixon's forehead more deeply. "You see," the ex-President said, "I'm stuck on a couple of points, I don't mind telling you, for the new book I'm writing. They have to do with the future of Central America, now that the Sandinista situation has been resolved. Well," he continued, "I'm betting you're onto the same things I see in today's picture, and I wanted to kick it around, just the two of us." Nixon studied Truman's reaction. "Know what I'm talking about?" he asked.

Here was a chance, Truman realized, to explore his own uneasiness about events in Central America, particularly Costa Verde, the unscratchable itches of his own intellect that occurred in private moments. Nixon was all ears tonight, and the man was a great geopolitical thinker. Truman decided to get Nixon's reactions.

"The hardware that's still parked in Nicaragua," he said. "That's what's got your attention, sir."

"You're damn right. Makes no sense in terms of communism, which is what it was supposed to have all been about in the first place." Nixon waved his hand in disgust, "You know, comradely aid to the Sandinistas, and all that crap-ola. Tell me, T-Square," he said, draining his glass, "how've you doped it out?"

His take, Truman said, on the interminable skirmishing between the Reagan-backed Nicaraguan Contras and the communist-sponsored Sandinistas was that it bored the American public stiff. They understood the danger of direct Soviet intervention in Cuba, ninety miles from Florida, but didn't follow the ball when the Kremlin pirouetted and began using surrogates in Central America—Cuba to supply manpower, and East Germany to funnel massive arms shipments.

"Pirouetted!" Nixon cried. "That's it exactly!" he said, standing and throwing his arms upward and out in the famous Nixon victory salute. "Oh, they simply pirouetted," he said, and whirled around in his mandarin robe.

Nixon sat down and cocked his head to one side. "Those armaments," he said, "are the elephant in the parlor nobody wants to acknowledge."

"The real elephant," Truman said, "is the overkill they represent. They're the heaviest available—long-range field artillery, main battle tanks unsuited to the terrain." "What do you make of it all, T-Square? What was the real purpose of that incredible arms build-up?"

The sound of a downpour intruded on their conversation, and they stopped to listen. Lightning as white as strobe lights lit the kitchen for several seconds, and when the thunder claps came, they sounded like aerial bomb blasts. Truman evaluated his own thoughts. Troubling questions were suddenly nagging him again, as he sat at a kitchen table with the country's foreign policy oracle.

Who could profit from bleeding East Germany white, as it was getting ready to implode any day or week anyway? Truman decided to reveal his inner thoughts to the master geopolitician. "I can't shake the thought," he said, "of something more sinister than a last-gasp Soviet policy being the reason for the gargantuan shipments of hardware originally intended for a massive European land war."

"Then what's the hidden agenda?" Nixon asked. "Whose agenda? Who's going to use the stuff, with what troops?"

"I don't know the answers to your questions, sir," Truman admitted. "The whole thing has never made any logical sense—unless you start thinking a little crazy," he said. "Unless you start thinking out of the box. Rest assured, though, Mister President, I'm damn well going to find out, because a lot of that hardware is being maintained in battle readiness by the current, supposedly friendly Nicaraguan government. At least, the State Department thinks they're friendly."

"You're not so sure?" Nixon asked.

"Not really," Truman said, draining his glass.

Nixon stifled a yawn. "The Secret Service fellows will get you back to the Pierre," he said, standing. "Thanks for coming here, on this Edgar Alan Poe kind of an evening. Poe lived just a stone's throw from here, you know."

"Glad I came," Truman said.

Nixon led the way down a hallway toward the back door. He suddenly stopped and took hold of Truman's elbow. Up close, standing in the dim light, Truman thought he looked much older, and definitely needed a shave and haircut.

"Army sergeants," Nixon said, "don't end up atop the military hierarchy, unless there's been a popular uprising to turn the social order on its head. No sign of that, though, in Costa Verde. Right, T-Square?"

"Exactly," Truman agreed. "With the officer corps going along the way they did, I still think this was sealed and delivered with outside money, though they're trumpeting it as a grassroots thing, of course."

"You don't think a foreign power is behind it?"

"No," Truman said. "This isn't the work of any other country. I'd know if that were the case."

"So who's the culprit, then?" Nixon queried.

It flashed in Truman's mind that the scene here was a dreamlike experience. He recalled Poe: *all that we see or seem is but a dream within a dream.* He dismissed the thought of shaking himself to make sure he was really closeted with Richard Milhous Nixon in this hallway in the middle of an electrical storm. He decided to say what his instincts told him.

"Nazis!" he said.

"NO!" Nixon was flabbergasted. His head jerked about and his lips moved silently as he searched for words with both of his hands in the air. The idea apparently hadn't entered his mind and had slammed him in the solar plexus. He began to scratch his cheek.

Truman guessed Nixon was mentally disemboweling his Nazis-under-the-bed theory. He regretted it the moment he said it. "There're lots of Nazis, and neo-Nazi groups, these days," he parried, "in Europe, South America, even America. Some of these Nazi covens have tons of money."

In fact, nothing suggested Nazi involvement in either the Sandinista buildup or the coup in Costa Verde—no supporting logic, no evidence whatever. It was intuition, a kind of spiritual prompting, that set off Truman's alarm system. He could sense Nazi fingerprints the way forest animals sense danger, without sight or smell.

"Goddammit, I hate Nazis," Nixon growled. "Commies are bad, but Nazis are the embodiment of evil itself. You must root them out. Find and destroy them before they multiply."

"I'll do my best, sir," Truman said, a little surprised at the vehemence of Nixon's reaction.

The former President extended his hand. "You've given me much to chew on. I hope you'll forgive the eccentricity of an ex-President who rousts people at night, but . . . ," he smiled, "you were in the neighborhood."

"Good to see you, sir," Truman said.

"Good night, Mister President," he called, as the old man padded away, his leather slippers making a sandpapering sound on the hardwood.

He seemed frail all of a sudden, and Truman wondered if he would see Nixon alive again.

The ex-President suddenly stopped and turned around.

"Nazis? Hell, T-Square, suddenly these ideas of yours are scrolling around in my mind like great banks of tuna in mid-ocean." He gave a salute that was somewhere between a military gesture and a Papal blessing.

"Whatever else, T-Square, you follow those instincts of yours that serve our country so well."

Truman made the decision to transfer Wade Holloway, his best Latin American station chief, from Nicaragua to troubled Costa Verde as soon as possible. Getting it done without a flap was going to be touchy because Bill Burton, Holloway's immediate boss, was nonchalant as hell about the coup, as if nothing bad could happen to *Pax Americana* on his watch.

Dream on, Truman thought, as he wondered what kind of a malignant dream within a dream was metastasizing down in Costa Verde.

EIGHT

MEXICO CITY

Werner Tolt contemplated the twilight skyline of the smog-bound city from the terrace of his forty-first-story penthouse above the Paseo de la Reforma. It was a far cry from the pure air of his native Bavaria, but this was where his destiny had taken him. He smiled as he savored the anonymity he had achieved here in the Mexican capital, essential to his far-reaching scheme, the major elements of which were in place. No one in the megalopolis stretching in every direction knew him for who he was, one of the ten richest men on the planet and the undisputed leader of a secret hierarchy known to its power elite as the *Kohorte*.

At a towering six-seven, with straight black hair and ramrod posture, he bore his sixty-nine years well, with the driving energy that would enable him to carry out a cabal that he visualized on a Napoleonic scale. *Reichsführer* Tolt was pleased with himself and excited about the future. Returning to the seating arrangement on the terrace, he stood facing one of his sycophants. Heinrich Kaalten was seated patiently in a lounge chair.

"Brigadefuhrer," Tolt beamed, "I want you to know how pleased I am that your mission went flawlessly."

Kaalten basked in the compliment. "Yes," he beamed, "you may activate the master plan now whenever you wish."

Tolt dropped into a chair. "I will, soon enough, yet it seems like only yesterday that Hitler was so good to me."

Kaalten had heard Tolt's story many times, but his face never showed it. He swished the drink in his hand and waited. If it was ambrosia to the Reichsfuhrer to tell it, the brigadefuhrer didn't mind, and maybe most of it was true. But he couldn't help wondering how much was made up, for Tolt had changed his name since his days in the SS.

"I delivered maps to the Fuhrerbunker one morning near the end," Tolt began, "when the Fuhrer called me to his quarters and launched a verbal rampage against his generals. `The disloyal fools don't deserve to carry on my legacy,' he roared. `However,' Hitler continued, `I have observed your loyalty and discipline, Tolt.' He spoke with me as a man speaks to his friend. `You, Tolt, will serve in their place after my death. You will lead my SS Kohorte.'

"Hitler informed me what I should have known from a dictionary: a kohorte was a band of soldiers, a unit of three hundred men in the Roman legions. The secondary meaning of 'accomplice' was acquired later. The Kohorte would perpetuate his *Kampf.*"

Kaalten tried to catch nuances here that might be different from previous versions of the story.

"Even as Eva Braun sat on the sofa filing her nails, and his shepherd dog Blondi sniffed at my boots, Hitler shuffled to a wall safe and withdrew a briefcase.

"'I promised the German people a Thousand-Year Reich,' he lectured, `but I never claimed it wouldn't hang by a thread at times.' The Fuhrer banged his fist atop his desk. `A thread, Tolt! A people's struggle can take lifetimes. My struggle must continue when I am gone. Do you understand, Tolt?' he suddenly shrieked."

The Reichsfuhrer fixed Kaalten with his gaze as if expecting him to answer Hitler's question, too. The brigadefuhrer nodded eagerly but inwardly he was unsure. *Was this gospel of Tolt's just bunkum? No way of telling*, Kaalten decided. Tolt was simply larger than life.

"Well, Heinrich," Tolt continued in his seductive way, "Hitler opened the briefcase, and I was delighted to see that it contained hundreds of cut diamonds. `Finance my Kohorte with these!' he ordered me."

"How magnificent!" Kaalten offered, "to receive gems worth millions!"

"It wasn't the first time," Tolt snapped, "that I knew financial power." He rose and began to pace. "Hitler couldn't know about the fortune I made by cornering Berlin's black market in fuel that winter. My fortune was already safely tucked away in Switzerland."

Kaalten raised his eyebrows. This was new material, he realized, so he decided to pander. "And since that day so long ago, you have acquired major industrial holdings in a dozen population centers around the world. Today the Kohorte is a major economic entity, truly a hidden empire.

"Still," the brigadefuhrer continued with a wave of the hand, "we've long since discarded Nazism, as such."

Tolt stopped his pacing. "Absolutely!" His eyes narrowed. "Nevertheless I shall continue to preach Nazism the way false teachers wield the Bible for their own profit." Tolt templed his hands in mock reverence. "There being no dearth of mulish thugs in the world, why not feed them the slop they like? Harness them to our objectives?"

Viktor, Tolt's dour-faced, mountainous bodyguard and butler, appeared and announced the arrival of former SS General Klaus von Keitel. Whether von Keitel had actually been an SS-general, as he claimed, or was related to Hitler's armed forces chief of staff, was murky. Tolt knew for sure but wouldn't talk about it. The fact that von General, as Kaalten and others called Keitel behind his back, was useful to him was all that mattered to the Reichsfuhrer. And von Keitel, who liked to create the impression he was Tolt's Deputy, had settled into a high-priestly role as keeper of the glorious heritage of Hitler's SS—the dreaded unit that was cloaked in quasi-religious ritual and charged with protecting the Fuhrer's person. As rumor had it, von Keitel knew some dark secret of Tolt's, which was the cause of an ill-defined tension existing between the two.

"Some of us," Kaalten ventured, "think von Keitel fails to comprehend what the Kohorte is all about, that he's overly enamored of his various gangs of jackbooted morons."

Viktor returned with the general, a wiry, diminutive man sporting the classic belted black leather overcoat once favored by the Gestapo, which he seldom removed. Von Keitel stepped forward, clicked his heels, and gave the Nazi salute. "Reichsfuhrer! I just came from Chicago, where I created apparatus to link together all the major neo-Nazi groups in North America."

"Good evening, Klaus. Have a seat, enjoy a cigar from Viktor's tray," Tolt said, waving him to a chair.

"*Nein!*" von Keitel snapped, waving Viktor away.

Tolt bristled. "I thought I had made it clear that we converse in English, the *lingua franca* of the global economy I am maneuvering to control from behind the scenes."

"Relaxation is difficult these days," von Keitel said, "knowing how far we two have grown apart concerning the mission of the Kohorte. Despite my knowledge that others were better suited, the Fuhrer passed his mantle to you, Tolt. And what have you done about restoring the Thousand-Year Reich? What about your SS Oath Unto Death? Your loyalty to the Fuhrer? What has happened to your beliefs?"

Tolt's lips pursed as he regarded the birdlike man. "You're forgetting, Klaus, that profit is power! We have had this discussion before, and I am beginning to lose patience." He punched out his next words. "ONE, I no longer consider any oath I took to be binding. TWO, my loyalty is no longer to Hitler but to myself. THREE, my beliefs are well defined. Nazism, fascism, communism, they're irrelevant now, just like

Christianity. But I shall succeed where Hitler failed, by manipulating the global—"

"Outrage!" von Keitel screeched, leaping from his chair. "Nazism dead? Have you gone mad, Tolt?"

"Do you know Shakespeare, General? 'Though this be madness, there is method in it.' I assure you, there is much method in my madness."

Von Keitel's knuckles rippled within the black leather gloves he hadn't removed. "There's been a turning point with you, Tolt. Just what heresy has beguiled you?"

For some reason—perhaps because it felt pleasantly dangerous, like high-stakes wagering—Tolt for once opted for candor. "You see," he snarled, advancing to tower above von Keitel, "you are a fool whereas I'm not." The general's pickled-onion eyes bulged with hostility as Tolt unloaded. "Perhaps, Herr von Keitel, it is your upper-class background that causes you to live in the past. Otherwise, you would comprehend that Nazism is reduced in practice today to the tawdry religion of street gangs of smelly criminals."

Ignored by the other two, Kaalten cringed in his chair, and it crossed his mind that von Keitel hadn't a concealed weapon, else he would use it on the Reichsführer.

If Tolt was aware of the shock in von Keitel's eyes he never showed it, but drove his point home instead. "I don't buy Nazism any longer, you damn fool!" he exploded. "I peddle it! I finance your currying the thousands of faceless, jackbooted thugs the world over who crave a modicum of status." He relaxed and placed a hand on von Keitel's shoulder. "Don't you see, Klaus? All this widely publicized Third Reich nostalgia today, well, it's just a means of controlling the cretins who buy into your slop!"

Wordless sounds issued from von Keitel's throat as he slapped Tolt's hand away and seemed to flail his arms like an enraged bird.

Tolt shrugged. "Well now, Klaus," he said, "perhaps I was a little too harsh with you just now." He indicated the open double doors of his penthouse. "If so, the fine dinner Viktor is preparing for us, preceded by some of my 1954 champagne and caviar, Giant Beluga caviar, should restore the proper balance between us. After all, haven't we both pulled together harmoniously these many years?"

Von Keitel backed out of Tolt's space a little, as Tolt guided him toward the railing with a comradely hand again placed firmly on his shoulder.

"Come now, Klaus," Tolt offered. "Let us both try to get a hold of ourselves, shall we? Then after dinner I shall reveal the true brilliance of my plan."

They stood at the railing where a soft breeze was flowing in the gathering darkness, as Tolt gestured out over the city. "See, there is Chapultepec Park, and right there is the palace where Maximillian and Carlotta lived," he said, pointing to the west. As the little general followed with his eyes, Tolt reached down and grabbed the rear of his coat with one hand, its collar with the other, and launched the little man out into thin air.

Von Keitel's screams faded as he plummeted hundreds of feet toward the busy street below.

"Goodbye to our ersatz general!" Kaalten crowed, as they entered the penthouse and approached the bar.

Tolt corrected him. "More than that, goodbye to our pretense of loyalty to the past!"

He nodded toward the railing outside. "Sadly, a suicide, due to all the open windows downstairs."

"What about the neo-Nazis and Skinhead gangs he fostered in Europe, the UK, the States, and here in Latin America?" Kaalten asked. "They're all chafing for action."

"Zeal can be put to good use," Tolt said. "Von Keitel's deputies will accept the challenge."

Tolt smiled as he took the bottle of champagne from its ice bucket and produced two glasses. He loosened the cork, which fired off like a cannon and bounced off the ceiling.

"That may not be the shot heard around the world," he observed, obviously delighted with the sound, "but it will be heard in some unsuspecting places."

Kaalten touched his glass to Tolt's. "To our empire, then!"

A Mona Lisa–like expression appeared on Tolt's lantern face, or so it seemed to Kaalten.

"To *my* hidden empire!" Tolt corrected him.

NINE

Mallory took the Interstate 5 off-ramp onto the Coronado Bridge spanning San Diego harbor in a high, gracefully curving arch, glad to be driving Luisa's yellow Mustang convertible with the top down. He filled his lungs with fresh sea air and glanced down at the shimmering waters, host to every conceivable kind of watercraft: sailboats, power boats, fishing boats, and a variety of gray naval vessels. A commercial jet on final to Lindberg Field cautiously wove its way above the forest of tall office buildings in downtown San Diego to the right. Coronado, with the quaint, historic Hotel Del Coronado and the Pacific beaches of the Coronado Strand, lay just ahead.

His decision to retire a few months ago had been a good one. His daughter was married and lived in Texas, his son was at UCLA, and he realized that if he were now deploying for another WestPac cruise, Luisa would be a very lonely Navy wife rattling around their home in La Jolla all by herself for the next eight or nine months.

Yes, he had made the right decision. He was married to Luisa, not, like some of his old shipmates, the Navy. It had been a good career, one that he could be proud of, but it was time to turn the page to a new chapter in his life. He would miss flying and he would never be an Air Wing Commander, but he had been a squadron commander with three stripes and now he would be able to sleep in the same bed with his wife every night for the rest of his life.

This would be his first visit to the Officers' Club at Naval Air Station North Island since his retirement party. Civilian dress was quite common at an Officers' Club in the evening, and his present attire of blue blazer with miniature gold wings in his lapel, striped tie and gray slacks would blend right in. The difference was that tomorrow he wouldn't be in uniform and morning muster would be with Luisa at the breakfast table.

He thought about the call he had received from Mel Peters, his old squadron XO. Mel had the squadron now and was about to deploy in *Kitty Hawk,* which was in port for perhaps the last time. As one of the few remaining nonnuclear-powered carriers, she was due for reassignment to nuclear-free Japan after home porting in San Diego for more than two decades.

"Hey Skipper," Mel had said on the phone, "the drinking lamp's lit this Friday at 1700, and I'm buying whatever you're drinking these days. Make sure you get that civilian butt of yours over to the O-Club. You copy? Otherwise, if you're a no-show, I'll just have to assume that waltzing lookie-loos around town is more exciting than having a drink with your old shipmates."

Mallory smiled. He wasn't going to miss this, he thought, as he gazed from the concrete ribbon high above the surface of the water and was able to pick out *Kitty Hawk*'s island superstructure rising above the yellow buildings at the quay wall at the far end of North Island. He was happy for his old XO's rise to squadron command, and he figured Mel would surely finish up as a four striper and maybe even get a couple of stars before retirement. In the meantime, Mallory was glad to be seeing him again, a welcome counterpoint to the take-no-prisoners world of real estate brokerage.

He braked at the toll booth on the Coronado side of the bridge, paid the toll, and drove through the familiar residential area to the main gate, where a Marine sentry in combat fatigues noticed his retired officer's parking decal on the windshield and passed him through with a snappy salute and a "Welcome to North Island, sir."

The road circled the runways counterclockwise, winding a couple of miles past various newer buildings set among those from the World War II era and before, when the sole runway had merely been a huge circular apron of concrete. The road ended atop a slight hill overlooking the southeast end of what was the main runway, not a popular one with local pilots, who as soon as they left the deck had to wrap their aircraft into a tight left turn to avoid flying over some retired admiral's house on Point Loma to the north.

He parked in the lot fronting the Officers' Club, a pleasant-looking, mustard-brown 1930s affair of indistinct Spanish-Moorish architecture, topped by a red tile roof. As he climbed the concrete steps to the entrance, a Lockheed S-3B Viking anti-submarine plane approached for a landing. From the distinctive, whisper-whine of its engines that sounded like a vacuum cleaner, he identified it without looking around. Hoover, of course, which was the fleet's nickname for the stubby plane.

Mel Peters was presiding over a large table near the bar. A quick glance told Mallory he knew most of the other officers at the table, but he found it difficult making his way there, as he was stopped time and again by former shipmates and acquaintances wanting to say hello, shake his hand, and ask how he was doing.

After a round of drinks and some banter at the table, catching up on everyone's activities and their flying stories du jour, Mel asked him to step outside to the tiled terrace for a private chat. They picked up another round at the bar and found a place outside where they could lean against the rail and talk privately.

"I want to know how you're really doing, Skipper." Mel asked. "Seriously."

Mallory collected his thoughts. It wasn't clear cut in his mind. He hadn't yet concocted a pat answer to the question everybody kept asking, ever since his decision to hang up his flight suit.

"Seriously, Mel, I'm doing fine," he said, "but I'd be lying if I told you it's real easy to slip right into civilian life after the kind of adrenaline levels you and I maintained for so many years." He tasted his drink. "Fact is, though," he continued, "retirement is a part of service life, I guess. Everyone has to face it sooner or later. Maybe sooner is best, when you're a little younger like me. Maybe not. I don't know."

"Yeah, that makes sense," Peters said. "I don't know how I'll handle it when my time comes. Anyway, I just wanted to know how you were doing and how you were handling not pushing the envelope all the time. We'll be under way in a couple of days, won't be back for the usual nine months, and I didn't want to sail away into the sunset without knowing if you were really up to the rigors of civilian life on dry land." Peters smiled. "I understand it can be pretty rough on an old salt like you."

"Thanks, Mel," Mallory said. "I'll do my best and try to bear up."

Back at the bar, Mallory felt a hand on his shoulder. He turned around to see his old Air Wing Commander, Conrad Frazier, smiling at him.

"Commander," Frazier said, addressing Peters, "may I commandeer your old skipper for a few minutes?"

"Be my guest, Admiral," Mel said. "But you should know that Mister Mallory here has achieved celebrity status somehow and expects people to buy him drinks these days."

Frazier laughed and guided Mallory to an unoccupied table in the corner.

"I'm buying this one," Mallory said, "in honor of your two stars."

Frazier grinned. "Right," he chuckled. "Far be it from me to argue with civilian control of the military in such an important matter."

Mallory caught a waiter's eye and pointed at Frazier and himself. "The admiral will have a Bombay Sapphire martini, straight up with two olives," he said, "and I'll have a Glenlivet, neat."

"Good memory!" Frazier said. "And my memory's pretty good too. You were just Four-O when we served together, Deke, and I haven't forgotten. I had a meeting at ComAirPac today and I heard you'd be at this watering down, so I thought I'd drop in and have a little chat about the Navy's participation in the new Joint Strike Fighter Program."

Mallory looked blank for a moment. "I know a little bit about it, I guess. Should I know more?"

"Yes, Commander, I think you should," Frazier said. "I know you're retired now, Deke, living the good life in La Jolla. Hell, maybe that's what I'd be doing if I were in your shoes, but I'm not. I'm still strapped in, not in the cockpit where I'd like to be but in Washington, in charge of creating the protocols and building a team for the Navy's part in testing Boeing's and Lockheed's JSF prototypes when they're rolled out mid-year 2000. It's going to be a big job, and the winner probably won't be selected until 2002. That's where you come in," Frazier continued. "I can use your experience and expertise as a civilian on my team. I know you took early retirement to spend more time with your family, but I think you and Luisa would enjoy living in the Washington area, perhaps in Virginia, where I live now."

Mallory was caught off-guard. As their drinks arrived he tried to think how best to respond to this out-of-the-blue proposition. "This is a real compliment, sir," he said. "I really appreciate it, but I've got a good life here, sir, playing golf and tennis, swimming at the club whenever I want, catching a wave or two, and selling some real estate now and then."

"When you see the specs on these new birds," Frazier said, pulling some documents from his attaché case and giving them to Mallory, "selling real estate will seem about as exciting as tic-tac-toe. You have all the qualifications for what I have in mind," he continued. "I've recently re-read your Officers' Service Record. You had a good balance of sea and shore duty, a good combat and command record, including

Command-at-Sea, four rows of merit badges, including a Silver Star, two DFCs, and a flock of Air Medals. And you've flown McDonnell's recent stuff: the Phantom and the Hornet. McDonnell is part of Boeing now."

"They're real good birds."

The admiral set his martini aside. "Damn it, Deke, you've a master's degree in aeronautical engineering from MIT, for crying out loud. You've been at the Pentagon before and know the pecking and pissing order." He leaned back in his chair and studied Mallory. "I'm sure you've learned how to deal with incoming waves of bureaucratic bullshit."

"Yes, Admiral, I've been there and done that, but you should know one thing about me. I have a tolerance level for bullshit of just about zero."

Frazier laughed. "That's what I like about you. We're definitely in the same percentile." He leaned forward across the table. "I'm offering you the opportunity to come aboard as a civilian on my staff and get a taste of the absolute ultimate in aviation experiences. There's plenty of time for you to wrap things up around here. You and Luisa could come back east next week, find a nice place to live, then come back here and sell or rent your house."

Frazier ordered another round as Mallory brooded and tried not to show it. In spite of his excitement about the opportunity, he realized he was mentally inventorying reasons that he shouldn't take the job. He sighed and handed the papers back to Frazier. "It's a real honor to be asked, sir, but I have to say that I'm really happy enjoying life with my wife. I'm not sure I'll ever get over that time aboard *Kitty Hawk* when Luisa and the kids were in Costa Verde in the middle of a bloody revolution while we were bobbing around in the middle of the North Pacific. It's supposed to be the other way around, sir, with the fearless warrior doing battle and the faithful family at home worrying about him."

Frazier slowly nodded his head. "Yes, I remember."

"Admiral, I appreciate your offering special duty to an old salt, but I think I'll play out the hand I've got."

"I think I understand how you feel, Deke, and I knew this wasn't going to be an easy sale. But think about it, will you?"

"Yeah, I will, but don't get your hopes up, sir."

Frazier nodded. "That's all I ask. But you should know one thing about me too." He popped an olive into his mouth. "I'm a persistent devil, remember?"

TEN

WASHINGTON, D.C.
1999

St. John's Episcopal Church is an attractive brick-and-cream Colonial structure located across Lafayette Park from the White House. Every President since 1815 has attended, some regularly, occupying Pew 54, marked with a plaque as "The President's Pew." Most Americans have seen pictures of their favorite First Couple strolling to services there, accompanied by the Secret Service, White House Press Corps, and the usual bevy of photographers.

Sunday mornings in downtown Washington are nearly devoid of traffic, especially in winter, although today was bright and clear with the temperature in the low fifties. Terry Truman found a parking place on 16th Street almost in front of the church. His wife Sarah was quickly out of the car and waiting as he joined her on the sidewalk. They were early for the second service and went to the basement parish hall, which was packed with people chatting animatedly over coffee. Except for the institutional floor covering, bulletin boards, and the china cups and saucers in everyone's hands, the scene was much like a stand-up cocktail party.

Sarah disappeared into a crowd of friends as he hung their coats. This was their customary entrance. He was an infrequent churchgoer and didn't mind people assuming golf was the reason. Once he had invited Father Tom, the rector, to a member-guest tournament at Burning Tree to reinforce the impression. Besides, Truman was Roman Catholic; she was the Episcopalian. In any event, his Sabbath distractions were serious national security matters, not golf or denominational differences.

He exchanged small talk with acquaintances until people began guiding each other toward the stairs leading to the sanctuary above. Then he approached the coffee table, where a lady wearing a Hospitality Guild name tag was seated by an impressive antique silver service he hadn't remembered seeing, a recent bequest to the parish, he guessed.

She poured regular coffee, added a dash of cream, and handed him the cup. "Sorry, it's the dregs, I'm afraid," she said, "and none too hot."

"Doesn't matter," he said, accepting the cup, "I've already had my quota." Truman knew there could be but one reason for her calling to inquire if he might be accompanying Sarah today. It had happened before when there was something she thought too sensitive to discuss at the office. They had worked hand-in-glove for decades, and St. John's was her meeting-place equivalent of the proverbial park bench.

"What's the good word, Gretchen?" he asked, selecting a cookie.

Gretchen Reece was a formidable intellect, with iron-gray hair and a precision mind. She had joined the CIA in the early days, when she was one of a bevy of administrative assistants in daily contact with Director Allen Dulles, until his retirement. He was her hero. As far as she was concerned, the course of intelligence was downhill ever since. Now she was in charge of vetting high-level personnel for the Company, and she knew everyone's secrets.

"Oh, just boys being boys," she said pleasantly. Truman was startled. "Boys being boys" was Gretchenese, and it meant she suspected someone of being a mole or double agent. *No wonder she picked this place,* he thought, where the risk of even electronic eavesdropping is next to nonexistent.

"Really?" he inquired, as if enjoying pleasantries. An usher swept by, reminding them the service was about to commence. "Yeah, right," Truman called over his shoulder.

"It's Billy Burton, this time," she purred, reaching for her coat, as Sarah headed their way. Burton was in charge of the Company's activities in Latin America.

The news hit Truman like a karate chop to the neck.

"Hmm," he said, trying to get a grip, while his mind stalled at the idea of Burton being disloyal and seemed to go blank momentarily. Bill Burton had been an usher in the Trumans' wedding, when they were all in their thirties, years ago, and Truman regarded him as one of his closest friends. Burton was already a flourishing agent in London when Truman's first boss moved from the Department of the Navy to the CIA as an Assistant Director and brought his administrative assistant, the hard-working "T-Square" Truman, along with him. Truman's rise within the Company was another story, turning on his ability to quickly cut through a complex situation and articulate the bottom line, while others were still bogged down in detail or off on tangents. That and a willingness to risk his career time and again on the correctness of his own analyses. While Burton shone in the field, drawing increasingly important assignments, Truman became "Mr. Inside," guiding successive CIA Directors and Presidents with his incisive judgments.

Gretchen made no bones about disliking Burton and they clearly had a personality conflict, yet Gretchen was a professional's professional and he never knew her to be in error when questioning someone's loyalty. But he couldn't help balking at the notion of Bill Burton being disloyal. *It can't be,* he thought, as Sarah joined them and they headed up the stairs for the service.

"How about brunch?" Sarah asked, as they joined the line waiting to greet the rector following the service.

Gretchen beamed. "Love to," she said.

"Sure," Truman added. "Why not the Hay-Adams?"

His mind raced with questions about Burton as they crossed 16th Street to the Hay Adams Hotel facing the church and Lafayette Park. He shepherded Sarah and Gretchen into the smallish, dark-walnut paneled lobby. As they checked their coats and took the carpeted stairs to the second floor dining room overlooking the park and White House, the leaden feeling knotting his stomach told him that the last thing he could tolerate right now was the sight of food.

After years as wife of America's top spymaster, Sarah knew how to read his mood and how to handle herself at such times. After they were seated at a window table and placed their orders, she excused herself to go to the ladies room.

"Okay," Gretchen said, leaning closer to Truman. "Wade tipped me off last month, when he was here, so I began a thorough work-up." Wade Holloway was station chief in San Marcos, the capital of Costa Verde, and worked directly under Burton, who was based in Mexico City. Burton's purview was all of Latin America; Holloway's was Central America. Interesting, Truman recalled, as Gretchen paused for effect, that Burton had objected when he insisted on transferring the very able Holloway from Nicaragua to Costa Verde following the coup against Peralta.

"Next," Gretchen purred, "is a real gem from the Jeweler." The Jeweler was a former Stasi bureaucrat who now lived in a lakefront estate in Zurich. He had cunningly privatized his Stasi operation after the Wall came down and set up shop in the West. A blind chain of Swiss and other bank employees the world over fed his computers information, capitalizing on the fact that banking transactions are electronic nowadays. Each link knew only one or two of the others, and hardly any of them knew the Jeweler even existed, much less his identity. For a hefty price, the Jeweler could determine the owner of a numbered Swiss account and trace the actual source of money deposited to the account. If the name of the game was "follow the money," the Jeweler was its reigning Grand Master. If he reported that Mother Teresa had diverted funds to a secret account for Saddam Hussein, it was probably true. Needless to say, the Jeweler sold his services to anyone able to pay for them and was suddenly very rich. Actually, exposing the ownership of a numbered Swiss account was a simple matter, Truman knew. Numbered accounts are secret only to the lower levels of bank management. It was the Jeweler's capability of tracing the origin of funds that was his unique contribution to the black world of intelligence.

"Billy's the proud papa of a brand spanking new Swiss account," Gretchen announced. "There's almost four hundred thou in it, and I've got the access numbers, too!"

"So who's paying Bill off?" Truman asked.

Gretchen rearranged her silverware. "The Jeweler said the money came from the G-mo," she told him, meaning the self-proclaimed Generalissimo of Costa Verde.

The cryptic exchange told Truman all he needed to know in order to give the matter his urgent attention. *By God! I'm damn well going to get to the bottom of this personally,* he told himself.

"But Bill?" he protested. "I still can't—"

"I've nailed him, fair and square," she said.

Truman knew that "fair and square," in Company practice, meant she would have developed at least three separate strains of evidence supporting the conclusion that Burton was a traitor. Truman mentally reviewed the bidding. First, the tip from Holloway, which he sure as hell wanted to know a lot more about. Second, the Jeweler's evidence. Impressive, but circumstantial. *What other evidence does she have?* he wondered.

"Third?" he asked pleasantly.

"Third, is the source of the G-mo's own abundant wherewithal these days. I'm afraid I've busted your budget this time, T-Square," she said, "but the Jeweler came through in grand style."

She smiled as a waiter hovered to top off their champagne. Truman caught sight of Sarah entering a phone booth in the hallway outside. *Good, she's making use of the time to call her mother or one of the kids,* he thought.

73

Gretchen paused while the waiter moved out of earshot. "The G-mo gets his from the Kohorte," she said.

Truman's mind spun as the revelation blindsided him. As far as he was concerned, the Kohorte might as well have floated somewhere between Saturn and Uranus—ephemeral, part myth, part gauzy Hitlerian legacy. All he actually knew was it was supposed to be some kind of secret businessmen's society of obscure origin and purpose, if it even existed. Nothing was documented, he realized, just something in the files about an elusive, supposed multibillionaire, a murky figure if there ever was one, who was thought to be its leader, and entries about suspected members being sympathetic to various neo-Nazi causes. *It was all confined to Western Europe,* he thought, *until now.* In fact, the information from the Jeweler was the first hard evidence suggesting the Kohorte was real.

"Find out the Jeweler's price for a full financial report on that bunch," Truman told her, as Sarah strode toward them. It angered Truman to cozy up to the ex-Stasi ferret in order to get the information he needed, but no one else had a network of banking interconnects like the Jeweler's. He reached across the table and touched Gretchen's wrist. "Hell," he said, "if the sonofabitch says he can do it, pay whatever it takes to lay the Kohorte bare-ass naked."

Light snow was falling as Truman headed west on K Street. He turned north on Wisconsin Avenue through Georgetown, on the way home to Kensington, across the District line in Maryland.

They rode in silence as Sarah, who sensed something unsettling had happened, left him to his thoughts. Passing the wooded grounds of the National Cathedral, he wondered how reliable the Jeweler's information was this time. Well, he'd go to the office this afternoon and sort through the printouts himself. No need to call Gretchen at her Washington apartment. He knew she would be at the office, waiting for him. His mind was occupied for the next couple of miles. He didn't remember Bethesda's business district stretching along Wisconsin or passing the Naval Hospital looming on the right just before the suburb of Kensington, as he tried to test the logic of Gretchen's allegations.

She might be right, he admitted. Holloway was a crackerjack agent, and the tip from him about Burton's possible disloyalty was disquieting, especially given Burton's resistance to stationing Holloway in Costa Verde. Though nominally the station chief in Costa Verde, Holloway was running several strings of agents in Central America, keeping tabs on any developing post–Sandinista era threats to the region. Holloway had lots of sources of information and his finger in enough pies to stumble onto Burton's slight of hand, if there was any.

Could be, Truman had to admit, as he found himself turning into White Flint Road, where they lived.

He knew from experience that it could take as long as a year to compile and evaluate the charges against Burton. Meanwhile he would pick the time for a surprise personal visit to Costa Verde to get firsthand knowledge of the current situation there before pulling the trigger on his friend. And getting to the bottom of things would have to be done with deliberate speed, not hasty moves. The lives of a dozen agents could be jeopardized, to say nothing of America's national interests in Central America. A botched job of removing a rotten apple from the Company's barrel could do more damage to vital interests than tolerating a known double agent, whom you could work around until you built-up a parallel network to replace his. *It's a case of the devil you know being better than the unknown,* Truman mused, *so long as you're forewarned he might be a devil.* Besides, he thought, if one of his close friends was on the take from the Generalissimo, he should be able to sense it somehow, in the man's actions and demeanor.

Still, maybe it's all a frame-up, he thought, as he slowed the car near the house. There was precedent for despoiling an agent by opening a Swiss privacy account in his name, then arranging an information leak. In such cases, if there were no withdrawals of the money, it always came down to whether you still trusted the person.

He pulled into the driveway and stopped to let Sarah out, and had parked in the garage, locked the car and taken the back steps when the obvious occurred to him. Gretchen, he remembered, had found out more than the bare fact of a privacy account in Zurich in Burton's name. The Jeweler also provided the access code for the account. With it she could make withdrawals or deposits.

He recalled the gravelly voice of his high school coach saying, "Always take advantage of what the defense gives you." *Okay, why not deposit some money?* he pondered. *Watch to see what happens?* No, not just any amount, which could be a bank error, he mused, but something calculated to get Burton's attention, let him know someone's onto him. If he's culpable and, HELLO, scary deposits start popping up in his numbered account, it ought to jar the hell out of him. *But, what's a scary deposit?* he wondered. What amount or amounts would tip him off that somebody knows his secret? Minutes later he used his scrambler and called Gretchen's safe line at the office.

"This is Gretchen," she said, emphasizing the word "is" in her inimitable way.

He told her the plan. "And, if Bill's a bad apple, we can't wait around for him to make a withdrawal. Look," he said, "if he's clean, he doesn't know the account exists. No withdrawals. If he's sold out, he's too smart to withdraw anything until he retires. Either way, we sit on our hands. I'm for action, instead," Truman said. "What's to lose, anyway?" he asked.

"Money," she said.

He gave her the amounts of several cash deposits, each to be made separately in Swiss francs, on successive Mondays. That way, the pattern would be clear, and it wouldn't suggest bank errors.

She read the figures back to him. "Nineteen hundred forty, nineteen hundred sixty-two, nineteen hundred sixty-five, nineteen hundred sixty-nine, nineteen hundred seventy-six, and nineteen hundred ninety-four.

"Okay, T-Square," she asked, sounding a little weary. "Why these particular numbers, anyway?"

"They're the years he was born, graduated from college and from law school, was married, his only child was born, and his wife Peggy died. That should get his attention," Truman snorted. "And don't worry," he said, "Bill's a half-assed numerologist. He bought me dinner once simply because it was July seventh, nineteen-seventy seven. Seven, seven, seven, seven, get it? He'll take notice, all right."

"You think this is going to add enough pressure in Bill's life to do us any good?" she asked.

"Well, Gretchen, as you're so fond of saying," he chided, "nothing ventured, nothing gained. Maybe, if he's worried enough, it'll reflect in his demeanor somehow. At the very least, if he's playing more than one side of the street, it should slow him down, make him more cautious, assuming he's really on the take. And, if someone's set him up instead, it'll give them some real heartburn too. I know it's a shot in the dark, but my instincts tell me it could flush something out for us. What the hell? It's a real freebie, isn't it, so far as we're concerned?"

"Sure," she said, "give or take about eight grand, at the current exchange rate. Look, Terry, isn't this all pretty obvious? Won't Billy suspect you of doing this?"

"It's all public information," he reminded her. "Why suspect me more than an unseen enemy who's simply pulled a credit report on him?

"Just do it!" he ordered. "Be sure we deposit cash."

"Okay, T-Square. Let me call you back."

A few minutes later, she called to confirm that the Company's Zurich Station chief would send a man to make the first cash deposit when the bank opened in the morning.

Truman thanked her, switched the phone off, and poured himself a drink. He smiled as he tasted it.

Even the Jeweler couldn't trace cash deposits.

ELEVEN

BAHIA PAJAROS, COSTA VERDE

Elena Peralta lay sprawled on the bed where she finally fell asleep late at night fully clothed. She wore white cotton pants, matching blouse, and her feet were bare. Her body was sticky in the late summer heat, even though the ceiling fans were set on high here in her house on the white sand beach at Bahia Pajaros.

She stirred to consciousness and reached out and twisted the digital clock around to look at it.

4:07 A.M.

She sighed and pushed the red liquid crystal display away, closed her eyes and drifted back into a light sleep.

The house was perched on the hillside below the road and was cantilevered over the beach on concrete piers. Beyond the uncovered decking that extended the bedroom out over the sand, a light surf pounded rhythmically and palms rustled in the breeze, which was why she was here in the airy house where she could try to get a decent night's sleep. When her husband Roberto and their twelve-year-old son Cesar were slain earlier this year near one of the remote villages where they went to treat the poor, her brother Nacho had forbidden her to come here alone. Nacho had never been married and didn't understand her need to feel their presence here in the cottage at the edge of the water on the lonely stretch of beach a mile north of the new marina. It was Roberto's retreat before their marriage and their weekend getaway ever since.

The large firm bed, the musty ocean smell of the place, the comforting sounds of the Pacific pouring through open louvers—even their old black lab's occasional snorting as he lay near the door fidgeting in his sleep—seemed to be the only things doing her good in these awful months of grieving.

The whine of a mosquito woke her first. She slapped at her cheek and pulled the pillow across her face.

She awoke fully when the first bottle clinked against the rocks below. *Damn,* she thought. Some drunken fisherman returning from the cantina up the road.

She sat upright when the second bottle broke to the accompaniment of muted chuckles.

"Couple of cretins," she muttered, and touched the gun beside the bed, checking it by feel. The Colt .32 automatic, a weapon favored by gangsters in the thirties, had belonged to her husband. Roberto claimed he bought it because Bogart shot Major Stroesser with one in *Casablanca.*

Diego, Nacho's bodyguard, had added a silencer, figuring correctly it would encourage her to shoot if necessary, and trained her to use it skillfully.

She crossed to the deck, crept outside, and peered over the railing at the beach. She could see only the moonlight's path on the water and heard nothing but the surf washing the rocks in darkness. After a minute, she decided they were gone and returned to bed, placing the gun under Roberto's pillow this time.

She was semiconscious when the man threw his thick, muscular body onto her, knocking all the breath from her lungs, and forced the serrated edge of a knife against her neck. He reeked of sticky sweat and cheap rum.

"Bitch," he croaked, and pushed himself up a little, the better to examine his prey in the faint moonlight.

It was a mistake.

She was right-handed, but her left found the Colt. She shot him through the heart. The silencer did its work, aided by her having pressed the muzzle against him.

She rolled quickly out of the way, avoiding the main weight of his body collapsing against her.

She bounded to her feet, too frightened to scream, when she saw the other intruder, standing stark naked near the door. He had cut the harmless old dog's throat and was kicking the carcass with his bare feet, making sure it was dead. The hollow thudding made her feel sick.

"Ernesto!" he called softly, gutturally, slurring the syllables.

"Your friend's dead!" she spat.

He emitted a throaty gasp and lurched toward the stairs. Judging from the sound of his flying feet, he was sobering up quickly.

Months of pent-up rage erupted inside her, canceling all good judgment, and she flew after him. She reached the damp sand just as he dove toward a pile of combat fatigues and army boots lying on the beach. She stopped short, about twenty feet away, realizing now they were soldiers from the nearby garrison. She held the Colt behind her, in her right hand this time.

"Get up!" she demanded in a hoarse voice she barely recognized as her own.

He tugged a crumpled jacket toward himself on the sand, and pulled an Uzi from its folds, frantically toggling off the safety. He jumped to his feet and spun toward her.

She dropped him with a shot in the forehead. He jerked backwards onto the sand and lay motionless.

She turned away, sinking to her knees, and vomited.

Diego loaded the bodies into a skiff and disposed of them at sea. They wouldn't be missed. Desertions were frequent in the military, ever since the former army sergeant who led the coup against her father had proclaimed himself a generalissimo, for godsake, suddenly gotten rich as a pharaoh, and ruined any sense of military discipline. When he returned, Diego scolded her for not rousing him from his room downstairs and told her he was going to tell Nacho when they returned to San Marcos this morning that this place was indefensible and to forbid her to come here again. The skin tightened slightly around her high cheekbones, and she finished the rum she had poured herself to ease her shock. She dismissed it with a carefree wave.

"Fine with me," she said. "I'll handle it, though I'm not looking forward to confession with Bishop Subueso."

THE HIGHWAY FROM BAHIA PAJAROS TO SAN MARCOS

Diego threaded his way expertly through the lackadaisical Sunday traffic on the main road to the capital. Elena rode in the passenger seat of the Mercedes 450SL her father gave her when she left for college in the States. She looked out the side window as trees flew past. *The years are flying past like that,* she thought.

She thought about the dog's grizzly death, herself trembling in the dark on the beach. No one was any safer than Roberto and Cesar had been from a rogue military that violated its own people instead of protecting them.

She ground her teeth, muttering to herself.

This absolutely does it, GODDAMMIT!

It's no longer a question of Father's ouster, she realized, *and his dying in exile of a broken heart because he failed his people, or my pride at losing my professorship at the university, courtesy of the Generalissimo's stupid toadies— it's not even a question of my darlings' deaths anymore,* she whimpered. *Evil has seized us by the throat! The marauding goons they call an army just proved it all over again. . . . They're not like father's army. . . . They're scum, animals, have been bought with their pay doubled, and they think they can just get away with anything, anything at all.*

She suddenly resolved that she would not move to Madrid and safety, as Nacho insisted. She would stay right here in Costa Verde, instead, where she would overthrow this evil regime or damn well die in the trying.

Funny, she mused, as raindrops began to dampen the pavement. *In the movies the hero leaves his homeland because he kills a man—a bad man, he tells the heroine—but I'm staying here because I killed a couple of rapists.*

Diego braked suddenly, then accelerated around a weaving truck whose sleepy or drunk driver lolled at the wheel.

To the good, she and Nacho still owned much of the country, were wealthy enough to finance a small war, and sustain it a while as well. For whatever reason, the Generalissimo hadn't seen fit to jail them or drive them from the country. Nacho thought it was because of the Americans, who wouldn't like to see such a sign of repression, and might cut off foreign aid to the Generalissimo's government.

Watching the wipers lazily sweeping the light raindrops, she began thinking about how she would do it.

By force of arms, of course! There wasn't another way.

The trick in organizing a bloody coup of her own, she realized, would be milking the best from Nacho's volatile personality. She loved him very much, of course, but she was realistic about him and knew he couldn't contribute the necessary vision and judgments that she would need. *Dear, irrepressible Nacho,* she mused. He could be counted on to win all the best medals in any man's war. Nacho was like that, a natural-born gold medalist, whether flying a plane or shooting a gun, or soaring from a ski jump, but he was instinctively an individual performer. He wasn't the kind of man who was a natural at generalship, and his playboy years certainly hadn't been a training ground for the kind of leadership she considered important.

She knew she herself would be the moral authority and the driving force in recovering their country, but she would need a tough general by her side, a man of cool courage and stout heart who wouldn't flag no matter how dark the situation might become. A man like that would train a lifetime for such a job, would be able to find a crevice in the enemy's strength and slip a whole army through it. She knew all the former commanders of the Costa Verde military; none had the timbre she visualized.

Out of the corner of her eye she caught sight of a Costa Verde Air Force jet descending through the scattered rain clouds to nearby San Benito Air Base, a ray of sunlight glinting from its canopy.

The idea leapt naturally to her mind. Yes, if she played her cards right, maybe she could get the Mallorys to agree to an extended vacation as her guests here in Costa Verde. Deke could be their sounding board on strategy, logistics, and the other aspects of war planning. And, just maybe, if Luisa didn't stand in his way, Mallory might even warm to the challenges of generalship.

"Diego," she said, turning to look at him.

"Yes, *Señora?*"

"I'll need a complete dossier on Commander Mallory. You remember who Commander Mallory is, don't you?"

"Yes, *Señora*. Of course. The American whose wife and children were your guests during the coup."

"He has left his career in their Navy, Diego, so the information I'll need may be difficult to get. I want to know all about his Naval career, especially what commands were his, and war colleges attended, that sort of thing, in detail. Discreetly, of course."

Diego glanced at her. He flexed his driving gloves and gripped the wheel more tightly. He switched the wipers to full speed as heavy rain began pelting the car and smiled as he peered at the road ahead.

"I have my sources, *Señora*. They will need a few days, of course."

"Thank you, Diego."

TWELVE

CIA HEADQUARTERS, LANGLEY, VIRGINIA

Terry Truman hunched in his chair with one leg on his desk, balancing a laptop on his thigh. His office at CIA Headquarters had been a small dining room. A fire burned in the small fireplace behind him, which was why he had surrendered a large corner office for the cloister. He had furnished it in eighteenth-century antiques and hung oil paintings of World War II and Korean War Navy and Marine Corps subjects.

He had just returned from the White House where the President had sought his advice on handling questions about the Panama Canal that were sure to be asked at a press conference later in the week. The Senate Majority Leader was raising a ruckus about a Hong Kong company with ties to the Chinese military bidding to obtain a twenty-five-year contract to operate the Canal after the scheduled return of control of the vital link to Panama at midnight December 31, 1999. The Majority Leader's grim vision of Chinese pilots guiding U.S. warships, not to mention a significant share of American imports and exports, caught media attention. Truman had difficulty with the President's "why worry" attitude about the Canal, and limited his advice to suggesting that he stick to the fact that in 1977 the Carter administration

signed the treaty surrendering the Canal, and a companion treaty rec-
ognizing the right of the United States to reopen the Canal in the event
of an emergency, presumably by force of arms.

His duty done, he thought it prudent to memorialize the morning's
discussion in a half-page memo to the file. He was inputting this when
Gretchen quietly entered his office and seated herself across the desk.

"Give me a minute," he said, without looking up, as he finished typ-
ing, saved his work, and set the laptop aside. The expression on her face
told him something terrible had happened.

"Wade Holloway's dead," she said.

"My God! How?"

"Fell out of a goddamned helicopter. Jack Franck, his number two,
called and talked to me while you were on your way back from the
White House."

Truman was as inured to shocking information as a man could
become, but this was a hammer blow. Wade Holloway was one of his
brightest stars and had first tipped Gretchen to the possibility of
Burton's involvement with the Generalissimo or whatever dark forces
controlled Costa Verde. Truman had counted on Holloway to keep an
unbiased eye on developments in Costa Verde and Central America,
while he and Gretchen watched and waited for Burton's activities to
either indict him or clear him. Under these circumstances, Holloway's
rather strange death raised chilling questions to add to Truman's list of
worries about Burton's loyalty, and Costa Verde.

"Where's Bill?" he asked. "Has he called?"

Gretchen pursed her lips at the mention of Burton, crinkling her
nose as though smelling something rancid. "In San Marcos, too, according to Franck."

"Compile a thorough report and let me see it when it's finished,"
he told her.

———————

At home that night, Truman lit a fire in the fireplace and poured
a scotch. He could hear Sarah listening to TV in the kitchen as she

prepared dinner. He sat in his favorite chair, thinking. It had been a perfectly awful day, given the President's lack of national security vision and Holloway's seemingly inexplicable death. He sipped his drink and stared at the fire.

How the hell does an experienced agent, he asked himself, *simply haul off and fall out of a helicopter?*

No way did he fall, he decided, when his cell phone jingled. It was Burton, in Costa Verde.

"I just found a suicide note," he said. "He was tired and couldn't cope, it says."

A barking dog woke Truman at 2 A.M. He slipped out of bed and went downstairs to the refrigerator where he poured himself a glass of water and sat down at the kitchen table in the dark to collect his thoughts. *Shit, what a lousy damn year!* he muttered. His mother had died in February, his son was going through a divorce, and now the pall of the Burton question hung over him like a dire medical diagnosis.

He thought about the years he had headed all clandestine operations for the Company and quickly calculated it was twenty-four years, not counting the tough ones working his way up.

The Burton issue made his chest tighten involuntarily, as it had several times recently when he thought about it, and he shifted on the chair. He couldn't remember when, if ever, a problem or challenge caused a physical reaction.

Am I over the hill? he wondered. *Would this have rocked me so hard when I was younger?*

He didn't know, of course, but he guessed that what was really torturing him, aside from the strain on his friendship with Bill Burton, was the looming likelihood that the stench of high treason on his watch would destroy his spotless reputation. More than thirty years could be wiped out in no time, by another's misdeeds.

Goddammit, Truman, he told himself, *the wheels are about to come off your sanity . . . unless you find out the truth about Bill. . . . It doesn't matter that you've been thinking about maybe winding down next year or the year after. . . . This is the biggest goddamn crisis you've ever faced. . . . None of the others involved high treason.*

He thought of the ancient Chinese proverb *He who rides the tiger dares not dismount! You're sure as hell riding the tiger this time,* he told himself, *only this time you can't trust anyone at the Company anymore. You've even got to be careful of Gretchen.*

He finished the water and put the glass in the sink.

Can't afford to wait for Bill to screw up . . . time to go into the field myself, he muttered, as he climbed the stairs to bed.

THIRTEEN

THE VATICAN

Monsignor Albert knelt in the privacy of his quarters with his mind a jumble of conflicting thoughts. He kept trying to settle down and pray, but he found that he was too agitated to concentrate.

My God, the very magnitude of the sins I've committed! He covered his eyes with both hands, trying vainly to erase the images of today's meeting in Guilianni's office. The Little Pope had called him to watch as he proudly and with flourish signed the citizenship papers for the East German priests. "God is so gracious, isn't he?" Guilianni had beamed. "I'm giving these to you instead of sending them through channels," he had bubbled, as he handed Albert the passports destined for Tolt and the others. "No doubt you'll want to transmit these with a note encouraging our German brothers in their ministry to the poor."

Trusting the monsignor as blindly as he did, the bouncy Little Pope hadn't a possibility of knowing that Albert's glowing reports of the former East Germans' Mother Teresa–like activities were fictitious. And for his own part Albert had told and embellished the story so many times that he was as much at ease with the fable as with the truth that Tolt was living like a Ming emperor in his pleasure dome in the Mexican capital, where he was plotting some clandestine operation that Albert could only guess about. But it didn't require guesswork for him to realize that when the time came, the Kohorte inner circle would be sallying forth, masquerading as priests. Vatican citizenship was obviously a linchpin of whatever Tolt was planning, that much was sure, as Albert had known from the beginning. It was equally obvious, from the tidbits that Sturmbannfuhrer Staib had dropped, that Tolt's move would be huge when it came. Clearly the Reichsfuhrer had marshaled his resources and was throwing everything into whatever the plan was.

It wasn't that Albert hadn't been anticipating their citizenship being finalized so soon; he just hadn't foreseen that Guilianni would make such a show of signing the passports. It seemed to Albert that his friend had somehow unwittingly struck the chords of a resounding coda, ending the game whereby he had managed to string out the citizenship question for years. He had smiled and feigned pleasure for the cardinal's benefit, but his heart had sunk with foreboding now that the Kohorte had what it had wanted. Would they regard him as a man who knew too much? He hoped that Guilianni hadn't sensed the fear in his heart.

"We're so privileged to serve God," Guilianni had beamed as he capped his pen, "in even a small part of the working of His Plan for the lives of these dear brothers who've been transplanted so far from their beginnings and whose cause you so correctly championed."

Albert had been thinking about the dirt-level contrast between his friend's godly bearing and his own craven duplicity, but he had quickly refocused on the conversation. "You know," Guilianni added, scratching his chin, "I really want to meet them when they visit Rome, as they no doubt will one day."

"But of course, Eminence," Albert had assured him, "I'll convey your invitation with the passports."

He had faked his emotions well enough, he decided on reflection, but he was definitely relieved when Guilianni had been summoned to the Holy Father's apartments and he could sequester himself here in his own quarters to feign illness and plan his next steps. The general contours of his survival plan were clear enough in his mind, though he hadn't figured out the details. His strong suit was his pivotal position in the Church hierarchy. A man in his position could sidetrack any inquiries that might arise concerning the bona fides of Tolt and his brood of vipers. And there was the further fact that they would need a mentor to teach them the do's and don'ts of priest craft as long as they pretended to be priests. Then it had suddenly dawned on Albert that he had already created the necessary role for himself and that he was filling it nicely. *Yes,* he thought, *I need only continue, with just a touch of arrogance, what I have been doing right along and the Kohorte will continue to accept me as an important part of their plans.* He smiled and rose to pour himself a sherry from a decanter he kept in a bookcase. *Surely they understand, he muttered to himself, that I have protected them from scrutiny because I have kept them directly under my authority so that they haven't had to report to the Church hierarchy in Mexico.* Albert had been assuming that Guilianni would transfer Tolt and the others to the diocese of Mexico City once the issues affecting them were resolved. But now Albert had a better idea. Yes, he, Monsignor Siegfried Albert, would personally supervise their ministry to the homeless! He knew he would be able to figure a way to get Guilianni to agree. *Yes, that's the solution!* he decided, as his old self-confidence suddenly returned. He now saw clearly the opening bid he would make when meeting with Staib to give him the passports. He would tell him he could cover Tolt and the others in the short term by continuing to keep them under his personal authority. Later, he could pull strings, he would assure him, to get the Reichsfuhrer and his staff assigned to any diocese anywhere in the world, to any kind of ecclesiastical or administrative duties they might want.

He felt very relieved to have gained a handle on extending his own life expectancy—until his eyes fell on the passports laying on his desk, as the peeling of dozens of noonday bells throughout the city announced the hour.

He suddenly knew that everything was very wrong with his think-ing. *Oh, God!* he gasped, *how could I entertain these thoughts of encouraging your enemies?* It seemed to Albert that the cacophonous bell chorus was convicting him, cutting through everything to remind him that though he had once been a Nazi, now he belonged to Christ. Clapping his hands over his ears and bursting into tears, he threw himself onto his bed, tormented by the silence after the peeling of the bells.

Who will deliver me? he sobbed, *from this hell of my making? Dear God, can you forgive . . . treachery?*

After a few minutes he pulled himself together, washed his face at a small basin in the corner, tugged the heavy drapery aside, and cranked the window open. Normally, fresh air and the sight of the bustling city would have helped clear his head. Unfortunately, the weather matched the foul state of his mind, for it was unpleasantly humid and smoggy. He peered beyond the Vatican walls at the gray city of Rome spreading into the distance and glanced at the courtyard below where queues were beginning to form, as a greater than usual number of people assembled for the afternoon tours.

Yes! he remembered. *It's Annunciation Day,* the day of the angel Gabriel's announcement to Mary that she would give birth to the Lord Jesus—a special day of new beginnings foretelling man's deliverance.

As he closed his eyes in prayer, the solution to all his inner turmoil entered his mind as softly as the murmur of the doves roosting under the nearby eaves: *I must confess everything and trust in God's unfailing mercy that at the last I may enter with the saints into His glorious Kingdom.*

He felt better immediately and closed the window. "Catharsis!" he cried, joyously raising a fist.

It lasted but moments. The crack appeared in his resolve when he picked up the passports, felt them lying in his hand, and remembered that he was about to meet with the assassin.

FOURTEEN

MEXICO CITY

Former Stasi General Fritz-Julius Karpf certainly dressed the part he affected as a septuagenarian *bon vivant*. Two-tone wing-tip shoes and a gold-tipped walking stick, which he wielded like a riding crop, accented an expensive pearl-gray suit, ascot tie, and thousand-dollar plantation-style Montecristo *fino*-grade Panama hat. But the cruel grin on his face was to any kind of real joy as is vinegar to whipped cream. Using the stick, he pressed the bell at Tolt's penthouse on the Reforma. Viktor bowed approvingly as he admitted him.

"A very good evening to you, Herr Steiger."

Steiger was Karpf's alias in Mexico City, where his cover was acting as business manager for his reclusive host. In reality these days, Karpf was the Kohorte's Chief of Intelligence with the SS rank of Obergruppenfuhrer.

"Herr Staib is already here," Viktor proclaimed. "He has joined the Reichsfuhrer in the dining hall." He took Karpf's things and led the way, opening the room's tall double doors. The huge formal room lent an elegant though lonely air to the occasion. Staib sat at the side of the table, equidistant from the ends. He nodded brusquely as Viktor guided

Karpf to the place set for him at the far end of the table. They dined silently. Staib figured that Tolt liked it that way. In fact, the table was of such great length he had to relay some of Tolt's and Karpf's words to each other. Afterwards, with Tolt leading, they crossed the oak-paneled hallway to the Grand Salon overlooking the Reforma. Tolt adjusted the air conditioning, lowering the temperature. The others fell silent as Tolt strode to the hearth and turned to face them. All accepted cognac from a tray passed by Viktor, the former SS-sergeant.

"As you know, I retreat before a fire at night, whenever possible," Tolt told them, stooping to poke the glowing coals before adding wood himself. "Perhaps this originates from happy memories of my grandfather's hunting lodge in Bavaria, but I have found that a hearth fire facilitates brotherhood, as it did among our Teutonic tribal forbears and heroic Germanic knights of ages past."

Staib stifled a smile. He hadn't heard of an ancestral hunting lodge among the versions of his upbringing Tolt put about over the years. *So what?* he thought. A Great Man is entitled to embellish here and there. He grouped it with Tolt's well-known paranoia, as a concomitant of the man's genius.

"This is how the heroic Teutons," Tolt continued, "always conducted their important ceremonies. Yes, they sought their gods before a blazing log. This wood," he told them, tenderly displaying a short piece in both palms, like a jeweler showing his work on a velvet pillow, "is from Germany, Frankfurt Am Main, specifically. I have it aged and cut to my specifications and shipped in crates. I've a whole year's supply on hand. See the fine, almost crystalline coals it makes," he continued, selecting one with tongs. "Quite suitable," he allowed, "for the Sacrament of the Coals."

Karpf stiffened at mention of the Kohorte's ultimate sacrament, which was reserved for sealing the lips of Kohorte warriors swearing to suicide missions. Staib of course resonated with the thought. To Tolt the sacrament was simply a matter of ridding the Kohorte of the Jewish notion of the sanctity of human life. His analysis was linear and practical. A judicious suicide mission simply meant that one prepared the casualty list before rather than after battle. What possible difference could that make in the perspective of a Thousand-Year Reich? *None,* he thought. The SS-Oath Unto Death, based on the German officer's oath, had long since supplanted religion in the Kohorte.

> I swear to Thee, Adolf Hitler,
> As Fuhrer and Chancellor of the German Reich,
> Loyalty and Bravery.
>
> I vow to Thee and to the superiors
> Whom Thou shalt appoint,
> Obedience unto death.
> So help me God.

Tolt had improved the oath by capitalizing Superiors, dropping the plural, and deleting the "So help me God." Thus amended—with God out, and Tolt in—the oath served precisely his intent concerning apostolic succession. It bridged Hitler's mortality nicely and put Tolt in the Fuhrer's chair for life.

He replaced the glowing ember in the fire and accepted a cigar from Viktor's tray, produced a remote and clicked the lights off. His cruel features glistened in the fire's orange glow as he bent to replace the tongs in the nest of fire tools. Viktor, a death-squad veteran and one-time violinist with the Berlin Philharmonic, strode to the far end of the room, placed violin to jowl, and commenced a slow, haunting rendition of Wagner's *The Ride of the Valkyries*. A spotlight in the ceiling illuminated his bullet head as he faced the timbered wall with his mountainous back to them. Tolt grimaced. "Somebody placed a tiny microphone in the wall there once, years ago," he said. "Whether it was the CIA or the KGB, or even the British, I don't know, but they picked it up with a receiver in an apartment in the hotel next door. So I bought that building too, and that's why Viktor turned his back to us."

Staib and Karpf exchanged glances. The Reichsfuhrer's night-blooming paranoia was blossoming like jasmine.

Tolt held up his hand for silence, though neither deigned to speak. He lowered his voice, his eyes dancing about in search of offending microphones. "I give them chicken feed, you know. That's spy language, I believe," he glanced at Karpf, who slumped next to Staib on a sofa, "for mildly interesting disinformation to justify installing microphones but throw them off the track. You must never discuss business in this room," he scolded. "You may safely assume they are always listening."

Karpf seized the opportunity to impress the Reichsfuhrer with his own background in secret intelligence. "My compliments," he said, his death-skull countenance glistening in the fire's glow. "You are right to play them like a trout until they finally conclude you are the reclusive real estate tycoon you claim to be."

Staib bristled at the transparent attempt to curry favor. "Them?" he snorted, loud enough for Karpf's ears but not Tolt's. Not deterred, the former spymaster couldn't resist elaborating on Mexico City's role as the base where the CIA and KGB introduced illegals into the Western Hemisphere. "KGB had way too many assets here," he expounded, waving a hand, "for their own good. So did the CIA, not to mention MI6. They were intercepting every possible source of electronic intelligence here in the *Districto Federal,* which was much more intel than they could ever hope to process. The CIA is still so engaged."

"That's history!" Staib fumed aloud. *What does this old fool,* he asked himself, *bring to the table anymore?* His assassin's hormones were stirring within him.

"By the way," Karpf said, turning to face Staib and clink his glass against the younger man's, "you'll never be able to go back to Germany. You did such a good job of reforming the Church there, they're still looking for you!"

"It doesn't matter," Tolt interjected, ignoring the humor. "Staib's priorities lie elsewhere today."

"That's right, Herr Karpf," Staib snarled. "Stasi is history, and so are—"

Tolt extended a hand to shush Staib, who squirmed in his seat and composed himself. Tolt set his snifter aside and hugged himself, rubbing his palms together.

"Reichsfuhrer," Staib ventured, changing the subject, "would you care to mention when we may expect Case Green—"

"NO!" Tolt shrieked. "Never say that here! I sense," he announced, touching finger to temple, "they're listening at this very moment." He lowered his voice. "I will impart Case Green when the others arrive tomorrow," he whispered.

―――――――

Lung Fan's Chinese restaurant was next to a dry cleaning establishment on a back street not far from Tolt's penthouse on the Reforma. Fan beamed as a party of six strolled by, examined the entrance, and came inside. The acrid odor of diesel fumes from the smoggy street invaded Lung Fan's, too, until a lazy mechanism finally closed the door. Tolt took in the red lanterns and large gilt dragons adorning the ceiling of the empty dining room. He dissected Lung Fan with his eyes until the little man bobbed his head and led the way to a private room having a lone window fronting the alley outside. The plaster walls looked greasy and probably hadn't been repainted in years, nor had the window been washed recently. An ancient electric fan hummed in the corner, its blades spinning invisibly inside their dirty wire safety cage. Tolt nodded approvingly.

"Es adecuado," Staib told the owner, in the neutral accent of the Mexican capital, as the others found places at the lone table. "Viktor said the food is good," he said.

They were dressed as small-time businessmen. Only Staib and Tolt wore jackets, which they draped over their chairs as the others seated themselves. On the threshold of his eighth decade, Tolt remained a remarkably energetic physical and intellectual presence.

"Bring us tea and egg rolls, to start," Staib said, glancing at the food-stained menu. "Then we'll have, yes, number four, the businessman's lunch." Wearing a cheap shirt and tie, he looked the part of a local accountant conferring with his clients. Pens and pencils protruded from a plastic holder in his shirt pocket. He placed a pocket calculator on the plastic tablecloth and garnished the scene with a gum eraser. Reaching into a battered briefcase, he produced a printout of columns with numbers, and plopped that onto the table.

Fan's sparse eyebrows arched. "Ah!" he exclaimed, suitably impressed that confidential business was to be discussed, and scuttled toward the kitchen. His wife brought an aluminum teapot to the table and retreated.

"These people only speak Spanish and Cantonese, Viktor assured me," Tolt told the others in English. "They've no employees, just a daughter in the kitchen. It's best to be taken for Americans," he added, "should the question arise. In fact, this set-up is quite good," he continued, as he circled a finger in the air. "I have always made it a practice to disclose the deepest secrets in a public house selected at random, like this one, even in plain view of strangers that might be present. This way, I control the situation, appearances are entirely consistent with people's normal behavior, and I can always abort, if necessary."

Staib smiled. *I doubt,* he thought, *this greasy, fly-ridden dump is a regular watering hole of the worldwide intelligence community. This is ridiculous overkill, thanks to his runaway paranoia.*

Gruppenfuhrer Otto Kreeber rubbed his hands excitedly, as Brigadefuhrer Heinrich Kaalten and Oberst Wilhelm Rolfe looked on. Like Staib and Karpf, they were anxious to learn Tolt's reason for meeting in this improbable restaurant. Kreeber was head of the Kohorte's geopolitical think tank in Munich. Kaalten and Rolfe ran the Kohorte's legitimate business operations from bases in Zurich and Istanbul. Kreeber, Kaalten, Karpf, and Staib were the tiger-team Tolt hand-picked to serve as his immediate staff for his decisive move. He loved symbolism and told them he chose the name Case Green according to Hitler's system: Case White for invading Poland, Case Yellow for the invasion of France. Even in the Kaiser's Germany, he reminded them, the color green signified the German Empire; green ink, for example, being reserved for the exclusive use of the Kaiser and his principal ministers.

"Therefore," he bridged to the present, "green evokes my decisive stroke, as well as the target country's verdant landscape." He looked each man in the eye and lowered his voice. "As surely as multinational corporations acquire one another in Darwinian fashion," he seemed to hiss like a snake now, "I am acquiring Costa Verde!"

Fan and his wife returned with the order, which they deposited on the table and briskly rearranged, as waiters the world over do to make a show of their importance. "Leave us now," Tolt growled in Spanish, "and leave the dishes. I will not be interrupted this afternoon." He returned Fan's smile as the man left, trailed by his wife. When they finished the meal, Tolt paced the floor, as Staib hunched with pen and paper and the others waited.

"To understand Case Green, the takeover of Costa Verde, which has been quietly in progress for several years already," Tolt began, "you must understand that my purpose is to influence world politics on the grandest scale. Recall the American adage about money as mother's milk in politics," he lectured.

"I am going to do to the Central Americans what advanced people always do to their inferiors. Recall what the Americans did to the Native American Indian. They took his land and pushed him aside, to the point of extinction." The others nodded expectantly. "If you think that was unique in the hemisphere, nothing could be farther from the truth. Why, in Argentina and Chile the white man put a bounty on the head of the indigenous Indians—one pound sterling for each genital or pair of ears. As a result, there is not one indigenous native left in Argentina today, and only nine individuals are thought to survive in Chile."

"Are we going to kill off the population of Central America?" Kaalten asked with childlike innocence, as though that were a possibility.

"Better!" Tolt told them. "We are going to do by financial and economic means what has formerly been accomplished with the sword.

Warfare, properly understood, is the extension of politics by all available means, including the proper use of money. Gentlemen, the Kohorte already owns or controls the principal industries and infrastructure in Costa Verde, except for what is owned by the Peralta family and a few other wealthy individuals.

"When I am finished, the Kohorte will own everything of value throughout all Central America! Obviously, such a thing couldn't be accomplished in more mature economies during our lifetime. But it's going to happen in Central America because of Case Green and the force of my unshakable will!" He paused, letting that sink into their minds. "To take this next step," he concluded, "I require behind-the-scenes control of one of the family of nations."

They were visibly startled by his bold proclamation, as he paused with his lips slightly separated, then continued as though they hadn't the acuity to connect his thoughts.

"The first phase of Case Green—the remaking of Costa Verde as a Teutonic country—will lay the foundation for my master plan to acquire Central America as a Nazi Reich. "In short," he waved his hand as if dismissing the past, "we have arrived at a place where the Kohorte needs the facilities of nationhood, beginning with a national bank and memberships in the international financial community, including its network of treaty organizations, such as the World Bank and the International Monetary Fund."

Kaalten, the most impetuous of the inner circle, lifted his hand slightly, thought better about asking a question, and suppressed an imaginary sneeze.

It was a defining moment for the Kohorte. Unlike the Moscow-based international communist movement, the Comintern, thriving on a world scale in the 1930s, the Kohorte hadn't a host country. That made it an organism of the shadows like the Sicilian Mafia's Cosa Nostra. The difference was that Tolt wasn't interested in the underworld. He would rule as surely as Hitler, but very subtly this time, behind the scenes. He paused by the window to peer into the street. A squadron of dead flies littered the sticky window sill, and the filthy venetian blinds cast parallel shadows on his cruel face, as if revealing the scars on his soul.

"Case Green," Kreeber recited, in case the others missed it, "requires international legitimacy, since it involves manipulating the finances and politics of other Central American nations. The Reichsfuhrer selected Costa Verde, with its Atlantic and Pacific coasts," he continued, "as our host country due to its strategic location and susceptibility to military coups."

Tolt gestured impatiently for him to get to the point.

"We are definitely satisfied," Kreeber continued, "with progress to date in manipulating Sergeant Drago, the current Generalissimo. We financed his overthrow of the elected leader, Edwardo Peralta, and have supplied money for arms and some bank accounts for him and his henchmen. Needless to say, we've led the cretin to believe his money comes from certain commercial interests." Tolt looked on, enjoying the surprise and pride registering on his lieutenants' faces, and motioned for Kreeber to continue. "Several of our young business professionals," Kreeber said, "have been transferred from Europe to San Marcos, the capital, and they've obtained control of important enterprises. Sometimes, the previous owners were unwilling to sell," he exchanged eye contact with Staib, "so other means were used to remove them from the scene." Staib smiled as Kreeber rubbed his hands together and parted his lips to continue.

"I caution," Tolt interrupted, "that our men in Costa Verde don't know what you are being told. They were transferred from Kohorte businesses in Europe and told to establish branch operations. To maintain security, they must never find out the part they're playing."

"Costa Verde," Kreeber continued, "has a central bank, *Banco Central de Costa Verde,* with the international memberships the Reichsfuhrer mentioned, and a national airline, Aero Verde, that flies domestic and international routes. It has agreements with JAL, KLM, American, and British Airways to fly anywhere in the world."

"This surprises you?" Tolt exclaimed, gesturing impatiently toward Staib's briefcase. The assassin reached into it and produced packets of papers bound with rubber bands. He turned them over in his hands, like a postman sorting mail, and passed one each to Kaalten and Kreeber.

"There you will find," Tolt continued, as they inspected them, "suitably aged East German identity cards—with photographs of your more youthful selves—proper birth certificates, a personal letter or two from authorities in the Roman Catholic Church and, most importantly, passports issued by the Vatican in Rome. All are authentic originals. Karpf provided most of the documents years ago in accordance with my plan, but the Vatican citizenship and passports came through recently.

"Kaalten, Kreeber, and Staib will accompany me to Costa Verde, where we'll occupy the National Cathedral. Karpf takes over here in Mexico City, while Oberst Rolfe moves to Zurich to run our European operations from there."

Judging from the detached expressions on their faces, Tolt's listeners seemed to have been transported to the other world where he lived. "The Vatican coup"—Tolt wrapped his tongue around the word "coup"—"was accomplished by Monsignor Albert, the longtime personal assistant of the Vatican Secretary of State, who is regarded as the power behind the Pope for good reason. Monsignor Albert was a corporal under my command in the war. He served me well," Tolt now stretched to his full height, "when I was in charge of the Special Squads in Poland. Before the war's end, I dispatched him to Rome to study for Holy Orders. Now you see the rewards of my foresight, for we not only have Vatican citizenship and passports, but the Archbishop of Costa Verde is welcoming us to his staff at Rome's direction."

Staib raised his hand. "I'm wondering about the gap in years," he said, "between our defections from East Germany and the present time. Perhaps—"

Tolt cut him off. "Here is proof," he said, producing a letter from his jacket and waving it, "that ever since our heroic defections, we've been under Cardinal Guilianni's authority. Should anyone make inquiry about that, Monsignor Albert will confirm it. In fact, we'll rendezvous at the cathedral in San Marcos, where he'll conduct orientation, since there are no German-speaking priests in Costa Verde." Tolt hovered above his chair, restuffing the letter into his jacket, and continued pacing, as the others waited. He stopped by the window again.

"Staib and I are fluent in Spanish, but that will be a secret until we are well established as priests. Monsignor Albert's true purpose in coming to Costa Verde will be to teach us enough priest craft so we can get by. He's confident the other clergy there will ascribe whatever our shortcomings may be to differences in practice between Catholicism in Germany and the Church in Central America, which of course are worlds apart culturally."

Tolt pointed at the packets laying on the table. "You also have," he said, "a copy of Stasi's dossier on the unfortunate priest whose place you are taking, along with some personal effects Staib removed from the bodies—crucifixes, eye glasses, fitted with your own prescriptions, and other such personal things."

A heavy truck rumbled by in the alley outside, rattling the window and stilling conversation.

"Kreeber," Tolt announced, "you will be called Father Klaus. Kaalten, you will be called Father Josef, and Staib is Father Martin." Tolt produced his own passport and waved it. "And, henceforth I am Monsignor Schmehr."

"Excellent!" Karpf croaked, catching the others' excitement. "With Vatican passports and an international airline, you're free to travel anywhere." He shot a finger in the air. "Who would suspect humble priests of anything untoward? This is masterful, Reichsfuhrer!"

"Yes, it is," Tolt said, donning his coat as the others rose. "However, I have given you only a foretaste. There is more to reveal, when you have need to know."

They didn't ask him how he would pull off the final phases of Case Green with the puny resources of Costa Verde, though each knew a different piece of the answer, for Tolt was a master compartmentalizer.

They took it as an article of faith he alone held the key to the critical questions.

Tolt read their thoughts, and was pleased he held the reins, as they filed out of Lung Fan's.

———————————

The Boeing 737's beat-up aluminum doorsill showed the ravages of a couple of decades of hard use, as Kaalten boarded, wearing a priest's black frock for the first time. He crossed himself as a flight attendant examined his ticket and waved him aft aboard the daily Aero Verde flight from Mexico City to San Marcos. Tolt, Kreeber, and Staib were already seated to the rear of the aircraft. Otherwise, the cabin was almost empty, except for a sprinkling of business passengers up front.

A man wearing headphones entered the cabin and waved a clipboard. "We must ask you to leave the airplane," he said. "This flight has been cancelled, due to a mechanical problem with the aircraft. There'll be a replacement in two hours. Please return to the terminal building at this time. Don't worry, your baggage will definitely be at the airport in San Marcos when you arrive."

Tolt and his party collected their belongings, waited for the other passengers to exit, and went forward, but the man with the clipboard barred them from reaching the door.

"It seems the problem's fixed now," he said. "Please take any seats you like. You'll be flying alone today."

"Excellent!" Tolt said after the man left.

"Yes," Kaalten agreed, "he just received a phone call from his superior in San Marcos. Two calls, actually; the first ten minutes ago, telling him of the `grounding mechanical,' and the second just now, telling him it was fixed, and that the archbishop is expecting us for dinner."

They seated themselves at the table in first class, as the lone flight attendant served mineral water and bowls of fruit and nuts. Being given to understand clerical matters were to be discussed, she retreated to the rear of the airplane and curled up with a book.

Staib pulled out their tickets. "We'll be in San Marcos in less than four hours, then change to a commuter plane for the flight to Bahia Pajaros on the Pacific coast. The archbishop is vacationing there," he told Kreeber and Kaalten, "at his seaside retreat house. Don't worry, Monsignor Albert will meet this plane and then fly with us to Bahia Pajaros."

As the Boeing lifted from the runway, the portly Kreeber loosened his seat belt. "Reichsfuhrer," he ventured, "is there more you would wish to divulge to us about Case Green at this time?"

Tolt swigged his mineral water. "Well," he said, "aside from the obvious benefits of Vatican passports, you may have been wondering why I decided we would masquerade as priests down there." They nodded enthusiastically. "The answer is simple. The great sweep of our undertaking requires matching stealth. We would be quite visible locally as investors, leaders of a movement, or even as teachers or philosophers. But as priests in a Roman Catholic country, we will be in the local community without being either a part of it or complete outsiders. It's the perfect protective coloration, and the cathedral is the perfect place from which to conduct our operations on site without suspicion. Just think of it. Who would suspect simple men of the cloth, such as ourselves, of buying up and running their country? No one!"

"What about the archbishop?" Kaalten asked.

Tolt looked at him and smiled his usual thin smile.

FIFTEEN

BAHIA PAJAROS

Luisa Mallory and Elena Peralta hugged one another at the small airport at Bahia Pajaros, Costa Verde's premier resort on the Pacific.

"Well, I gather this visit was more relaxing than the last time you were here," Elena said, with a laugh.

Luisa nodded. "That's for sure. Watching sunsets from your yacht was a lot more fun than escaping over rooftops and hiding in the bushes. But I think the best part," she said in her soft Castilian Spanish, "was conversing in my native language."

They stopped at the gate where Luisa showed her passport and ticket. "You couldn't see it from the yacht," Elena said, "but there is violence and unrest everywhere. Unfortunately, the leaders of the elements opposing the Generalissimo have been systematically eliminated. Many of our more thoughtful younger citizens have simply disappeared since he came to power. The Disappeared, we call them."

Luisa hugged her. "I'll be praying for you and Nacho."

The DeHavilland Twin Otter turboprop had landed and was taxiing toward them. The pilot spun it around in front of the thatched roof terminal where it stood vibrating on the sun-baked tarmac with one engine still running.

"I wish Deke could have come," Elena said. "We were really looking forward to seeing him again."

"I know," Luisa said, "but the death of his friend changed everything. Mel Peters was Deke's Executive Officer in his last squadron. He was killed in a landing accident at sea, and Deke felt he had to help arrange the memorial service. They flew together in Desert Storm, and the bond among Naval Aviators is very strong."

Elena nodded. "I understand," she said. "I hope there'll be another time when Deke will be able to come."

While the DeHavilland discharged its passengers, and Luisa stood in line to board, Elena reflected on the demise of her plan to get Deke Mallory to Costa Verde under the guise of an extended vacation. Her reason, unknown to Luisa of course, was to pick his brain about the counter-revolution she and Nacho were hatching. Their preparations cried out for professional military skills far beyond Nacho's experience. He was an expert pilot but, despite his dedication to avenging their father, Nacho had spent most of his life as a playboy whereas Diego's report on Mallory's background showed that he possessed the professional expertise to plan and carry out successful military operations. *Mallory's are the qualities of a great fighting admiral, had he remained in the service,* she thought. And years ago he had served as U.S. liaison to their Air Force's *Pajaros de Fuego* flight demonstration team. Nacho had commanded the Fire Birds then and pulled strings to get Mallory assigned. Mallory had even logged about a hundred hours in the propeller-driven Grumman Bearcats the Fire Birds flew. Eventually the Fire Birds switched to Lockheed F-80 jets and the Bearcats were sold to other users but, following the coup, Nacho had been able to track down most of the Bearcats and was secretly restoring them to battle readiness.

From the reports Diego obtained from his sources in the States, Elena also learned that Mallory had attended the Naval Post Graduate School, the Naval War College, and held staff positions at the Pentagon under the Deputy Chief of Naval Operations for Resources, Warfare Requirements and Assessments. Those very words: resources, warfare requirements, and assessments convinced her of the wisdom of her decision to somehow draw Mallory into the counter-revolution. She knew his retirement was prompted by the desire to spend time with his family, but she suspected he missed military aviation.

Luisa picked up her shoulder bag and threw her arms around Elena. "Deke's going to be sorry he missed out on this," she said.

As she made her way through the arriving passengers, she turned to wave to Elena and collided with a tall, elderly monsignor, one of a party of clergy on their way to the terminal building.

"Oh, *perdoneme, Padre!*" she said, backing away. "*Lo siento.*"

She thought the priest stared at her a moment, before he continued toward the terminal. "*No problema, Señora.*"

Luisa walked toward the plane and then, in a flash of inspiration, she pulled her tiny Minox spy camera from her purse and ran after the group of priests.

"*Padres! Momentito, por favor,*" she called. "*Solamente una fotografía, por favor?*" She pressed the Minox to her eye and snapped a picture. "*Muchas gracias,*" she called, waving to them.

She ducked into the plane, found her seat, and settled back to relax as the passenger door was secured. The woman seated next to her looked up from her magazine. "Are you a journalist?" she asked. "I noticed you taking those priests' picture."

"No," Luisa said. "I'm not really in the habit of photographing strangers. I'm an artist and I like to capture scenes I think will make an interesting painting." She rubbed with her thumb some oxidation from the little gold-plated camera. It wasn't much larger than a pack of chewing gum. "Like those workmen back there, stringing palm trees with Christmas lights in humid, ninety-degree weather. And the priests in their heavy black cassocks, against such a colorful background of exotic flowers, thatched roofs, and people in brightly colored shirts and blouses. A great study in contrasts."

The woman returned to her magazine.

Luisa closed her eyes, suddenly feeling uneasy about her encounter with the priests. *Yes, there was contrast all right, but it was more than just the colorful background.* She recalled the tall monsignor's piercing eyes. *They weren't the eyes of a priest,* she thought. *No, there wasn't even a trace of Christian love or pastoral concern there.*

She reached for her crucifix necklace and clasped it to her until the chill of evil passed.

The Lincolnesque-appearing priest and his companion lagged behind their party as they entered the terminal. "Before we meet the archbishop," the tall one whispered, "slip out on some pretext and use your cell phone. Give the order to find out who that woman was."

"As you wish, but what risk is there? She's just a tourist capturing local color with her camera. It merely proves our appearances are all in order."

"Yes," Tolt snapped, "our credentials are in order, but that's not the point." He stopped and grabbed Staib by the arm. "You see that woman over there in the tan silk slacks?" He pointed to Elena, who was waving to the airplane as the pilot advanced the throttles.

"Yes, I see her," Staib said. "So?"

"She is the daughter of the former president we so efficiently removed from office. Her brother is the Ignacio Peralta whom our intelligence confirms is itching to back a counter-revolution in this country one day soon."

"How do you know this?" Staib asked.

"I have studied Karpf's latest reports. We have dossiers on all the major factions here in Costa Verde: military, industrial, and political, including photos of the key people. This Elena Peralta is a smart woman. Some say she's tougher than her brother and should never be underestimated. The woman who took our picture may be a threat to us since she's obviously connected with the Peraltas somehow."

"I see," Staib muttered.

"No, you don't see," Tolt snarled. "You didn't see what I saw in her face. She knows we are not real priests. I saw it in her eyes. Make no mistake, Staib. She knows!"

They watched the Twin Otter accelerate toward them and leap into the air, passing almost directly over the terminal building. When the decibels subsided, Tolt spoke into Staib's ear. "Find out who she is," he ordered, "and have that film recovered before she can get it processed."

SIXTEEN

PACIFIC COAST HIGHWAY NORTH
FROM LA JOLLA TO LOS ANGELES

Driving up the coast was pleasant in spite of the heavy traffic, but Mallory was in too good a mood to let occasional Southern California gridlock bother him, even as he passed through the art colony of Laguna Beach, which was always backed up through the center of town. He thought of Laguna's legendary town greeter, a tall, bearded man who looked like Father Time, who for years had smiled and waved to each passing car as if the passengers were old friends.

Mallory had come to appreciate such simple bliss. His Navy career had taken him overseas many times, but Luisa was always there for him, caring for their two children, managing their affairs, and trying to pursue her fragmented career in art when time allowed. This would be a wedding anniversary to remember, a small reward for all their times of separation. They had reservations for two nights at the Century Plaza Hotel, tickets to an acclaimed production of *The Nutcracker* at the Shubert Theater, and reservations for an after-theater supper at L'Orangerie, a five-star restaurant a friend recommended. The next day they would visit their son David, who would graduate from UCLA soon.

Yes, Mallory thought, as they drove past the rolling surf of Corona del Mar, with the reflected light from the afternoon sun glistening on the water, *life is good.*

Passing through Newport Beach near Balboa Island brought back memories of lazy days of sailing and surfing when he was in high school, and later when he was at UCLA. That lifestyle ended with the necessity of military service during the latter stages of the conflict in Viet Nam. He had spent most of the time since then in the cockpits of carrier-based fighters, but those were closed chapters.

Traffic was backed up for a mile or two in the Los Angeles Harbor area but thinned out as they neared LAX. Being in no hurry, Mallory stayed to the right in deference to impatient drivers who had to get to wherever they were going right now.

His fighter pilot's peripheral vision caught something, and he was suddenly aware of a vehicle to his left passing, then slowing down and passing again. He saw what appeared to be five or six scowling skinheads in a large mud-splattered pickup. Its huge knobby tires were making a dreadful whining noise at freeway speed. Three of the occupants were riding in the truck's open bed, facing backwards with their backs braced against the cab, wearing black leather boots and jackets with the sleeves cut out. One had a swastika tattooed on his upper arm. Their animated conversation was punctuated at one point by one of them flipping him the finger.

"Oh, charming," Luisa said. "What's their prob—"

"Don't worry," Mallory said. "We'll let them do their thing up ahead."

He eased off the accelerator and, as traffic from an on-ramp blended in, he moved into one of the left lanes.

"Should be at the hotel in about twenty minutes," he said. As he turned toward Luisa, the rude tire noise intruded again, and he noticed the truck overtaking on their right now. As it passed, one of the punks waved a handgun.

Oh shit, he thought, *that's all we need.*

He'd outgunned Syrian MiGs and flown dangerous missions in Desert Storm, but this was Los Angeles and a Saturday Night Special in the hands of an inner-city thug was almost as dangerous. He figured he could lose them in the increasing airport traffic. He floored the Mercedes.

The pickup accelerated to keep pace, its tire noise even louder now. As Mallory began to change lanes to the left again he heard a loud POP and the shattering of glass. He turned quickly to see Luisa slumping toward him.

———————

Mallory sat on a bench next to a vending machine, staring at the floor, unaware of the blood on his hands, shirt, and pants. The emergency room waiting area at Harbor General was noisy, with redundant paging of medical staff, ringing phones, and the sounds of human anguish. After an hour, he had tuned it out. Somewhere in the distance he thought he heard his name being called.

"Mister Mallory?"

He felt a tap on his shoulder and looked up to see a pair of feet under a green surgical gown. He raised his head and saw that the legs were connected to a torso and finally to a head with a red mustache.

The head said, "I'm sorry, Mister Mallory. We did everything we could do."

LA JOLLA, CALIFORNIA

Everyone said the service was beautiful and just what Luisa would have wanted. He remembered being there but little else about it. The night Luisa was killed was spent with David at his apartment in Santa Monica, the two of them sleeping fitfully, fully clothed atop the bed. He refused the sedative the doctor offered and was rewarded with some kind of natural narcotic the body brings forth at such a time. David saw that his father had clicked onto emotional autopilot, and took over driving the car and making lists of what needed to be done.

More than three hundred attended the funeral in the quaint little Catholic church in La Jolla. His old friend Nacho Peralta came from Costa Verde with his sister, Elena, whom Luisa had visited the week before her death.

Elena spoke briefly at the service, following tributes from David and Mallory's daughter Laura and Laura's husband, Mike. Mallory remembered sitting in the pew, absorbing the warmth of their words, but not what they said. He couldn't recall what Elena looked like, not that it mattered. But he appreciated Peralta's strong presence, along with dozens of old shipmates, both officer and enlisted, who assembled from near and far.

The Mallory house on La Jolla Shores Drive was quiet the following week. David stayed for a few days before returning to UCLA, and Laura and her husband flew back to Fort Worth. Luisa's relatives had come and gone, and the mail brought stacks of condolences that needed to be acknowledged. Friends brought copious supplies of food, most of which remained uneaten, and the accumulation of dirty dishes had reached critical mass in the kitchen.

He was surprised to find himself rather calm and collected, in a surreal, fuzzy way. He even accepted the complacency of the California Highway Patrol investigators, who seemed to treat the whole scenario as an incident to be documented as another drive-by shooting, then filed away as a statistic. Even the shock of returning home from dining out after Luisa's return from Costa Verde and finding the place burglarized had nearly faded from his mind. From the list of missing items, the local police suspected teenage drug abusers known to be operating in the area. Things like Mallory's .38 caliber service revolver, a video camera, and Luisa's Minox—a gold plated model he'd given her as a birthday present—could be readily converted to cash or traded for narcotics. He regretted not being able to see the pictures she took on her trip. The exposed film was still in the camera.

He knew he had to get on with his life, somehow rouse himself and begin to fill the vacuum, a step at a time.

Mallory's phone rang as he unplugged the coffee pot in the kitchen. *Better get used to answering it again,* he told himself, after avoiding the thing for several days.

"Deke!" The voice was Peralta's.

"Hello, Nacho." Mallory took the hand unit with him outside to the pool, where he plopped onto a lounge chair.

Peralta sounded much as he did back when they went through flight training together. Foreign cadets were not uncommon in the Training Command then, and a trickle of students from Mexico, Brazil, Costa Verde, Panama, and Argentina returned to their countries wearing U.S. Navy or Air Force wings, courtesy of the U.S. taxpayer and whatever trade agreements were being renegotiated. The Latin Americans were well connected at home or they wouldn't have been there in the first place, but even among this group Peralta enjoyed special influence, and always stood out among the foreign cadets. Tall, trim, and devilishly handsome, the son of his country's president, with a suave manner and bedroom eyes, Ignacio Guiterrez de Peralta was always the first to be inspected by the girls whenever they entered a room. He and Peralta had spent their off-duty time together, with Nacho footing most of the bills for their partying.

"Deke, I'm in the car," Peralta said, "headed your way, right now. Listen, I know with what you've been through, my timing is probably very bad, but I think I found a real tonic for you at this terrible time in your life."

Mallory sighed almost involuntarily, hoping it wasn't audible at the other end of the line. Peralta's hair-brained, jet-set schemes were seldom of interest to him anymore, though they shared plenty of adventures in years past.

"I thought you went back to San Marcos," Mallory said.

"I got sidetracked. I've found this beautiful Bearcat," Peralta purred, "at Chino Airport, east of Los Angeles. Needs lots of work, of course, but she's absolutely beautiful."

Mallory wasn't surprised anymore. Peralta was a sucker for the Navy's last, and finest, propeller-driven fighter, the Grumman F8F Bearcat, not that Mallory wasn't enamored of the rare bird himself. Luisa had reported that Peralta owned a small collection of flyable Bearcats he kept at his plantation in the Costa Verde countryside. She had the feeling that something was brewing down there, perhaps involving the Bearcats. She had said she thought Nacho was putting together some grand scheme to depose the present government.

"I thought you had some Bearcats, Nacho?"

"Yes, I have several, but you don't have one, and you should!" Peralta continued. "Let's go partners on it. You buy and I'll restore her. Or I'll buy her and you pay for the restoration. Don't worry about operating expenses once she's flyable. I can handle them in one of my companies. Just take a look, okay?" he pleaded.

"Partners?" Mallory asked.

"Sure, we can buy it for $95,000, and it'll cost that much to restore."

Mallory found himself paying attention. No other adrenaline rush could compare with flying a Bearcat off a short field under full power, and climbing to 10,000 feet in a minute and a half. And adrenaline had always been Mallory's drug of choice. This could be something to throw himself into for a few months, until he was ready to face the future without Luisa at his side.

"Another thing, Deke. We'll flip a coin to see who races her next September. I've already paid the entrance fee for the Reno Gold Trophy! Of course we'll have to qualify and—"

"You've entered a plane you don't even own?"

"I entered one of the Cats I have in Costa Verde. But I might not to be able to get the proper approvals to export her when the time comes, due to the gangsters who are running my country these days!"

"Hey, I'm turning into your street right now. Just wait till you see this beauty!" He hung up before Mallory could respond.

Mallory looked at all the dishes and casseroles in the sink. *What the hell! I've got nothing else to do today.*

He grabbed his old flight jacket from the hall tree in the entry and headed for the front door.

SEVENTEEN

SAN MARCOS, COSTA VERDE

A carnival atmosphere prevailed in the city. Most shops were closed and shuttered, but it wasn't the midday siesta when most businesses close, it was nine o'clock in the morning. Vendors sold ice cream and cola drinks, and children ran about squealing, as young mothers with black shawls about the head and shoulders tried to control them.

It wasn't a saint's day or fiesta, though in San Marcos nearly any excuse would justify an impromptu celebration. This was a funeral.

Terry Truman stood at the entrance to the Cosmopolitan, the only four-star hotel in the downtown area. He had arrived at daybreak on a commercial flight from Miami, after a flight from Washington aboard a military jet. He thought about Gretchen's conviction that Burton had sold out to the Generalissimo's government, but despite all major efforts to uncover the truth about Burton's loyalty, the evidence remained inconclusive. Truman wasn't much nearer getting to the bottom of the matter than he had been in the beginning. Maybe this trip would result in uncovering some scrap of information to move things one way or the other. Though Gretchen remained adamant, he still found it hard to believe Burton was a traitor. There hadn't been any withdrawals from the Swiss account she alleged was Burton's, and the bank account itself didn't prove he was getting payoffs. It could have been established without Burton's knowledge by someone seeking to discredit him.

Truman reviewed the elements of the surprise visit he would make to Electricos Verde, S.A., the electronics distributor and local CIA front where Jack Franck, formerly the deceased Holloway's number two, was holding forth as station chief. He wanted to debrief Franck without Burton being in the loop and possibly filtering whatever Franck might say about the situation here in Costa Verde. However, Truman hadn't foreseen the whole city's closing down for the archbishop's funeral, so he would wait until tomorrow to drop in on Franck.

The crowd pushed slowly along *Avenida de Los Santos* toward the twin towers of the Cathedral at the far end of the Plaza a few blocks away. A single bell pealed, slowly and monotonously. The people in the streets had come from everywhere in the country and were being watched by soldiers and the government's civilian informers. *There shouldn't be any trouble today,* Truman surmised, *since it isn't a politically important funeral.*

The morning was hot and a strange, dry wind prevailed. This wasn't the usual humid weather by any means. There had been a middling earthquake just after dawn which heightened the surreal quality of the moment. Truman overheard someone in the crowd say God was hurting today, grieving with them. He watched as a man ducked into a cantina across the street and emerged wiping his mouth on his sleeve, hurrying to catch up to his wife and children. He remembered Burton telling him about the local *Aveita*. The "little bird" was a rather good beer that, according to the Generalissimo's decree, sold for a mere peso. Bill laughed when telling him the decree also required the Aveita to be chilled at forty-five to fifty degrees, which rumor had it the G-Mo had read on a Heineken bottle. Truman wondered whether Electricos Verde had benefited from a corresponding demand for more commercial refrigeration units.

He stepped back through the revolving door and headed for the modernistic brass and marble bar just off the lobby, where he ordered an Aveita and sat watching the crowd through the window.

As he sipped his beer, he reviewed what he had learned from Burton in the past year that might shed some light on the loyalty issue. Burton had told him about his suspicions that the Generalissimo's regime wasn't the garden-variety Central American military government it appeared to be on the surface. Burton claimed Holloway's plunge from the helicopter was a suicide and he derided Franck as being too shifty an operator to be trusted as a station chief. Nevertheless, Burton reluctantly agreed to elevate Franck to Holloway's spot at Truman's urging. Truman knew the way to get to the bottom of things was to leave the puzzle as intact as possible, and he had insisted on the continuity that Franck represented.

Ever since the Generalissimo's coup, Burton had speculated the former sergeant was actually a front man for someone behind the scenes. It only makes sense, he had argued, given the G-mo's lack of education and command experience. Truman had greater respect for the native ability of a born tyrant, but whenever he pressed Burton for information to support his guesswork, Bill backed off and straddled the fence. "Well, it's just a gut feeling, really," he'd say, "but I'm working on it." And whenever Truman demanded specifics about Burton's plan to uncover the truth about the Generalissimo and his junta, Burton would say he was trying to help Franck find a way to get closer to the army colonels and generals who might provide clues. Then, last month, Burton proposed meeting the Generalissimo himself and becoming chummy with him. Truman had vetoed it on the grounds that if Burton's true identity wasn't already known to the Generalissimo's intel people, they sure as hell would find out when he started cozying up to their leader.

Finally, Burton's increasingly indifferent performance was leading Truman to the conclusion that either he had lost his professional effectiveness or Gretchen was right about his being in the Generalissimo's service. Either way, Truman would have to relieve Burton of his duties

THE HIDDEN EMPIRE

before long, but not until he could satisfy himself about Holloway's death and Gretchen's allegations. There was too much at stake here in Costa Verde and across the border in Nicaragua not to follow up every lead, specifically including Burton's activities, whatever they might be. Relieving Burton would remove all possibility of uncovering the truth about him. In fact, if he canned Burton he would lose perhaps the last chance of finding out if there was another power behind the Generalissimo.

Outside, one of the military's ubiquitous four-door Jeep Cherokees gradually pushed through the throng and stopped in front of the hotel. *Now I've seen it all,* Truman thought, shaking his head. *Where but in this mad Banana Republic would army vehicles be painted pink, accented with gold trim, and fitted with white sidewall tires?* But then, the G-Mo was only a semiliterate sergeant until grabbing power a few years ago.

The Jeep's rear doors discharged two soldiers, wearing designer sunglasses and carrying Uzis, which they held at high port. The soldiers' white garrison caps, web belts and boots contrasted with their medium-blue uniforms. Truman thought it a halfway decent, if prissy, combination. A heavyset, bearded man in civilian clothes slipped from the front passenger's seat and pushed his way into the lobby. Dark glasses and a planter's hat shielded his features. The soldiers reentered the Jeep and it crawled forward, to the obvious relief of those in the slow-moving crowd.

To hell with it, Truman decided, and motioned for another beer. He rarely traveled anymore. He knew too much to hazard himself in situations where his security wasn't guaranteed. Besides, he realized he was getting too old for field operations anyway. Ignoring the advice of his experts, he thought this time his safety would best be served by traveling alone with the simplest cover. He was Harry Fram, a retired banker from Indiana. And here he was, without so much as the Colt .45 automatic he had carried as a Marine platoon leader in Korea. Modern handguns were more accurate and carried twice as many rounds, but Truman didn't care about that. The .45 fitted his character, which, despite his Georgetown doctorate in foreign affairs, was Irish Catholic, uncomplicated and street-smart, unlike the ubiquitous Ivy Leaguers who always seemed to permeate CIA culture. If he ever used it again he knew it would be up close where the unmatched energy of the military .45 made exit wounds the size of footballs. He could have sent it in the diplomatic pouch but didn't abuse the privilege.

This is dumb, he thought, *America's chief spook sitting at the bar like a cheap gumshoe. No,* he told himself, *it's necessary.* The Company's operations in Central America are at stake and the lives of a dozen agents are jeopardized. If his oldest living friend was on the take from the Generalissimo, Truman was confident he would sense it somehow. What nagged him, as he sat staring through the plate glass separating him from the passing throng, was the apparent lack of any motive Burton would have for selling out. Bill was independently comfortable from family money, and had experienced enough excitement and success to satisfy anybody's ego. He was by no means the archetypal traitor, a mid-level loner bureaucrat whose hope of making it big in life lay in selling what he knew to a foreign power.

Whisky breath filled Truman's nostrils as a man slid onto the next stool. "T-Square, you old son-of-a-gun, what brings you out of the shadows?"

Truman turned on his stool and was shocked to encounter Burton. *My God,* he thought, *he's put on tons of weight.* Burton's eyes were red, yet he seemed to be in control of himself. Truman hadn't seen him for a couple of months, though they were in touch regularly by telephone.

"Hello," Truman said. "Harry Fram's my name."

Burton seemed bewildered.

"From South Bend," Truman continued in a warm voice, and gave him a business card. Burton glanced at it. "Fram & Co., Investments," it read, "Harry G. Fram, Principal."

Burton recovered quickly.

"Yeah, right," he said. "I'm Bill Winslow. Sorry, but I thought you were someone I knew." He extended his hand. "Glad to know you,

Fram." Burton's cover was William G. Winslow, a tire distributor from Mexico City.

Truman's mind raced. *Was it Burton who had emerged from the Jeep in front of the hotel?* He thought so. *What the hell's happened to him? Why hasn't anyone tipped me to his condition?*

"Say, Fram," Burton said, "why don't we get out of here to where we can talk?"

They joined the huge throng moving toward the National Cathedral and the archbishop's funeral. Truman could hear blaring loudspeakers in the distance and judged the area was already overflowing and the army was trying to control the sea of people.

He turned to Burton as they stopped at an intersection. "You don't look so good," he said. "What the hell have you been up to?"

"I figured you'd notice," Burton laughed, as they stepped from the curb and headed across the street. "It's all in the line of duty, believe me. I just left an all-nighter at Colonel Benes' estate. He's commander of the local military district but handles the major purchasing contracts for the military. He's my customer for truck tires. More importantly," he continued, "Benes is a pal of the G-mo's, so guess who was there? The big man himself!"

Truman's eyes flashed with anger. "Damn it, I told you to stay away from the Generalissimo!"

"Relax," Burton parried, "I didn't know the great man was going to be there, and I only shook hands with him."

Truman tugged Burton into a doorway. "What the hell's wrong with you, Bill?" he demanded. "You're not yourself."

"So I had too much to drink last night," Burton scoffed. "Wade Holloway was a friend of mine and I'm still pissed off about his death. Even though I think it was suicide, I'll never know for sure. Franck is a sneaky little bastard, and I still resent your overriding my decision to put a trustworthy man on station here."

"Are you finished?" Truman growled. "None of that justifies pulling your Lone Ranger act on me!"

Burton's eyes flashed. "Then here's the real answer to your question," he said. "I'm working on uncovering a murky foreign investor, who's backing the Generalissimo. Whoever he is, his fingerprints are all over the place down here. The whole damn country has been taken over by a bunch of smart-ass whiz kids from Germany, who are running one hell of a lot of the industry and commerce here from behind the scenes. None of this could happen without the Generalissimo's blessing. So, what's in it for his royal highness? Money, that's what. Lots of it."

He held up his hand, as Truman glared at him. "I'm not finished, T-Square. Hear me out. There are nine or ten of these *wunderkind,* all about thirty years old. They're not working for any of the corporations or investors known to be operating in Latin America, because I've checked it out. And here's the topper," he continued. "These guys operate in the shadows. They're so reclusive that no one can get close to any of them. Holloway tried and I've tried.

"But guess who's the exception to the rule, T-Square? Jack friggin' Franck, that's who! He's got a relationship going with at least two of them, that I know about so far. When I question him about it, he says they're just friends, that's all." Burton shook his head emphatically. "Bullshit! So, I figure to get closer to the G-mo, which enables me to observe these young hotshots more closely, and start finding out what the hell's really going on."

"Okay, okay," Truman said, "but why not have Langley or some contractor dig the facts out for you? You've got two dozen agents down here. Why are you up to your ass in this personally?"

"Because I think Franck's gotten himself involved with the blitzkrieg somehow, and I don't want the word spreading around Langley until I can prove it."

Truman nodded thoughtfully, and decided if he was going to get any results from this trip he'd better finesse this confrontation and avoid having it out with Burton prematurely. "Okay," he said, "let's see what this funeral is all about."

They reached the Plaza in front of the cathedral as a cardinal intoned the liturgy. *"Yo soy el resurreccion y la vida. . . ."*

Ancient morning-glory shaped loudspeakers were strung from buildings surrounding the huge Plaza and transformed the voice into a staccato, cursed with multiple echoes. Below a dais placed atop the cathedral steps, the archbishop's ebony, gilt-trimmed coffin rode on his pallbearers' shoulders. Four to a side, they stood on the steps, bracing upward. He couldn't have been a heavy man, Truman judged, since they were keeping the casket steady at such a high angle. The pallbearers were all short, elderly priests, except for one who seemed to tower above them. Stationed at the foot of the coffin, the tall man had some difficulty maintaining his shoulder at the proper height.

"The real tall one," Burton said, "is from East Germany, one of four priests who defected in 1989. They came here recently from Mexico City."

Interesting, Truman thought. He hadn't heard about any priests defecting from East Germany and it was his business to know. He made a mental note to have someone confirm this curiosity he should have known about at the time.

The cardinal finally finished and went before the casket into the Cathedral, followed by a score of clergy wearing ornate vestments. As they disappeared inside, the loudspeakers shrieked with feedback from microphones picking up the service from the altar. The stillness of the morning ended abruptly moments later when a chill breeze suddenly buffeted the throng waiting in the Plaza. Women tightened their shawls as dirt and paper bits rose in the air.

"Well, there he goes again," Burton quipped, waving his hand. "God, I mean. First a quake, now this. Makes a memorable day for the locals, though. They're superstitious as hell about portents, you know."

As they walked back toward the Cosmopolitan, Truman decided to press home to the heart of the matter. "What the hell really happened to Holloway, anyway?" he asked. "How could he have somehow fallen out of a helicopter?"

Burton stuck to his story. "He didn't fall. He jumped," he said. "The note I found said he was tired of lingering illness and couldn't cope any longer."

Truman had recently reviewed Holloway's medical records and knew better. It was true the man had contracted malaria once, but he had been certified to be in good health by Company physicians just a few weeks before he died. *Was Holloway mentally ill? Is Burton lying?*

"That's bullshit, Bill! He was healthy as hell."

"Just face it!" Burton snapped. "He jumped from the cargo door of the big chopper that Electricos Verde charters to deliver heavy equipment to remote sites. It happened over the rugged mining district south of here, so they never found the body. I discovered the note in his briefcase."

Truman stopped and glared at Burton. "What the hell are you telling me?" he demanded. "That a healthy man up and left a note claiming he was sick?"

"Well, that's the way it was."

"Who else was aboard that helo with Holloway?"

"Franck and I were," Burton said.

─────────

The ceiling fan spun noiselessly in Truman's room at the Cosmopolitan when he returned from his meeting with Franck at Electricos Verde. He pulled off his bow tie and loosened his collar. The meeting was fruitless. Holloway's successor seemed every bit as slick as Burton claimed. "Remember, Franck isn't always frank," Bill liked to say. *Maybe it's the man's lousy personality,* Truman thought, as he checked his airline tickets for the departure time to Miami. *Or maybe Franck just didn't know anything helpful.* At least his version of Holloway's death matched Burton's, which Truman found neither suspicious nor comforting. It bothered him, though, that Franck had initially told Gretchen that Holloway fell from the helicopter. Now they claim he jumped.

Maybe it was just a lapse due to the excitement of the moment, but Truman wondered. With an hour to spare before leaving for the airport, he stepped into the shower, feeling lousy about the lack of progress in achieving closure. One thing continued to strike him as odd as hell. Burton never once asked him the reason for his being here. Was it to avoid further questions? Was Bill aware he was under suspicion? If so, who, other than Gretchen, could have tipped him? Then there was his physical appearance. He had an explanation for his whisky breath, but why was he suddenly overweight? Was his meeting the Generalissimo at Colonel Benes' home simply fortuitous?

He toweled off and was uncapping a beer when he had an inkling he was missing something in the bigger picture. It hit him in a flash.

No one saw Holloway jump or fall!

Instead of suicide or foul play, Truman realized, maybe Holloway had parachuted to safety!

EIGHTEEN

THE CATHEDRAL, SAN MARCOS

Kaalten ventured outside after sunrise and decided to explore the cathedral gardens, comprising a half dozen acres enclosed by a high adobe wall in downtown San Marcos. He entered a maze of narrow clay paths, bordered with smooth stones set in the earth and realized that here was an amazing collection of tropical and nontropical trees and plants, representing all regions of this small but geologically diverse country. Elderly gardeners tended shrubs and raked leaves as downtown traffic noises poured over the wall.

He fingered the leaves of a large coffee tree. The scarlet beans were of commercial grade, he guessed, touching a cluster, although the plantations were high in the mountains. A small boulder with a bronze plaque indicated the tree's donor.

A LA GLORIA DE DIOS.
Regalo de La Iglesia de Santa Fe de Las Montanas
23 de Mayo 1933

A peacock spread its wings and rattled its tail feathers nearby, reminding him of visiting the Berlin Zoo when he was a child. Hearing someone on the path, he looked about and saw a priest approaching.

His hand flew instinctively to his clerical collar for assurance. *There's no need to be concerned,* he told himself. Adjusting the spectacles on his nose and strolling toward the other, he pretended to read his missal. As the other priest offered a greeting Kaalten turned a page, moving his lips to the Latin. The priest continued on his way, apparently not wishing to interrupt the newcomer's devotions. He found Staib—*Father Martin,* he reminded himself—sitting on a stone bench near the wall, with his eyes closed, sunning himself like a crocodile on a rock.

"Guten Tag," Kaalten offered, looking about to make sure they were alone before making conversation. "As I suppose you know, I just returned from Mexico City and missed the big funeral."

"Yes, I know," Staib said softly.

"Did you kill him?" Kaalten asked.

Staib straightened himself as the brigadefuhrer sat down on the bench. "Kill who?" he parried.

"The archbishop, of course."

"Of course I killed him," Staib snapped.

Kaalten's eyes narrowed. "Was it necessary?" he asked. "Doesn't it make things more difficult? We were in the archbishop's personal care here."

"First of all," Staib sighed, "you realize it was an order, don't you?"

"Of course, I don't imply—"

"Reichsfuhrer Tolt is always right," Staib reminded him. "He determined we could operate more freely with the archbishop out of the way, since the Vatican will control things until they consecrate a successor. Monsignor Albert in Rome has supplanted the archbishop, so far as the bishops of Costa Verde are concerned. He will remain the ultimate authority until the process is completed, which will take years, if he handles it properly, as of course he will.

"Monsignor Schmehr," Staib said, using Tolt's priestly appellation, "calculates that insinuating new faces, like ours, into a bureaucracy is best done when there's a leadership vacuum, rather than with a steady hand at the helm, as was true of the archbishop. Tolt knows that when an official is removed from a hierarchy, like the Church," Staib gazed at Kaalten condescendingly, "and the question of his replacement is made to linger, then those on lower rungs will find themselves in a perpetual state of wanting to please whoever has power to influence the appointment. In fact," he continued, "the more aggressive ones, who may covet the appointment themselves, can become especially subservient to higher authority, as they play out the game, hoping to win approval."

"That may be true," Kaalten said, "but why trade a known situation, like a benign archbishop, for the unknown?"

"Someone's coming," Staib interrupted.

The two moved off together on the path and opened their missals. Kaalten spoke when they were alone again. "Weren't you concerned about the risk, at all? I mean you obviously poisoned him?"

"A rare type of toxin, yes. It simulates a heart attack fairly well."

"Only fairly well?"

Staib stopped on the path, and beamed at Kaalten.

"Just when do you suppose," he asked, "were the sanctified remains of an archbishop subjected to the indignity of autopsy in a country like this?"

"I see what you mean," Kaalten allowed, his brow furrowing in thought. "Yes, I see," he continued. "Rome puts its imprimatur on the temporary order of things in the Church here in Costa Verde and the Reichsfuhrer ends up controlling everything due to Monsignor Albert's influence with Cardinal Guilianni at the Vatican!"

"Exactly!" Staib snapped. "Until Rome consecrates an archbishop, by which time Case Green will have succeeded."

"Excellent!" Kaalten exclaimed, spraying saliva.

As they neared the side entrance to the cathedral and were about to go inside, Kaalten grasped Staib's elbow. "Tolt's no priest," he snapped. "Neither are we, for that matter, but the charade works for us because we're merely administrative assistants. But how can Tolt even pretend to head the Catholic Church in this most Catholic country?"

"Simple," Staib told him. "Tolt won't be concerned with priest craft due to an edict of Cardinal Guilianni's effective today. The edict makes each Costa Verde bishop his own authority in matters of spiritual concern, for the time being, subject to supervision from Rome."

Kaalten seemed to be confused again.

"However," Staib told him, "the same edict makes our own Monsignor Schmehr the chief executive of the Church here pending a successor to the late archbishop. This means," Staib continued, his eyes narrowing, "that for our purposes the Reichsfuhrer just became the de facto Archbishop!"

Kaalten stiffened. "Why wasn't I told these things?" he demanded.

"You just were," Staib grunted, pulling his arm loose.

"Wait!" Kaalten said. "Isn't Tolt concerned about Monsignor Albert operating alone, half a world away? How can we trust him there at the Holy See of Christian piety?"

Staib blew through his teeth. "I have Monsignor Albert under good control," he said, with an evil smile. "In fact, he has become rather dependent on me recently."

Kaalten was nonplussed as Staib disappeared into the building. *What the hell does that mean?* he wondered.

THE VATICAN

Monsignor Albert splashed cold water on his face with both hands. He was too depressed to concentrate on anything beyond the water, and he was beginning to feel sick in the stomach. On his desk lay a treatise on the sin of suicide, which he had obtained from one of the Vatican libraries. He had been searching it for a loophole letting him slip the bounds of this life without eternal consequences, but he hadn't found one. He rubbed his eyes, trying to erase images of his visit to Costa Verde and the memory of his complicity in Tolt's scheme to occupy the cathedral.

A knock at the door startled him. He slowly rose to his feet and straightened his cassock. "One minute, please," he called, in a voice he hoped didn't reveal his emotional state. He quickly shoved the treatise into a drawer and opened the door.

Cardinal Guilianni's elderly male secretary smiled at him through his seemingly bloodless lips. He handed him a small parcel wrapped in brown paper with colorful postage stamps. It was addressed in green ink. "This package from Costa Verde is for you, Monsignor Albert," he croaked.

Albert thanked him and opened the package at his desk. An elegant longhand note in green ink offered a humble gift of native Costa Verde spices, in gratitude for his many courtesies to the Church there. He found a gift box of polished wood containing three little hand blown bottles. He read their colorful labels: garlic powder from Costa Verde's sun-drenched garlic fields; comino, a cumin favored in Costa Verde's finest seafood dishes; and cream of tartar, a by-product left from the fermentation of grapes into wine, used in making the finest local pastries.

Albert selected the cream of tartar, removed the cork stopper, tasted it and felt better immediately. Cream of tartar is odorless and indistinguishable to the eye from the highest quality cocaine. Net weight 109 grams, the label said. About a quarter of a pound, he realized. He had exhausted his own meager cache of cocaine the week before.

A few minutes later he spread the dossiers of the seven Costa Verde bishops before him and began examining them with relish. From the raw materials in these thick files he knew he could manufacture sufficient doubt about their qualifications to derail Guilianni's plan for the Pope to speedily appoint one of them as the new archbishop.

In his newfound exuberance, Albert no longer seemed to care that Staib, whom he had every reason to dread, had introduced his recent habit and become his supplier.

NINETEEN

Tongues of yellow flame shot past the open cockpit, followed by blasts of thick black exhaust, as the Grumman F8F Bearcat's Pratt & Whitney engine roared to life. The exhaust thinned as it settled down to idle. A brief scan of the instruments assured Mallory that all was well with the 2250 horses living under the engine cowling.

Pulling out of the chocks, he glanced at the packed grandstand. The American flags flying from the top of the grandstand snapped in the brisk desert breeze, heralding the intense energy of the audience. People came from all over the country for the National Championship Air Races, and he felt like a celebrity as he waved to the crowd.

Like a thoroughbred that preferred the track to the paddock, the Bearcat expressed its discontent with its serpentine progress down the taxiway by coughing, vibrating, and backfiring. This engine was built for speed, not taxiing, and if he weren't off the deck soon, he would have to apply brief bursts of power to keep it from loading up.

The other contenders in the Unlimited class—two P-51 Mustangs, another Bearcat, two British Sea Furies, a P-38 Lightning, and an F4U Corsair—all seemed ill-at-ease too, as they taxied to Stead Field's Runway 28.

As he maintained his place in the aeronautical conga line, bitter memories invaded his thoughts. Luisa's death had left a mark on him like a cattle brand, a malignant tumor of the soul that had not been assuaged by more tennis, more swimming, more golf—and more drinking. Nacho was right: readying the Bearcat for the race had been welcome therapy for his loss. He had obsessively thrown himself into the restoration of the aircraft, working long hours, often spending the night on a cot in the corner of the hangar at Montgomery Field in Southern California.

Closing the canopy and clearing the engine with a burst of power, he was suddenly seized by the thrill of coming home to the world of high RPMs, high octane, high G-forces, high pulse rate, and sweaty palms on the controls—the aeronautical tonic that was missing in his life.

His Navy retirement pay, along with some decent investments they had made over the years, provided a comfortable living, but the cost of all this was only possible through Luisa's inheritance from her father. The Bearcat had cost a hundred thousand, and Peralta had put an equal amount into the restoration. He would rather have Luisa alive than a racing aircraft, but he was learning to live with the new reality.

The annual races attracted two kinds of entrants. There were the serious contenders, with the drive and the money to win. Modified engines, canopies, propellers, and airframes were costly as hell, but were the ticket to fame and a hefty share of the purse. Mallory's crowd, on the other hand, flew solely for thrills in World War II "warbirds" like his Bearcat, near stock with only slight modifications, but meticulously restored and carefully fine-tuned for top performance. Some bore nostalgic decor like Mallory's, which carried the markings of his old Navy squadron, VF-263.

The Lockheed P-38 ahead of him lifted off, and Mallory was cleared onto the runway. He ran through his prelaunch checklist, with final emphasis on full right rudder throw and trim, and locked the tail wheel as soon as he was on the runway's centerline. Without full right rudder on takeoff, the incredible torque of the 18-cylinder engine put the aircraft into a skid to the left as soon as it left the deck, and the incredible acceleration prevented the left gear from retracting against the slipstream into the wheel well. Acceleration set the Bearcat apart from these other fighters. Bearcats were designed to climb from a carrier deck to 10,000 feet in 94 seconds to meet the Japanese Kamikaze attacks in the Pacific, but by the time they joined the fleet in 1945 the war was over. The Navy's Flight Demonstration team, the Blue Angels, flew them in air shows from 1946 to 1948, pushing them to maximum performance until 1949, when they were replaced by Grumman F9F Panther jets.

After a final check of the engine instruments, Mallory eased the throttle forward to takeoff power and released the impatient Bearcat into its element. He left the deck in less than 300 feet, accelerating rapidly in a puddle of sweat and a state of euphoria, which he likened to a sort of aerial orgasm. Retracting the gear, he swung wide to the west over the desert, powered back for the formation start, and joined up on the aircraft ahead of him, flying a loose right echelon on the pace plane, a metallic silver T-33. In previous years the pace plane had been a P-51 Mustang but with the advent of highly modified aircraft that could touch 500 miles per hour, it was replaced with the Lockheed jet.

They were soon joined by a Sea Fury, a Mustang, and the Corsair. The pace plane swung the eight aircraft in a wide turn to the left, toward the first pylon. When they were reasonably arranged in a line abreast formation, their headsets crackled with the traditional declaration. "Gentlemen, you have a race."

Mallory's adrenaline surged as the airspeed needle passed 365 miles an hour and he positioned himself for the first turn. The highly modified Mustang immediately pulled ahead of the pack, followed closely by the modified Bearcat, with its tiny "Cosmic Wind" canopy, clipped wings that shortened the wingspan by about four feet, a propeller spinner, and a tail cone fairing covering the port for the stinger tail hook.

A glance in the rearview mirror showed the P–38 and the Corsair coming up close behind, while his peripheral vision caught the black and white invasion stripes on the highly modified Royal Navy Sea Fury as it began overtaking on the left. The cockpit noise increased as he eased the throttle forward carefully—but not all the way. Hardly a year passed at Reno without someone firewalling the throttle too early in the race. The powerful engines simply couldn't sustain full engine power throughout the entire race. Thrown rods, cracked stress points, blown gaskets and oil lines caused an engine to seize up in seconds, and many an aspirant wound up in the Nevada desert with a windscreen covered in oil.

As the Sea Fury passed, he focused on the first of the eight orange pylons on the nine-mile course. He swung wide on the turn at an altitude of about a hundred feet, behind the Sea Fury and ahead of the P–38. Rounding the pylon in a slight wingover meant gaining altitude and losing a little ground in the race, but it was preferable to "mowing the sagebrush" and dipping a wingtip into the sand. Heading for the second pylon, he slowly closed on the Sea Fury and pulled away some from the P–38 and the Corsair.

The first casualty came on the fourth lap. A Mustang blew a gasket and trailed a plume of coolant from its Rolls Royce Merlin engine. Mallory rounded the next pylon, this time only fifty feet above the deck, and for the next lap held his own in the middle of the pack. Rounding the fifth pylon with just three laps to go, he felt a powerful urge to throw caution to the wind, firewall the throttle, and go for it. His inner voice of prudence said NO, but rounding the next pylon closer to the deck than ever, a plane length behind the Sea Fury, the urge to push the envelope overcame the prudence.

Alive with energy, he carefully advanced the throttle, giving full rein to his eager team of 2250 wild horses. He retrimmed for the increased speed and the Bearcat moved forward in the pack. He was still a lap behind the major contenders but, by God, he was now in a position to beat all the other warbirds. He had a silly grin on his face as he darted past the Sea Fury, and took the lead among the amateurs in the race.

The grin disappeared the instant the oil hit the windscreen.

He pulled up immediately, instinctively trading airspeed for more altitude, as he keyed his mike to announce his predicament. "Mayday. Bearcat three zero one, pulling off course." He continued his climb to buy a few seconds in which to set up for a wheels-up landing in the desert below, but he couldn't see much through the oil-splattered windscreen. Fortunately, he knew the pace pilot would soon be on his wing for whatever guidance was necessary.

"Three zero one, you're too low and too far to make the runway, but you've got a smooth spot of real estate dead ahead and slightly to your left."

Mallory corrected slightly to his left and thought he could make out a clear spot ahead through the smudged windscreen. Quickly opening the canopy, he dropped the wing flaps and reached for the mixture control, hoping to shut down the engine before it seized.

He was too late. *Shit!*

The huge, four-bladed Aeroprop ground to a halt, and the only sound was the airstream whistling through the cockpit. With wings level, the Bearcat's nose was slightly below the horizon, and dropping fast. Unpowered flight was not the Bearcat's forte, and pilots used to joke that it had the glide angle of a free-falling safe.

He tightened the harness for impact. As the Bearcat plowed into the desert, his ears were bombarded by the sound of metal tearing on rocks and sand. The propeller blades bent back as the massive engine weight dug the aircraft's chin into the earth in a cloud of flying soil and sagebrush. He was still in the cockpit, slowly shaking his head at his misfortune, when the pace pilot flew by close to the deck and rocked his wings.

The lounge at Reno's Holiday Inn was noisier than ever, as racing tactics were debated and tales of the old days told and retold: the P-40s and the P-47s that had raced in the years following World War II, the legendary Paul Mantz, who always flew his Mustang wearing a coat and tie, Bill Fornoff's bronze Bearcat, and Clay Lacy's purple Mustang. How airspeed had increased over the years, with Darryl Greenamyer's Bearcat, Number 1, setting a speed record in 1975, to be topped by Lyle Shelton's Bearcat, Rare Bear, in the late 1980s. Mallory had heard it all before and after receiving condolences from his fellow pilots, he had retreated to lick his wounds. He stared into the mirror behind the bar, swirled the ice cubes in his glass, and was sipping his scotch when he felt a hand on his shoulder.

"Deke, I'm really sorry about what happened today."

Mallory looked up to see Peralta sliding onto the next barstool, wearing an impeccably tailored blue blazer, his trademark spread collar and an outrageously expensive Italian silk tie, in sharp contrast to Mallory's rumpled khaki slacks and Hawaiian shirt.

"May I join the wake and pay my respects to our beautiful Bearcat?" Peralta asked. "May she rest in peace," he intoned, solemnly crossing himself.

Mallory shrugged. "Don't forget to bring flowers for the gravesite," he said, as he caught the bartender's eye and pointed to his glass and then to Peralta. He sighed and shook his head. "Dammit, if I just hadn't tried to overtake that Sea Fury so close to the finish."

Peralta shrugged. "Hell, I would have done the same thing. We've always shared the same demon, the one that wants to push us right through the envelope. That's what makes us tick, you know. And don't worry too much about the cost. The money is not important. Entering the race was."

Mallory sighed. "So was finishing it."

"I'm glad we still share the taste of good scotch," Peralta said, as he accepted a Glenlivet single malt, "although last night you didn't share my enthusiasm for the plans that are gelling in my country."

"Of course I didn't. That's because you're certifiably insane." Mallory turned on his stool and surveyed Peralta. "I would think the son of the former president of Costa Verde, with a Harvard education and bottomless pits of money, would have something better to do than dreaming up revolutionary jungle war games."

"There's nothing more worthy of my time, or my life, than what I'm planning," Peralta said. "Nothing!"

Mallory eyed his friend. This certainly wasn't the Peralta he had known over the years, the sybaritic, skirt-chasing playboy whose personal agenda left no room for anything but the immediate pursuit of pleasure.

Peralta had spent the last several evenings in a passionate dissertation on his revolutionary movement to retake control of Costa Verde. According to Peralta, the country had been taken over by a shadowy group of German businessmen who now controlled the banks, the national airline, hotels, public utilities, the major commercial enterprises, and maybe even the church. The Peralta family still controlled many of Costa Verde's plantations and distilleries, but Nacho seemed convinced they were in the path of an economic invasion launched by a murky underworld organization. He was bent on organizing a squadron of mercenary pilots to fly his collection of Bearcats in an all-out attempt to overthrow the existing military government and restore a democratic regime.

Peralta glanced at Mallory. "Look, Deke, I can't sit by and do nothing. I'm no longer the playboy you once knew. The coup against my father changed everything in my life."

"How could I forget the coup," Mallory interrupted, "with Luisa and the kids missing all day, and me helpless in the middle of the Perfect Storm in the North Pacific?"

Peralta sighed. "I can imagine how you felt. As you know," he continued after a thoughtful pause, "my father died in Spain last year." Peralta took a sip of his scotch and stared into space. "I was with him when he died with the terrible realization that he failed our people. I don't want to end up like that. I must do something."

"Of course you'll do something," Mallory said. "I'm curious, though, about what the hell this Bearcat squadron of yours is going to be able to do. Fly against the Air Force from Captain Midnight's secret base in the jungle? Costa Verde still has an air force, right?"

Peralta nodded. "Cessna A-37B Dragonflies and North American T-28D Counter Insurgency aircraft. When a village is thought to be dis-loyal, they commandeer a farmer's truck for gunnery practice. Strafing the poor bastard's pickup convinces the villagers what the next step will be if they don't shape up."

"Any jets?"

"Yes," Peralta acknowledged, "some F-80s, including the very ones that belonged to the Fire Birds demonstration team, and a couple of helicopter gunships, Soviet Hinds, actually, like the ones Nicaragua got from East Germany."

Mallory knew from Navy briefings that the Sandinista hardware couldn't have simply vanished but he was mildly surprised that some helicopters had ended up in Costa Verde.

"Okay," he said, "but the air force isn't going to let you blast them out the sky without a fight."

"Of course not. But as you know, the Bearcat is perfect for taking out equipment like that."

"I understand that," Mallory said, "but with all your means, why don't you get some Russian MiG-29s for the job? They're readily avail-able these days, real cheap."

"I couldn't get jets into the country unnoticed," he said. "And they would need longer airstrips than the ones I maintain, runways that could easily be taken out.

"Look, Deke, I already have my Bearcats. Six so far. I've been col-lecting them for several years now. The Generalissimo, as he calls him-self, doesn't seem concerned about them. He thinks they're merely my toys, and up to now he's been right. In fact, I've put out disinforma-tion that because of their age only one or two are flyable; that I'm stripping the others for parts to keep the flyable birds going. I can operate my Bearcats from small strips, all within easy striking distance of the capital and the military bases." Peralta paused to let that sink in. "This has been in the works for some time, you know."

"Obviously."

"I already have several pilots, besides me, who are very proficient handling a Bearcat. They're damn good!"

"What about the army? They have tanks, right?"

"Damn right. When they rumble into a village the peasants pee in their pants and give the army whatever it wants. My Bearcats can easily neutralize them with rockets. And when I've leveled the playing field and taken care of those bastards in the Presidential Palace, the people will arise and take back our country, and reinstate a legitimate government. The people are ready but they need to be galvanized into action."

"Okay," Mallory said, as he took a sip of his drink. "But your preparations can't have gone unnoticed. As soon as you launch, they're going to bomb your secret bases right off the map, amigo."

Peralta grinned. "Not these secret bases!"

"Why haven't they dropped the net on you yet? They must have some idea of what you're planning. If they've taken over everything as you say, how come you're still running around loose?"

"Because they think I'm the foppish son of a wealthy family, content with jetting around the world and pursuing nubile maidens. Elena and I own major portions of land, plus most of the silver mines, banana plantations, breweries and distilleries. We produce revenue—through exorbitant taxes, of course—and the Generalissimo doesn't want to disturb that. And he can't do a high profile takeover of private property and still get aid from the United States. He definitely doesn't want to do anything to discourage the rapidly growing tourist industry. Americans are flocking to our new Pacific beach resorts, and they're bringing lots of Yankee dollars with them."

"Why don't you just assassinate the bastard," Mallory snapped, "and take your country back with another coup? Isn't that what Latin Americans usually do?"

"I wish it were that simple but, considering what we know about the enormity of the operation, the present junta would just be replaced by others."

Mallory nodded as the bartender brought another round.

"What will you do now, Deke?" Peralta asked.

"After I've finished the insurance paperwork on our bird, I'm looking forward to taking a risk-free vacation with David. A week in Cancun. Sand between my toes, the sound of waves on a white sand beach, punctuated at frequent intervals by industrial-strength libations. David just graduated from UCLA and, considering everything that's happened, we need some time together."

"Of course," Peralta said. "But after a few days of toasting yourselves in the inferior Mexican sun, and exercising your livers, why don't you drop down to Costa Verde for a little fishing on my yacht? After all, you'll be in the neighborhood and a day or two at sea would do you good. And I'm sure David would enjoy a visit to Costa Verde when we're not in the midst of a revolution."

Mallory was careful to avoid any response that even bordered on acceptance.

"And while we're fishing," Peralta continued, following an expectant pause, "considering the relaxed state you will be in, I may be able to pick your brain a little. You've had training that I could never hope to have. Naval War College, TOPGUN, strategic and tactical planning at the Pentagon, experience that I could benefit from in running an effective campaign. I could learn a lot from you."

Mallory realized now that Peralta had obviously done his homework. Perhaps this had been in the works all during their partnership in the Bearcat. Maybe he didn't know Nacho as well as he thought, but one thing was certain; there was a hidden agenda here somewhere.

"And when you and David come to Costa Verde, you'll meet La Pantera."

"You've got a panther? Hell, we had a cat once."

"I'm not talking about any pets. You obviously don't know your Latin American history. La Pantera was the nineteenth-century liberator of my country. She led the revolution which ended 300 years of Spanish rule."

"She?"

"Yes, she. La Pantera was the Simon Bolivar of Costa Verde. The peasant women expect her to return in their hour of need. They pray for her to liberate us again."

Mallory raised an eyebrow. "You're bullshitting me?"

"No. It's true. She and her ragtag army sprang from the jungle like panthers. They destroyed the enemies of the people in colonial times. When responsible leaders were in place, she disappeared. She is going to reappear," Peralta continued with a broad smile, "just in time for my war of liberation."

Mallory snorted. "Don't you think she's a little past her prime for a return engagement? I suppose you've got Spiderman and Wonder Woman waiting in the wings, too?"

Peralta shrugged. "Okay, I'm sure you find this an amusing fantasy, but you'll understand when you're my guest. You might even meet La Pantera."

Mallory laughed and shook his head. "You've always provided good entertainment for your guests, Nacho, but really, this takes the prize. By the way, I thought panthers lived in Africa."

"That's true but a *pantera negra* is a black jaguar, native to Central America. Jaguars are spotted but occasionally one's born pure black. That's a very special cat, a magic cat, and its black coat makes it revered by our people. Naturally, legend has made La Pantera larger than life but the peasants know she is coming again to save them from oppression. And she will."

Mallory sighed. "If you say so, Nacho."

TWENTY

David Mallory looked down from his window seat at the blue-green waters of the Gulf of Mexico as the Boeing 767 banked slightly to the right. Gin and tonics and some airline mystery chicken had produced a relaxed feeling of euphoria he hadn't known recently.

"You look like you're finally beginning to unwind," his father told him.

"I sure as hell hope so," David said, continuing to stare down at the water.

Mallory regarded his son thoughtfully. A strapping six foot three, he had his mother's eyes and olive skin, a constant reminder of Luisa's Spanish beauty. She had insisted on proficiency in Spanish for their two children, and David's was good enough that he could shed his gringo persona whenever he wanted and emerge as a genuine Latino. Mallory's bumbling Spanish had led to his meeting Luisa in the first place, but he spoke with the fluency of a Spanish national now, and he liked the idea of his children sharing their mother's heritage.

"Taking the Graduate Record Exam," David said with a grin, "then the LSAT and applying to a dozen law schools doth not a tranquil summer make, to say nothing of beginning to sweat out getting some acceptances. I'm sure as hell ready for some serious beach time and checking out the bikini-clad maidens, assuming there are any in the area."

Mallory smiled. "I've a feeling you'll encounter some," he said, as he passed their trays to the stewardess.

David turned serious. "Dad, I'm glad you finally told that admiral that you'd go to work for him at the Pentagon." Mallory listened without comment. "Sis and I both felt it was the right thing for you to do after Mom's death; you know, get out of the old neighborhood, get a new start. Plus you love that kind of stuff anyway."

Mallory nodded. "Right. I wouldn't have told him yes if your mom had lived. But now I'm looking forward to it."

David snapped his table into the back of the seat in front of him and stretched his legs. "You know," he said, "I'm still trying to figure out your old buddy Nacho. There wasn't much chance to get to know him at Mom's funeral, and I missed him that weekend I came down from UCLA to see your Bearcat. I vaguely remember him as a playboy-type around the house when I was a kid, and I recall you and Mom talking about him a lot. He was in Europe or someplace when Mom and Laura and I visited Elena. Wow! That was really something. Tanks firing right into where we were staying and scruffy-looking soldiers pointing machine guns at us, not to mention escaping across the roof. Mom was really cool-headed."

"She always was," Mallory said softly, slowly nodding his head.

"But this private war of Nacho's he told you about in Reno . . . is it a payback for them overthrowing his dad's presidency or has he gone bonkers or something?"

Mallory sighed, "I think he knows what he's doing. He's had an epiphany of sorts and feels guilty about having frittered his life away playing with his toys and chasing skirt. His plan may sound like a bad movie plot, but he seems to have thought it through and planned it pretty well. When we were in Reno he said he wants to pick my brains on things like logistics and strategy, things I studied at the War College or handled at the Pentagon. I don't know where he got that idea, but

I'm going to stay out of the picture. There are just too many risks involved, even if he is an old friend. I'll say one thing, though," Mallory added. "He can fly circles around a lot of Naval Aviators I've known."

David cocked his head and looked at his father. "I know you were in flight training together, but the Bearcat's an old World War II plane. Where did you both fly it?"

"It was a long time ago," Mallory recalled with a smile. "I was a junior officer in a squadron at Miramar, and one day I received orders to be the Navy Liaison Officer to a flight demonstration team being formed in Costa Verde. Most countries with a real air force have them. We have the Blue Angels and Thunderbirds, the Canadians have the Snowbirds, and the Costa Verdeans had just formed their Fire Birds, the *Pajaros de Fuego*. I couldn't believe I had been selected for such choice duty. I mean, they could have sent down a former Blue Angel, someone with more experience, but I got all the procedures from the Blue Angels, and your mom and I went to Costa Verde for several months. Your mother was pregnant with Laura, and it was an incredible time.

"Of course," Mallory added with a smile, "the fact that Nacho's father was President of Costa Verde and a fishing buddy of Dick Nixon had a lot to do with it. You weren't born yet."

"That must have been fabulous duty."

"It was, indeed," Mallory said. "I checked out in the Bearcat and flew it almost every day. Your mom and I swam in warm water from white sandy beaches and, because we both spoke Spanish, it wasn't anything like being in a strange foreign country. Nacho and I flew together later, too. When I had shore duty in Washington at the Puzzle Palace he was there a lot with his embassy, on trade missions or just partying in the power circles. I needed at least four hours flight time a month to keep my flight pay, so we'd get together and sign out planes at NAS Anacostia: old SNJs, TV2s, T-28s, and F-5s, all good fighter trainers. Nacho had his pair of Navy Wings, was an officer in his own navy, and also in their air force, a nephew of his country's ambassador, and the son of its serving president. Between the two of us, we could get the keys to most anything we wanted. He wasn't always properly checked out in what he flew, but by the time we landed he knew the bird almost as well as I did."

"Sounds like a couple of kids in the bumper cars at the county fair."

"Something like that," Mallory laughed. "Anyway, we'd check out a couple of planes on a Saturday, head out to sea and mix it up. That's what he wanted to do, and I was always antsy from flying a desk, so needless to say, we had a ball. He never flew combat, of course. I've been a fighter pilot my whole career, but he always gave me a run for my money. David, the guy was awesome, a natural."

David nodded thoughtfully and looked down at the water. "I think I'm a natural for that water down there. I can't wait to hit the beach."

CANCUN, MEXICO

The beach boy ducked under the thatched roof of their *palapa* on the beach at Cancun. *"Otra cerveza, señores?"*

Mallory turned to David, who appeared to be dozing in his beach chair, his heels dug into the sugar-white sand. "Want another beer?"

David looked up and blinked. *"Por supuesto!"*

Mallory smiled. *"Dos Coronas, por favor,"* he said.

David sat up and stared out to sea as the beach boy headed across the sand to the outdoor bar. "A medicinal beer is just what I need. I think I may have exceeded my rum quota last night."

Mallory smiled. *"Es posible."*

"Hey, Dad. This has been a great trip, and I really appreciate it. We sure did everything there is to do around here." He pointed out to sea where a pair of Hobie Cats sliced across the turquoise Caribbean, hard on the wind. "Sailing those Hobie Cats yesterday was really cool, to say nothing of the parasailing—cruising along up there with the frigate birds. I'd do that again, any time."

Mallory nodded. "Yeah, me too."

"You know," David continued after a pause, "we really should accept Nacho's invitation to stop by on the way home. It's really not so far out of our way."

"David, it's a thousand air miles, each way." Mallory glanced at his son, and then turned to stare out to sea.

"It's only a two-and-a-half-hour flight on Aero Verde. There's one every day, at noon."

"How do you know?"

"I checked at the desk," David said, looking sheepish. "Hey, let's do it," he grinned. "Nacho's boat is probably the size of a cruise ship, with guys in mess jackets serving hors d'oeuvres and drinks. It's the chance of a lifetime."

Mallory drained his beer. "I don't think it's a good idea. I don't want to get mixed up in his private war."

"It hasn't even started yet."

"That may be, but I don't want to be in the position of lecturing him on the fine arts of logistics and strategy."

"Come on, Dad," he pleaded. "Let's push the envelope. You were always for doing that, right? I mean, where are your basic principles anyway?"

Mallory turned to look at David and saw him grinning, and Luisa's dark brown eyes looking back at him.

He scratched his cheek, as David waited. *What the hell,* he decided, *maybe it'll be a great father-son memory.*

"Okay," he said, "we'll pay Nacho just a quick visit, then we'll execute the world's oldest military maneuver."

David seemed puzzled.

Mallory grinned. "We'll get the hell out of there."

––––––––––––––

Glancing out the window of the old high-wing, twin-engine DeHavilland Otter they had boarded for the short hop from San Marcos to Bahia Pajaros, Mallory could see the thick, green jungle give way to the bright blue of the Pacific and Bahia Pajaros in the distance. He was assaulted by a nagging feeling that he had given in to David too easily, that they should be flying north in a 767 instead of south in this

ancient bird. Just then a sign on the overhead lit at the tone of a pseudo bell. *Abroche su cinturon.*

"What's Nacho got going here at Bahia Pajaros?" David asked. "We
stayed in San Marcos during the coup."

"This is where he keeps his boat, although he's taken it to the Med
a few times. He still has the family compound in San Marcos, although
he lived in the Presidential Palace when he was growing up. And, of
course, they have a *finca,* or country home, somewhere in the interior,
and plantations where they grow coffee and bananas. They acquired
some of them when United Fruit packed up and left. Then there're the
breweries, distilleries, and mining interests, and probably more. He's one
wealthy guy, that's for sure."

"It seems odd to me," David observed, "if the government is as cor-
rupt as he claims, that they haven't expropriated the hell out of his
whole operation."

"He says they leave him alone," Mallory explained, "because they
don't want to do anything that could discourage their booming tourist
trade, to which we're about to contribute. I suppose that makes sense,
but I agree he's in a pretty precarious position. They could change their
mind and exile Nacho and his sister any time they want."

The aircraft banked for its final approach to Bahia Pajaros. The jungle ended abruptly at the edge of town, held in check by an advancing
wave of condominiums. A large, tile-roofed Colonial-style hotel complex dominated the white sandy beach, surrounded by a golf course,
tennis courts, and swimming pools. Another hotel was under construction farther along the beach to the south. To the north, in the lee of a
small spit, a modern marina housed a hundred or more pleasure boats.

Mallory kept a weather eye on the cockpit and would be glad when
they were finally on the ground. The young co-pilot had flown the
entire way from San Marcos, and his disheveled appearance seemed to
say more about his professional expertise than the two stripes on the
epaulets of his soiled shirt. From his seat, Mallory could see past the
open curtain behind the pilots and on several occasions he noticed the

captain's gnarled right hand dart across and correct the co-pilot's use of the throttles. Mallory's hope that the captain would take over for the landing was in vain and the touchdown was reasonably safe at best.

BAHIA PAJAROS

After a spirited 180-degree turnaround at the end of the runway, the plane taxied to a parking area in front of a terminal building still under construction and rolled to a stop as the engines shut down. Their luggage was yanked out of the aircraft and piled on the tarmac as the passengers deplaned.

David retrieved their bags and they headed for the terminal building. Pushcart vendors peddling *helado* and a half-dozen urchins selling chicle surrounded them like a swarm of bees. Mallory scanned the crowd for some sign of recognition from whoever was to meet them. At the sidewalk they were accosted by cab drivers extolling their expertise as guides and pointing out the virtues of their dilapidated vehicles. Mallory waved them away and spotted a swarthy giant of a man headed towards them. He wore black trousers, black-rimmed sunglasses, an open-neck shirt framing a gold chain on a mat of black chest hair, and the look of one who is used to being at the head of the line.

"*Señor* Mallory?"

Mallory smiled and waved.

"*Bienvenidos, Señores,*" the giant called out, returning the wave and extending his hand.

"*Buenas tardes,*" Mallory replied, as they shook hands. "*Tengo mucho gusto.*"

"*Señor Peralta,*" the man said, "*dice que su Español es perfecto.*"

Mallory shrugged. "*Adecuado, tal vez, no mas,*" he said. "*Esto es mi hijo David.*"

David stepped forward. "*Mucho gusto, señor,*" he said, shaking hands.

Their new acquaintance turned to Mallory. "Your Spanish is more than adequate, *Señor* Mallory," he continued in English. "I am Diego. Here, I'll take your luggage. The car is right over there."

155

Diego led the way to the parking lot and pointed to a Mercedes parked in the first row. He placed the luggage in the trunk and opened the rear door for them.

"It's only a short ride to the boat," he said.

The car's air conditioning provided relief from the oppressive humidity. The narrow road contained sharp curves but Diego maneuvered the big car expertly, dodging a pig that suddenly crossed the road to whatever porcine pleasures awaited on the other side.

The contrast between the old village and the trendy shops and boutiques of the resort complex was striking. Pulling into the marina, Mallory noticed the working fishing boats moored to buoys at the far end of the lagoon. He assumed they belonged to fishing families who had made their living from them for generations, but couldn't afford the pricey new dock space. The boats occupying the slips and side ties were an expensive mix of power craft and blue water sailboats. Mallory recognized Swans, Columbias, a couple of Morgans, and a Santa Cruz. The power boats were state-of-the-art fishing machines making a strong statement that this was marlin country.

They drove past the berthing areas and pulled up to the transient dock where several runabouts were tied. Diego stopped at the head of the gangway and waved to a man seated in a highly varnished Italian mahogany speedboat with sparkling chrome fittings. The man in the boat, dressed in loose-fitting white cotton pants and matching shirt, darted up the gangway and took their luggage.

"Alberto will take you to *Señor* Peralta's boat," Diego said, as he handed over their bags.

Alberto waved them down the gangway to the boat and placed the luggage on the forward seating, ahead of the amidship engine compartment. He motioned them to the after seating compartment and set about throwing off the lines. Mallory noticed the name on the boat's transom, *Gustito*, meticulously inscribed in gold leaf. "Little Pleasure," *what an appropriate name*, he thought, considering its owner. "This is great!" David whispered. "Can't you picture James Bond speeding through the canals of Venice in this thing? Or bikinied beauties cruising the bay in Monaco?"

"I think you have the picture," Mallory laughed.

A little cloud of exhaust rolled across the surface of the water as Alberto started the engine, a familiar sight from Mallory's many years at sea. As they headed out into the bay he experienced a flash of déjà vu, as if this were the officers' shore boat leaving the quay wall at a port of call to return to the carrier at anchor. As they approached Peralta's yacht it appeared to be about two hundred feet overall and capable of round-the-world cruising. Nacho had said it was built at the Benetti yard in Italy.

As they neared the yacht, Alberto reduced power and Mallory could hear the unmistakable sounds of a party drifting across the water. The guests he could see on the afterdeck were attired in colorful tropical prints. The scene easily fit the image of Acapulco, Majorca, Monte Carlo, Cap Antibes, Corfu—anywhere the ultrawealthy gather to reaffirm their lives of privilege. He was not surprised to see the name *Gusto* on the towering transom.

Alberto brought the runabout smoothly alongside the gangway, where a waiting crewman secured the launch and ascended the ladder with their luggage. As they headed up the boarding ladder, for a split second Mallory saw himself saluting the national ensign and then the Officer of the Deck. Stepping onto *Gusto's* spotless teak deck, he saw Peralta striding their way.

"Deke!" he shouted, approaching with open arms, and squeezing Mallory in the customary Latin *abrazo.*

"Bienvenido a mi barco!" he said. Releasing Mallory he turned to David, and extended his hand. "It's so good to see you again, David. I'm so glad you have come."

David smiled and shook his hand. *"Con mucho gusto, Señor Peralta."*

Peralta leaned back to survey David. "Ah, yes, you are quite definitely the son of your most beautiful mother."

157

TWENTY-ONE

THE ARCHBISHOP'S PALACE AT THE CATHEDRAL

Kreeber and Kaalten edged forward on their chairs, as Tolt pushed his dessert aside and smoothed a place on the tablecloth. Staib closed the doors to the archbishop's quarters on the cathedral grounds and fetched a decanter.

"Muscatel?" he asked, pouring some for Tolt, who beamed, as he lit a cigar and blew out the smoke. He was wearing pseudo archbishop's attire, consisting of a fitted jacket with salmon piping and buttons, a clerical shirt of salmon silk, salmon cummerbund, and black trousers. His wardrobe, styled to resemble an archbishop's, had just arrived from Rome, and he was using it the first time. Monsignor Albert had apparently overlooked nothing, except the fuchsia color denoting a true archbishop, specifying the salmon color of a monsignor instead. The others wore their priests' black suits and clerical collars.

They were comfortably ensconced in the archbishop's palace on the cathedral grounds, and a palace it was, although on a relatively small scale. Elegant carved paneling and fine marble clothed the interior in a style more Italian than Spanish.

Tolt traced a map of Costa Verde on the table cloth with a spoon handle, as the others looked on.

"The Americans," he lectured, "expect the populations of third-world countries to be neatly divided into two camps, those locals who agree with American foreign policy, and bad guys, they call them, whom they assume are working in the interests of a competing foreign power.

"I will play to their weakness by giving the CIA everything it would expect to find here in Costa Verde. Then, I will complete Case Green without CIA interference. The Americans will never find out I created and manipulate the local political figures they will so quickly embrace as friend and foe. Thus, I shall raise up two very different charismatic resistance leaders, who will stir up antipathy toward the military government."

The others were conditioned to hearing outlandish plans from their visionary leader and rather enjoyed the fact his horizon seemed broader than theirs. So they smiled as though they saw the logic of his thinking, which they didn't. But they knew he always ended up making things clear, and even obvious in hindsight, so they listened attentively.

"One of my puppets is to be a wild-eyed appearing youth," he rhapsodized, waving his cigar, "in the Che Guevara mold the peasant class here in Latin America seems to revere. He is to attract at least moral support from Beijing, in order to alarm and distract the CIA. However, Washington will embrace my other popular political leader, due to his having been educated in the States and his more conservative stance."

Tolt tapped his glass and Staib hastened to refill it.

"My little strategic deception must be accomplished before the CIA succeeds in identifying and raising up a political leader of their own choosing. They've already made attempts, of course, but have failed thus far to produce a charismatic underground leader." A smile creased Tolt's hatchet face. "For some reason, their efforts along these lines have been half-hearted to date."

"Reichsfuhrer," Kaalten asked, "do we understand you to mean that you intend to raise a Resistance opposed to the Generalissimo, whom we already firmly control?"

Tolt smiled. "You see," he said, "you have not acquired the concept of strategic deception, have you?"

"Strategic deception?" Kaalten mumbled.

Tolt tasted his wine and set the glass aside, enjoying the moment and yet another chance to demonstrate his intellectual superiority. "Strategic deception is best described by an example of the work of Felix Dzerzhinsky, the legendary founder of the modern Russian intelligence services," he told them. "When the Bolshevik regime was threatened by several million White Russians, at home and abroad, he masterminded the creation of an organization inside Russia that was dedicated to overthrowing the Bolshevik regime. It was called The Trust, and it was bogus, of course. But no one knew it except Dzerzhinsky and Lenin, and the upstart Stalin. The Trust neutralized all the hostile activity threatening the regime, kidnapped the top White leaders, and persuaded the British not to attack the Soviet government, in deference to a promised internal uprising, which of course never occurred. In a similar fashion, the Americans perpetrated a strategic deception involving non-existent invasion forces, misleading our commanders concerning the importance of the landings at Normandy. We withheld our best divisions, anticipating even larger landings to occur elsewhere.

"When I was gathering intelligence in Poland early in the war," he continued, "I became intrigued with the uses of strategic deception myself. Naturally, I had to be circumspect, since the idea is assumed to be of communist origin, though it was practiced five thousand years ago in ancient China."

The others gave the appearance of understanding this monologue, as they tried to sift and remember the kernels.

"But the Generalissimo?" Kaalten asked, when he was able. "Won't he nip your popular movements in the bud?"

"Ha!" Tolt snorted. He tapped the ash from his cigar. "The Generalissimo," he said, accepting a light from Staib, "is a disagreeable cretin and has outlived his usefulness."

Kreeber and Kaalten edged forward on their chairs. This was new. They had thought the Generalissimo was all the puppet the Kohorte would be needing in Costa Verde.

"I created him, of course," Tolt scoffed, "although the fool still doesn't know where his money comes from.

"Strategic deception flourishes best in the aftermath of shattering events," he explained, "like the Bolshevik takeover or the Normandy landings, in my examples.

"Now, here comes the point," Tolt continued. "The Americans have grown accustomed to the Generalissimo, and recently resumed the foreign aid they used to give the Peralta regime. They will be disconcerted, to say the least, if the Generalissimo is suddenly overthrown. In the aftermath of such an unexpected development, they will not question the emergence of my newest puppets.

"Staib," he said, "the time has come to activate Operation Mauser to rid us of the Generalissimo.

"Mauser will shock the American's perception of stability in the region and create a situation where the appearance of resistance groups will seem very plausible."

Staib bowed slightly, as the others bristled. He was obviously in on the plot and they weren't.

"Mauser," Tolt told them, "is my code name for Colonel Benes, who commands the army barracks here in San Marcos. He is a former mercenary—Czech father, Costa Verdean mother—and a virulent neo-Nazi, though he conceals it quite well, which is all to the good. A Kohorte agent, posing as a neo-Nazi businessman, recruited him in Miami several years ago, and pays him through one of our neo-Nazi groups in Germany. Although the colonel has proven reliable, he doesn't know we exist, nor shall he, as yet.

"Mauser," Tolt explained, "will seize the Presidential Palace and oust the Generalissimo in what will appear to be a strictly intramural coup, ostensibly to settle some kind of score within the ruling junta. It's well known the officer corps prefers one of their own class to our pock-marked former sergeant, anyway."

"Reichsfuhrer," Kaalten asked, "have you fully considered the tourism? This is one of our peak months and the hotels are filling with tourists, especially Americans."

"Tourists will be in no danger," Tolt answered, with uncharacteristic patience. "What's the worst that can happen?" he said. "Perhaps an American could disappear, should he unwittingly stumble onto a sensitive matter affecting our security, that's all, and that could happen with or without Mauser's coup. This is the Banana Belt," he reminded them, "and even Washington is inured to such cases happening in Central America.

"The point is," he continued, "Costa Verde will have a brand-new head of state who won't sell out to the Americans," he paused for emphasis, his thin lips slightly parted, "and who, unlike the Sergeant Generalissimo, can be trusted to faithfully execute my orders!"

Kreeber thought the Generalissimo must have committed some pivotal indiscretion to have brought all this about, but decided it wasn't worth risking a question. It would be better to contribute something new. "Permission to interrupt?" he asked, before continuing. "As I reported, Reichsfuhrer," he said, "the CIA's spymaster from Mexico City, Herr Burton, was in town earlier this week. He met with a man I've since traced back to CIA headquarters at Langley, in Virginia, though I don't yet know his actual identity. Reichsfuhrer, my point is that it was obvious to my watchers that Burton deferred to this man and seemed even to fear him. Have you taken this into account? Personally, I have never known the CIA to be so easily deceived as—"

Tolt stiffened. "I know where Langley is," he snapped. "The man's name is Terence Truman," he said, "as you would know had you inquired of General Karpf, who also called me about it yesterday. Herr Truman is the Assistant Director of the CIA, for Budget and Finance."

Kreeber appeared stunned by Tolt's knowledge.

"Obviously," Tolt sneered, "Herr Burton would show deference to a man who controls his budget! Next time, Kreeber," he snapped, "use properly trained watchers, who can not only tail people, but listen in on their conversations. Then you may learn something worthy of reporting to me!"

Kreeber's jaw clamped shut and he remained silent. It was no use reminding the Reichsfuhrer that his watchers were from Karpf's stable in Mexico City. His brow furrowed as he contemplated the likelihood that they provided Karpf a transcript of the Burton/Truman conversations. And he wondered how much of it Karpf shared with Tolt.

"Begging the Reichsfuhrer's pardon," Staib ventured, "but what is the plan for recruiting pro-American and pro-Chinese resistance heroes? Won't this take time?"

"That will be your assignment, Staib, after you have activated Mauser. You are creative, aren't you? And you have enough money available, don't you? Surely you have abilities in more than a single area of expertise?"

Tolt's eyes burned with intensity, and his voice took a hard edge, as he seemed to flare at Staib for no apparent reason. "I want my anti-Benes movements launched immediately upon the heels of the coup," he demanded.

Staib squared his shoulders.

"*Jawohl*, Reichsfuhrer!" he said.

Kaalten ventured to suggest Peralta as a candidate for leadership of the pro-American underground. "My young business experts," he said, "are impressed with his wealth and intelligence."

The corners of Tolt's mouth tightened as he seemed to contemplate an inference he might have overlooked someone who was bigger-than-life in the minds of the people in Costa Verde. "You should have realized," he answered, with vinegar in his voice, "I have known all about this Ignacio Peralta, and his conniving sister, Elena Peralta de Gomez, since I began evaluating this country as the locus of Case Green. I will certainly deal with them at the proper time, as the game plays out."

The others jumped to their feet, as Tolt pushed away from the table and stood.

"Staib, I want the coup to happen as soon as Colonel Benes can be ready to move against the Presidential Palace. You will unleash Mauser at dawn!" he ordered.

————

Staib rose early in the morning. He grimaced in the mirror as he slipped a silver chain around his neck and adjusted the antique crucifix suspended from it. Noticing dandruff, he brushed it from his black clerical shirt, removed a vinyl-covered metal briefcase from the closet, and took the stairs to the garden. He found the bench where he and Kreeber met earlier that week, and pushed a pair of half-frame reading glasses onto his nose.

The sun was low in the brightening eastern sky as he placed the briefcase on his lap, opened it and removed a couple of books, including a leather-bound treatise on monasticism, with colorful ribbon book marks, which he opened and placed on the bench by his side. He noticed a pocket-size Bible that was the original Father Martin's, and opened that too, momentarily recalling how quickly the garrote did its work in the little church in Stralsund.

There, he thought, satisfied with his appearance as a priest engaging in his private devotions.

From the briefcase he now took a satellite telephone, punched it on, and extended the antenna. He kept the case open on his knees, so he could stow the sat-phone if he should hear anyone approaching on the path.

Mauser would be activated according to a procedure Karpf devised, by setting in motion a series of telephone calls among Kohorte agents. He closed his eyes and rehearsed the procedure. The chain reaction would run, like cascading dominoes, straight to Colonel Benes. The beauty of it was that none of the talkers had any clue what was going on. They only knew that when they received a certain prearranged message they were to telephone a certain number and recite another prearranged message. The chances of anyone tracing or eavesdropping on so many seemingly random, innocuous calls was almost zero, and even in that unlikely event a transcript of the messages wouldn't reveal anything suspicious. Neither the CIA nor Colonel Benes could ever trace the chain back to the initial call Staib placed to trigger the coup. Even Benes wouldn't know the identity of his masters.

Staib's palms moistened as he contemplated the fact he was about to start a small war. It was a first and a high of sorts, he realized, but nothing compared to killing someone personally, he decided. He wiped his palms on his trousers, took a deep breath, and peered over his spectacles. He dialed 001-049-91-4548895, and waited for a phone to ring in Dortmund, Germany.

"Gehering and Sons, Wine Merchants," a woman answered.

"Do you have any Heilsburger, 1947?" he inquired.

"Wait, please," she said. Moments later a man came on the line. "This is Otto Gehering," he said. "May I be of assistance?"

"That depends," Staib told him, "on whether you have any Heilsburger, 1947."

"Very rare, the 1947. Who is calling?" the man asked.

"Herr Zimmermann," Staib told him.

"Yes," the man said. "It's very expensive, however. Two hundred fifty marks, the bottle."

"Then, I'll have to think about it," Staib said.

He hung-up and glanced about. He was still alone in a corner of the garden. He closed his eyes and tried to imagine the series of calls taking place in the next few minutes. A phone would be ringing in Rockford, Maryland, right about now, he knew.

"Guns of Fame. May I help you?" the proprietor, a gunsmith, would most likely answer.

"I wish to sell a rather excellent example of the 1896 Mauser military model automatic pistol," the caller would announce.

"Well, that depends," the gunsmith might tell him. "I could be interested, depending on the serial number."

"Let's see," the caller would say, and pause. "The serial number is NK-0347-22."

"Not interested," would be the gunsmith's answer. He would hang up, thinking. Then he would dial 011-503-77-37081.

"El Salvador Intercontinental Hotel." Staib imagined a hotel operator's voice. "How may I direct your call?" she might say.

"Let me have Esteban, in catering," would be a likely response.

"This is Esteban," he'd answer.

The caller would say, "I want to host a reception for seventy-four on Sunday afternoon."

"How many did you say?" Esteban would want to hear the number of guests again, since it was the tip-off, that and Sunday afternoon.

"Seventy-four," the man would repeat.

"I'm very sorry, señor," Esteban would tell him. "The rooms appropriate for a group that size are booked already."

In Staib's mind's eye, Colonel Benes was crouching to study the lie of his ball on a green at Las Linternas country club, located in the finest residential district in San Marcos. He would stand, grip his putter and address the ball, when his cell phone would ring.

"Colonel Benes."

"I would like to charter your jet, Colonel," the caller would say, "for several hours on the twenty-seventh of this month."

"My aircraft isn't available for charter," Benes would tell him.

"Excuse me, sir," the caller would apologize, "I was poorly informed."

The colonel would swear softly, Staib imagined, replace the putter in his bag, and tell his companions, "I'm sorry, my concentration's broken. Let's quit for today."

Staib opened his eyes, gathered his belongings and went to the archbishop's quarters, where Tolt was eating his breakfast. He patted his lips with a napkin, and spread it on his lap as Staib entered, carrying the briefcase.

"I have done as you instructed," he reported, patting the case with his free hand.

"Excellent," Tolt said, rubbing his hands together.

TWENTY-TWO

M.V. *GUSTO* ANCHORED AT BAHIA PAJAROS

The guest suite aboard *Gusto* was a study in efficient luxury, with paneled bulkheads, elegant carpeting, original art work, and a sitting area with a love seat, chairs, and a Louis XV table. The nearby shoreline and lush hills above Bahia Pajaros were visible across a private veranda deck.

Peralta knocked on the door and poked his head into the stateroom, as Mallory and David unpacked.

"I want you to meet my other guests," he said, as he led the way aft toward the main salon. The room was paneled in cherry wood, which served as a backdrop for historic nautical prints. The teak decking was covered with exquisite oriental rugs. Intricate cabinet work framed an extensive library, an entertainment center with a wide-screen TV, an elaborate music system, and a giant bar. Guiding Mallory and David effortlessly through the groups of guests, who seemed to wear their Gucci, Armani, and Magli coverings as comfortably as their own skins, Peralta introduced each with a succinct descriptive résumé.

"Don Guillermo Salazar, a partner in the Peralta rum industry. He's the one who keeps the rum so rich it leaves a bead on the side of your glass . . . Don Guillermo's daughter Teresa, and her husband Oscar. Both are doctors who are trying to keep our people healthy . . . General Francisco Mora. Retired, but a loyal officer of the true Army of Costa Verde . . . Carlos Iturbe, formerly the publisher of what used to be our free press . . . Doctor Julio Carrera, the former chair of philosophy at our university, who taught our young people to think clearly."

Carrera stopped playing the white lacquered piano long enough to shake hands, and returned to a Chopin nocturne.

The first half-circuit of the huge salon took them to the bar. "Glenlivet?" Peralta asked.

Mallory nodded.

"Of course," Peralta laughed. "With your usual single drop of water.

"And you, David. What will it be?"

"I've acquired a taste for rum since we left the states, sir. I understand that people here like it with Coca-Cola."

"A wise choice, indeed," Peralta said. "Americans regard rum and Coca-Cola as a silly nostalgic drink, or a corny song from the era of that Disney abomination *Saludos Amigos,* but we Costa Verdeans consider it a special nectar of the gods." He turned to the bartender. *"Reserva Especial, con Coca-Cola."*

He turned to David. "Our family makes this, you know."

As they stepped from the bar, Mallory sipped his drink and surveyed the guests. He noticed a tall woman in a blue silk top tied above her bare midriff. Her back was to them, but when she turned and started towards Peralta, he was taken by her striking, doe-eyed, olive-skinned beauty.

"Sorry I'm late," Elena said, touching her brother's arm. "I was on the phone longer than I expected."

"With Colonel Fuentes?"

"Yes. Everything's fine now."

Although he'd known Peralta for years, Mallory hadn't seen much of his younger sister Elena since she was in her early twenties, save at Luisa's service, and because of his daze then he hadn't much memory of her presence. Years of sea duty made for a disjointed social life, where Luisa maintained friendships, like hers with Elena, while Mallory was scripted-in but hardly ever on stage.

She turned to face Mallory. "Deke!" She said, as she hugged him. "I'm so glad you've finally come," she said, kissing his cheek.

She turned to David "And, Dah-VEED, it's wonderful to see you again."

David shook Elena's hand, startled but pleased to hear his name pronounced so softly in Spanish. He hadn't heard it since his mother died.

The warmth of Elena's greeting seemed to free Mallory's restless spirit, and he began to relax for the first time since coming aboard *Gusto.*

"This is just awesome!" David said, exiting the shower. "I'll have severe withdrawal when I get back to the states."

"Then enjoy it while you can," Mallory said, as he buttoned the front of his *quayabera,* a light, hip-length shirt with a pleated front, worn as evening wear.

"Nacho's guests seem like a decent bunch," David said, as he slipped into white duck pants and a reverse print Hawaiian shirt. "Do you think they're part of his revolutionary plan? Are they really going to don jungle cammies when the time comes to take out the bad guys?"

"Could be," Mallory said with a shrug, "but I'm hoping Nacho's pretty much over his freedom-fighter phase and working for some kind of peaceful transition from the military government. On the other hand, it's pretty obvious these people wouldn't be here if they weren't sympathetic to his cause, but they don't look like the kind who would participate in a full-scale revolution."

"Diego does," David said. "Did you notice the bulge under his shirt? He's carrying a gun. I noticed it when he handled our luggage. I'll bet his job profile includes more than chauffeuring."

Dinner was extravagant, a grand buffet in the dining salon, served on an elegant, oyster white table service with a gold and green border with a compass rose in the middle and the name "Gusto" on the flat rim. The flatware was obviously sterling with a gold compass rose on the handle. The crystal was Waterford, etched with "Gusto," like the china. Mallory helped himself to yellowfin sashimi and some *langostina,* a succulent fresh-water shrimp, larger than prawns, smaller than lobsters, and more delicious than either. The main dish was *pargo roja,* red snapper, served with *gallo pinto,* a combination of rice and black beans.

"I don't know why we call it gallo pinto," Elena said. "As I'm sure you know, it means spotted chicken, but that's what it's called in many Latin American countries."

Dinner was capped with a serving of mango, papaya and sweet fried bananas. Elena and Mallory finished and were having coffee together, when Peralta joined them.

"The younger set wants to attend the opening of a new disco tomorrow night," he said. "It seems they're bringing in a European headliner who's all the rage of the under-thirty crowd these days. David said he'd like to go, and I haven't an objection to postponing the fishing for a day."

"Fine with me," Mallory said, glancing at Elena. "I'm certainly enjoying myself as it is, and I doubt if David wants to stray very far from that girl he's talking to."

"Bianca, of course," Peralta said with a smile.

"Bianca's my daughter," Elena interjected. "She just turned twenty-one."

"She's really lovely," Mallory said.

"Diego will take the group ashore tomorrow night," Peralta said, "and remain until they're safely back aboard. Don't worry, Diego knows what to do."

Mallory nodded. "I'm sure he does."

A few new arrivals were greeted with bloody marys on the fantail the next morning. Mallory thought the new group, including several more near David's age, appeared about as affluent as the other guests, and he couldn't help wondering where they all stood concerning Nacho's hope of one day dislodging the government.

Peralta glanced at the white MD-520 helicopter parked on its raised pad above the midships area.

"Diego will be flying David and Bianca and another couple to the finca," he said, "for a look at the horses and some country cuisine for lunch. It's about an hour round trip, so he can return for any who would like to join them. Dinner tonight will be at seven," he continued, "a little earlier than usual so our intrepid youths can enjoy the disco scene and be back aboard in time for a 3 A.M. departure. The older folks," Peralta flashed a smile, "needn't worry about getting their beauty sleep," he said. "Gusto is as silent as a thief, when getting under way."

Mallory watched the helicopter lift off to a safe height. Diego expertly maneuvered the craft sideways to clear the yacht, before dipping the nose to pick up speed for an en route climb to the northeast.

"When Diego has ferried the last of them to the finca," Peralta said, "we'll take the helicopter. I want to show you some of our plantations and our beautiful beaches," he continued with an expansive wave, "and overfly one of the landing strips I told you about."

"Sure, Nacho," Mallory shrugged. At mention of one of the secret landing sites, his stomach tightened and an uneasy feeling came over him.

Mallory awoke before dawn with a start. Something was wrong. Nacho said they would weigh anchor but *Gusto* wasn't under way. *Are we still at Bahia Pajaros?* He switched on the bedside light and saw David's bed was undisturbed.

Peralta was on the bridge with the captain when Mallory found him. "Nacho, what the hell's happened?"

Peralta held up his hand for silence as the radio crackled with a voice in Spanish. The transmission was breaking-up, but Mallory caught the essence. ". . . *no es possible hoy. . . es absolutamente final—*"

Peralta flipped the mute switch and turned to face Mallory. His face was ashen as he spoke. "There's a military coup going on in San Marcos. That's a patrol craft on the radio. They won't let us put to sea today."

173

"Holy shit!" Mallory exploded. "We're right in the middle of another damned coup? Where's David?" he demanded.

Before Peralta could answer, a pair of Costa Verde Air Force jets screamed a hundred feet overhead, rattling the windows and the instruments lying on the chart table.

"Coincidentally," Peralta said, "there was a drug bust at the disco early this morning. Diego got out with Bianca and two of the girls, but David and the others were taken to police headquarters. But don't worry, Deke, they were released an hour ago, and Diego has gone to get them.

"Except . . ." Peralta's face twisted in pain. "Except that David was apparently taken to San Marcos."

"Are you telling me my son's being held prisoner right in the middle of a fucking war?"

"Now calm down, Deke!" Peralta blurted, holding up his hands to Mallory. He took a deep breath as Mallory riveted him with blazing eyes.

"I've got many influential friends in San Marcos," he continued, "on every side of the politics. Deke, I'll see to David's release. Don't worry. Diego will whisk him out in the MD, and—"

"When?" Mallory demanded. "How can you do that in the middle of a war? For God's sake, Nacho . . ."

He was suddenly aware of Elena standing behind him. She slipped her arms around him and rested her head on his shoulder. "Take courage, Deke," she said. "Everything's going to be all right."

TWENTY-THREE

CIA HEADQUARTERS, LANGLEY

Truman dried his hands and stepped from his private bathroom at CIA Headquarters in Langley. He poured water from a carafe on his desk and began reading a report he needed to sign off on before forwarding it to the National Security Council. The Latin America phone chirped. He reached for it without looking. Each of the instruments on his desk had its distinctive ring.

"Truman."

"Hey, T-Square," Burton said, "there's an attempted coup in Costa Verde, going on as we speak." He sounded energized.

"Oh, yeah? Where are you?"

"Mexico City. That guy Benes, the colonel, has surrounded the Presidential Palace and fired a few rounds from a couple of tanks. Blew out a couple of offices on the second floor. That's about all, though, so far."

Truman pointed a clicker at the TV across the room, found CNN and adjusted the volume.

"*We interrupt* Morning Business Report *and go now to CNN's Washington Bureau, where Ramona Diaz is standing by with news of a coup attempt this morning in Costa—*"

He tapped the mute button.

"Tell me more," he said.

"It's the usual Banana Belt internecine bullshit, I think. You know, strong man versus strong man, thug on thug. It's pretty much plain vanilla this time."

"What's your guess on the outcome?"

"I'm betting on the colonel. Remember, he commands the army forces in the San Marcos Military District. Unless the air force decides to weigh in on the Generalissimo's side. That's the wild card, but I don't think they'll interfere. The Generalissimo's got some real warts, as far as the airedales are concerned. He hasn't increased their budget since he came to power, which pisses them off.

"Now, this guy Benes, on the other hand, is a jet-qualified private pilot. Keeps an old Lear 35 at the San Benito Air Force Base, which he sure as hell couldn't do without being in tight with General De Silva, the Air Force Chief of Staff."

"Did we have anything to do with this thing?" Truman asked.

"You know we didn't!" Burton sounded defensive.

Truman wondered. Was Burton covering over his tracks by instigating a coup?

"Just how well do you know this Benes fellow, again?" Truman asked.

"Holloway knew him pretty well, actually. They belonged to the same golf club, played together sometimes. He introduced me to him once at the bar. Then, when Benes took over procurement for stuff like tires, he became my customer. I know you're still upset I went to his home that time, but the guy invited me. What was I supposed to do, alienate him?"

"Okay," Truman said. "But, what's he like, this Benes?"

"Intense kind of guy," Burton told him, "not your usual Central American military type."

"What does that mean in plain English?" Truman asked.

"I digested Holloway's file on him," Burton said, "and updated it since. Benes just doesn't seem to have any personal weaknesses. He's married and doesn't womanize or abuse drugs or booze, or even toys, except for the Learjet. No, he's as professional as they come, especially considering his soldier-of-fortune past. But he's got a reputation as one mean sonofabitch, if crossed."

"What do you mean, soldier of fortune?" Truman probed.

"Well, that's the unusual part. Benes resigned his commission once. He was a captain at the time. It's all pretty murky, but he was in Angola and Afghanistan, that we know about so far."

"On whose side?" Truman asked.

"Not ours, not the Soviets' either. The best I can track it all, from what our people in the field knew at the time, Benes' gig was placing himself in the service of whatever private interests had a stake to protect, and paid him enough. Put it this way, he was sort of a one-man Pinkerton's for various European financial interests."

"A mercenary?" Truman wondered aloud. "How could a guy like that suddenly wash the dirt from his face and re-enter the army to become a respected colonel?"

"I can't figure that one either," Burton said. "But, he did is all I know. He must have had some kind of pull."

Or someone was pushing, Truman thought.

He glanced at the TV screen. A female reporter dressed in safari khakis stood in front of a photo mural of the Costa Verde capital. She glanced at her notes, apparently speaking with someone on the telephone in San Marcos; someone who didn't know squat, he guessed. He touched the mute button again, confirmed his impression, and clicked the power off. Give CNN ten minutes, he decided, and they'll have live feed from the scene outside the palace.

"You going down there?" he inquired.

"Naw, not now, anyway," Burton said. "I'll give it a chance to settle out first. Hell, we don't even have the winner yet."

Truman wondered. *If Burton is on the take,* he reasoned, *then he's sold out to whoever controls things from behind the scenes, not to the Generalissimo, who's a front man by all logic.* He closed his eyes and pinched the bridge of his nose, thinking. He knew the amazing economic and cultural progress taking place in Costa Verde was beyond the capacity of a thug like the former sergeant. *If this coup really is an intramural shakeup,* he reasoned, *then Bill's involvement won't be affected by it. And, if Colonel Benes succeeds, there's more reason than ever to get to the bottom of it before the scent of treachery fades—or Bill creates another diversion to throw me off the track.*

"Keep me posted."

"Like always, T-Square."

A few minutes later, Truman pointed the remote at the TV and clicked.

"*. . . here in San Marcos. We return you now to CNN Atlanta for a news summary, and more on the successful coup this morning in Costa Verde.*"

TWENTY-FOUR

M.V. *GUSTO* ANCHORED AT BAHIA PAJAROS

The sun neared the horizon as Mallory and Elena stood at *Gusto*'s bow watching. News that David was released from custody and was returning from San Marcos with Diego in the helo had released the tension in Mallory, and he felt drained of energy. His emotions had been severely taxed by keeping vigil on the bridge while Peralta talked for hours on his satellite telephone, playing out a bureaucratic game of cat-and-mouse to secure David's freedom. He looked up to see Peralta sprinting towards them, waving his cell phone.

"Here's David!" he yelped, handing the phone to Mallory and dancing about with his arms in the air.

"David! Is that you?"

"Hi Dad!" The sound of his voice quickened Mallory's pulse.

"Are you all right? Where are you? What the hell happened? Did they treat you—"

"I'm fine, Dad. But I'm still in San Marcos." Mallory could hear traffic noises in the background. "Diego is driving me to Nacho's home here to spend the night. He says it's getting too dark to safely operate the helicopter, so we're going to lay over and fly out to the boat in the morning."

"David, what happened? Why did they—"

"I'm pretty beat, Dad. I'll explain everything in the morning."

"Okay, you're right. I love you."

"I love you too, Dad."

Mallory squeezed his eyes shut and gripped the railing so hard his knuckles turned white.

Shouts of glee rose from the other guests, who gathered around to congratulate him. Peralta returned and pushed through the crowd to hand him a double Glenlivet. Mallory feared it might floor him, given the roller-coaster emotions of the seemingly endless day, but the drink had a bracing effect instead.

"I need a shower and a nap," he told Elena, as the others drifted toward the main salon.

"Why don't you finish your drink first?" she said, sipping a glass of wine someone brought her.

"Good idea," he answered, "assuming someone can carry me to my quarters afterward."

She laughed. "I have more faith in the United States Navy than to think one scotch can do you in," she said, when they were alone.

"We missed the sunset," he said. "It's beginning to get dark. Maybe tomorrow we can see if we can catch that split-second green flash you sometimes see in the tropics, the instant the sun goes below the horizon."

"I've heard of that," Elena said. "Have you seen it?"

"Just once, in the Western Pacific. I have no idea what causes it. Some people say it doesn't exist, that it's just imagination, but that's not true. I've seen it."

"Oh, Deke, I'm so relieved about David," she said, suddenly brushing away tears. "Sorry," she continued, "but this whole experience brought back bad memories of my own."

They strolled aft and leaned on the taffrail. "How beautiful," Mallory said, sipping his scotch and surveying the darkening water and the last light on the verdant hills.

"Yes," Elena said, with a sigh. "We have a beautiful country, soiled by political ugliness."

"Yes, you do," Mallory agreed.

"I know Nacho did his best to recruit you," she said.

"Yes, he did. And I said no."

"I can't blame you. This isn't your fight. And you don't strike me as the Quixotic type, looking to tilt at other people's windmills."

"I know they're not just windmills. But, whatever they are, they're not mine."

"I know that," she said. "But Nacho isn't going to give up on our plan, no matter what. I won't either! I'm playing a part too!"

"Did you go to guerilla school?"

Mallory's unfortunate words just slipped out, and he instantly regretted them.

"No, I went to Columbia and got my masters at the University of Madrid. I returned to Columbia for my doctorate, and that was when Luisa introduced me to Roberto, my husband, who knew her relatives in Spain."

"I guess that was during one of my tours of sea duty," Mallory observed.

"Yes, it was. Roberto was finishing his residency in family practice. When we returned to Costa Verde, he opened a practice in San Marcos and I took a position at the university. I taught history, which I really enjoyed until I was forced out."

"Why were you forced out?"

"My views on politics and the lessons of history were considered treasonous by the Generalissimo's toadies, especially the President of the University, who's medieval at best in his thinking. The fact I was a woman in a man's world didn't sit well with others on the faculty either, but I felt I had something to contribute to the training of our young people.

"I was wrong, of course," she said with a sigh. "Maybe I was lucky. I was only removed from my position. I could have disappeared like

Juanita's older brother, who was a priest." Elena looked away and slowly shook her head. "You met Juanita the first night aboard, remember? Her brother was serving at the National Cathedral. One day recently, he simply vanished. We don't know how or why, but he's a Disappeared now. We suspect the regime," she said. "Who else would want to harm a simple priest?"

She turned to face Mallory. "He was a godly man, sensitive and thoughtful, with great love for the poor people, and was always pleading their cause." She paused and slowly shook her head. "A lot of people have disappeared, since my father was ousted."

"I gather," Mallory said, "you think this new guy, the colonel who took over this morning, is cut from the same cloth as the Generalissimo, that things in Costa Verde won't change much at all."

"It's all one and the same regime, really," she said. "The officers who have remained in our military are, as you say, cut from the same cloth. Today's shoot-out at the Palace wasn't a coup in the regular sense. It was all about the ranking members of the officer corps ridding themselves of a sergeant they detested."

"I gather too," Mallory continued, "that life isn't so predictable in this part of the world."

"That's true," Elena said, "except for the few of us who are insulated by great wealth. People here live in the midst of a power encounter between the successors of the Spanish *caudillos,* whose idea is to rule with an iron hand, and the liberal forces opposing them. Unfortunately, the so-called liberals—including communists like the Sandinistas who ruled Nicaragua—always say power to the people, but they too only want power for themselves."

"Yes," Mallory said, "but I can see that things in Costa Verde have been taking a rather different kind of direction since your father was ousted."

"Definitely," she said. "Even our informants—we've many well-placed ones, you know—haven't been able to agree about what's really happened since Father was exiled."

"I'm not much of an expert on Costa Verde," Mallory said, "but Nacho seems to think your military is just a pawn for a much darker force operating behind the scenes. He mentioned a band of young German businessmen."

"Nacho's informants tell us lots of things," she said. "But I think they're right about those people."

Mallory decided not to pry. "How long have you been committed to Nacho's counter-revolution?" he asked instead.

"Since . . ."

In the darkness, Mallory sensed her swallowing hard.

"This is my vengeance too," she continued. "It's personal to everyone you've met here. We've all lost someone or something important to our lives."

"All these people aboard Gusto are involved with you?"

"Of course."

Mallory's mind went blank for a moment, and he realized how tired he was. He shifted his weight and tried to clear his head. "I guess I really didn't know what to expect. After my heated exchanges with Nacho in Reno, I wasn't sure I should even come here. But time heals, and David thought it would be a grand finale to our vacation."

"I'm glad you came," she said, taking his arm. "I'm sure you and David will finally have a good time now."

She looked away, and released his arm. "Nacho can still be gracious, witty, and charming," she continued, "but now it covers his guilt for doing so little for so long. I found it easy to look the other way myself. Life was good, it was fun, it was easy. We lived the good life. I enjoyed my work and Roberto loved his practice."

"Tell me about your husband."

"He was a wonderful doctor," she said, "although he got bored with most of his upper-class patients. He began to care for the poor people in the outlying villages. They have little hope of receiving proper treatment, you know, except from volunteer doctors. Some he cared for were suspected of antigovernment activities, and the army warned him to stay away. Roberto found he just couldn't do that and kept going back. One day he took our son, Cesar, along for the experience and to help out. Cesar wanted to be a doctor like his father."

"You must be very proud of your boy." Mallory said.

"Yes, I was." She stared out across the bay. "Their bodies were found outside the village of Santa Isabel. Their throats were cut with one of his scalpels."

Mallory was stunned. He managed to say he was sorry, and in the silence that followed, he turned Elena around so she faced him, and gently wrapped her in his arms.

"When? Why wasn't I told?" he mumbled.

"It happened a few weeks after I returned from Luisa's service," she said. "Since there was nothing you could do, we didn't want to intrude on your own grief."

She kissed Mallory's cheek as he released her.

"Anyway," she continued, "this little Shirley Temple who grew up in a Presidential Palace . . . is a bomb-throwing revolutionary now."

Mallory nodded silently. "I understand, having lost Luisa the way I did. . . ."

She reached out and took his hands in hers. "Let's go inside with the others," he said, "and change the subject."

———————

The energy of the cocktail hour and dinner conversation subsided and the atmosphere in the main salon became that of a reading room. Professor Carrera lolled at the piano, toying with what may have been his own composition. Nacho was engrossed in an intense backgammon game, and the others who hadn't already retired were reading or conversing quietly. Mallory knew he was operating on adrenaline and should turn in for the night. As he and Elena approached the bar for a nightcap, they were joined by General Mora.

"Commander Mallory," the general said, as he reached for the unordered drink the bartender handed him, "I would enjoy exchanging war stories with you over this cognac."

"I'd be honored, sir," Mallory said, accepting a snifter like the general's.

Elena excused herself. "I'll see you gentlemen in the morning," she said.

Mallory wondered whether the general was assigned to try his hand at recruitment now. The image of a switching zone basketball defense somehow leapt to mind. He decided letting the general do the talking was the best way to shorten their encounter.

"One drink, then I'm off to bed," he said. "I'm pretty tired after the ordeal of my son's capture and release."

"But of course," Mora said, with a warm smile.

The cognac opened the door to some of the general's war stories. Although his were local yarns, they gave more insight into the Peraltas' cause. "I envy you, sir," Mora said. "You fought the good fight against dark forces in the far corners of the globe, while my own military experience is very provincial by comparison. I gained a general's stars struggling with nothing more dangerous than our quaint destiny here in little Costa Verde. Sadly, though, sometimes the enemy turned out to be a close friend."

"That must have been difficult for you. At least my combat experiences were pretty impersonal."

"I gather," the general said, glancing at Peralta across the salon, "that Nacho made you privy to our emerging effort to put things right here?"

Here it comes, Mallory thought. "I hope you pull it off, General," he said, "though I can't be part of it, as I hope Nacho understands."

"Of course he understands," Mora said with a nod. "This is our struggle, not yours. Our good friend Nacho is an incurable romantic, like his father, although he's tougher and better organized. I am sure he thought recruiting your assistance was a natural thing to do. By the way, he recently recruited a top fighter pilot who also has an excellent war gaming and logistics background."

Mallory shrugged. "That's good."

185

"Yes, his name is Maldonado. He distinguished himself with the Argentine Navy in the Falklands War."

Mallory nodded. "Well, Nacho is persistent."

"Yes, definitely.

"But Elena," Mora's eyes sparkled, "is the truly tenacious one in the family, and the born orator, too. She'll stir the hearts of our people. You'll see. They're flocking to her cause, to drive these traitors from power."

". . . Elena?"

"I thought you knew," Mora said. "She's the one the people in the villages throng to hear. The *campesinos* love her for her gentle strength, and because she shares their suffering through her own loss."

Mora's eyes moistened, "They bond with La Pantera."

Mallory's eyed widened. "Elena is La Pantera?"

The pride in Mora's eyes answered for him, then he cocked his head to the sound of rapid throttle changes of a small boat being docked at the boarding ladder in haste.

"There must be a problem," Mora said, as he started for the passageway to the deck outside, with Mallory at his heels. Peralta reached the railing at the same time and, as they peered down into the darkness, Diego leapt from a launch still rocking side to side. He rushed up the ladder and burst onto deck, his clothes soaked with sweat.

"Where's David?" Mallory shouted. "What's happened? Where the hell is David?"

"The goddamn army pulled him out of bed," Diego stammered, trying to catch his breath. "A truckload of soldiers burst all through the house, waving automatic weapons everywhere. I couldn't do anything to stop them. Their officer said there was new evidence of David's role in a drug deal at the disco."

"Where is he now?" Mallory demanded, squaring off in front of Diego.

"I don't know, *Señor* Mallory. They took him with them. They yanked the phone lines and cut the car's tires. When I finally got to the airport, I had to kick in the fence and dig under it with my bare hands. I took off without permission. I didn't want to use the radio, so I landed at the marina and hot-wired a launch."

"This is bullshit!" Mallory screamed, his face twisting in agony. "David's never even smoked a cigarette in his whole life!"

"I know, *señor*," Diego said, nodding his head.

———————

Mallory awoke to the sound of knocking on his stateroom door. He realized he had drifted asleep wearing his clothes, without switching out the lights.

"Yeah, come in," he growled.

Peralta entered with General Mora. "We've found out where they've taken David," Peralta told him. "He's been transferred to Prison Num—"

"Taken to prison?" Mallory demanded, leaping to his feet. "What prison?"

Mora spoke, as the two of them stood at the foot of the bed. "It's called Prison Number Five. Many leading citizens have been held there for years, incommunicado."

"Where is it?" Mallory demanded, his eyes ablaze. His heart skipped a beat and he felt a twisting in his guts, as it crossed his mind David wasn't in harm's way until Peralta's bodyguard took charge of him.

"It's deep in the jungle," Mora said, "close to the Nicaraguan border."

Mallory sank onto the bed in the grip of a paralyzing pain he knew only once before in his life, that horrible day on a Los Angeles freeway.

"The jungle there is impenetrable," Peralta exclaimed.

Mora gathered himself.

"So is the prison," he said.

TWENTY-FIVE

THE CENTRAL JAIL, SAN MARCOS

Wearing a flowing black cassock and broad-brimmed priest's hat, Staib ambled the short distance from the cathedral to the *Presidio Central* toting a suitcase-like portable chapel containing everything needed for a Catholic service. He smiled and nodded as people stepped aside deferentially to clear his path. The streets here were spared any of the fighting and, except for an occasional truckload of soldiers rumbling by, things seemed normal enough. Pausing at the entrance to the Central Jail, he mopped his brow, then walked straight to the reception counter where he opened the case and made no little show of checking its contents.

"What brings you to us, Padre?" the desk sergeant asked, as Staib snapped the case shut again.

"The Archbishop," Staib told him, "has directed me to hear the confession of certain prisoners." He produced an envelope from his cassock and handed it over. "The ones named in this letter to your commandant."

An officer joined the sergeant and read Tolt's letter. "Of course," he said, smiling. "It will take a few minutes to assemble them for you."

The visitation room was dismal, hardly larger than a closet, with a rough concrete floor, garish blue walls with plaster in need of repair, and a dirty light bulb dangling from the high ceiling. A wooden table and two metal chairs completed the furnishings. Except for the Generalissimo's portrait still gracing the wall, it could have been any jailhouse anywhere, Staib thought, recalling his night in the cooler at the Volksmarine base. He placed the portable chapel on the table and sat down to wait for the first of three prisoners a police official denounced as enemies of the government. Staib smiled as he recalled eliciting the information in the confessional. *Maybe one would make a suitable resistance leader,* he thought. The first wasn't very intelligent, he decided, and he hurried his confession.

When Patrick Batista entered and sat as the guard left, Staib knew this was a man he could use. The illegitimate son of an American father and Costa Verde mother, he attended high school in Dallas and completed two years of college until deciding to run guns to the highest bidder in Central America, including the Nicaraguan Contras in their struggle with the communist-backed Sandinistas and, unfortunately for Patrick, the meager criminal element operating in the Generalissimo's Costa Verde. He seemed proud of his American connections and hated the local military with passion. Staib promised to get him released and arrange for money to fund a campaign of opposition to the government, should Patrick agree, for appropriate compensation, of course. Staib implied that the CIA was involved, which it would be soon enough when Patrick's democratic cause emerged from the Central Jail. They shook hands on it.

Arturo Hung didn't impress Staib at first, but he was the son of a Chinese father and Costa Verde mother, and he certainly looked like the wild-eyed liberal of Tolt's specification. A graduate student at the university, he was jailed for punching a policeman. There was a surly self-confidence about Hung, a wry rebelliousness. Probing his view of the government, and getting satisfactory answers, Staib asked what would be needed for subversive activities.

"Fifty thousand, U.S. should do for a while," Hung breezed. "It'll get me started."

Staib decided to take a risk on this brash young man.

"Could you approach representatives of the Chinese government," he asked, "get Beijing to lend moral support?"

"Not for fifty thousand."

"Say money were no object," Staib pressed. "Have you the necessary connections?"

"Sure. Chinese are as racist as anybody. My name is Hung, isn't it? You've heard of the Hung Dynasty, haven't you, Padre?"

Staib had to admit he hadn't. But they shook hands, with Staib promising to get Hung, and anyone else he named, released within hours, and come up with the fifty thousand.

"May I call you Arturo, my son?"

"Sure, Padre. For fifty thousand, you can call me anything you like."

A guard shoved Arturo back into his cell, where he sank onto his grimy cot amidst the penetrating odor of stale urine and the incoherent muttering of the elderly prisoner in the adjacent cell, who had begun babbling days before.

Arturo rose and banged on the wall. "Don't worry, old man," he called. "You'll sleep in your own bed tonight."

The muttering stopped and Arturo flopped onto the cot again and lay staring at the ceiling. Moments later, hilarity tumbled him onto his stomach, washing over his body like the huge Pacific combers at his favorite surfing beach. He stifled the sound of it by forcing his mouth onto his fist, and lay there rolling with joy.

He hadn't heard of the Hung Dynasty either.

TWENTY-SIX

THE AMERICAN EMBASSY IN SAN MARCOS

The streets outside were strewn with debris from the fighting when Mallory arrived at the embassy the next morning. He waited under a smiling portrait of President Foxlee until Ambassador J. Frederick Cathcart II arrived and he was shown in to meet him. According to Peralta, Cathcart's wealthy family contributed to Foxlee's campaign in order to secure a position for J. Frederick, who wasn't very able in their eyes. Peralta regarded him as the modern equivalent of the British "remittance man" of past centuries, who was kept safely out of the family's way with a sinecure of some kind.

"You must call me Fred," Cathcart told his visitor, extending his hand. Mallory took him in at a glance. "Fred" was a large, well-proportioned man of perhaps forty, well tanned, firm of jaw, wearing tennis warm-ups. Entering his office, Mallory noted the beautiful rugs and antiques and assumed they were some of the family heirlooms. "I'm not a by-the-book foreign service officer, you know," Cathcart said, smiling broadly and arching his bushy eyebrows. *He must have a match this morning,* Mallory thought, noticing the tennis racket enclosed in its zipper cover atop the papers on the Louis XIV desk, which didn't appear to be a reproduction.

"Mister Ambassador," he said, "I'm here to ask you to intercede on behalf of my son, David. He was seized—"

"Yes, Commander, I know about the unfortunate incident at the disco. I'm sorry, of course." He motioned toward a chair and seated himself behind the desk.

"Mister Ambassador . . . Fred, they're holding David in Prison Number Five."

"Indeed?" Cathcart was impressed. "Yes, Prison Number Five. I've heard of that one, all right. Maximum security, I gather. I doubt they'd put you in there unless there was good reason."

Mallory was dumbstruck by the man's nonchalance, then outraged that the U.S. Ambassador apparently thought a military junta deserved the benefit of the doubt against an American tourist. *Doesn't this asshole realize what's been going on in this country?* he thought. *How the hell can he smile and play tennis with burned-out vehicles, broken glass, and rotting bodies lying all over this part of town?*

"As I was saying," Cathcart continued, "your son's unfortunate situation has come to my attention."

He folded his hands and rested them on the tennis racket. "These things take time, Commander Mallory, as I'm sure you understand, of course. They have to be resolved through proper channels. The first thing I will do," he continued, "is to set the ball in play." He jutted his chin and gave Mallory a fraternal look. "I am going to call the Minister of State right away and tell him the United States will be watching with interest, and concern, the treatment your son receives while in the custody of his government. I think that should be enough to assure that no harm will befall David while he is in their custody."

"I'll appreciate that, sir," Mallory said. "But, Ambassador Cathcart, sir, the main thing is to get him released as soon as possible. This morning, sir."

Cathcart's eyes darted to the ceiling for a moment, then he took a breath and continued. "You see, Mallory," he nasalized, "drugs are something of a problem here in Central America these days." He straightened in his chair. "I am doing my part in the war on drugs," he continued. "I'm giving full reign to the DEA agents Washington assigned to my staff here in San Marcos. Working together with their Costa Verde counterparts, they'll look into the matter, quite urgently I can assure you. Hopefully, by this time next week—"

"Next week!" Mallory exploded. "By next week David could be dead in that hellhole!"

"Well, I certainly understand your concern as a father," Cathcart said. "Please understand, however, your son matches the agreed law enforcement profile of a drug-type person. Superficially, of course," he smiled, "due to his age and college background. Why, even as long ago as when I was at Yale, colleges and universities were hotbeds of experimentation with all manner of illicit substances."

"I thought the criminal element sprang from the streets, not Yale," Mallory said, in an even voice, realizing his own ambassador wasn't assuming David's innocence. From the depths of his combat experience, he pulled himself together emotionally. He wasn't going to lose control and burn bridges here, so he urged Cathcart to greater efforts and looked for a pleasant way to end their encounter. Rising to leave, he noticed an antique print hanging on the wall behind Cathcart's desk, a battlefield scene unfamiliar to him.

"Well, of course, now," Cathcart told him, as though Mallory should have known, "this depicts the Battle of *Quezaltenango,* from which is derived a good deal of Central American legend."

"Interesting," Mallory managed to say, as he shook Cathcart's hand.

Peralta's Mercedes SL was waiting in the embassy driveway where Mallory had left it. He got in and slammed the door and pounded the steering wheel with his fist.

Shit!

Mallory felt lucky to find a parking space across from his destination, the *Posada Primavera,* a small inn just off the Plaza. He locked the car and waved away several urchins who offered to guard it for a fee. In some countries his attitude could result in slashed tires but he thought the regime here, eager for the tourist dollar, could be relied upon to prevent such activity.

He found the inn according to the address system used in San Marcos, which was no address at all. The odd numbered *calles,* or streets, ran north and south; the even numbered *avenidas* ran east and west. The inn was on Avenida 2 between Calle 3 and Calle 5. The system functioned without benefit of street numbers.

He entered the patio of the inn and paused just inside the wrought iron gate, until he spotted Elena at a small table next to the fountain in the center. The sun seemed to cast an aura on her black hair, shiny as a raven's wing, and highlighted a profile of classic Latin beauty and gentility. He took a moment to savor the scene—the high cheekbones, the flawless olive skin, the upturned patrician nose, and the delicate hands, as they held the jasmine she had taken from the flower vase on the table—and then crossed the patio to her table. "Sorry I'm late," he said, touching her shoulder as he sat down.

"I've been here only a few minutes," she said, reaching across the table to take his hand. A waiter brought her a tall drink and looked inquiringly at Mallory.

"Ron y tonico con lima, por favor."

The waiter nodded and departed. "Pardon me for staring," Mallory said, "but you're a welcome sight after my meeting this morning with his numbness the ambassador."

She smiled at the compliment but turned serious. "It didn't go well?"

"Hell no! He's a pompous dumb-dumb who wants nothing more than his file to look good. I've known career officers like that. They always find reasons to delay command decisions for fear of making a mistake that could show up on their record. That kind of weaseling procrastination in combat costs lives, and that's what scares the hell out of me in this situation. I feel I'm back in combat again, only this time it's David's life at stake."

Elena reached across the table again and put her hand on his. "I'm sorry," she said.

"That stupid ass instructed me in the evils of drugs in Latin America." Mallory shook his head. "David couldn't possibly be involved in anything like that," he said, as his voice rose with irritation. "He was never out of my sight. But Cathcart's mind-set filtered that out."

"I know," Elena sighed. "Nacho told the same thing to the mayor and a local judge and got the same reaction."

"They seem to consider David in a category with the Colombian cartel," Mallory said, as his drink arrived. He stared at the bubbling fountain and shook his head. "This whole situation down here is so damned surreal! Here we are in this beautiful setting but David's in a filthy prison. And you, the most beautiful woman I know, are deep in preparations for a new civil war." He shook his head. "I find it bizarre, frankly," he lowered his voice to a whisper, "that you're going to play the Joan of Arc role."

Elena shrugged. "Well, I am. Look, the La Pantera thing's a long story. Let's not talk about it now."

They sipped their drinks in silence.

In the ambiance of the colorful luncheon atmosphere, he decided to try to relax while he could and enjoy the company of a beautiful woman.

When they finished their meal, he paid the bill and they walked slowly through a live carpet of pecking birds on the patio and out into the street. With the exception of the churches, the Cathedral, the *Teatro Nacional,* and the *Palacio de Bellas Artes,* the rooftops of downtown San Marcos supported a sea of signage reminding Costa Verdeans of the world's products awaiting purchase: Sony, Toyota, Canon, Mercedes, Pepsi, Coca-Cola, Toshiba, Marlboro, and McDonalds.

They walked through the *Parque Libertad,* where black-clad matronly women, their rebozos drawn tightly around their wrinkled faces, huddled together on benches, quietly exchanging the gossip of the day. An intense guitarist, his guitar case spread open on the sidewalk, strummed his instrument, oblivious to the cacophonous honking of horns in the street and the bustle and chatter of pedestrians. An indigenous Indian woman with elaborately braided pigtails sat on a tile-covered bench nursing her child. As Mallory and Elena emerged onto the Avenida Central, urchins selling chicle from battered cigar boxes followed them. Vendors extolled the merits of their baskets, pottery, parasols and paper flowers. A young man wearing a black Hard Rock Cafe T-shirt sold brightly colored balloons. A young couple nestled on the edge of a three-tiered, tiled fountain, oblivious to the splashing of several small children dancing in the water.

"Despite the fighting yesterday, life seems normal enough," Mallory said.

"Things are meant to look good where the tourists spend their money."

"Maybe I'm finally beginning to understand Costa Verde," he said, as they stepped aside for a young mother with twins in a stroller. "And hasn't there always been a German influence here in Latin America?"

"Yes, right," Elena said. "For example, before World War II, the airlines in Ecuador and Colombia were German owned, with Luftwaffe pilots. They were thrown out, of course. The Colombian airline became Avianca while the Ecuadorian line was taken over by Pan Am.

"There were funny stories, too," she laughed. "For one, United Fruit was a big presence and Costa Verde became a leading banana producer. In the 1930s the Germans were just crazy about bananas." She glanced at him, as they paused at an intersection. "I'm not making this up," she laughed. "Germany was to build the company a ship in exchange for banana shipments. United Fruit learned the Nazis were going to expropriate the ship once they got the bananas, so they fudged on the shipments and demanded sea trials. They took the ship at gunpoint on the high seas and kept the bananas."

They turned into *Avenida Catedral*. Mallory grinned. "Terrific! Serves the bastards right."

As they strolled in silence a while, Mallory had a sudden premonition that he would be stuck in this town for months trying to get David out. *Probably into the new year, 2001, at the rate Cathcart moves,* he thought. *Well,* he realized, *there goes my job at the Pentagon.*

Elena must have sensed something at that moment, for she reached out and took his hand in hers. In spite of her own burdens, she exuded a calm and purposeful aura. He judged it was a quiet fearlessness coming from deep within, giving strength to her beauty. As they approached the National Cathedral and passed in front of the grilled openings in the high adobe wall surrounding the gardens, they paused to admire the serenity of the scene. Palm, frangipani and coffee trees punctuated the immaculately manicured grounds. One of the resident peacocks patrolled his domain on the verdant lawn as an aged gardener trimmed the tropical foliage. Statues of saints peered down from their niches in the ornate, sculptured facade of the Spanish-built cathedral.

"I'd like to go in for a few minutes," she said, taking the scarf from her shoulders and placing it on her head.

"Of course," Mallory said. "I'd like to join you, though I'm not a card-carrying Catholic like Luisa."

She smiled. "It makes no difference. God doesn't see our membership cards. Only our hearts."

They climbed the stone steps together, tugged open one of the heavy, intricately carved doors and were welcomed with the musty but refreshing coolness of the interior. A few worshipers were scattered throughout the shadowy nave, some on their knees, others sitting silently. The click of Elena's heels echoed against the stone walls as she led the way to a pew on the right side of the main aisle. She knelt and crossed herself, as Mallory seated himself beside her.

It had been a long time since he was in such a place, although he agreed Luisa would raise the children as Catholics. He was from a nominally Episcopal family, so the Catholic liturgy was familiar, but there wasn't a religious orientation in his life so far. Not surprisingly, though, he had found something approximating it in the air. Seeing the curvature of the earth from altitude, taking off for a night flight and seeing a second sunset from 40,000 feet, skimming the top of a cloud layer at twice the speed of sound under the light of a full moon, these were experiences lending a sense of identity with the Creator, and they left him with a holy sense of awe. Glancing at Elena, he realized her prayers must be focused on the fears and concerns of her life: her safety and Nacho's, the people who were committed to their cause, the loneliness after the brutal deaths of her husband and son, and yet there was serenity on her face.

Mallory's thoughts also revolved around his fears, especially David's safety. When Elena reached over and took his hand indicating it was time to go, he realized he had been praying too, without thinking of it as prayer.

TWENTY-SEVEN

The flight attendant worked her way toward the rear of the plane as the last of the passengers boarded Aero Verde's inaugural flight to New York, found their seats, and stuffed belongings into the overhead compartments. She stopped at Kreeber's seat on the aisle and touched his arm. "There's room for you two in first class today. We're upgrading you." She smiled brightly.

Kreeber and Kaalten retrieved their briefcases and went forward. None of the passengers seemed to mind that the priests received special treatment. Kaalten took a window seat across from and two rows behind the nearest passengers where they could talk without being overheard. Kreeber dropped into the aisle seat beside him. The Boeing 767 swayed gently as it moved away from the gate and took the taxiway bordering the new runway. This was nonstop service from San Marcos International Airport to New York's JFK.

"We've already overbooked the return leg this afternoon," Kaalten beamed, as they passed a Boeing 737 taxiing toward the terminal.

"When we add the second 767 next month, we'll be competing on a level playing field with American Airlines, Avianca and KLM."

Kreeber, knowing the brigadefuhrer's constant need for approval, readily agreed. "You were brilliant," he said, "ordering the runway extension two years before we even arrived in Costa Verde, and contracting for first-rate equipment. It's too bad Aero Verde's board can't toast you properly!" he laughed.

"Makes no difference," Kaalten replied, "they're my puppets anyway, though they don't know I exist."

Kreeber realized he was in for one of Kaalten's self-congratulatory recitations of information he knew as well as Kaalten. For once, he didn't care, as he settled in for the long flight. "Only Alvarez," Kaalten purred, "the chairman, and Muller, the president, know a consortium in Germany controls the airline. Their modest Swiss accounts depend on their discretion, of course. This Muller," he continued, "was terminated by Lufthansa last year for suspected embezzlement that was never proved and for involvement in neo-Nazi causes. Muller knows the international airline industry as well as anyone in the business."

"Well, this has certainly been your pattern, hasn't it?" Kreeber said, stroking him. "You find an expert who's fallen into disfavor, then you buy his loyalty."

"Except for the regrettable case of Doctor Richter, the lawyer. He had more scruples than we thought."

"What's happened to him?"

"Oh, I think he disappeared," Kaalten said, crossing himself and winking at Kreeber.

Kreeber stretched out and closed his eyes as the plane accelerated and lifted off. Though he outranked Kaalten, two stars for a gruppen-fuhrer to one for a brigadefuhrer, he seldom lorded it over him since they had essentially equivalent assignments. Tolt had put Kreeber in charge of cleaning up the banking industry and managing the country's fiscal affairs. Kaalten was in charge of Germanizing the country. As to banking, Tolt had decreed that Costa Verde rid itself of the reputation of a Cayman Islands look-alike, when it came to loose banking practices favored by fraudulent business empires and criminals. Germanization meant Costa Verde would assume the coloration of Germany-Austria-Switzerland as to efficient public services and a notable hospitality industry. Kreeber's program involved gaining control of banking in Costa Verde, starting with buying off the Chairman of Banco Central, the government-owned central bank, and using that power to reform the various private banking institutions. The goal was to transform the shady business practices of the past and adopt the Swiss model of circumspection and privacy. Banco Central hired American and Swiss bankers and laid down the law: no more drug money, no more laundering of currency, efficient service, and Swiss-type privacy accounts. Kreeber had managed the early stages of the banking transformation from his office in Munich prior to moving to Costa Verde. Working through various Kohorte business fronts in Germany, Canada and the United States, he gained controlling interests in Costa Verde banks wherever he could, then drove the others to the wall, where they either conformed to the new order or they ceased to exist. Today he was traveling to New York to make the rounds of the banks and investment banking firms, testing the water for a massive new offering of Costa Verde bonds. Not that the Kohorte needed the money; it didn't. Instead, Kreeber sought validation of Costa Verde's role as the bright spot in Central American banking and finance. This would be confirmed if Costa Verde's international debt could be floated on advantageous terms, especially if the offering were oversubscribed by foreign investors. Kreeber needed an occasional foray into the financial community to counterbalance his almost monastic lifestyle. In fact, his new life at the cathedral differed little from the one he chose to lead in Munich. It was there that he first developed the art of "unseen management." With Tolt's blessing *ungesehen behandeln* was applied to the Kohorte's entire portfolio of business interests. By definition, unseen management was the antithesis of hands-on management, and its effectiveness depended on the keen inputs he gathered from experts living in the real world of finance.

Kreeber performed these periodic reality checks by changing identities in New York, where he became Dr. Wilhelm Weiss, a lawyer-banker from Dortmund who regularly surfaced two or three times a year. Dr. Weiss always stayed at the Waldorf and made the rounds midtown and downtown, renewing his contacts within the commercial and investment banking communities on behalf of his employer, a German consortium that was a Kohorte front. This trip he would announce the purchase of a controlling interest in *Banco de Libertad,* a San Marcos bank with branches in several cities and towns. The comments and reactions he received would enable him to assess the progress to date of his "de-Caymanization" program, which hinged on the financial community's perceptions every bit as much as it did on actual changes wrought in the system. He suspected if there were negative sentiments they would center on the Generalissimo's image as an uncultured bully, who hadn't made enough progress in returning power to the elected officials. The Generalissimo had been the fly in the de-Caymanization ointment.

Kreeber smiled. *Well,* he thought, *it turns out the timing of this trip is perfect. Mauser has unsettled the equation and I'll be there in New York to soothe the financial community power brokers and convince them of brighter prospects under Colonel Benes.*

"Hot towel, Padre?" the stewardess asked, as Kaalten awoke with a start.

"Thank you, my child," he told her, accepting a towel.

"It strikes me," Kreeber said, "that your trip to Europe combines the sublime and the ridiculous."

"Definitely," Kaalten laughed.

He was going to Rome for an audience with Cardinal Guilianni who had reissued his invitation to meet with one or more of the former East Germans.

"Are you concerned about the meeting?" Kreeber asked.

"Monsignor Albert will insulate me from difficulties that may arise," Kaalten snapped, seemingly offended.

Kreeber glanced at his watch, saw that there were more than two hours to go, and decided to flatter him once more. "Well, I'm amazed you've accomplished so much Germanization already considering that you had to do it using my *ungesehen behandeln* methodology, and so much of it before we ever arrived in San Marcos. How did you know to concentrate your efforts on Costa Verde before the Reichsfuhrer announced Case Green?"

"I concentrated equally on all the candidate countries," Kaalten told him.

"But where else except in Costa Verde is the process so far advanced?" Kreeber waved his hand expansively. "The hotels, even the ones we don't own, are managed by Swiss, the restaurateurs are European, the phone system is quite efficient, street cleanliness is becoming superb, the busses and trains run on time, with new first-class equipment—all this in only two, three years time!"

Kaalten beamed at the accolades. "As the Reichsfuhrer is so fond of reminding us," he said modestly, "much can be accomplished in very little time if you have all the money in the world and a deep well of neo-Nazis to draw from. I merely listed the country's needs, used our business connections, and spent the money.

"The hospitality industry was the easiest. Any billionaire could get the same results. The public sector was more difficult. However, not even the Generalissimo was so stupid as to ignore the unmatched luxury of a couple of Swiss bank accounts. I always made sure his payments coincided with the suggestion of a particular improvement needing to be made to the infrastructure or public services. The unmistakable implication," Kaalten smiled, "was that contractors and equipment manufacturers were paying him to obtain the consequent contracts. The same holds true of Colonel Benes now, of course. In fact, this is why I brought Herr Hesse to Costa Verde from Munich and had him function as a manufacturers' representative in San Marcos."

"Ah," Kreeber said, "I remember Gerhardt Hesse, as crooked a man as there ever was. How can you trust him?"

"Actually, I don't trust him. Staib takes care of ensuring his continued loyalty."

They chuckled about that.

———————

Kaalten jarred Kreeber awake as he climbed into his seat from a trip to the lavatory. The gruppenfuhrer opened his eyes as a stewardess moved toward them in the aisle.

"Would you like a complimentary pisco sour?" she inquired, holding a tray of Latin America's version of the whiskey sour, containing pisco brandy instead of bourbon.

"We'll have a bottle of champagne, instead, assuming you have some good caviar as well," Kreeber said.

"Oh, yes. As it happens, Padre, catering did place a jar aboard just before we sealed the aircraft."

"Thank you, my child. That's nice," he said, glad he'd thought of caviar earlier in the day.

Kaalten leaned toward her from the window seat, smiling beatifically.

"You see, this is our little chance to enjoy ourselves," he said.

Minutes later, when they were alone, their glasses clinked. "What shall we drink to?" Kreeber asked.

"Case Green, of course," Kaalten proposed.

"Case Green!" they agreed.

TWENTY-EIGHT

LANGLEY

Truman stood at the rain-splattered window in his fifth-floor office on a dark afternoon, staring down at the wind-whipped trees dotting the wet parking lot. He thought about the unresolved question of Burton's loyalty and reviewed the bidding for what seemed like the hundredth time. His own foray into the field, resulting in their encounter at the bar at the Cosmopolitan, hadn't led to a damn thing, nor had the business of the deposits to Burton's Swiss account produced any discernable result, if it ever would.

He turned and began to pace the floor, frustrated by the lack of any progress toward resolving the potential ugliness on his hands.

"Bill's always so damn prescient," he muttered. "The son-of-a-bitch catches every little scent on the wind. I still don't dare enlist Franck or anyone from the Company." He pounded his fist into his palm. "Damn it, I've simply got to have someone on the scene there in San Marcos."

Recruiting an American living in Costa Verde was far too risky, he knew, since you never know who's doing what to whom in a tight little place like Costa Verde.

"Shit," he said under his breath, "I've got to come up with an agent in place ASAP . . . or the trail, if there is one, will fade and be lost. Yes, that's it!" he stroked his chin, "somebody antiseptic as hell, without any connection with the Company, but savvy as hell about the country."

The next morning Gretchen entered Truman's office and closed the door. "Here's the list of Americans now visiting in Costa Verde that you asked for," she said. "Got it through MI6 in London since our embassy in San Marcos is dead on its ass, apparently. Seems the Director de Pasaportes in Costa Verde has been on the Brits' payroll for ever." She slid the file across the desk and drew up a chair. The list included hometown, declared purpose of visit, length of stay, and the usual passport information.

"There must be two hundred, almost three hundred," Truman said, turning pages.

"They're vacationers," she said, "except for a few visiting their relatives and a half-dozen corporate people checking on their local operations. I've marked a couple of them, though. See page nine, for example."

Truman turned to page nine.

"Decatur Mallory. Hmmm," he said, tapping the page, "this sounds familiar, I think."

"Retired Navy Commander," she said. "Here's a vitae I pulled together on my computer from Navy Department records." She slipped a sheet of paper to him on the desk. "He has an interesting service record," she continued, "and was recently hired as a civilian employee at the Pentagon with the Navy's JSF fighter procurement team. He's supposed to go to work for an Admiral Frazier there, but Mallory's son is being held locally on a drug charge, so the commander is temporarily in San Marcos working on the boy's release. But what really caught my eye was his service in Costa Verde as a young liaison officer with the Costa Verde Air Force flight demonstration team."

"Got a Silver Star in Desert Storm, I see."

Gretchen smirked. "And that Syrian MiG above the Med a few years back. Unofficially, of course."

Truman frowned at her, then brightened. He clasped his hands behind his head, recalling the scene in Nixon's kitchen in New York and the former President telling him about the younger Peralta's nocturnal visits to the White House during his administrations.

"Do this," he told her. "Find out if this is the Deke Mallory who was a friend of Edwardo Peralta's son Ignacio. If so, prepare a full dossier as quickly as you can."

"What about the other names I've marked?" she asked.

"Forget them for now," he said, returning the file. "Commander Mallory is our top candidate," he told her. "We may have lucked out here."

"All right, Terry," she said. "But how are you going to convince him to become a spook?"

"Oh," he said, with a gentle smile, "I'll think of something." Gretchen left and he picked up the phone.

"This is the President," Nathan Foxlee answered.

"Truman here, sir. I need to ask you to intercede with the Department of the Navy on something."

Foxlee laughed. "T-Square, I thought you had a clean service record. Or was I misinformed?"

"Clean as a latrine, sir. Marine, I mean."

Foxlee laughed again. "Okay," he said. "What's up?"

"I'm in need of someone I can trust to do some investigating for me down in Costa Verde, completely outside of CIA channels. I might have a bad apple on my hands this time, so I can't risk using Company personnel on this one."

"What's the Navy Department got to do with it?"

"The man I need is a recently retired Naval Aviator, a Commander Mallory, Mister President, who has a strong background involving Costa Verde. He just hired on to work for the Navy as a civilian on the JSF program, but I need him recalled to active duty."

"Why?" the President asked. Truman heard him yawn.

209

"So that you, Mister President, can order him to do whatever's needed in this matter. Civilians are too independent for my taste this time, sir. I can't risk him tossing his head and just saying no."

"Does this have to do with that Burton guy you told me about the other day? The fellow you said may have compromised himself down there?"

Truman smiled. Foxlee had lowered his voice just a touch and was paying attention to their conversation now. The President loved playing amateur spook, Truman had discovered, and his proclivity was about to pay off.

"Right. That's what it's about, Mister President.

"Sir, please remember, so far you're the only one, other than Gretchen Reece, who knows about this."

"Can I do it, Terry? Can I recall a retired military person to active duty?"

"No you can't, Mister President, absent declaring a national emergency."

There was silence on the President's end.

"What you can do, though," Truman told him, "is instruct the Secretary of the Navy that Commander Mallory is to be offered a captaincy, if he agrees to re-up."

"Consider it done!" Foxlee said. "Gotta go now."

"Thank you, Mister President." Truman hung up and opened his road map of Central America.

TWENTY-NINE

THE ARCHBISHOP'S PALACE AT THE CATHEDRAL

Tolt scowled as he finished reading Karpf's weekly intelligence summary. Rising from the archbishop's massive desk, he crossed the room to where Staib was seated at a computer and slammed the report down on the table. "I assume you've read this?" he demanded.

Staib glanced at the report. "Of course I've read it."

"Then it should be obvious to you that the time has come to put an end to Peralta's meddling sister."

Staib shut down the computer. His hard, thin lips gradually widened into a satisfied smile. "Give the order, Reichsfuhrer, and it shall be done."

"This confirms my suspicion," Tolt said, as he paced the floor and addressed the ceiling. "Elena Peralta no longer spends her time shopping in fashionable boutiques and lunching with her society friends. Karpf's information proves she is the one behind this pitiful Joan of Arc caricature, La Pantera, who is supposed to emerge from the jungle to lead the simple peasants in a full-scale revolt."

Tolt burst out laughing. "Doesn't that strike you as amusing?" he asked. "A revolt against whom? In reality, I am the government of Costa Verde." He bowed theatrically, as he continued in a mocking tone. "A simple man of God, playing out my destiny on the stage of this small country, ably assisted, of course, by others such as you, Father Martin, bringing a new destiny to this little country . . . through irresistible forces," he shrieked, "unleashed in support of Case Green!"

His manic laughter continued as he crossed to the hearth and turned to face Staib with his hands clasped behind his back in the Hitlerian pose.

"This pathetic little princess," he said, "and her imaginary panther friend remind me of Don Quixote and Sancho Panza, because the government she's so upset about is but a pitiful windmill itself." Tolt let out a maniacal whoop. "And what would her followers think if they knew the windmill is owned and operated by me? This spoiled society matron thinks she can thwart my unstoppable destiny, does she? Yes, I find that very amusing."

Staib stood and faced Tolt. "Give the order" he said as he clicked his heels, "and I will devise a death scene for her to enhance your mirth."

THE PERALTA FAMILY COMPOUND

Elena inspected herself in the mirror of her dressing room, gathered a black lace mantilla over her shoulders and tied it off to one side. She adjusted her small veiled hat and wondered what Mallory would think of the effect. She had worn only casual wear aboard *Gusto* and since, but a christening at the cathedral called for a definite formality and she felt he would relate to such occasions. After all, he was a senior naval officer and must be used to the niceties of formal affairs.

As she selected gloves, she thought of what a happy occasion this would be, the christening of the first son of her cousin Alicia and her husband. Family and friends were coming from near and far to attend the service, and Bishop Subueso was coming from Pacifico Provence to perform the rite. He was an old family friend, a special confidant of her father, and her and Nacho's confessor. She looked forward to seeing him again.

Her mood darkened as she recalled the christening of her son Cesar at which Bishop Subueso also officiated. She solemnly crossed herself and willfully banished the thought from her mind. This would be a joyous occasion, one in which the bishop, a dear family friend, would receive a child into Christ's church. Satisfied that she looked her best, she picked up her purse. The extra weight reminded her it contained the silenced Colt .32 Diego insisted she carry at all times. Removing it from the purse, she weighed it in her hand and put it in the drawer of her dresser. It wouldn't be needed in God's house.

THE CATHEDRAL

Monsignor Schmehr preened in the mirrored robing area of the sacristy in the rooms behind the altar, as he adjusted the fit of his vestments. He knew his salmon colored acting archbishop's cap and stole were supposed to be impressive to Catholics, but in reality he preferred the black and silver of the SS uniform, with an Iron Cross worn at the throat instead of a silly crucifix dangling from the chain, but it was a small cost to pay for masquerading as a high officer of the Church. *I am archbishop here,* he muttered, *and I shall act it to the fullest today.* In the back of his mind the day would come when the Church here would break with Rome and he would be proclaimed its Supreme Pontiff, a role he recently decided fit his destiny better than head of state, of which there were hundreds at any time in the fractionated modern world.

He turned from the mirror as Staib entered the sacristy and locked the door. "Did you bring the poison, Father Martin?" he inquired with a smile.

"Of course." Staib produced a tiny vial.

"This is the same as you used for the late archbishop?"

"Better," Staib said. "Little more than a trace amount is necessary and death is certain within fifteen minutes, producing the same effect as a coronary thrombosis." He smiled, savoring the image. "And best of all, it leaves no trace that can be detected, except by the most sophisticated laboratory, and this assumes that the physician performing the autopsy has near mystical intuitive powers."

"Excellent!" Tolt said. Staib held the vial up to the light and produced a small hypodermic needle from the folds of his cassock. Carefully uncapping the vial, he withdrew a small amount into the needle.

"A wafer, if you please, Archbishop Schmehr," he said, as he put out his left hand. Tolt took a communion wafer from the supply in a cabinet and with mock solemnity placed it in Staib's hand. The assassin placed the wafer on a folded paper towel and carefully squeezed one drop onto it.

"There," he said with a satisfied smile. "We have what I believe they call the Transubstantiated Body. The Body of Death in this case."

"You have done well, Father Martin," Tolt said, as he inspected the lethal wafer. "I know you prefer to do these things yourself, but in this case I am the only one who can administer the wafer."

"I shall be close at hand, watching your performance," Staib said, feigning wistfulness. "And how did Bishop Subueso react to your decision to participate today?"

"Most graciously, of course. What else could he do? I made it easy for him by explaining I have been so busy with burdensome administrative matters I sorely miss performing my priestly duties, and requested his permission to assist with the mass following the christening. I said I knew he was an old friend of the family, and I wouldn't dream of intruding during the christening itself.

"I will appear at the altar just prior to his blessing of the elements," Tolt continued. "I said I would prefer that he offer the chalice, while I distribute the wafers to the family at the rail."

Staib was enthusiastic. "Perfect!" he said. "By the time the potion has done it's work the ceremony will be over. She will collapse as the party leaves the sanctuary."

Brilliant shafts of sunlight emanating from the stained glass window behind the altar penetrated the dim interior of the cathedral.

Elena smiled as she observed that some of the laserlike beams of light came to rest almost as a halo on the child presented for baptism. Her mind wandered to pleasant memories of her childhood in this holy place, and for a moment she was back at the christening of her son Cesar, with happy feelings this time.

The words of Bishop Subueso drew her out of her reverie. "Dearly beloved, forasmuch as you have brought this child here to be baptized, and have prayed that our Lord Jesus Christ would vouchsafe to receive him, and sanctify him with the Holy Ghost—"

Elena's mind wandered and she suddenly saw herself marrying Mallory at the altar. She blinked and shifted in her seat, trying to pay attention.

"Dost thou, therefore," Subueso asked the infant's parents and god-parents, "in the name of this child renounce the devil and his works, and the sinful desires of the flesh, so that you will not follow, nor be led by them?"

A few moments later, he asked the same question of the people assembled, and Elena heard her own voice blend with those of the small congregation. "I renounce them all, with God's help."

"Wilt thou keep God's holy will and commandments, and walk in the same all the days of thy life?"

"We will, with God's help."

Elena took in the assembled group of family and friends, most of whom she had known all her life, and felt a surge of happiness. She looked up again to see the magnificent stream of colored light still spot-lighting the child, and returned to the present, as she heard the familiar words: "I baptize thee in the Name of the Father, and of the Son, and of the Holy Ghost."

Bishop Subueso made the sign of the cross on the infant's forehead with holy water from the baptismal font. "We receive this child into the congregation of Christ's flock, and do sign him with the sign of the cross."

The rite of baptism concluded, the party moved to the chancel rail to receive the Eucharist. Elena knelt in prayer with the others, as the ancient rite was recited by the bishop. She happened to look up as the elements were about to be blessed, and was startled to see the acting archbishop standing behind the altar with the bishop. She sensed, not for the first time since his arrival in Costa Verde, that there was something sinister about this cold, towering presence, about which rumors were flying within the community of the faithful.

Her hands began to tremble and she felt a cold chill. *What's he doing here? Why has this holy moment been fouled with his presence? How can Bishop Subueso seem so perfectly at ease with him? Doesn't he sense the presence of evil?*

Subueso blessed the elements and the archbishop walked to the right side of the rail with the tray of wafers in his hands. Subueso followed a step behind and met her gaze with his benevolent smile, as he waited to offer the chalice to the communicants.

Unaccountably, Elena began to feel a growing terror as the archbishop approached, distributing wafers to those keeling to her right. She closed her eyes and willed the fright to pass, but she couldn't help stealing another glance. A woman next to the man on her immediate right received the wafer, as the archbishop paused and looked back briefly to smile at the bishop. In doing so, she saw him withdraw a wafer from the folds of his robe and palm it with the third and little finger of his right hand.

Elena gasped and covered her mouth, as she watched out of the corner of her eye.

With his thumb and first two fingers, the archbishop selected a wafer from the tray for the man kneeling beside her. Then she saw him retrieve the hidden wafer, poised now to place it in her upturned palms.

She looked up into the face of evil and leapt to her feet, holding her mouth with both hands.

She realized people were staring at her now, and she feigned she was about to vomit. She bent from the waist to cement the impression.

Quickly assessing possible escape routes, she ran to the aisle on the left side of the sanctuary. Seeing Father Martin waiting in the shadows there, she headed for a door leading to a maze of rooms located behind the altar. It was familiar territory from her days of service on the Cathedral Women's Guild, which was responsible for maintaining the altar, vestments, and utensils of worship.

No one followed, which was a tribute to her compelling performance as the victim of food poisoning; no one, that is, except Staib, who nodded reverently to the congregation, and bowed toward the altar before departing the service, ostensibly to render assistance.

The first room she encountered was an anteroom to the sacristy, and beyond that were storage rooms for altar pieces. She could hear Staib's footsteps behind her now, and instinctively knew one of the archbishop's lieutenants was in deadly hot pursuit. Turning a corner, she entered a hallway with several doors. The first, she knew, led to storage areas. The door across the hall led to a small vestibule, and on outside to the back street.

She opened the first door and quickly tossed in her mantilla, which fluttered to the floor. She left the door slightly ajar, crossed the hall, entered the door of the room leading to the outside, and quickly closed and locked it. She prayed her pursuer was unfamiliar with the layout of this part of the cathedral, would take the bait, and by the time he discovered his error, she would be safely away.

Once on the street, she mingled with the passing crowd, but soon broke into a frightened run, putting as much distance as possible between herself and the cathedral. Looking over her shoulder to see if she was being followed, she collided with an elderly woman. Her hat caught in the tip of the tortoise shell comb the woman wore in her hair, and her hat fell to the sidewalk.

"Señora!" she heard a man's voice calling. "Señora, su sombrero—" But she raced on.

Two blocks later she slowed to a walk and stopped in front of a store window to catch her breath. Glancing at her reflection in the glass, she saw her hands and shoulders were trembling. She clasped her hands and willed the trembling to cease. When she studied her reflection again, she saw a disheveled Elena Peralta de Gomez, but she also saw a woman marked for assassination. *Yes,* she thought, *the supposedly invincible La*

Pantera met her nemesis just now; but such a horrifying thought soon turned to elation, as it dawned on her that the dark powers ruling Costa Verde regarded La Pantera as a threat to their reign.

She quickly ran her fingers through her hair and straightened her dress and, with a satisfied smile on her face, she turned to hail a passing taxi.

On the way to the Peralta compound, she concluded that the embarrassment of explaining her behavior at the christening was of no real importance. She would merely say she hadn't felt well that day. People would soon forget.

The trees lining the boulevard were flying past, reminding her of the morning she and Diego returned from the horrible episode at the beach house at Bahia Pajaros. She would probably never know whether the terror that night was part of a plan to assassinate her or just a chance encounter with drunken soldiers.

Today's encounter was different, though. The acting archbishop actually tried to poison her with a communion wafer. Maybe others would think she was paranoid, but she saw it with her own eyes.

Stopping at an intersection, the driver looked up into the rearview mirror. "Do you think the colonel will prove to be a good man, compared to the Generalissimo?" he asked.

"I have no idea," she said, not wanting to reveal herself politically.

"Well, I think they're all just the same," he said. "My wife is praying for La Pantera to return. I only wish La Pantera were real," he sighed.

Elena averted his gaze and looked out the window, as his eyes returned to the road. Minutes later, when they stopped at an intersection near the family compound, she got out and paid the fare, preserving her anonymity.

"Your wife's right," she said. "La Pantera is coming soon."

"How do you know?" the driver asked.

She thought of the brood of vipers at the cathedral.

"Because God is not mocked," she told him.

THIRTY

THE AMERICAN EMBASSY IN SAN MARCOS

Mallory listened as Cathcart chatted on the phone with the new military government's Interior Minister, reportedly an air force crony of Colonel Benes, thrust into the role following the coup. His mind wandered as he gazed out toward the embassy gardens while Cathcart delicately thrust and parried, occasionally winking at him, as if they were scoring point-after-point in an arcane parlor game Mallory should be enjoying, which he wasn't, since he doubted the ambassador was making any progress toward David's release.

Mallory compressed his lips and inspected his nails, wondering if Cathcart would get tough and threaten to cut off foreign aid or use the weight of the U.S. government to demand David's immediate release. The ambassador was as conciliatory and cautious toward the new regime as ever. Mallory doubted he was ever going to ask Washington for instructions on handling David's situation.

Mallory's own urgent telephone calls to Senators and Representatives brought sympathetic responses and some promises of help but nothing was happening as a result. He guessed it was a long way from Capitol Hill to Foggy Bottom, in terms of politicians altering the glacial progress of a perennially aloof State Department. And

Nacho's sincere, often heated, attempts to secure David's freedom through his local connections were proving equally unfruitful.

"Well, now!" Cathcart announced, replacing the receiver. "The new Interior Minister, Colonel Alvarez himself, mind you, has just assured me he will personally look into the question of David's well-being and call me back about it in a day or two." He raised his bushy eyebrows and winked conspiratorially.

Mallory's heart sank as he realized the man actually thought he accomplished something toward the main objective. "That's nice of him, Ambassador," he said, "but the goal is getting David released, don't forget."

"Now, you just rest assured, Commander, obtaining the release of your son into my personal custody, as the proper representative of the United States legal system, remains my absolute highest priority."

Cathcart pretty clearly thought David was part of the drug culture, so Mallory took it as a hollow assurance. Nevertheless, he forced a smile, shook Cathcart's hand firmly, and gave him a knowing look in the eye, as he had seen the upper-crust do when stroking one another.

Cathcart jutted his chin at him, and smiled vacuously. "And please extend my continuing sympathy to your—"

He's forgetting Luisa is dead, Mallory thought, and took him off the hook by interrupting. Cathcart's mind was elsewhere, but Mallory felt there was no alternative but to play out his hand to the fullest here at the embassy.

"Fred," he said, selecting chumminess this time, "the receptionist said your naval attaché wants to see me. How do I get to his office?"

As Cathcart led the way, Mallory got the feeling he wouldn't normally be doing so, but was maintaining the appearance of bending over backwards. He seethed as he followed Cathcart down the hall. The ambassador was coatless but wore the pants to a three-thousand-dollar black silk suit and a custom-made white shirt that formed to his athletic body, with a pale yellow collar to frame his very expensive Italian silk tie. Despite the humidity, the shirt looked crisp and had the military three-crease press in back. *I'll bet he changes shirts three or four times a day,* Mallory thought, *to intimidate his staff.* Marine drill instructors did that when Mallory was in OCS prior to flight training at Pensacola, for the sole purpose of intimidating their sweaty young charges. Cathcart had no military background, Mallory knew, but he judged him to be the type of high-powered fop who would use any crutch he could in order to maintain the appearance of his superiority to others. Mallory bit his lip in a state of controlled anger. *And what the hell does the attaché want with a retired officer?* he fumed.

A trim young woman wearing Navy tropical whites came around from behind her desk and shook Mallory's hand. He noticed her Naval Academy ring.

"Commander, I'm Lieutenant Commander Ruth Tanaka, our naval attaché here in Costa Verde," she said. "I remain shocked and angered about your son's treatment, sir."

Tanaka closed the door and sat in a chair as Mallory dropped onto the couch and declined coffee.

"Thanks," he said. "It's in the ambassador's hands, for now, I guess. What can I do for you, Commander?"

Tanaka took a sheet of paper from her desk and handed it to Mallory. "I received a coded E-mail this morning," she said, "from Vice Admiral Frazier, at the Pentagon. Here's the translation. It's self explanatory, sir."

Mallory scanned it. Frazier was arriving at Howard Air Force Base in the Canal Zone in the morning and was sending a plane to San Marcos to fetch Mallory for a meeting over lunch. There was no indication of the subject of discussion, which Mallory assumed was his civilian employment on the JSF Evaluation Project. *Why the hell would Frazier fly 2,500 miles just to see me?*

"What's this all about?"

"I've no idea, sir," Tanaka said. "But if you don't mind, I'd like to come along for the ride. There's nothing for me to do here for a while until the Benes government settles in and we find out who we're supposed to be working with in the new regime.

"And maybe I can help if there's any problem of getting you into Costa Verde's San Benito Air Base where the plane from Howard will pick you up."

"Sure," Mallory said. "Glad for the company."

Inwardly, he felt sick. Tanaka was right. Nothing could be done by Cathcart about David's release until the United States recognized the new government and the game played out for a few days or weeks.

SAN BENITO AIR FORCE BASE

The four-engine U.S. Air Force C-130 Hercules prop-jet landed short, reversed pitch, and taxied to the tower at San Benito, the Costa Verde Air Force's main base, where Mallory and Tanaka were waiting with an officer who met them at the main gate. Mallory noticed that none of the plane's four engines shut down. They thanked their host and trotted toward the aircraft's rear cargo ramp where they were met on the tarmac by the aircraft commander as the crew off-loaded a crate that Mallory guessed might contain jet engine parts.

"I'm Major Billings," he said in a southern accent. "Business as usual," he added, thumbing toward the crate. "Those parts were promised before the coup, I guess."

They followed him up the ramp and went forward. "Just buckle yourselves into one of the seats behind the flight deck," he told them, "and we'll be out of here in a jiffy."

The flight to Howard Air Force Base took less than an hour, during which Mallory learned a good deal from Tanaka about the U.S. military's disengagement in the Canal Zone.

"What do you think of us turning the canal back to Panama?" he asked. Tanaka turned in her seat and faced him. She looked pained.

"It's okay, Commander," Mallory assured her. "I'm not going to repeat anything you say."

Tanaka took a deep breath. "President Carter never should have sold Congress on the treaty in the first place," she said. "Panama's self-image is all wrapped up in the canal, but it accounts for just seven percent of their economy. They've got massive unemployment there and our base closures are going to make it a lot worse. And the Panamanian police force—they have no army—is no match for anybody, yet they're supposed to be guaranteeing the canal's security. Carter must have forgotten everything he learned at the Naval Academy," Tanaka said, smiling weakly.

Mallory was surprised to learn the reason they were flying courtesy of the U.S. Air Force was that Rodman Naval Base had been closed a few months before. Worse, Howard AFB was due to be closed in a couple of weeks, before the handover of the canal at noon on December 31.

"You can assess the damage to our national security as well as I," Tanaka said, "but what you may not realize is that our entire war on drugs down here has always been projected from Rodman and Howard. We're talking thousands and thousands of air and sea sorties every year. So the Colombian drug industry mushrooms and what do we do about it? We quit and retreat to Florida, that's what. All those sorties will have to be run out of there now.

"It's the worst possible thing for us to be leaving Panama," she continued, "and when you factor in the Chinese having negotiated twenty-five-year contracts to manage the Canal . . . and our former bases as well . . ." Tanaka's voice trailed away. "Anyway, you asked what I thought."

"You forgot to mention the instability of the whole region," Mallory said, shaking his head sympathetically, "of which we've just had a prime example in Costa Verde, in Colonel Benes' little coup."

HOWARD AIR FORCE BASE, PANAMA

The Officers Club was almost deserted at noon when Mallory strolled in looking for Admiral Frazier. In a matter of days it would be deserted permanently when the base was closed and the property turned over to Panama. He found Frazier at an isolated table overlooking the lawn.

"Any progress getting your boy released?" Frazier asked, after they ordered Bombay martinis, straight up with two olives.

"No, not yet," Mallory said. "I keep trying everything I know to do but I'm sort of stuck in the mud so far."

"I wish there were something I could do to help," Frazier said. "I guess you want to stay there in Costa Verde until David's release?"

"No way am I leaving without my son, sir. I'm sorry but this thing has to take precedence over my working for the Navy." He paused as their drinks arrived. "Why in the world did you fly all the way here to see me?" he asked, as they clinked glasses.

"First," Frazier said, "your staying in Costa Verde isn't a problem right now. You're still the man I want and you know that the Navy always takes care of its own. I'll keep your slot on my team open for you as long as I can. Now to your question: something new has come up." He reached in his pocket and produced a pair of silver captain's eagles. "The Secretary of the Navy has authorized me to give you these if you'll re-up for active duty. They're yours to wear when you report to my office at the Pentagon," he said with a smile, pushing them across the table to Mallory. "They were mine and I'd consider it an honor if you'd accept them."

Mallory was stunned as he stared at the eagles.

"You see," Frazier said, "you really needn't have been concerned about that little incident with the Syrian MiG denying you your fourth stripe. The scuttlebutt at the time was that it had to be one of the reasons you took early retirement and settled for three stripes."

Mallory shrugged. "Well, the Syrian thing wasn't exactly in the same category as my Silver Star medal. And anyway, there were other reasons."

"Of course there were," Frazier agreed. "I hope the sight of these eagles in front of you will put that issue to rest, though." The admiral leaned forward and lowered his voice. "Truth be known, I did the same thing in Viet Nam. These things happen and you aren't the first guy to push the envelope on the rules of engagement and take out one of the bad guys under less than authorized circumstances."

Mallory laughed. "'Less than authorized circumstances.' You have a way with words, Admiral. Anyway, I just felt at the time that I should turn the page on a new chapter in my life and spend more time with Luisa. Given what happened to her, I'm sure glad I did."

Frazier nodded. "Of course. Well, in any event, these silver birds are yours . . . and don't worry about remaining here for David. You can be assigned to temporary duty at the embassy in San Marcos. Don't worry," the admiral winked, "you won't really be working with that asshole of an ambassador, since all this is classified Pentagon material and he isn't cleared for it." He opened his briefcase and plopped a stack of files on the table.

"This is damned unusual, Admiral," Mallory said.

"Hell yes, it is. Let's just say you've got friends in high places. What are powerful friends for anyway?"

"And just what friends would these be?" Mallory asked.

Frazier shrugged with upturned palms. "Damned if I know," he said. "But I'm not complaining, since I want you on my team. As an active duty officer you will get a lot of flight time in the new prototype birds, including CarQuals, and connect with the project much more directly than you could ever do as a civilian on my staff."

"There's got to be a catch to this," Mallory said, thumbing one of the silver eagles.

"The catch," Frazier said, leaning forward to jut his chin in his characteristic pose, "is that civilians can tell me to go to hell but Naval officers do as they're told."

Why do I smell a rat here someplace? Mallory wondered. He thought of the emptiness of his life without Luisa and remembered that when David was released he would be off to law school somewhere. A civilian job would pale compared to his love affair with Naval Aviation.

He nodded and put the captain's insignia in his pocket. "Welcome aboard, Captain," Frazier said, as he reached for the stack of documents on the table.

Mallory interrupted him, still thunderstruck by the chance to re-up as a four-striper. "Admiral, you came all the way from Washington today just to recruit me?"

"Sure. Besides," he chuckled, "I'm going to personally swear you in right after lunch. The Base Commander here has agreed to let us use his office, and he'll witness the blessed event along with his senior JAG officer."

Mallory drained his glass as they placed their orders. Frazier pulled a file from the stack and handed it across the table to Mallory. "Here's your job profile on the JSF evaluation team. Pretty interesting stuff, I'd say, and right up your alley. Look it over and try not to drool on the tablecloth."

Mallory read through the material until their plates arrived. In spite of his obvious excitement about the project, he kept wondering how he could have been granted this unheard-of invitation to active duty after more than a couple of years in retirement.

David's voice replayed in his head: "Come on, Dad, let's push the envelope. You were always for doing that, right?"

The admiral signaled for coffee. "Remember," he said, "Boeing hasn't proven they can make one of these things right. Neither has Lockheed Martin, but that's the job Congress gave me; to prove that one of them can—and on budget. "Congress doesn't give a shit if the thing actually performs, you know, just that the price is right. But, dammit," Frazier said, raising his voice, "I care and so do the Marines, the Air Force and the Royal Navy." He took a sip of his coffee. "There'll be three versions. One for our use aboard ship, a slightly different version for the Air Force, and a special version for the Marines and the Royal Navy to replace their STOVL Harriers."

"Congress is usually obsessed with cost," Mallory offered, "but that's the thinking that gave us the stupid Brewster Buffalo." They both knew about the contract given to Brewster Airplane Company in the late 1930s against more qualified competitors, ironically including Boeing. The result was the infamous "flying coffin" of the air battles at Midway and Wake Island. Any surviving Marine aviator would have found the Buffalo's designer and strangled him.

"I'm glad I never had to fly in combat in a turkey like that one," Mallory said.

"So am I," Frazier sighed. "But just look at these specs," he said, tapping a file with his finger. "These JSF proposals are risky designs, too. That's why we've simply got to spend the money to find out how they perform, especially in carrier ops, whether Congress likes it or not.

"The Boeing design is supposed to have the best weapons-carrying capability," Frazier continued, "but it appears to be a little short on speed. Lockheed expects to deliver around Mach 1.6 compared to Boeing's projected 1.4. There are lots of tradeoffs. They both have internal bomb bays to add to their stealth capability, which is roughly the equivalent of painting a sea gull on radar. One of the problems is that Boeing, as you know, hasn't built a fighter since the 1930s. Sure, they turned out sturdy and reliable fighters for the fleet back then but, hell, it was peacetime stuff with flashy chrome yellow wings and vertical stabilizers painted in primary colors to identify the carriers they flew from.

"Boeing has come up with a single-piece wing," Frazier said as he passed a schematic across the table to Mallory, "which they say offers greater fuel capacity, but the concern here is the difficulty of repairing battle damage. Frankly, I like the existing F-18's concept, where there aren't any lefts or rights in the parts bin, just a unisex thing that makes for quick and easy repair on either side. Lockheed has built fighters since World War II, damn good ones too, but not for the Navy. Well, it's a whole new ball game in this day and age, and we've got to select the best plane and make sure of the cost."

Mallory nodded.

"Captain, you're going to help me determine which of these entries is up to snuff, can really do the job, with proper maneuverability, combat range, efficient battle damage repair, and ground support capability—the whole enchilada, under fleet conditions, with real deck crews and live ordnance, not just computer simulation bullshit."

Taking the oath in the base commander's office was as Frazier had described it. Mallory couldn't help thinking that re-upping on the spur of the moment in resort togs in Panama was the military equivalent of getting hitched by a justice-of-the-peace in Nevada.

What the hell! he thought, as he surrendered to feeling damn good about being back in the saddle with four stripes!

SAN MARCOS

As he dropped Tanaka off at the embassy's main entrance, one of the marine guards saluted and stepped forward. "Commander Mallory, sir, Ambassador Cathcart thought this might be urgent." He handed Mallory a sealed manila envelope. It was stamped DIPLOMATIC POUCH in block red letters. Mallory's heart leapt. *Something to do with David's release,* he thought. Inside he found a hand-written note asking him to meet "a good friend of the President of the United States" aboard the yacht *Power Play,* arriving at the marina in Bahia Pajaros in the morning. The note was signed "W. R. Cabot."

Who the hell is Cabot that he's got access to the diplomatic pouch? Talk about "friends in high places!" In a nanosecond he realized that the "immaculate reenlistment" was a set-up for some purpose he didn't understand.

What the hell am I being drawn into?

THIRTY-ONE

THE PERALTA FAMILY COMPOUND

Mallory jogged up the driveway toward the main house. Ancient bougainvillea clumps cascaded over the high adobe walls on either side of him and tall palm trees filigreed the morning sunlight as he passed by. Everywhere well-manicured tropical plants produced a vibrant palette of greens, yellows, orange, and red. As he reached the porte-cochere and stopped to rest, the massive, carved wooden door was opened by Santiago, the aged butler.

"Señor Peralta asked for you to join him and the others in the library as soon as possible. This way, sir."

Santiago led the way across the huge, tiled foyer, opened tall, intricately paneled doors, and stepped aside to allow Mallory to enter. Against a backdrop of hundreds of leather-bound books and classic prints of race horses and polo matches, Peralta was engaged in intense discussion with Elena, General Mora, Diego, and two other men. He looked up from the maps spread out on the huge trestle table.

"Deke, meet the general's son, Major Alejandro Mora. As you can see, he's wearing the honest uniform of the peasants who suffer at the hands of the regime."

The major was of medium height, deeply tanned, and appeared hard as nails. He wore loose-fitting cotton trousers and a peasant's pale blue shirt. "Alejandro," Peralta continued, "was Professor of Military Science at the university until he was arrested last year. He escaped, took to the jungle and become a leader of our people."

"*Mucho gusto,* Captain," the major said. "I've heard so much about you, I feel we are already comrades in arms."

"I'm with you in spirit, Major, but my active duty orders are already cut."

"The major's *nom de guerre* is Carlos," Elena said.

"Yes," Carlos smiled, "I lead our guerrilla forces in what you Americans call the boondocks."

"Believe me, Major, many wars have been won in the boondocks."

"And, Deke," Elena said, "here is one of my former students. The best, I might add. Meet Arturo Hung."

Arturo smiled and nodded. "*Mucho gusto,* Captain." He wore jeans and a polo shirt.

"Arturo was a student activist at the university," she continued, "and was imprisoned for his efforts. He was released under incredible circumstances and has the distinction of being a double agent now." She smiled as Arturo related his release by Father Martin. "If he gains their confidence," she said, "it will give us a window on what's going on inside the cathedral."

Arturo frowned. "After what happened to *Señora* Peralta there, it will be a privilege to screw them."

Mallory turned to her. "Can't you alert the Vatican?"

"That's another subject," Peralta snapped. "We need to stay focused here. We were discussing the commencement of actual hostilities when you came in."

"We were discussing the first phase of our battle plan," General Mora said, "which includes freeing the captives in Prison Number Five."

"Carlos has learned," Peralta said, "that some people we thought were dead are held there, including a senator and the owner of a bank taken over by German interests."

"There are three Americans besides your son," Carlos said. "An archeologist from Cal Berkeley and two medical missionaries who supposedly died when their plane crashed. I plan to free them once actual hostilities commence."

"There is always a sort of vacuum following a coup," Peralta agreed, "when new chains of command are not yet firmly in place and a degree of mistrust exists, even among the perpetrators themselves. We're hoping Colonel Benes won't be able to quickly implement the necessary command decisions in the face of swift, powerful attacks."

Carlos turned to Mallory. "The present plan is for my northern column to take the prison on the fourth day of battle," he said. "They are trained in jungle fighting and can cut the prison off from the nearby government garrisons, once the air force has been neutralized." He paused. "Thanks to your CIA, I have ground-to-air Stingers to shoot down the army's helicopter gunships."

"That's only if the Bearcats don't get them on the ground first," Peralta chortled, raising a clenched fist.

Mallory realized as an active duty officer he shouldn't be privy to the details of their battle plans. "Look, Nacho," he said, "you know that I'm back on active duty now as a captain in the U.S. Navy. I shouldn't hear this, since we're officially neutral. I'll need to pack and catch a plane to Bahia Pajaros before the shooting starts. I'm meeting someone there tomorrow."

He couldn't read Elena's reaction.

"No need for catching a plane," Peralta said. "Diego is flying Elena and me to the finca in the MD. There's room for you, and he can continue to the coast for your meeting." He pulled a paper from his shirt pocket and gave it to Mallory. "We may not see each other for weeks, so here are phone numbers of some of our people. Announce yourself with your nom de guerre."

Mallory's irritation at being given a nom de guerre for a war he couldn't join was obvious, as he stared at Peralta.

231

"Oh, hell, Deke," Peralta laughed. "Lighten up. Just consider it your new call sign, that's all."

Mallory started to speak, but thought better of it.

"You are QUETZAL," Elena said. "Q-U-E-T-Z-A-L."

"Whatever," Mallory said. "I'll go pack."

Elena walked him to the door. As they stepped into the hall, she slipped her arms around him. "I wish we had met under better circumstances," she said. "I wanted to see that green flash at sunset with you."

THE FINCA

The Peralta estate in the country was as Mallory imagined it. From the air it reminded him of Casa Pacifica, Nixon's Western White House in San Clemente, which he overflew many times in his years at NAS Miramar. The extensive grounds included a polo field, surrounded by a training track and stables. The short airstrip seemed adequate for Bearcats, and Mallory noticed it was marked off in increments of about thirty feet to sharpen the short field landing skills of Peralta's pilots. The main hacienda was of typical Spanish Colonial design, with thick stucco walls, mission tile roof, and shady porches on all sides, set among palm trees, bougainvilleas, and manicured gardens. Diego eased the MD-520 onto a paved helipad on the front lawn and shut down. As the rotor blades spooled down and began to sag, a fuel truck painted green jungle camouflage appeared from behind a hangar at the far end of the runway, which Mallory assumed housed the clandestine air force.

"While Diego attends to refueling," Peralta said, as they climbed out of the helicopter, "let me show you something of the plantation, which has been in our family for generations. They'll probably bomb the hell out of this place, so I've had the family valuables put in an underground bunker they'll never find. If we're still around after this is all over, we can rebuild and restore it to what you see today."

Mallory had the feeling of being at *Guernica* or some other tragic place just hours before the bombs fell.

The great hall was mercifully cool. A covered porch supporting a jungle of bright red and purple bougainvillea vines extended out about eight feet around the entire perimeter of the house. Thick, hand-adzed beams emerged from the thick plaster walls and crossed the room at a height of about twelve feet. The tile floor was partially covered with the soft colors of antique Persian rugs. Some of the furnishings appeared to have been custom made of native woods in counterpoint to period European antiques, including a rosewood concert grand.

"Our art collection was always a great pleasure to me," Peralta said, noticing Mallory's interest in the furnishings. "It included Picassos, a Degas and a Monet, and this one above the mantle."

A carpenter was about to crate the work. He moved aside and Mallory found himself staring at a huge oil painting of an exotic trop-ical bird, with iridescent emerald green feathers. "This is by Costa Verde's greatest artist, Octavio Ramiriz," Peralta continued. "His works hang in many museums, including the Metropolitan in New York."

"I can see why. What's this fantastic bird?"

"The *quetzal*," Elena said, joining them, "as in your new call sign. The Mayans revered it as a sacred bird to protect them in battle. According to legend, when the Spanish conquistadors fought the Battle of Quezaltenango in Guatemala, the Mayan chieftain, Tecun Uman, was wounded in the chest. His guardian quetzal covered his chest where he lay, and when it arose its once white breast feathers had turned to the bright red you see here. You probably know the quetzal also as the monetary unit of Guatemala."

Mallory moved for a closer look at the painting.

"The bird is small, like a robin," Peralta said, "but, as you can see, the green tail feathers are two feet long."

Mallory turned to face them. "I hope he'll protect you in the com-ing days."

Peralta nodded thoughtfully. "Let's hope there's truth to the legend."

THIRTY-TWO

BAHIA PAJAROS

Diego set the helicopter down on the helipad adjacent to the parking lot at the new marina and shut down.

"Thanks for the lift," Mallory said, as he picked up his luggage. "I'm not sure where I'll be going from here."

"Good luck, sir," Diego said, extending his hand.

Mallory nodded. "I want you to know, I'm sure you did everything you could that night in San Marcos."

"Thank you," Diego said. "There were just too many soldiers for me to deal with."

Mallory nodded.

"There were no drugs at the disco either," Diego continued. "It was staged for your Drug Enforcement Agency. I think in America you call it grandstanding."

As Mallory headed for the Harbor Master's office, he admired a flight of black frigate birds passing overhead, majestic creatures with long forked tails and scimitar shaped wings sometimes approaching a span of eight feet. The Bay of Birds was well named.

His instructions were to meet Mr. Cabot aboard a yacht in the harbor. Not much to go on. As he approached the Harbor Master's office, he decided to introduce himself to the local authorities in English, just another gringo tourist who doesn't speak Spanish.

He found a door marked *Capitan del Puerto* and entered the office. A clerk came to the counter.

"Good afternoon. My name is Mallory. I'm supposed to meet a Mister Cabot aboard the yacht Power Play."

"Momentito, señor." The man left the counter, opened the door to a private office, and returned with a portly man who sported a black handlebar mustache.

"Good afternoon, *señor*," the man said. "Welcome to Bahia Pajaros. I am Captain Mendoza, Harbor Master of our port and new marina. Señor Cabot's yacht is indeed here," he said, pointing out the window. "The big white one you see there in the middle of the bay."

It was a luxury fishing machine with the requisite outriggers on each side of the superstructure and a large, open fantail for dueling game fish. A small helicopter was secured to a pad projecting over the afterdeck.

Captain Mendoza picked up the radio telephone and raised *Power Play*. After hanging up, he told Mallory a boat would be sent for him right away. After exchanging pleasantries with Mendoza, Mallory could see a sleek runabout heading from the yacht toward the dock area.

"It looks like that's your boat," Mendoza said. "Enjoy your visit with us, *señor*."

Mallory retrieved his bag from in front of the counter, stepped outside, and continued down the stairs to the dock.

Mendoza watched him walk toward the waiting launch, then picked up the phone and dialed a number in Mexico City. "He just left my office, sir," he said. "Yes, of course, I'll check on that right away. You can always count on me, *Señor* Steiger."

———

Crossing the bay toward *Power Play,* Mallory filled his lungs with salt air, momentarily enjoying the familiar sound of the gulls and the slap of the water on the bow of the runabout. As they neared the yacht, he noticed she flew the U.S. ensign on the stern staff, the flag of Costa Verde on the starboard spreader, and a triangular yacht club burgee on the bow staff. At least the owner knew his flag etiquette, which was more than could be said for some of the American boats in the harbor. One of them flew a pair of pink panties and a bra from the spreader.

As they approached the accommodation ladder the bowline was thrown to a waiting crewman who secured it while the runabout was brought parallel to the grated step and held there with rudder and reverse power. Mallory stepped to the boarding platform.

"I'll take your bag, sir," a crewman said, as Mallory started up the ladder. As he reached the main deck, he was greeted by a tall man in a light tropical suit and bow tie, who appeared to be in his fifties.

"Welcome aboard, Captain. I'm Terry Truman," he said, extending his hand. "Let's go to the main salon."

They entered a spacious cabin opening to the afterdeck. Dozens of well-maintained deep-sea-fishing rods were neatly stowed in overhead racks. Mallory scanned the framed photographs of prize fish and smiling fishermen, including one of Richard Nixon linking arms with two others, with a huge marlin dangling from a winch in the background.

"Mister Cabot on the right," Truman commented, "and the former President of Costa Verde, Edwardo Peralta. The three of them were good friends."

Truman motioned for Mallory to take a seat on the sofa. "Mister Cabot is recovering from hip surgery at his home near Palm Springs," he said, as he sat down on an adjacent chair, "but he was kind enough to let us have the use of this yacht, which is currently based in Mexico, at Cabo San Lucas." Truman removed his coat and tie and turned back his shirt cuffs. "The helicopter you saw topside picked me up yesterday while *Power Play* was off the Mexican coast en route here."

"What's this about my meeting a close friend of the President?" Mallory asked.

237

"I guess I do qualify as his friend," Truman said, "that is, if anyone can claim to know President Foxlee very well. At least, I'm the only one at Langley he's remained on speaking terms with since he took office."

Mallory tried to remain calm as he boiled at the realization he was caught up in the grasp of the CIA.

"Here, have some coffee," Truman said, reaching for a carafe and cups.

"Since I'm here having been suckered into reenlisting," he said, "I assume this is all going to make sense to me."

Truman shrugged. "I don't blame you, Captain, for being sore about a number of recent developments, so let's get right down to the business at hand. I'll fill in the details later over drinks and dinner, and you'll spend the night aboard. Your luggage is already in your stateroom."

"Well, I'm afraid I have a problem with that," Mallory said. "How the hell do I know you're the genuine article? For all I know, the real Cabot and Truman are bound and gagged below deck!"

"Fair enough!" Truman said, nodding his head.

He reached into his pocket, produced a small phone, and activated a number. Mallory could hear it ringing.

"Mister President," he said. "T-Square here. I've got Mallory with me now on Mister Cabot's boat. Yes, we're in Costa Verde . . . right, sir . . . yes, here he is, sir."

He handed the phone to Mallory. "Here, he wants to talk to you."

Mallory was momentarily paralyzed by the unfolding situation. He slowly took the phone. "Captain Mallory."

"This is the President, Captain. I want you to know I share your concern over your son, and we're going to do everything we can to get him the hell out of there. After Mister Truman explains our situation, I'm sure you'll understand the unique position you're in to help us sort out this mess. Your relationship with the Peraltas, and your knowledge of the country, can help us clear things up in Costa Verde. America needs your help."

Mallory managed to say something in acknowledgment.

"Captain, I can't go public with this yet," Foxlee confided, "but I want that damn colonel down there thrown out on his ass. I'd like to see your friend Ignacio Peralta elected fairly, soon as it can happen. And I want to know why all these faceless Germans are buying up the place."

Mallory's mind was racing as fast as the signals relaying the conversation.

"Mister President, I'm a Naval Aviator. I have no training for intelligence operations. . . .

"How do I know it's really you on the line, sir?"

"Damn good question, Captain. There's someone here who can answer that for you."

Mallory could hear the President chuckling as he spoke to someone. "You got a good man down there," he heard him say. "No bullshit for the captain. Damn, I like that." The President laughed. "Why, hell, I just got carded! He wants to know who the hell I really am."

The unmistakable, gravelly voice of Admiral Frazier came on the line, with the President chuckling in the background. "Captain, I know what the President has in mind seems a little bit out of your line but, as he says, you're uniquely positioned to ferret out what he and Truman need to know. I'm confident you can handle it. And don't worry, I'll keep your seat on the JSF Team warm for you."

"Aye, sir. I understand."

"Consider anything you hear from Mister Truman to be a direct order from the President," Frazier said. "Now the President wants to talk to Mister Truman again."

"Understood, sir."

Truman listened for a moment, then folded the phone, stretched, and clasped his hands behind his head. "Life's full of little surprises, isn't it?" he said. "Now, let's get to the damn point, which is serious as hell. I have a problem with my top field agent, Bill Burton. I've known him for a long time, and I'd like to think he hasn't been turned, but if he has, I have to know by whom and why."

Mallory felt silence on his part was the wise posture.

239

"Here's the picture." Truman refilled Mallory's coffee and explained the scenario of Burton's suspected disloyalty, and the conflicting and inconclusive reports of Holloway's death. "Since both Burton and Franck were aboard the flight with Holloway at the time, I may be dealing with a murderer at the very least and high treason at worst." He paused and shrugged his shoulders. "A third possibility is Holloway parachuted from the helicopter. Maybe there's a fourth or fifth possibility. Any of them leaves me with a huge, nagging WHY?"

Mallory shifted on the sofa. "I still don't see how I come into the picture. Even though I know the Peraltas, something of the country, and speak the language, I'm just a Naval Aviator. You're the spook, Mister Truman."

"Please call me Terry or T-Square." He leered at Mallory. "Captain, I seem to recall you have just been assigned Temporary Additional Duty, as a spook, by your Commander-in-Chief."

"TAD, I understand, but the question is, why me?"

Truman stabbed the air with his index finger.

"Because, *one,* you're here. *Two,* you speak fluent Spanish. *Three,* Admiral Frazier thinks highly of you and feels you can handle it. And *four,* you can keep your mouth shut, which is critical in this business."

"How do you know I can keep my mouth shut?" Mallory snickered. "Maybe I'm a congenital gossip."

"You used to drink with Dick Nixon after hours at the White House, you and Peralta, and you kept the confidences."

"How did you find out about that?" Mallory gasped. "We never told anyone."

An enigmatic smiled formed on Truman's face.

"I'll share that with you over a scotch before dinner."

"*Five,* and most important, I have to have someone with no relationship whatsoever to the Company, somebody antiseptic as hell. Look, we don't know who's in bed with whom down here. If I try to investigate this mess using my own assets, I'll never know if I'm getting the runaround."

"Okay," Mallory said with a sigh, "I get the picture, so far. I don't like it, but I think I get it."

"There's another element in this picture," Truman said, sliding the coffee carafe across the table to Mallory, "and it's not a pleasant one. There's an extensive network of Germans operating here in Costa Verde. They might be agents of an organization called the Kohorte. We don't know much about the Kohorte, just that they're a bunch of Nazis, led by an elusive multibillionaire named Werner Tolt." Truman shook his head. "The Israelis think he's the same guy as a young SS-officer who was indicted *in absentia* at Nuremberg for war crimes. The Kohorte may have infiltrated the Costa Verde banks and several large businesses, including Aero Verde. For all I know, Colonel Benes is in their pocket. I just can't wait any longer to find out the answers to these questions," he said. "If Burton's sold out to the Kohorte directly, or indirectly through the Generalissimo and Benes, it's critical to uncover it now." Truman rubbed his hands together. "I need a total outsider to penetrate the situation and make sense of it."

Mallory set his cup aside and studied Truman. "Okay, I do know something about the German connection," he said, and related what he learned from Nacho and Elena. Truman was silent as he digested the circumstances of Arturo's release from the central jail and Elena's bizarre experience at the christening. He was used to distilling the wild yarns of excited field agents to extract the truth.

"You mean to tell me," he said, suddenly sitting upright, "this priest or archbishop or whatever the hell he is actually tried to murder her?"

Mallory nodded. "Elena's sure. She was there."

Mallory watched as Truman closed his eyes in thought.

"Okay," he finally said, "but how do the Peraltas fit into the picture? I gather they want to overthrow the regime, which seems to be a moving target these days."

"They're hot to trot," Mallory said, and briefed him on what he knew of their plans. "D-day can't be more than a couple of days off, and

Carlos plans to seize Prison Number Five the third or forth day of hostilities, I think."

"Oh, shit!" Truman growled, shaking his head. "That's an extremely dicey kind of operation. I hope this Carlos character knows what the hell he's doing." His face darkened and he got up and paced the cabin, before turning to face Mallory. "Okay," he said, "you have your orders, as I have mine, but this time there's a little extra incentive I can offer. It may be the only time in your career you're going to get a *quid pro quo* for following orders."

Mallory wondered what was coming. "How so?"

"I'm going to ask the President to commit Special Operations Forces to assist Carlos in rescuing your son and the others. We have specially trained units that can neutralize a stockade before the guards can even think about killing the prisoners or using them as human shields."

Mallory's heart sank as he realized more fully the risks but steadied as he heard Truman speak with Foxlee again and get the approval. Truman dialed another number and told someone about Carlos' plan. Mallory assumed he was in touch with the Special Operations Command somewhere.

"Don't worry," Truman said, switching off the phone, "the SOF people will contact Carlos right away."

Returning from the head, Truman outlined a plan for Mallory to find out everything he could about Holloway's disappearance. He produced a passport with Mallory's picture, documents certifying Mallory as an insurance investigator, and a full dossier on Holloway with photos.

"Okay," Mallory said. "How do I proceed?"

"We start with this sat-phone. "This is more than state-of-the-art. It's a special Qualcomm digital GSM, good for secure communication to any other phone on earth. The numbers you'll need to reach me and others are in its memory, even the President's direct line." He ran a brief demonstration.

Truman produced a silenced handgun with extra boxes of ammunition, and handed it to Mallory, who was more apprehensive than ever about the unfolding scenario as he fondled the Browning 9mm automatic.

"I assume you know how to use it, Captain?"

"I always carried a sidearm as part of my survival gear," Mallory said, "but not with a silencer."

"Of course," Truman said. "Let me show you how to attach it, and make sure it's secure." He did a quick demonstration and watched as Mallory repeated the steps.

"Okay," Mallory said. "Now that I'm armed and dangerous, what the hell am I supposed to do with this thing? Terminate suspected double agents with extreme prejudice?"

Truman smiled. "It's a good precaution," he said.

"You were certainly prepared for this meeting."

"We try to think of everything," Truman said.

"Look, all this really is out of my line. I've always been a by-the-book Naval officer."

Truman burst out laughing. "Bullshit," he said. "I know all about you. Just what the hell did you think you were doing when you unloaded your ordnance on that off-limits ammo dump in downtown Baghdad, when you were supposed to be patrolling a hundred miles to the south?"

Mallory tried to appear thoughtful.

"Or back in 1986 above the Eastern Med, when you suddenly turned ninety degrees and made a high speed dash at Syrian radar?"

Mallory studied the fishing poles suspended from the overhead. "I was trolling for MiGs," he said. "I got one, as it turned out."

Truman got up and stretched. "Well, now that you're fully briefed on your spook duties," he said, "as Mister Cabot's lawful representative, I hereby declare the sun is over the yardarm. Let's open his bar!"

"Thought you'd never ask."

243

"What'll it be?" Truman asked, walking inside to the salon, and opening a bulkhead cabinet that revealed an extensive bar. "Let's see, Glenlivet single malt scotch, with a single drop of water. Correct?"

"My God," Mallory said, "is there anything you people don't know about me?"

Truman poured Glenlivets and handed one to Mallory.

"Not much," he said.

—

THIRTY-THREE

THE VATICAN

Monsignor Albert hurried half a step ahead of the portly Kaalten as they strode along a wide upper-floor corridor in the romanesque building housing the offices of the Vatican Secretary of State. Kaalten's head swiveled this way and that as he listened to Albert while taking in the scene. Doors to offices, meeting rooms, and specialized libraries lined the wall to their left, while to their right a colonnade of pillars supported arches open to the weather. Through them could be seen the tile roofs of other wings of the sprawling building and patios and rose gardens below. Little groups of clergy and visitors flowed both ways, reminding Kaalten of university students late for classes.

"Pardon, Father," Kaalten called over his shoulder, as he brushed a priest while trying to keep up with the longer-legged Albert. For some reason the incident rattled him and, for the first time since arriving in Rome, he felt like the imposter he was.

The monsignor briefed him as they hustled along. "You're penciled in with Cardinal Guilianni at 3:15," he said, glancing at his watch, "for ten minutes. He's meeting with the ambassador of Brazil at 3:30, and he'll want time to review the file and pray before greeting the Brazilian.

"Just keep the conversation simple," Albert counseled, gesturing with his hands. "And, remember, answer Yes or No, whenever possible. Let Guilianni do the talking."

They stopped at what Kaalten thought was the lobby of a small hotel, complete with front desk and comfortable chairs and coffee tables. Potted palms completed the impression.

"Here are the State Secretary's diplomatic reception rooms," Albert said, taking Kaalten's arm and pulling him aside to where they could talk safely. "Because of his meeting with the ambassador, he'll be meeting you in one of these rooms, rather than his office or apartment."

Albert bent closer and lowered his voice. "Try to keep the conversation centered on the work of the Church, especially the needs of the poor in Costa Verde," he instructed. "Don't let him probe into your life as a priest behind the Iron Curtain."

"My God!" Kaalten said, paling visibly. "What do I tell him about those years?"

Albert grimaced and threw up his hands. "I would think, Herr Brigadefuhrer," he whispered, "that you would have thought up a good story years ago, one to keep at-the-ready, precisely for times like this.

"Look," Albert continued, "just keep it simple." He closed his eyes in thought, then fixed Kaalten with his gaze and continued. "Tell the cardinal that one day when you had gone out to shop for groceries a parishioner warned you that Stasi men were waiting at the church to apprehend you when you returned. Being anticommunist," Albert continued, drawing a breath, "you had the foresight to keep your papers and money on your person at all times. Your parishioner took you as far as the Baltic in his truck, where a fisherman relative of his smuggled you to Sweden. Tell him that."

"Yes, yes," Kaalten agreed excitedly, having recovered his poise. "That's just about what I was planning to say."

The damn fool, Albert thought, staring at him and deciding there was no point challenging him since the objective was to get the meeting over with and Kaalten the hell out of town as fast as possible.

The ornate diplomatic reception room featured a pair of gilt Louis XVI chairs, upholstered in tufted silk, facing each other across a low table, under a huge crystal chandelier. Otherwise the room was bare of furnishings. Guilianni and Albert occupied the chairs. A floral arrangement occupied the table, and Albert occupied behind the cardinal, prepared to orchestrate Kaalten's performance with hand signals if necessary.

"And so," Kaalten bubbled, "Hurricane Mabel last year was devastating to our poorest people—*los pobres de la tierra,* we call them in Latin America. Most of the money the Church had accumulated over many years was distributed for food, medicines, and clothing in the rural areas. Only recently has our treasury been replenished."

"Pray, tell," Guilianni asked, "about your part in the work, Father. Monsignor Albert tells me you are personally responsible for the growing finances of your archdiocese."

What if Guilianni knew the truth? Albert thought. *What if he knew the Kohorte simply commingled some of its funds with the Church's, since Tolt thinks he owns them both?*

"Oh, by no means, Eminence," Kaalten said, placing his hands together reverently and smiling sweetly. "God alone sustains us, you see. I was merely privileged to receive his blessings on behalf of the Church."

Good answer, Albert thought, as he nodded at Kaalten.

"You do well," Guilianni said, rising from his chair to terminate the interview, "to cultivate such modesty, Father, for we know that God is opposed to those who vaunt themselves. However," the cardinal continued, "there is a kind of pride that is sometimes appropriate, and you may be appropriately proud of your contributions. In fact," he said, taking Kaalten's hands between his, "I intend to mention your daring escape from the East German secret police, and your good works in Costa Verde, to the Holy Father himself, when I dine with him this evening."

Kaalten beamed, as Guilianni continued.

"Good reports about the work of the Church," the little cardinal said, beaming himself, "strengthen His Holiness to persevere in his heavy burdens."

Albert wasn't beaming. His spirits sank as he contemplated the fact even the Pontiff himself was about to be touched by the dark side of his double life here at the Holy See. As Guilianni turned to go, Albert found himself unaccountably short of breath. He wondered how much of a role stress was playing in shortening his life on earth.

Afterward, as the cardinal's driver picked his way through the aggressive Roman traffic, Albert and Kaalten conversed in the back seat of the black Mercedes S Class on their way to drop Kaalten at Leonardo da Vinci airport. Other drivers gave way to the yellow and white Vatican pennants flapping above the big car's front fenders. Kaalten was impressed and suddenly waxed manic.

"This reminds me of films of the war years in occupied Europe," he chortled, bouncing on the seat, "when SS officers displayed little swastika flags on their staff cars. Well, I tell you, Herr Albert, it will be like this in Costa Verde one day soon, you can be sure of it."

Albert nodded in silence as Kaalten, obviously buoyed by his successful encounter with the cardinal, regaled him with tidbits of his successes with Aero Verde and other ventures in Costa Verde.

Albert hardly listened as he watched the buildings and sidewalk scenes pass by. He was relieved to be seeing Kaalten off and to be able to close the book on years of duplicity. He had accomplished everything demanded of him by the Kohorte and thought that at long last he could refocus on his life's work as Guilianni's confidant. Still, he realized, as Kaalten's words flowed in one ear and out the other, he was the only living person who might have a motive to reveal the murders of the priests and expose Tolt's and the others' fraudulently obtained citizenship. He clenched his jaw and renewed his decision to take it all to his grave with him. The truth was too horrible to reveal to a good man like the cardinal, much less would he do anything to stain the Pope's reign with dark scandal. He silently asked Merciful God to forgive him, a miserable sinner, and cleanse him of his sins—and to protect him from a Kohorte that might not be willing to trust him to keep the great secret.

The car pulled to the curb outside the terminal building where Albert was relieved to shake Kaalten's hand while the driver fetched his luggage. Kaalten took the bags from the driver but set them down on the sidewalk for a moment. "By the way," he said, touching his clerical collar with a pudgy finger and squaring off in front of Albert, "Father Martin wanted me to be sure to tell you that he always remembers you in his daily prayers." Kaalten seemed to leer at Albert. "Yes, every single day."

Mention of Staib's relentless control over his life shattered Albert's frail composure and he returned to the Vatican in torment. *Dear God,* he prayed, as the car rolled along in traffic, *you always look upon men's hearts and know everything. You know me to be a despicable sinner. I'm too cowardly to die, too cowardly to repent of my secret life and face my cardinal with the truth.*

For no apparent reason the hiding place where he kept the cocaine leapt to his mind, together with a strong physical reaction like a sugar low. *Oh God!* he blubbered into his handkerchief. *Oh, God!*

The car passed through the Vatican gates and up the driveway, pulling slowly around toward the porte-cochere where the door would be opened and he would be saluted by the Swiss Guards, which he knew would only heighten his sense of guilt. In that moment a pain gripped his arm, traveled toward his shoulder and migrated to his chest. He toppled onto the floor, choking on air, as the car drew to a stop. An officer of the guard opened the door and found him crumpled there with his damp face drained of blood.

"Oh my God!" the man shouted. "Get a doctor, quick!"

THIRTY-FOUR

M.V. *POWER PLAY* ANCHORED AT BAHIA PAJAROS

Mallory's hopes of a good night's sleep aboard Cabot's yacht were dashed by vivid dreams of David being held below decks in the engine room, with the yacht itself somehow being a jumbled extension of Prison Number Five.

After a hearty breakfast served by a silent steward, Truman accompanied Mallory to the accommodation ladder with a final word of advice. "You won't have a wingman covering your six this time," he said, "so stay on your toes."

Mallory shrugged, patted the silenced Browning in his jacket pocket, shook Truman's hand and started down the accommodation ladder to the runabout. A few minutes later, at the car rental office he told the clerk a car was reserved for him by the people aboard *Power Play*. He signed the paperwork, and was shown to the parking area. Most of the rental cars were white, tan or gray. The agent smiled broadly as he handed him the keys to a fire engine red Toyota sedan. Mallory asked for one of the others.

The clerk frowned. "It's not possible, *señor,*" he said. "These are all reserved for customers. But this is a free upgrade to a larger size car, *señor.* I am sure you will like it."

Mallory doubted the explanation but accepted the keys, threw his bag in the back, and climbed into the driver's seat. As he drove past the Harbor Master's office he glanced up to see Captain Mendoza looking down from his office, smiling and nodding.

The map indicated a fairly direct route on Highway 7 from Bahia Pajaros to San Marcos and he had little trouble finding his way to the main highway. What it didn't indicate was the road's tortuous path through the rugged countryside. After nearly three hours of white-knuckle driving, swerving to miss livestock, dogs, and farmers' trucks, he decided to find a place on the outskirts of San Marcos to stop for the rest of the day.

He turned off the road at La Fonda Obregon, which appeared to be a relatively decent-looking roadside inn, and registered for a welcome break and a chance to assemble some of the pieces of the puzzle that had been handed to him.

Over a beer and a sandwich in the adjacent cantina, he pored over the material Truman gave him. It included papers identifying him as Philip Malcolm, an insurance investigator with Atlantic Fidelity, based in their Miami office. He wondered if such a company even existed. His new passport featured a horrible picture laminated on the inside front cover, and the entry and exit stamps of a fictitious itinerary in Central America, which he carefully memorized. The dossier on Wade Holloway included photographs and information about Electricos Verdes' employees, including his secretary, Ann Graham, who was later fired by Franck.

MIRAFLORES, COSTA VERDE

Mallory drove into the upscale suburb of San Marcos late the following morning. The commercial center of the small community featured a branch of Banco de Libertad, a supermarket, a pharmacy, a church with adjoining school, a small hospital and medical center, a Mercado Video store, and a couple of automotive repair shops. Circling what appeared to be the central district, he noticed a Texaco station and StarMart, and some shops featuring native crafts. He found what he was looking for at the edge of the residential section, next to the public library. Holloway's secretary had opened a dress shop in Miraflores, and Mallory entered as the lone customer was paying for her purchase.

As he waited, he checked the brightly embroidered skirts and blouses, the native jewelry, and a display of antique baskets in the front window. Through the window, he noticed a Chevy wagon draw up to the curb, as a man and woman in the front seat opened up their road map. *Well,* he thought, *there aren't any urchins to bother them here.*

The customer left and Ann Graham, easily identified from the photo in his file, approached him. She wore a loose-fitting, brightly colored dress embroidered with birds and flowers that masked her plump figure pretty well. Silver jewelry adorned her hands, neck, and ears. She appeared to be in her fifties, but it was hard to tell.

He introduced himself as an old friend of Wade Holloway. He would like to speak to her regarding family or business assets and obligations Holloway may have had in Costa Verde. As executor of the estate, he would appreciate any information she could provide.

"Why don't we go across the street to the cantina and have a drink and a bite to eat?" she proposed. "It's about time to close for siesta, anyway."

She placed a *Cerrado Hasta Dos* sign in the window, and led the way to the cantina. They were shown to a booth, where she ordered a rum and Coke. Mallory ordered a beer.

He let her do the talking, making mental notes as she rambled. Yes, she knew something about Holloway's private life, but not much. Yes, he was a pretty private person. Yes, it was sad about his death, and she wasn't sure she should be talking about it. Yes, it was ridiculous to have leapt from a helicopter. Yes, he'd dabbled in some investments in Costa Verde, but they were losers. No, she didn't think he had any major debts. No, he didn't have any other life insurance policies she knew of. And, yes, she'd have another rum and Coke.

Truman's report correctly assessed her bondage to the sauce, and Mallory ordered another rum and Coke.

"You probably know," she said with a giggle, after several healthy quaffs of her second drink, "that the sly old stud kept a mistress across the border."

Bingo! He shrugged, as if the news was regrettable, but stale. *Keep talking, lady, I'm all ears.*

She drained her glass and smiled. "He tried to hit on me a couple of times," she said, "but I wasn't interested. He seemed to prefer these hot-blooded Central American girls with big boobs." She gave vent to rampant laughter. "A wife in California and a cutie pie in Managua. At least I think it was Managua! He used to burn rubber on the Pan Am Highway every time he could manage a break from work. It's only a three or four hour drive from here, and. . . ."

Mallory nodded expectantly, gesturing for her to continue. No, she didn't know the honey's name or her phone number, but she must be good in bed. No, she had no idea where Holloway stayed in Managua, which was about once every week or so. And, yes, she would like another drink.

He excused himself to go the men's room. When he returned, she was halfway through her drink. He left money for the bill on the table and thanked her for her help.

"Sure, Hon," she managed, raising her glass.

ROUTE ONE NORTH TO NICARAGUA

A good return on a modest investment in rum and Cokes, Mallory thought as he drove north toward the Nicaraguan border, analyzing the bits of information he received from Ann Graham. If Holloway was alive, he was likely holed up with his mistress in Managua. If he traveled there as often as his secretary said, he might have left some kind of a trail that could be picked up at this late date. Even if Holloway were dead, the trail could still lead to the girlfriend, who could possibly shed some light on the situation. The traffic began to slow as he approached the border checkpoint. A rusty bus in front of him, with its loud muffler spewing black exhaust, eased off into the lane for taxis and buses where it was immediately surrounded by a gaggle of vendors hawking their wares to the passengers who were stuck waiting their turn at *Immigracion*. Elsewhere, the scene resembled a permanent swap meet, with stalls massed on both sides of the road, displaying everything from cold beer to souvenirs and clothing. As he eased forward, he saw that the lane for passenger cars was being directed by soldiers. One directed him to a parking lot off to his right where tourists were being stalked by a horde of eager teenage boys willing, for a fee, to act as *agentes* to guide them through the immigration and customs procedures. He smiled and waved them away as he locked the car, making sure the Browning was well concealed under the seat.

He produced the Malcolm passport at the counter. The officer held it in one hand as he turned to a three-inch-thick book of computer printouts. He opened it and began scanning the columns, comparing names and numbers.

"You keep everything in that book?" Mallory asked.

The man grunted and explained that the names of persons who were *persona non grata* for any reason were in the book.

"You have that many?" Mallory asked.

"Sí, señor. If a person's name is found here, he will be detained until the matter is cleared up." He shrugged and continued checking the list. Although the book was upside down to Mallory, he quickly scanned the list of Ms to see if "Mallory" was entered. It wasn't.

Closing the book, the officer looked at him vacantly and then slowly and officiously stamped the passport for exit. "You are not in the book, *Señor* Malcolm."

So that's how the system works! There would be no record of Holloway's transit if he's not in the book, which he wouldn't be if he passed through as often as he did.

Mallory had clipped a fifty-dollar bill to the back of one of the photographs of Holloway. He withdrew it from his briefcase and showed the border agent his insurance investigator's identification.

"I'm working on an important case," he said, "and my company is offering a reward. I can reward any information that would help us find him and I'd appreciate it if you could check it for me. We don't know what name he uses, but I understand he has traveled through here quite often."

Mallory slid the photo and money across the counter.

The man studied the photo while carefully unclipping and pocketing the bill. "I'll be right back," he said.

Mallory could see him showing the photo to others, whose heads bobbed excitedly like barnyard chickens attacking kernels of corn. The man returned smiling.

"We have all seen him from time to time, *señor*, but nobody remembers his name."

"When was the last time you remember seeing him?" Mallory asked, trying to remain cool.

The agent yawned. "Maybe a month ago."

"Are your sure?"

"Sí, señor. Absolutamente."

Bingo again! Holloway's alive!

"I appreciate your help," Mallory said, and retrieved the photo.

He continued on to customs, was waved through without luggage inspection, paid a seven-dollar exit fee, and continued north on the Pan American Highway to Nicaragua.

The two countries' border checkpoints were several miles apart, with the actual border in the middle of a no-man's-land which, according to Truman, was loaded with land mines left over from the Sandinista days.

He entered the checkpoint on the Nicaraguan side, with the same result. Holloway was recognized but no one knew his name. The customs agents had no difficulty accepting dollars instead of Nicaraguan cordobas, *mordida* being the same the world over, whatever the coin of the realm.

North of the checkpoint, roadside stalls selling everything imaginable stretched for several hundred yards into Nicaragua. The last vendor, an enterprising fellow selling edible animals, displayed an iguana in one hand and an armadillo in the other, held high for inspection by passing motorists. Mallory noticed their mouths were sewn shut, a precaution against being dined on by one's meal.

Since Holloway wasn't in the *persona non grata* book either side of the border that route was a dead end now.

But what if his raging hormones required a faster route? It was less than an hour by air from San Marcos to Managua. Next stop, Managua International Airport.

The highway skirted the western shore of Lake Nicaragua, the largest fresh water lake between the Great Lakes and Lake Titicaca in the Peruvian Andes. Fresh water, yes; clear water, no. The brackish expanse was a muddy brown from volcanic deposits over the centuries.

He continued north to the capital, skirting the southern shore of the smaller Lake Managua, and drove to Los Mercedes airport. He found the immigration office and asked to see the officer in charge. A young man appeared at the counter. "I am Lieutenant Carrera," he said.

Displaying the Malcolm passport, his investigator's ID, and the photo of Holloway, Mallory explained his company's offer of a reward for information leading to the whereabouts of the man in the photograph. He explained he had driven from San Marcos himself but this man probably flew here from Costa Verde several times a year.

Carrera frowned. "Is he wanted in either Costa Verde or the United States on charges of any kind?" he asked.

No, that was not the case, Mallory told him. Instead, this was merely a matter of an insurance claim. The officer examined Mallory's passport and ID again and seemed pleased to notice the two fifty-dollar bills Mallory placed atop his attaché case. Carrera took the photo, consulted with several clerks, and disappeared into a back room. He returned to the counter and pocketed Mallory's money.

"This man has entered and exited our country on AeroVerde flights on several occasions. We think he is a Mister John Anderson and he lives here in Managua."

Makes sense, Mallory thought. If Truman can transform Mallory into Joe Blow Malcolm, insurance investigator, then Holloway can just as easily become Anderson.

"We have a record of all Americans who have resided in Nicaragua for any length of time," the officer continued. "We show this address in Managua for Señor Anderson." He passed a slip of paper across the counter to Mallory.

"Thank you, sir," Mallory said enthusiastically, as he retrieved the photo. "I appreciate your splendid cooperation, Lieutenant, uh . . . Car . . . re . . . ra?"

"You pronounce it correctly," the lieutenant said, smiling broadly.

"I will definitely acknowledge your assistance," Mallory told him, "when reporting to the Company." He wondered how Carrera would feel about it if he knew that Company was spelled with a capital letter.

THIRTY-FIVE

THE ARCHBISHOP'S PALACE

Staib burst through the door of Tolt's study in the Archbishop's residence on the grounds of the Cathedral, balling his fists and seething, as Karpf, just arrived from Mexico City, dropped into a chair across Tolt's massive desk. The ex-spymaster cut a dapper figure in his white Panama suit and two-toned wing-tips.

"Reichsfuhrer, why wasn't I informed the gruppenfuhrer was expected today?" Staib demanded.

Tolt glared at him. "Sit down!" he snarled, indicating a chair by the door. Staib knew that Tolt habitually played him and Karpf off against each other, and he was again humiliated that Tolt had left him out of something confidential. Sighing audibly, bowing to reality, he dropped onto the chair, a victim of Tolt's insatiable thirst for information, which he couldn't expect to satisfy himself. He was flying solo here in Costa Verde whereas Karpf ran networks of agents worldwide.

As he waited for Karpf to proceed, Tolt smiled at Staib paternally, removing something of the sting he was feeling. As if on cue, the assassin got up and moved to the chair next to Karpf, the better to protect his turf.

Karpf unsnapped his briefcase and produced several large black-and-white photographs.

"First of all, Reichsfuhrer," he asked, without so much as glancing at Staib, "is this the man?"

"Yes!" Tolt sneered. "That is the man I saw in the company of Elena Peralta, praying in the main sanctuary recently. They sat near the aisle, so I saw him quite clearly as I looked in. He is an American, you said?"

"Yes, an American," Karpf confirmed, opening a dossier and adjusting his reading glasses. "My agents in the United States have compiled the necessary information about him. His name is Decatur Mallory. He is a retired Navy commander and a Naval Aviator. But I am getting ahead of the point." Karpf could tell at a glance that Tolt was paying rapt attention to him. He took his time, enjoying upstaging Staib in the latter's domain.

"First," he continued, "I will state the most important fact about this Mallory, Reichsfuhrer. Then I will supply the details. This man is none other than the husband of the woman who photographed you and Staib at the airport in Bahia Pajaros. Do you remember the occasion, Reichsfuhrer? It was the day you arrived in Costa Verde. You ordered that she be eliminated, as you may recall."

Tolt's eyebrows arched. "Of course I remember the incident," he said, scowling at Staib. "I wanted to find out who she was and have the film recovered before she could have it processed, nothing more."

Staib bristled. "I thought, Reichsfuhrer," he said, "your request carried an amount of leeway so I used my discretion. I concluded that with her alive we were running an unacceptable risk of her being able to identify us one day in the future. I merely eliminated that risk."

Tolt stared at him a moment, then rubbed his hands together. "It's of little consequence," he said, and turned his attention back to Karpf. "Why is this Mallory here in Costa Verde?"

"It appears," Karpf told him, "that Mallory and Ignacio Peralta have been friends since they were flight cadets together. Mallory's wife had visited Peralta's sister in Bahia Pajaros on the occasion in question.

There have been various contacts between Mallory and Peralta since," Karpf continued, turning pages. "They formed an air racing partnership, for instance. Mallory and his son, who recently graduated from college, came here as weekend guests of the Peraltas."

"Then why is he still here?" Tolt interrupted.

Karpf shrugged. "It seems the younger Mallory was in the wrong place at the wrong time," he said. "On the eve of Mauser's coup, he was seized by the police for drugs. He remains incarcerated at Prison Number Five. That is why the commander remains here, trying to gain his son's release."

Tolt exploded. "Then have the little bastard released," he shouted at Staib, "and they will catch the next flight back to the States."

"Begging the Reichsfuhrer's pardon," Karpf ventured. "It is not so simple as that," he said. "The drug raid was staged by Mauser for a definite purpose, though it was botched. The target that night wasn't Mallory's son. It was Elena Peralta's daughter, Bianca, who has since been spirited out of the country, to Spain I believe. Operation Mauser needed a bargaining chip, should Peralta become a problem in terms of the coup. More recently, the need for bargaining chips has become even more important, since we now know that Elena Peralta is the mastermind behind the looming Peralta threat."

"Then we'll let the son rot in prison!" Tolt decided, "and find another way to rid ourselves of Commander Mallory. After all," he leered at them, "a bargaining chip is still a bargaining chip, isn't it? Even if this particular one is of dubious value."

"Do not forget," Tolt told Karpf, "to keep track of this Bianca Peralta so she can be kidnapped when it serves my purposes."

Karpf uncapped a fountain pen, scribbled a note in green ink, and placed it in a pocket of his briefcase.

"Why are we wasting energy on Mallory?" Staib interrupted. "Release his son and he will go home. Elena Peralta's daughter is the only bargaining chip that counts." Tolt glared at him. "Perhaps," he lectured, "but not everything is always as simple as you, Sturmbannfuhrer

Staib, have gotten into the habit of supposing. For example, Mallory could be involved in the Peralta conspiracy to take over the government. He and Peralta are air racing partners, as the Gruppenfuhrer said. If they are partners for one purpose, they may be partners in other ways too.

"Furthermore," Tolt seemed to raise his voice an octave, "if your agents, Staib, botched that woman's death," he snapped, "and left a trail for Mallory to follow, you can be sure he is here in Costa Verde with revenge on his mind."

"That's impossible, Reichsfuhrer," Staib pleaded. "There's no way that such a—"

"Silence!" Tolt hissed. "Nothing is impossible. That is why I shall go very slowly in deciding just what to do about Mallory, until I am certain of his motives." He scratched his cheek in thought. "As for his son, it turns out to be a good thing he is being detained where his fate can be determined at a time of my choosing, in a way that is useful to me." He motioned for Karpf to continue with his report on Mallory.

"Commander Mallory may have CIA connections," Karpf said. "He met an as-yet unidentified man aboard a yacht, the *Power Play*, in Bahia Pajaros, just the day before yesterday. This yacht, which put in at Bahia Pajaros for less than twenty-four hours, is known to have been chartered by the CIA on previous occasions."

Staib's eyes flashed with anger. He could not abide being kept in the dark about anything, especially by Karpf, whose position as Chief of Intelligence he coveted.

Karpf smiled patronizingly at him, enjoying his advantage. "The *Power Play* is based at Cabo San Lucas," he continued, "at the tip of Baja California, in Mexico. Employees of a boat yard there were useful in providing information, as was the harbor master at Bahia Pajaros."

Rising to pace the floor, Tolt made a decision. "Karpf," he ordered, "you must have your very best surveillance team follow Mallory until we know everything there is to know about what he's involved in down here in Costa Verde. However, there must be no mishaps by which Mallory discovers he's being followed."

Karpf's reptilian lips parted as pure pleasure swept across his face. "But I have already anticipated that! The finest surveillance team in the whole world has been following Mallory for two days."

Staib was aghast. Costa Verde was his turf even if Karpf had the rest of the world to himself. "What!" he blurted angrily. "This is my domain! I absolutely—"

"Don't worry," Tolt assured him. "You shall definitely have your usual decisive part when the time comes to eliminate Mallory. And I am quite sure," he nodded to Karpf, "that the Gruppenfuhrer will gladly instruct his men to report directly to you, Herr Sturmbannfuhrer, while they are operating here locally."

"But of course," Karpf agreed, knowing he controlled the surveillance team no matter what Tolt or Staib thought.

Mollified for the time being, Staib shifted in his chair and pretended to be composed. "Now, about this surveillance," he asked Karpf, "how many are involved?"

"Two only," Karpf said. "They're called Tristan and Isolde for code names. They were trained by the best street man in all of Stasi, and they have worked since for the KGB, the French, and the Israelis, but always as independent contractors. Tristan and Isolde know nothing of the Kohorte, of course. I simply bid for their services as I need them. Fortunately, they were available."

Staib was incredulous. Tristan and Isolde, he knew, were lovers in Wagner's opera of that name. "A woman?" he demanded. This Isolde is a woman?"

"Yes," Karpf told him politely, "she is a most efficient assassin and as proficient with the Uzi or a knife as any man. More to the point, the stealthy Tristan and Isolde are undetectable when following a mark."

"Good," Tolt breathed. "Yes, quite excellent indeed!"

Staib's pulse throbbed as he contemplated the fact Isolde might get to kill the American instead of him.

Tolt read his mind. "There will be no killing unless I say so, Ludwig. Just control yourself for the time being."

Karpf thought better of mentioning that Tristan and Isolde reserved the right to kill the mark in case of a mishap making it possible for them to be identified.

THIRTY-SIX

MANAGUA, NICARAGUA

The Hotel Corona had known better days but so had a lot of buildings in downtown Managua. Several decades of repressive regimes, from the Somozas to the Sandinistas, had drained the country's economy. Although the Sandinistas had received an enormous military build-up from Cuba and the Soviet Union, little money and energy survived to build a vigorous society. Not only had the seesaw of bloody politics discouraged foreign investment, but an earthquake in the 1970s left 6,000 people dead and 300,000 homeless. And the brackish waters of Lake Managua had little appeal to tourists who preferred the white sands and clear blue waters of Cancun, Acapulco, Cozumel, Bahia Pajaros, and other destinations where investment had produced modern hotels and condominiums with the expected amenities.

The hotel's once bright blue stucco had faded to a dull blue-gray, portions of which had fallen off, leaving exposed areas of gray concrete block. Most of the paint was peeled from the shutters, the iron grill-work was rusted, and the window sills were covered with a protective layer of black volcanic dust accented with undisturbed bird droppings.

The lobby was sparsely furnished and sparsely populated. A man in a rumpled seersucker suit and open-neck shirt sat in a corner reading the *International Herald Tribune.* Two older men sat frozen at a chess board at the window facing the street. The bar could be seen through a door to the right.

Mallory took a seat at the bar and ordered a beer. As he nursed his drink, he realized he damn well better put on a good performance or Holloway would see right through him, and he'd never get the truth. He was struck with the irony of the situation: a professional naval officer, on the cusp of a choice high-tech assignment in Washington, sitting at a seedy bar in a drab Banana Republic with a silenced gun in his attaché case, about to test himself against a renegade CIA agent who's gone underground. *Holy shit!*

He sipped the beer and decided that surprise, shock and serious intimidation—all successful military tactics—were the key to softening up Agent Wade Holloway.

If John Anderson was Wade Holloway.

He paid for the beer with an American fifty-dollar bill and let the change lie on the counter in front of him. He caught the bartender's eye and nodded toward the money. "Another beer, *señor?*"

Mallory shook his head and produced a small photo of Holloway. "I'm looking for this man. Do you recognize him?" he said in Spanish.

"*Sí,*" the bartender nodded. "*Señor* Anderson."

"I understand he has a room here." Mallory glanced at the money and then at the bartender. "It's important that I see him privately."

"How important?" the bartender said, eyeing the money. Mallory pushed the pile of bills toward him.

The bartender palmed the money like a professional magician. "Room 218, *señor,*" he said. "He's usually there this time of day."

The stairs creaked in protest as Mallory climbed to the second floor and followed the room numbers toward 218. The Browning was holstered on his belt, under his cotton jacket. He had to assume that Holloway was more skilled in the use of handguns than he, so he intended to brandish the Browning before Holloway could go for a weapon. He positioned himself close to the door, with one foot poised for quick insertion should Holloway slam it on him. From Holloway's photos, he'd recognize him in an instant.

He knocked on the door. No response. He knocked again. He heard mumbling from within, the door opened, and the unshaven face of Wade Holloway appeared in the opening.

"Doctor Holloway, I presume," Mallory said in a voice that carried no trace of uncertainty.

The look on Holloway's face left little doubt surprise and shock had been achieved. Mallory inserted his foot in the door, shouldered his way into the room, and closed the door behind him. He quickly scanned the room for any sign of menace, and Holloway for hint of a weapon. The room smelled unmistakably of spilled beer.

"Who the hell are you?" Holloway said, as he wiped his lips with the back of his hand.

Mallory pulled a copy of the phony suicide note from his shirt pocket. "You addressed this To Whom It May Concern," he said, holding the note in front of Holloway's face. "Let's say I represent those who are concerned about your disappearing act. We are going to have a talk," he continued, "and you are going to sit. . . ." He produced the Browning and motioned with it toward a frayed upholstered armchair in the corner. "Right there."

Holloway slowly backed up and sat down in the chair, obviously sizing up Mallory and his own lack of options.

Mallory took a chair opposite him and surveyed their surroundings. It was a large room, with a double bed, a sofa, a table and two chairs, a TV, a counter with a coffee pot, and a mini refrigerator. The door to the bathroom was open. A bra and panties were drying on a towel rack.

He noticed Holloway glance at a small desk that was out of reach. *Okay, that's where he keeps his weapon.*

"Put both feet up on the ottoman," Mallory ordered.

267

Holloway leaned forward as if about to get up. "Look, I've had enough of this shit—"

Mallory produced the silencer from his jacket pocket and without shifting his eyes from Holloway's he slowly attached it to Browning. He had practiced in the dark, thinking it could be an effective parlor trick for such a moment as this. "No, you haven't had enough of this," he said, through his teeth. "We're just getting started."

Holloway stared at the weapon. He exhaled a deep, pent-up breath and raised his feet up onto the ottoman.

"We'll start," Mallory told him, "by your telling me what brings you to this hole in the wall when your previous address was a townhouse on Avenida Florida in San Marcos."

Holloway sighed and stared silently at the wall, obviously considering how he might surprise his visitor.

"Silence, Mister Holloway, is not golden in your case," Mallory said, "and definitely not healthy."

"Okay," Holloway began, hesitantly. "I was about to be taken to the cleaners in a nasty divorce settlement. My wife bugged out three years ago, went back to California, and filed for divorce. I was fortunate to have a little action going here in Managua, so I decided to bail out and preserve at least some of what I had."

"Bail out? That's an interesting choice of words."

"Huh?" Holloway said with a puzzled look on his face.

"Never mind, we'll get to it in a moment." Mallory glanced at the panties in the bathroom. "What's her name?"

"Consuelo. So what?"

"So you just packed up and moved in here with the lovely Consuelo?" He stared at Holloway. "I'm sure it's a fascinating story of marital burnout, professional disillusionment, and star-crossed lovers, set in this tropical paradise, here in greater downtown Managua, but so far you haven't told me anything I don't already know.

"Screw you," Holloway sneered. "I don't know who the hell you are. You come barging in here like Rambo, pull out your pop gun and think I'm going to tell you the story of my life, just like that!"

Mallory smiled. He was beginning to enjoy this, but his attention was drawn to whatever Holloway was staring at. He glanced quickly to the right and saw a huge gray rat emerge from the closet and begin to slowly sniff its way along the baseboard.

"You've got two roommates."

Holloway shrugged. "Screw you," he said.

"You already said that," Mallory sighed. His elbow was resting on the arm of his chair nearest the baseboard.

Holloway's eye darted to the rat again.

Mallory slowly brought the Browning up and over to line up on the rat. With the gun and the long silencer in perfect alignment with his whiskered target, he squeezed the trigger. The high powered, hollow-nose round hit dead center, dematerializing the rat and sending a spray of blood and matter up the wall, and plaster dust everywhere. A dinner-plate-size chunk of baseboard and wall was suddenly gone, while a bat-shaped fur ball, consisting of the rat's head and still attached forefeet, flew up in a lazy arc and landed on the floor beside Holloway's chair.

Holloway's eyes bulged. He drew in his breath and appeared to be holding it, as his face reddened.

"I hope I have your undivided attention now," Mallory breathed. "This is your last chance to tell me the real story, including all the characters in your personal passion play: Burton, Franck, Graham, and local heavy hitters. So let's cut the crap and get on with True Confessions, starting with this bullshit note." He wadded the copy of the suicide note in his left hand and tossed it to Holloway. "I'm going to get the information I need, eventually. It'll be much easier on you if I get it here and now."

Holloway's eyes continued to register all the surprise, shock, and intimidation Mallory had hoped for, summed up as naked fear.

"Okay, okay," he gasped. He appeared to be on the verge of hyper-ventilating, and one of his eyelids was fluttering. "Okay," he said again. He took a deep breath, puffed his cheeks, and exhaled loudly. "There's a lot of German investment in Costa Verde these days. They own the banks, the airline, manufacturing companies, the TV and the radio stations. They have their own managers from Germany. These people were all brought in by one Heinrich Kaalten, a Nazi who is either a priest or, more likely, is posing as a priest. In fact, there're at least three phony priests at the cathedral. There's this one real tall guy, a monsignor who's acting archbishop, and another one, a Father Martin."

Holloway shrugged. "Damned if I know how it all squares with the Vatican, if it does."

Mallory exhaled. "Tell me something I don't know."

"I'm coming to that," Holloway said, testily. "One of the local Krauts is a guy named Gerhardt Hesse, a manufacturer's rep for construction equipment and building materials. I found out Hesse was funneling money from the Kraut interests to the Generalissimo. We're talking big bucks here. I assume it's the Krauts who got rid of the G-Mo after I bugged out, and they're the ones who put Colonel Benes in power."

Mallory thought of Elena's encounter at the christening and Arturo's with the so-called Father Martin. "Are you telling me Nazis are impersonating Catholic priests?"

"I'm telling you what Hesse told me. He could be lying. I don't really give a shit one way or another. The important thing is," Holloway continued, "Hesse was skimming some of the action into his own Swiss bank account. So I confronted him and he had to cut me in on it, too. Hell, Hesse is dead meat if I sing to the Krauts. But then, so am I if they ever find out."

"What about Burton?"

Holloway took a deep breath and continued. "I figured Franck might get wise to my personal retirement plan so I opened a Swiss account in Burton's name and put money into it. One of the analysts at Langley, a woman named Reece, was very eager to hear Burton was involved in something like that. It was the perfect smokescreen to cover my ass."

"And your suicide note?" Mallory asked.

"Yeah, the note," Holloway said. "Hell, it seemed like a foolproof plan. We'd be flying over some real boondocks and I thought it'd be a good time for my disappearing act. I left the note in the chopper, slid one of the cargo hatches open, and then stowed away behind a bulkhead panel I loosened before we took off. With them finding the note and seeing the open hatch, I figured they'd never think to search the aircraft. They never did, and I waited until after dark at the airport to slip out and split. I'd obviously jumped to my pitiful death. End of poor Agent Holloway. Home free with no trail and big bucks."

"Until now," Mallory said.

"Until now," Holloway echoed.

"What about Hesse?"

"He still skims. My cut still comes. I'm pretty close to my goal, almost to where I could be off to Argentina."

Mallory glanced at the lingerie in the bathroom.

"With cutie pants?"

"Are you kidding?" Holloway snorted.

Holloway's mood seemed to brighten. "Why don't you and I cut a deal?"

Mallory slowly shook his head.

"Then what the hell do I get out of this . . . for telling you what you wanted to know?"

"You get to stay right here at the luxurious Hotel Corona," Mallory told him. "You get to keep up your relationship with Hesse, exactly the way it's been. I don't want the pattern of Hesse's skimming operation upset or the flow of funds into your account disturbed in any way.

"If you do it my way, and don't rock the boat, you might just get to Argentina after all."

Mallory rose from his chair and backed toward the door. "Don't call us," he said. "We'll call you."

"Who did you say sent you?"

"I didn't," Mallory said. As he reached the door, he surveyed the splattered wall. "This place is a disgrace. You better call Housekeeping and get it cleaned up." He gestured with the Browning toward the rat parts beside Holloway's chair. "And have them send up a new rat."

THIRTY-SEVEN

DOWNTOWN MANAGUA

Main street was lined with Texaco and Arco mini-marts and McDonalds and Burger Kings offering high-calorie, high-fat fast food and One Hour Photos offering fast film processing. American, Japanese, and German products were advertised from rooftops and storefronts, but the grim aura of the war years still pervaded. In the middle of the traffic circles the requisite statue of the hero on horseback had given way to statues of Sandinistas brandishing assault weapons.

The Hotel El Camino Real was a modern structure with a colonial architectural flair, rejoicing in a concierge, a uniformed bellboy with a shiny brass luggage cart, a well-dressed receptionist at the desk, and an elegantly tiled lobby full of respectably dressed people. It was expensive but Mallory still had a good supply of American cash and felt some of the CIA's money should be put to good use. It had been a long two days since he left Truman aboard the *Power Play* at Bahia Pajaros. The meeting with Ann Graham in Miraflores, the drive to Managua through the border checkpoints and the airport, and his *tour de force* performance for Holloway's benefit had drained his last bit of energy.

His room was mercifully quiet, with a small balcony overlooking the lake. A short nap, a shower, and a change of clothes brought a new lease on life. He made his report to Truman on the sat-phone.

"You've earned your spurs on this one, Captain," Truman said. "You sure you wouldn't rather work for me than Admiral Frazier?" he joked.

Truman reported that the Special Operating Forces were close to being able to pull off the raid on Prison Number Five and were in training at a virtual reality facility in Mississippi, rehearsing the operation in great detail.

"You followed your orders and completed your mission," Truman said. "You may as well fly home from there."

"I'm not coming home until I know David is safe," Mallory said. "I delivered my end of the deal. Now it's your turn, and Foxlee's."

"I can't disagree with that," Truman said.

"I'll head back to San Marcos in the morning," Mallory said. "Right now, I'm going to head for the bar, then dinner and, God willing, a night's sleep. I'll have the phone on but don't call unless it's an aid to digestion."

The bar at the El Camino was more to Mallory's taste than the last few he was in. The walls and ceiling were of a rich, dark wood paneling, the clientele seemed upbeat, the tables and chairs matched, and there seemed to be an adequate supply of single malt scotch.

He ordered a double Glenlivet, neat, with a side of bottled water. Slowly sipping his drink, he amused himself by playing a mental video of the last two days against the context of his long Navy career. He recalled some strange duty over the years. As a junior officer he flew in an all-weather squadron with a skipper who was terrified of instrument flying. He flew with an executive officer who almost killed an entire flight by turning into a tight right echelon on approach to the carrier. He flew wing on a World War II ace who carried Jack Daniels in his flight suit. He tangled with MiGs, dodged SAMs, fired 20 mm and Sidewinder missiles, and dropped every kind of bomb on Iraqi troops.

But neither he nor anyone of his acquaintance ever took out a rat with a silenced Browning 9 mm. The thought of it left him fighting an outburst of laughter. It would make a never-to-be-topped O-Club sea story, unless, of course, Truman and Frazier decided it never happened.

"You were never there, Captain," he could hear the admiral saying. "You and your son had a nice vacation in Cancun. That's all there was to it, goddamn it. Now, let's get to work on these Joint Strike birds."

Aye, aye, sir, he said to himself, toasting his refection in the mirror behind the bar.

Mallory pulled the drapery aside, rubbing sleep from his eyes, and observed the morning's weather from his little balcony overlooking the plaza. Billowy white cumulus clouds hung over the mountains in the distance, and bright sunlight glistened on the otherwise gloomy surface of Lake Managua. He found the dining room attractively furnished, as was the hostess who showed him to a table by the window and left him with a menu and the Managua morning paper. A smiling waitress poured his coffee as he unfolded the paper and saw the headline.

AIR ATTACK ON COSTA VERDE AIR BASE

SAN MARCOS, Costa Verde—Propeller-driven fighter aircraft attacked the Costa Verde Air Force base at Mesa Del Norte yesterday, destroying jets and helicopters on the ground. The attacking aircraft, reported to be four or five in number, wore green jungle camouflage but carried no markings. Two Air Force fighters were able to take off from the base, but were shot down.

His eye went to a companion article on the front page, headlined MANAGUA HEARS RADIO PROPAGANDA. He scanned the article until he came to a reference to La Pantera.

SAN MARCOS, Costa Verde—Related to the attack on Mesa Del Norte Air Force Base yesterday, an unlicensed, pirate radio station calling itself *Radio Pantera* carried a message calling for the people of Costa Verde to rise against the regime of Colonel Hector Benes. A female speaker, claiming to be the reincarnation of La Pantera of legend, delivered a fiery oration calling on Costa Verdeans to revolt against their military government. The station carrying the speech went off the air shortly following her appeal.

In related news, there are unconfirmed reports of armed uprisings in Costa Verde's outlying provinces, including Pacifico Province, where rebels reportedly seized key road junctions.

The accompanying photo caption read "Rebels celebrate as they fire their weapons to shouts of *La Pantera Vive*."

Mallory skimmed the rest of the paper but there were no other reports of the fighting. However, one columnist speculated that long-time enemies of Colonel Benes were behind the attacks and mentioned the son of former Costa Verde President Edwardo Peralta.

Draining a final cup of coffee, his eye caught an item on page six, under the caption "News from the Region," about the death of a shop owner in the San Marcos, Costa Verde suburb of Miraflores. A female identified as Ann Graham, an American and former secretary at Electricos Verde, was found shot to death in her dress shop, the victim of a burglary, according to police investigators, the piece said.

He slowly put down the paper and stared out the window at the lake—with the sudden realization that he was probably being followed. Apparently Ann Graham hadn't cooperated by telling her killers what they wanted to know. Or had she? And who were they after, Holloway or him?

He packed, checked out, and headed south to Costa Verde, wondering what the situation would be at the border. He felt confident Holloway would stay in place, and keep his mouth shut, if no one else got to him. In spite of Holloway's strained display of bravado, it was obvious he would do exactly as he had been told.

The border was open on the Nicaragua side, leading to the likelihood of the Costa Verde border being open as well. Inquiring in

Nicaragua about the situation in Costa Verde brought shrugs and *"¿quien sabe?"* or *"no problema."*

On the Costa Verde side of the border he went through the same drill as before, showing the Malcolm passport and watching as the agent scanned the list for a matching name. He froze as he saw that "Mallory" appeared on the list of Ms. It had been entered since his departure yesterday.

The agent finished scanning the list, opened a drawer and withdrew a folder containing photographs. He studied one, which Mallory couldn't see, studied him, and replaced the folder in the drawer.

Mallory felt a sudden adrenaline rush. *Holy shit!*

It crossed his mind maybe Holloway was in-tight with the border guards and phoned ahead. No, he couldn't have furnished a photo. Only the government, the Kohorte, or the CIA could have done that. As the agent reached for his passport, Mallory's heart skipped a beat but the man slowly stamped the passport and handed it back to him.

"You may go, *señor,*" he said. "Have a nice day."

Mallory, who should have been elated, felt a numbing chill instead. The hunter was the hunted now. Once in the car, he found the Browning and cradled it in his crotch while he drove toward San Marcos with the doors locked. Even caked with mud and volcanic dust, the red Toyota stood out like a painted whore in church.

ROUTE ONE SOUTH TO COSTA VERDE

Driving toward San Marcos in a state of anxiety, Mallory turned on the radio to see if he could pick up any news, but all the Costa Verde stations were playing the same classical music. The Benes government had apparently ordered a news blackout until they could develop propaganda or report some military successes in the field.

With the exception of an occasional Army convoy, the traffic on the Pan American Highway south to the capital seemed pretty normal. From all outward appearances there was little evidence a revolution was under way. From what he read and heard, civil wars in Central America often presented a unique dichotomy. While opposing forces clashed on the battleground, the general population went about business as best they could, having learned through the years that this was the cyclic order of things.

Overhead, an occasional helicopter gunship surveyed the highway traffic but didn't appear to pose a threat to motorists. No one on the road seemed to be in a hurry. Suddenly, the London Symphony's recording of Vivaldi's *Four Seasons* was cut short during *Spring* by an announcer's stentorian voice.

"Vive La Pantera!" he proclaimed excitedly.

Next came Elena's calm, melodious voice. Mallory was startled, then transfixed. Her delivery combined the power of a skilled orator with the intimacy of a lover.

> "My people, listen to me. Listen as La Pantera speaks to her people. My eyes have seen your suffering. My ears have heard your cries. My face is against those who persecute you. You have cried out, and La Pantera has heard you. I grieve with you, and I feel your suffering. As you listen to my voice, the army of your redemption is springing forth from a hundred hiding places in the jungles to drive these evildoers from our homeland. No longer will evil men pillage our land. No longer will they torture our loved ones. Even as you hear this, my aircraft are growling from the sky, visiting destruction on the dark forces oppressing you. Rise up! Rise up, my people! The hour has come! Join La Pantera's righteous cause! Together, we—"

The London Symphony interrupted with a change of season, moving on to *Autumn,* as Mallory contemplated what had just happened. The lovely and caring Elena Maria Peralta de Gomez, who could have chosen the luxurious life in Paris or Beverly Hills or anywhere, had just turned down the one-way street to armed rebellion and would be shot on the spot if caught by the Benes forces.

He wondered how she managed to pull off the illicit broadcast, since she obviously outfoxed the government censorship, and he wondered if she was heard on other stations as well.

People tend to vividly recall exactly where they were and what they were doing when they heard the news of a great event or tragedy. As his eyes continued to follow the road ahead, Mallory realized that he would remember for the rest of his life that he was driving through the countryside of Elena's beloved Costa Verde on an otherwise unremarkable afternoon. He was always in awe of her beauty and her character but now—with the long talked-about counterrevolution a reality—he found himself in awe of her guts.

THIRTY-EIGHT

ROUTE ONE SOUTH TO COSTA VERDE

A glance in the rearview mirror showed Mallory only that light traffic was following him at a distance. Something caught his fighter pilot's eye, though, and he looked again. There, a few car lengths behind, was a tan Chevrolet station wagon. He suddenly remembered seeing such a car stop front of Ann Graham's shop. He remembered there was a man behind the wheel and a woman in the passenger's seat that day, and that they appeared to be studying a road map for directions.

My God! he thought, as the back of his neck tingled. His mind raced with the possibility they were connected with her murder and the appearance of "Mallory" on the *persona non grata* list. He tried to recall if the Chevy wagon he noticed in Miraflores had any distinctive marks. He barely noticed the car as Ann Graham greeted him. Yes, he thought, the front bumper was a little crooked, bent down on the passenger side. He glanced at the mirror again. The Chevy with the slightly crooked bumper was following.

Entering San Marcos about an hour later with the wagon still following at a discreet distance, he pulled the road map from above the visor and spread it on the passenger's seat where he could glance at it while driving. On the reverse side, he remembered, was a large-scale illustrated map of the city. He glanced at it repeatedly to re-orient himself: the Presidential Palace, the Palace of Fine Arts, the *Mercado Central,* the Cosmopolitan, the Holiday Inn.

He kept an eye on the rearview mirror.

Though other cars had filled in the gap between them, the man and woman in the Chevy still followed, more discreetly now. He was mentally searching for a way to lose them when he realized he was approaching a *redondo* or traffic circle. *What if they're just tourists?* he thought.

Better be sure they're a threat. Let them close up, for a good look at them. He slowed and let some cars pass him. The Chevy caught up until it was directly behind. Another glance in the rearview mirror.

No question about it, the man and woman both met his eyes, intensely. He had a tail for sure. The man was heavy set, with a black moustache. She was scrawny, with rimless glasses, and a scarf tied about her head.

Here comes the redondo. Maybe this is the break I need. He quickly studied the traffic flowing from left to right around the redondo and guessed he might get away with entering the wrong way and ducking out at the first on-ramp, which would serve him as an exit.

They were little more than a block from the redondo now. His pursuers were straining forward and watching him intently. The fixed expressions on their faces said he was the fox and they were bloodthirsty hounds. Their eyes met for another instant in the rearview mirror.

They want me to lead them to Peralta's supporters here in San Marcos. Or they want to kill me.

Mallory realized he had never tried anything very nervy when driving an automobile. He figured success would depend on drawing the Chevy right up to his rear bumper, then doing the unthinkable—suddenly swerving left, right into the oncoming traffic, just as his tail instinctively committed to merging with the traffic flowing to the right around the redondo.

He tightened his grip on the wheel, dropped the shift lever into LO for greater acceleration, and glanced in the mirror. The Chevy stuck to him now like it was being towed. He glanced to the left at the traffic on the redondo and gauged he could dart across two lanes of onrushing cars and trucks, then cut back against the grain and depart the redondo after a couple of hundred yards of hair-raising wrong-way driving.

There was no time to watch the Chevy as he suddenly yanked the wheel to the left and accelerated into the circle the wrong way in front of several cars that slammed on their brakes in desperate attempts to avoid broad-siding him and rear-ending each other. He sideswiped a portion of the guard rail lining the inside of the circle and darted back across the lanes of oncoming traffic to the outside lane where he departed the redondo and careened across a couple of hundred feet of grass before finding a clear space on a ramp leading onto the redondo from some other highway.

He didn't hear any collisions and hoped there weren't any, as he found himself going with the traffic again on a new unfamiliar highway.

He pulled into a Texaco station and StarMart, and parked the tell-tale red Toyota by a dumpster behind the station. The dumpster partially blocked the view from the street. He grabbed his jacket and duffel bag, shoved the Browning into it and walked to a nearby auto repair shop, where he paid a mechanic to drive him to a nearby hotel.

The tan Chevy wagon was not to be seen, and no taxis were waiting, but a bus was drawing up in front of the hotel. The destination sign above its windshield read *Districto Central*. Boarding it seemed to be the best move and he climbed aboard.

He rode the bus for several miles, catching his breath and trying to figure out his next move.

The unpleasant-looking couple tailing him was obviously following to see where he would lead them. He mentally reversed their roles; were he that couple, what would he be doing right now? He immediately concluded that they would go to the Peralta compound and wait for their mark to show up there. *Okay*, he decided, *the compound is off limits. The army has probably commandeered the place.* Nacho and Elena, he knew, were at one of their secret bases.

He decided against staying at one of the hotels. Even though his Malcolm identity couldn't be connected with the Peraltas, he wasn't just another traveling businessman stuck during a revolution telling war stories at the bar. He had a tail and they would damn well check the hotels.

The American Embassy was refuge, he knew, but he didn't want the ambassador involved in any way in what he was doing since Truman and the President recruited him. Showing up at the embassy, sweating and grimy, talking about a tail, would convince Cathcart he was a nut case for sure. Besides, Cathcart was a man with a congenital capacity for screwing things up, and he might do something through the State Department to spoil the Special Operating Forces' designs on Prison Number Five.

He remembered the list of phone numbers Peralta gave him and pulled it from his pocket. Other than Carlos, none of the names was familiar except Arturo, the young student he met in Nacho's library. Arturo seemed to be part of the inner circle and he lived in San Marcos. Even if he weren't at home maybe he carried a cell phone to stay in contact with the Peraltas. He dialed Arturo's number and a man answered.

"Arturo?" Mallory thought he recognized his voice. "This is Deke Mallory. Remember me?"

"Of course, Captain Mallory. What's happened to you?"

"It's a long story but, in short, I've got a tail, and I realize now I've been followed for a couple of days."

"Oh, shit! Okay, here's my address. Write it down. It's in the La Colina district. Do you know where that is?"

"No, but I'll find it." Mallory scribbled the address.

"Try to take a cab to my place. I'm the upstairs front apartment on the right."

Mallory turned the phone off and returned it to the pocket of his jacket. Most of his vacation wardrobe was still at Nacho's mansion. He was traveling light with only a few extra clothes in the small duffel bag. Taking off the jacket he reversed it from khaki to teal green, put on his dark glasses, and took out a light canvas sun hat from his bag and put it on.

He watched the stores and sidewalks passing by and reflected momentarily on how little effect the war was having on business as usual. Except for a few army trucks, and an armored personnel carrier parked in one of the intersections they passed through, there was no evidence of military activity on the streets.

After a few stops in the downtown area the bus slowed and drew to a stop across the street from the Hotel Cosmopolitan, which Mallory could see offered a line of waiting taxis. He got off the bus and crossed the street with the other pedestrians. He gave Arturo's address to the starter, who spoke to the waiting driver of the cab as Mallory climbed into the taxi with his bag.

"It will take about twenty minutes, this time of day," the driver said.

"I don't care what route you take," he told the driver, "but if we're followed by a tan Chevrolet station wagon, you will lose it . . . and get a tip of fifty dollars, U.S."

He could see a grin spreading the nodding face of the driver, who immediately scanned the rearview mirror.

THIRTY-NINE

LA COLINA DISTRICT, SAN MARCOS

The rickety wooden stairs of Arturo's apartment building in a run-down section of San Marcos protested as Mallory climbed them and knocked on Arturo's door. He quickly opened it and waved Mallory inside.

"I didn't expect to see you again so soon," Arturo said, "but then, the unexpected is always happening around here. Have a seat," he said, pointing to a worn sofa, "and tell me what's happened since you left for the finca and your meeting in Bahia Pajaros."

Mallory saw no reason not to relate at least some of what transpired. Arturo was obviously a trusted confidant of Peralta's or he wouldn't have been at the council of war that day. He told briefly of meeting Ann Graham in Miraflores and Holloway and the rat in Managua, his experiences at the border returning to San Marcos, the discovery of his tail, and ditching them in traffic.

Arturo was beginning to laugh by the time he finished. "You have obviously joined our cause," he said, "and the first shot you fired was at a rat with four legs instead of two!" He shook his head. "I'm sorry. I'm sure it was no laughing matter, but you'll admit it was pretty bizarre."

"Well, that's the way it went," Mallory said. "Now somebody's after me, and apparently the stakes have just been raised. I can only assume Miss Graham's killers were the people who followed me, maybe not to kill me but to see where I would lead them. Since shaking them at the redondo they know I won't lead them anywhere now, so they could change their minds and try to kill me after all."

Mallory could see a look of concern crossing Arturo's face. "Don't worry," he said, "I didn't lead them here."

Arturo nodded. "Good," he said.

"I suppose I could just get on a plane and fly home," Mallory said, "but I'm not leaving Costa Verde until I know my son is safe."

"Okay, you can crash here at my place. There's plenty of room. Relax and have a beer." Arturo opened a small refrigerator and uncapped two local brews.

Mallory surveyed the room. It was an organized mess with grungy furnishings befitting a nineteenth-century anarchist. Clothes appeared to have taken root on the floor and on the sofa where they were dropped. Books, newspapers, magazines, pamphlets, and maps were stacked to the teetering point. A Colt .45 automatic lay on a shelf by the front door. Stacks of posters rested against the walls. One protested the government's refusal to grant landing rights to a Chinese airline; one demanded higher pay for agricultural workers; another denounced the government as fascist. The firebrand revolutionary rhetoric was mixed with some prints of old masters, photos of jungle birds, an aerial photo of Hong Kong, a photo of a small restaurant, and photos of a handsome couple, who were obviously Arturo's parents. Mallory could see their racial features in Arturo's face; the smooth Asian skin of Arturo's father combined with the olive complexion of his Latin mother.

Impulsively, Mallory looked outside to make sure the tan Chevy wasn't cruising by.

He finished his beer and surveyed his new friend. "What's in this revolution thing for you? Are you involved for philosophical and idealistic reasons, or do you have some stake in this, like Nacho and Elena and the Moras?"

Arturo looked up from his place at the kitchen sink, where he was rinsing dishes. A minute or two passed before he spoke. "I would say, yes, I have a stake in it," he said slowly. "You have to go back a few years to understand it but, yes, I have a very personal stake in this war.

"My grandfather," he continued, "had a restaurant in Hong Kong. One of the best. A three-story restaurant in Victoria, on Hong Kong Island, overlooking the harbor. My father, Chen Quan Hung, worked there as a boy. I'm sure you know Chinese restaurants are always a family affair."

"Sure," Mallory said, nodding his head.

"When my father was about twenty, he heard there were great opportunities here in Central America for Asians. Costa Verde, being the most cosmopolitan of the neighboring countries, openly solicited immigration of Hong Kong Chinese, especially those who could bring professional skills or open businesses. So, my father came here in the 1970s. His first restaurant was very modest but it was in the center of the city near major businesses and became successful. By that time he met mother, whose family lived here in San Marcos, and they were married. She's Catholic, of course, which didn't seem to make any difference to my father, who considers himself a follower of Confucius."

"Didn't it present religious problems for them?"

Arturo shrugged and withdrew two more beers from the refrigerator. "Not really," he said. "Confucianism isn't really a religion, it's more of a philosophy. There's no priesthood, no hierarchy, no scripture, no church, no creed, no theology. It seeks the highest good, through what they call 'investigating the reason of things to the utmost.' Naturally, I was raised Catholic, but I didn't take it too seriously. I guess I gravitated more to my father's philosophy than Mom's theology. They both worked hard at the business, very hard, and it became a real success. Naturally, we lived above the restaurant. And as with many Chinese restaurants, it had private dining rooms on the second floor."

"Did you work in the restaurant with your parents?"

"Oh, yes, of course. Even when I was very young. There was always plenty to do. Naturally, my father wanted me to continue in the business, but by the time I was ready for college he could see I was headed in a different direction. I was more interested in political science and philosophy than cuisine."

Mallory smiled at the contrast. "Well, that's quite a difference there," he said.

"The restaurant was a popular meeting place, not only for business people but especially with faculty at the university. Many who opposed the regime met there pretty regularly. That soon became common knowledge, of course.

"You know what happened to Elena's husband and her son, how they were murdered when he went to treat poor people in the villages? Well . . ."

Arturo took a moment to control his emotions.

"One day I returned from classes and found that soldiers had beaten my father very badly. That was two years ago, and he's still bed-ridden. From then on, I was suspect of course. I probably followed my father's philosophy too well and investigated the reason of things too much. As you know, I was jailed for punching out a policeman who brutalized some students."

Arturo brightened. "Anyway, all this was before I found my new, high-paying profession of organizing left-wing resistance, under Father Martin's auspices."

"Why did you decide to do it?"

"Oh, I don't know," Arturo continued, with a smile. "I got out of jail and I've had some fun with it since, plus I've got plenty of money and a new motorcycle. And Elena and Nacho said go along with it, maybe my efforts would forge a student organization they could utilize when the time came. The students lean to the Peraltistas, you know."

Mallory finished his beer and set the bottle down. "Yeah," he said, "but you're supposed to be a radical, left-leaning tool of the Chinese government, and Peralta is a moderate, so it seems strange to me you could ever get students who favor Nacho to go along with such a program."

Arturo laughed. "That's true," he said, "so I offer them fun and games and they forget some of the politics."

Mallory checked the street again through the window.

"Like this morning, for example," Arturo said. "Six of us went to the government-controlled radio station, the one that's networked to all the others on the Emergency Broadcast Band. It's supposed to be used for hurricane warnings and things like that. It can automatically override all the other radio stations in the country so emergency news can be broadcast from a single source."

"I think I see what's coming," Mallory said, remembering Elena's radio appeal to the people.

Arturo laughed. "So we declared our own emergency and played Elena's tape until they got wise and went back to, what was it, Vivaldi?"

"Elena's appeal was carried to the whole country?"

"Hell, yes!" Arturo laughed. "We preempted all the broadcasts, just like in my father's favorite quotation from Confucius."

"Quotation?" Mallory asked.

"'A general of a large army may be defeated—but you cannot defeat the determined mind of a peasant.'"

Mallory grinned. His new friend was quite a guy.

"We came in as janitors," Arturo continued, "with pails and mops. One of the girls, made up like a fashion model, floated in a minute later and flirted with the guy at the control panel. She got him to take off his earphones while we switched the tapes and distracted him as long as she could. We all split, of course, and nobody got caught.

"Anyway," he continued, "I damn well have a stake in this war, for what they did to my father. Well, it's probably just a matter of time," Arturo continued, "before Father Martin finds out what I'm really doing. I think I'm okay for now, but I keep a bag packed so I can split at a moment's notice. So far, he seems to think I'm sincere in carrying out his orders. And if he comes here," he said, sweeping the room with his hand, "all he'll find are tools of my left-wing protests."

He swept his hand around the room. "Anyway, Captain, *mi casa es su casa,* for just as long as you want."

FORTY

THE PRESIDENTIAL PALACE, SAN MARCOS

Colonel Benes slammed the phone onto its cradle, grabbed his holstered sidearm from atop his desk and buckled it on. His neck and face had turned a deep red.

"Let's go!" he ordered his aide. "I'm going to Rio Rico. Peralta just bombed hell out of us there. Bearcats came in low and slow, as pretty as you please. And that's after they shot down an F-80 on their way," he added.

"Was there no warning?" the aide, a major, asked. The worried look on his young face said it all. Rio Rico Air Force Base was one of three government fighter bases and should have been able to protect itself.

"No! There was no warning!" Benes swore and kicked a wastebasket into the wall.

"This time," he said, "three or four Bearcats came out of the rising sun, well below our radar. A flight of four F-80s launched twenty minutes beforehand and should have intercepted them. But they didn't see the enemy until it was too late."

"It was bad?" the major asked.

Benes sucked in his breath and controlled himself. "Napalm," he said.

"They napalmed the hangars and repair shops and wiped out the flight line with rockets."

"Then Rio Rico's out of business?" the major asked.

"Yes, the surviving F-80s had to land at San Benito."

"Sir, our first priority must be to avail ourselves of the Nicaraguans' Russian-built radar sites. They paint every square inch of Costa Verde, night and day."

"I know that," Benes snapped. "How do you propose getting the Nicaraguans to do our bidding?" he sneered. The colonel obviously thought the idea was childlike. "Are you going to write to Saint Nicholas, Major?"

Benes hadn't picked a yes-man to be his aide, and Major Paco Martinez stood his ground.

"You should not dismiss the idea out of hand, sir," he said. "It would take many long months to construct equivalent radar facilities. And radar sites of our own would be attacked from the air the minute construction started. Sir, just think of the unparalleled advantage of using Nicaragua's radar network. Peralta wouldn't dare attack Nicaragua, with his limited resources."

Benes clenched his jaw. "I still say you're dreaming."

The major took another shot at performing his duty. "Sir, I strongly recommend you not go to Rio Rico today. There's nothing you can accomplish there."

Benes dropped into his chair. "You're right, Paco," he said. "It's better to go forward with today's briefing by my field commanders, as planned."

"I recommend a better idea," the major said. "If you cut short the briefing, which is a good thing anyway, you can meet with the acting archbishop at his request."

"He wants to see me?" Benes asked. The expression on his face could have been surprise or consternation.

"Yes, sir. I recommend you do it, too."

"Damn it, Paco, I'm not going to set myself up for the Church to intercede by demanding I negotiate peace with Peralta," Benes said. "I'll bet that's what the archbishop's up to, too," he groused.

"You've nothing to lose this time, sir," Martinez told him. "He wants to give you his blessing," he said.

"You spoke with him? When?"

"His aide, a Father Martin, called a few minutes ago. That's why I came in to see you."

Benes put his feet up on the desk, and smiled.

"Well, I'll be damned," he said. "His blessing could be golden, Paco. It could neutralize all this La Pantera bullshit from Peralta's camp."

THE CATHEDRAL

Benes fumed as he waited in one of the armored personnel carriers blocking entrance to the cathedral grounds. *This damn well better be worth it,* he thought, as he glowered at the entrance to the Archbishop's Palace where his aide stood talking to a priest.

"It's to be a private audience," Staib told the major in sepulchral tones, "only the two of them." He kept his hands templed by his large crucifix as he explained that the major could accompany Benes no further than Tolt's anteroom. Paco Martinez listened decorously and said he would consult with Colonel Benes about the arrangements and return in a few minutes.

Ah-ha! Staib thought, as he watched the young officer stride across the lawn toward one of the armored vehicles parked in the street. *That's the vehicle carrying Benes!* If the audience didn't go well, the plan was to assassinate him on the spot. Tolt would give the signal, which would be the invitation for Benes to receive a private mass and special blessing, and Tolt would serve the poisoned wafer as Staib followed with the chalice. That Tolt would botch the mass didn't matter because Benes wouldn't live to tell.

Staib gauged that Benes, were he led out onto the lawn soon enough, should collapse on the grass about half way between the Palace and his armored car. His eyes brightened as the colonel emerged from the vehicle and strode toward him purposefully with the major at his side.

He felt stirrings of the high that would come if the audience failed to satisfy Tolt's expectations.

Tolt dazzled Benes with the force of his will and the sweep of his accomplishments as Reichsfuhrer.

It all started when Monsignor Schmehr, wishing to confirm Benes' virulent neo-Nazism, asked if Hitler was divinely inspired. "If Hitler were alive today," he probed, "would you serve him or God?"

"Serving Hitler, Archbishop, would be serving God," Benes stated, diplomatically, he thought.

"But if you had to choose?" Tolt asked. "What then?"

Benes was nonplussed. The conversation was going in the wrong direction. If he answered "Hitler," how could he expect to get the archbishop's blessing for his regime? *Do I have to kiss his ass to get blessed?* he wondered.

Tolt's eyes suddenly blazed. "Answer my question, Colonel!" he demanded.

Something about the way he pronounced "colonel" seemed demeaning, Benes judged. Maybe the invitation to come here today was a trap of some kind. The promised blessing was the bait but the archbishop wasn't going to give it to him after all, judging from the man's demeanor, Benes concluded, preparing to storm from the room.

Damned if I'll kowtow to this churchman, of all people. What the hell can he do to me? I'm the chief of state here! "I have chosen Hitler!" he snapped defiantly.

To the colonel's amazement, Tolt sprang to his feet. On signal, Staib drew the heavy drapes and Tolt let his archbishop's cloak slip to the floor, revealing the black and white SS-Reichsfuhrer's uniform in every detail from Hitler Germany's highest decoration worn at the throat to the polished black knee-length boots.

"I am the Fuhrer's hand-picked successor," he barked.

Benes gasped. "Fuhrer!" he breathed.

Tolt imparted a short history of the Kohorte and administered the Oath Unto Death, to which Benes swore.

Afterward, Tolt sat behind his desk with his face electric with force and determination.

"What must you have to win this war in a few short weeks?" he asked. "Consider your response carefully, *Reich Marshal* Benes. Be succinct."

The colonel was dumbfounded to be called that but quickly composed himself and took a moment's thought.

"Five things," he said. "Money to pay my soldiers, fuel reserves for my tanks and aircraft, radar-controlled anti-aircraft guns to shoot down Peralta's planes when they attack ground targets, at least a dozen MiG 21 fighter aircraft, with ordnance supplies . . . and," he seemed to be hesitating about the fifth item, "the cooperation of Nicaragua in using its radar sites to track and report on Peralta's aircraft, from the very moment they take to the air until we can shoot them down."

Tolt studied him, leaning forward and scowling. "Is that all?" he demanded.

"It will be sufficient, Reichsfuhrer. With these things I could defeat Peralta's forces in fairly short order. With only the first four, it may take six months."

"You shall have all five," Tolt assured him.

"But Reichsfuhrer, how can you bend the Nicaraguans to your will?"

"My unshakable will," Tolt told him, his eyes ablaze, "is irresistible. My followers there will commandeer the radar installations."

It was the first that Staib heard of such a thing. He raised his eyebrows, thought better of it, and relaxed. From past experience, he could surmise Tolt meant they had the necessary *mordida* to bribe the relevant officers of the Nicaraguan military. *Yes,* Staib thought, *and have them train Kohorte personnel and turn the sites over to us.*

"What about the blessing?" Benes asked. "A photograph of the acting archbishop blessing the head of state would help dispel the scurrilous La Pantera propaganda my forces contend with daily."

Tolt was impassive. "All in good time, Reich Marshal. I walk a delicate line with the Vatican, you know."

"I see, yes. Of course," Benes said.

What he did not see then was that he had surrendered his independence and become a vassal of SS-General Werner Tolt, who now wore the mantle of military leader of Costa Verde as well as his archbishop's mantle.

Tolt and Staib watched from the steps of the Archbishop's Palace as Benes' column of armored vehicles rumbled away, trailing thin clouds of diesel exhaust. As the army left the area, police directed traffic in the streets and the Plaza sprang to life again.

"Reich Mar . . . shal?" Staib snickered. "Only the buffoon Hermann Goering ever had that title."

"That's true," Tolt said. "However, when you read a man's inner needs as I do, you know when flattery will succeed. Besides," he said, "he's Reich Marshal of Costa Verde only, and he cannot tell a living soul of his new title." Tolt smiled thinly. "Titles cost nothing, Staib. Still, you must remember Colonel Benes is no fool. The man has an incisive military mind."

"Why did you do it? Why did you reveal yourself?"

"There's a war to be won, Sturmbannfuhrer," Tolt said. "I cannot risk these Peraltas upsetting Case Green because of their little private war of revenge on the local military. I must crush them!"

"Remember what the World War I French Premier Georges Clemenceau said, Staib."

"Reichsfuhrer?"

"Clemenceau said, 'War is too important to leave to the generals.'"

FORTY-ONE

Burton seldom came to the Company's headquarters anymore unless summoned for a meeting and had long since surrendered his office on the sixth floor, where the lions and tigers held forth. Truman found him in one of the "hotel room" offices maintained on the fifth floor for visitors. "Let's get some lunch, a good one," he said, "get the hell out of here a couple of hours."

Burton shut down his laptop. "It isn't even eleven."

"Goddammit, Bill. Rank has its privileges, doesn't it? How long have we worked here, thirty years?"

"Well, since you put it that way."

Truman drove. He felt drained of energy and not a little queasy about confronting Bill directly. But there wasn't an alternative anymore. The cash deposited to the Zurich account registered in Burton's name—the scary deposits, Truman called them—hadn't produced a noticeable effect, if indeed Bill noticed. Of course, if he was innocent he wouldn't. But if the Zurich account was his little secret, and what they deposited to spook him really spooked him, he sure wasn't letting on. At best, the scary deposits increased the pressure in Burton's psychological hydraulic system; at worst, it wasted eight thou of the Company's money, as Gretchen believed.

It stopped raining by the time they reached the nearby on-ramp and took I-95 toward Washington, with Truman driving a motor pool Ford Taurus instead of calling up his chauffeured government Cadillac.

"I want a decent martini and some blue point oysters," he said, as mud from a truck ahead clouded the windshield. He cleared it with a long spray of blue washer fluid that left its own smear. "Why can't they just fill the thing with water," he opined, "like I put in Sarah's car?"

"Risk has rewards," said Burton, who liked playing the philosopher. "It's why the Company always goes first class. You know that, pal."

"I guess, but today's binge is on me personally."

"What's the occasion?"

Truman let a moment pass before answering. "It's been, what, almost four years since Peggy died? I wanted to talk to you about how you're doing these days."

"This is a performance review?"

"I don't know." Truman glanced at him. "I feel I still have a friend I really care about, but I don't have a sure-handed ball player, not like the old days."

"We were the best," Burton said. "Butch and Sundance. But, hell, we're old guys now, and still on our game."

Truman resented the ploy; get him to admit we're all slowing down at our age. *Bill is like that,* he thought, and noticed his own hands gripping the wheel tighter. He willed them to relax.

"I'm still the best, Bill. It's you we're discussing." He said this with a twinkle in his voice, regaining the initiative. "Let your hair down, won't you, *amigo?*"

Burton didn't answer, unusual for him. With the passing minutes and miles—they took the George Washington Expressway paralleling the Potomac, heading for the Key Bridge and Georgetown—he wondered if he shouldn't just get Truman to drop him off at his apartment in the Watergate after their wet lunch, and pick him up in the morning.

He broke the silence when they turned from the bridge onto N Street in Georgetown. "I miss Peggy more than I can say. It doesn't seem like four years, more like last month, really. Evenings are the hardest. I keep expecting her to be there, then I'll get into a book or something and another morning rolls around."

"Does it help, being in Mexico City? You could base here just as well, reverse the situation, if you like."

"Maybe when I retire I'll settle here, I dunno. Right now Mexico works best, since I'm in South America a dozen times a year."

Truman drew up in front of 1789, one of his favorite restaurants, and gave the car to the valet, a college kid with a textbook in one hand and a red vest over his print shirt. As Burton went to the men's, Truman slipped fifty dollars to the maître d', asking for no one to be seated next to them. When Burton returned they were seated in a corner and ordered Plymouth gin martinis and blue points. Burton took in the walls, which were literally covered with framed prints and art work, the heavy linen and fine crystal, and the air of timeless gentility.

"To spies like us," he toasted. "Ever see the movie, with Chevy Chase? *Spies Like Us?*"

Truman shook his head. "What kind of spies are we, Bill?" His tone required an answer, but if Burton was nonplussed it was hard to tell, as he waxed enthusiastic about the movie.

"I'm serious, Bill."

Burton looked him in the eye. "I'm an older, tireder spy, but I'm a smarter one. I work smart these days."

"I didn't like your relationship with Colonel Benes when I first learned of it, and I like it a lot less now. The man's obviously on some-body's payroll, as was the G-mo before him. Yet you seem to be pretty cavalier about the whole situation. Your attitude worries me."

"Oh, hell, T-Square, it's just Costa Verde, for crying out loud. It's a comic opera country with comic opera locals. Loosen up a little, okay? After Benes there'll be another, then another."

"Your job, Bill, is to find out who the puppeteer is down there, and there is a puppeteer, for sure. If you can't or won't penetrate the German influence and find him, then I'll find someone who will."

The waiter checked in and they ordered another round, with the smoked salmon appetizer, and asked for menus.

"What do you mean saying I won't, like I'm bucking orders or something?"

Truman tasted his drink and decided to let fly. "The old Sundance would pants those Krauts in a New York minute and give me a count of the hairs on their asses, that's what I mean. So I'm wondering, is there something that explains your `Mister Nice Guy, Finishing Last' routine?"

"Like what, for chrissake?"

"You tell me."

"Like you think I'm on the payroll in San Marcos too?"

"Are you?"

Burton didn't answer. Pledges or denials would be irrelevant. But the message was received: Don't Screw with Uncle T-Square.

Truman eyed him stonily. *No point,* he thought, *in telling Bill that Holloway was alive, had framed him.* Bill would deny they were in league, and there wasn't a comeback for that. Truman shifted the subject. "I checked," he said, "and there's no record of any priests defecting from East Germany in 1989 or thereabouts. London, Berlin, even Moscow, haven't a clue. These birds could be phony, Bill."

"Aw, come on, T-Square. Priests are, well, priests." He stirred the air with his hand. "A priest-is-a-priest-is-a-priest, for chrissake. This is what I mean about working smart. Why waste a minute's time playing an intergalactic long shot like that?" He toyed with his saucer. "The way I figure it, these guys slip into the West, through Sweden, say, and end up in Mexico City for a year or two before they go to Costa Verde. You know as well as I that the Mexican authorities didn't keep track of did-dly-squat then. That's why we and Ivan both used Mexico City as the

302

place to introduce human assets into the hemisphere. Besides, what do you want me to do about it, pants them, too?"

Truman smiled. Nothing to be gained by saying Holloway fingered the priests at the cathedral, he decided.

"You could check it out with the Church."

"Not me, T-Square. If you want to go ahead and piss off Foggy Bottom, just be my guest."

They both knew the State Department jealously guarded its proprietary rights in the Vatican's unique status as a nation state.

"Well, I'll turn to State, if there's no other way."

Burton snorted. "Oh, that'll be one for the books. I can't wait for her private Papal audience."

Secretary of State Sarah Wasserman was a suspected lightweight who reminded some people of Betty Boop.

"'Say, Popesy,'" Burton mimicked, "'be a dear, won't you? Please rat on those awful meanies the Company's got such a thing about these days, Boop-Boop-A-Doop. You know, dearie, the creepy ones with the Kraut accents?'"

Truman laughed, letting Burton off the hook, which was good for business. He touched his coffee cup to Burton's. "Say, why don't I drop you off at the Watergate now, and we'll drive in together in the morning?"

"Thought you'd never ask."

When they pulled into the circular driveway at the Watergate and Burton got out, he stuck his head back into the car before closing the door.

"I'll find your puppeteer for you, Terry," he said.

The man was lying. Truman knew it as soon as it poured from Burton's jolly lips. Well, maybe it wasn't a lie as such but he was buying time.

Truman was disappointed in himself as he drove home. He had thought that he could sense if Burton was off the reservation, but he had to admit to himself now that he really couldn't.

FORTY-TWO

ARTURO HUNG'S APARTMENT, SAN MARCOS

Mallory was startled by the sat-phone ringing in his pocket as he dozed on the sofa. "Hello Captain, T-Square here. Can you talk to me?"

"Yeah," he said, trying to wake fully. "I'm with one of Peralta's lieutenants."

"Good," Truman continued. "Don't worry. Our conversation is secure. What's happening down there?"

Mallory related his experiences at the border and acquiring and losing the tail.

"Good," Truman said, "stay out of sight now. Look, I called for another reason but first I want you to know the assets are now in place to get your son and the others out of Number Five. Our SOF people have achieved interoperability with a detachment of Carlos' forces. They're set for a GO in about seventy-two hours."

"That's great!" Mallory was joyous. "I sure hope you do good jail-breaks."

"The very best. Now here's the reason I called. I know you unlocked the Holloway thing for me and I'm much more than grateful for that." He paused. "But I still have an unresolved problem down there, one that just won't go away. I've been in this game long enough to learn to rely on my hunches, and I've got this niggling feeling we haven't really gotten to the bottom of things with Holloway. I mean, things don't add up, like itches you can't scratch."

"In what way?"

"For one thing," Truman continued, "Gretchen Reece, here at Langley, and Bill Burton, who you know about, are at odds about those priests at the cathedral, and I'm having a hell of a time trying to get to the truth. Gretchen checked them out with the Vatican, and they have a clean bill of health. She went through all the right channels and was told they're legitimate as hell. They escaped East Germany before the Wall came down, got retrained as administrators and sent to Costa Verde due to a lack of trained administrators there."

Mallory grunted, and waited for him to finish.

"On the other hand," Truman said, "Burton reports that General Fritz-Julius Karpf has been seen entering the archbishop's quarters but not leaving, as if on extended visits. He apparently stays days at a time."

"Okay," Mallory said, "he sounds German to me but what's the cause for alarm?"

"General Karpf is the former head of Stasi, the State Security Police in Communist East Germany, their equivalent of the Gestapo. He's a known butcher, so why the hell is he sleeping over at the cathedral?"

Mallory's eyebrows shot up involuntarily. "Holy Toledo!"

"Not only that," Truman continued, "but Jack Franck told me on the sly that Burton was observed entering the archbishop's quarters at the Cathedral. Of course, Bill claims he was snooping, pretending to be a staunch Catholic interested in learning something about the local Church."

Mallory sensed what was coming. "Look, T-Square, I'm really just a Naval Aviator, remember? I've done the TAD you got me assigned to accomplish."

"Relax, Captain. I want you to do something for me all right, but I'm not going to risk putting your ass on the line again. What I want is just real, real simple."

"I'm listening."

"I'm going to use the diplomatic pouch to send you a couple of state-of-the-art bugs to be planted in the archbishop's office complex. It should really be handled by a trained field operative, but you're smart enough to read the instructions and train someone to use them."

Mallory bristled. "Now hold on, T-Square. I delivered the goods on Holloway, as ordered, but no way am I going to be part of some half-assed Watergate burglary against the Church, even though I think the archbishop and the others are phony-baloney. I just told you I've got a tail, one I hope I've shaken for the time being. I'm going to lay low for a while until I know David's free."

"Now please hold on, Captain," Truman said. "I wouldn't dream of asking you do this personally. There must be someone you can trust. One of Peralta's sympathizers sharp enough to do it right, innocuous enough not to be noticed. A cleaning woman, someone delivering laundry. Whatever. These bugs are half the size of the battery in your watch. It'll be like putting a wad of gum under your desk in grammar school. The receiver is built into a Sony Walkman and the range of the bugs is more than a mile. You can put it in the hands of someone you trust."

"What's the duration of the tape?" Mallory asked, suddenly wishing he hadn't.

"The digital recorder and batteries will capture everything that's audible for a couple of weeks. We should know by then whether anything's going on with those priests.

"I can have this stuff there tomorrow, delivered to the Naval Attaché at the Embassy with instructions to get the package to you. How about it, Captain? Do you think you can find someone to do the job for me?"

Mallory was momentarily shaken by the thought of participating in yet another undercover episode. He got up and looked out the window for the tan Chevy.

"Deke, are you there?" Truman asked.

"Yeah, I'm here. Okay, so it's unfinished business from my Holloway gig, I suppose. Look, I'll try to get it done somehow, but it's obvious I have to keep a low profile."

"Well, for God's sake, just stay out of sight."

"I'll be here with Arturo for the time being, but I'll need some cash for this caper."

"Right. This is going to pay off, believe me. By the way, some Glenlivet will be in the pouch, too."

"Okay, T-Square, but what the hell are you doing about the Vatican situation? I don't care what they told what's her name. Gretchen? It's a bunch of bullshit!"

Truman paused. "Look, Deke. We haven't one shred of evidence against these people. The Church in Rome vouches for them. That's what the bugging is all about. Get me some evidence, Captain, and I may try to get Secretary of State Wassermann to make inquiries at a higher level."

"I hope she has a good bullshit detector. Anyway, thanks for filling me in on the prison raid."

He turned the phone off and sat staring at the floor. Looking up, he saw Arturo handing him a beer.

"Sounds like you could use this."

Mallory nodded and downed a healthy gulp. He related the conversation to Arturo.

"Bugging the bastards sounds great," Arturo said.

"Okay, it's a good idea but I'm holed up here. So how do I find somebody to plant the things?"

FORTY-THREE

THE WHITE HOUSE

Truman stirred to consciousness in a wingback chair in the first family's upstairs living room in the Executive Mansion. The room was dark except for a crack of light showing under the door to the hallway outside. He figured he had dozed off for a few minutes while awaiting the President's late-night return from a senatorial campaign fund-raiser in Miami. The First Lady was away on another of her trips to China. The Presidential helicopter, "Marine One," must have landed on the South Lawn, as he could hear its rotors spooling down. He shifted the First Cat from his lap to the floor, switched on the lamp next to his chair, and blinked the hands of his watch into focus. 2:20 A.M. The President would probably get a five-minute news briefing before coming upstairs to bed. Truman's mind returned to the Burton question as he waited. He blew out his breath and shook his head. The problem remained that other than Mallory and Foxlee, he didn't know who to trust anymore. If Burton was disloyal as Gretchen alleged—or if she was suspect as Burton claimed—either way Truman was going to have to solve the equation himself with only Mallory's help. He was sure of one thing: if a traitor flourished at the highest level, he still couldn't confide in his own people lest the merest echo carry to the miscreant.

He knew the key lay with Holloway, the human junction box all the wiring ran through. Yes, Mallory had found him and made him talk, but there had to be still more to the story. Truman's fingers drummed the chair-side table as he organized his thoughts. Holloway kicked off the whole imbroglio by accusing Burton of a tête-à-tête with the Generalissimo and possibly with the Kohorte as a consequence. But he told Mallory that he set Burton up. And, despite Holloway's confession, the fiery dart he had shot at Burton was corroborated by Gretchen's information from the Jeweler that the dictator was on scholarship from the Kohorte and had bought Burton in turn. Of course, Burton alleged that Gretchen was the one running the Zurich mystery man. To top everything off, this afternoon the Jeweler had returned a million-dollar fee from the Company, totally reversing field and now claiming that he couldn't verify the existence of any such thing as a Kohorte. Truman's brow furrowed as he contemplated that one. Was the Jeweler a member of the Kohorte? Was Gretchen? He was back to square one, and square one was still his one-time protégé Wade Holloway. True enough, Mallory's mission was a giant breakthrough, but questions remained—questions that Truman would have to ask Holloway personally.

First, there was an item of business to attend to here tonight. He heard footsteps in the hallway. The door opened and the President entered, wearing a rumpled tuxedo. His black tie was undone and dangled from his collar. The sound of Marine One lifting off filled the room.

"Aw, shit, T-Square, not again?" Foxlee flashed a weak version of his campaign smile, dumped himself onto the sofa and began pulling off his shoes. "It's been a long day, for chrissake. What's the matter this time?"

"Do you remember Mallory, the Naval Aviator you spoke with on the phone when I met him on Willard Cabot's boat?

"Of course I do. He carded me, remember?"

"He accomplished what we asked. He located my disappeared station chief and," Truman smiled, "pretty much cut him a new one. Scared the shit out of him and got the confession I needed."

"Good. So can I go to sleep now?"

Being de-facto national security advisor to five Presidents, and a fly fisherman himself, taught Truman about waiting for an invitation to proceed before setting the hook. And knowing a President's likes and dislikes was more than a little helpful.

Foxlee was removing his cufflinks when a waiter entered and quietly set two places on the coffee table. Another served Eggs Benedict with rye toast, returning with a silver bowl filled with cracked ice and long-neck bottles of beer.

The President grinned. "Now, why didn't I think of this?" he said, surveying his favorite meal. He stopped massaging his feet and swung them off the sofa to reach for the bottle opener.

"All right, T-Square, you win," he said. "Let's have it now. What's up at this ungodly hour?"

Truman reached for his portfolio-style briefcase, then pushed it aside. "I've got memoranda summarizing this situation, for the record, which you're not going to read at this hour. Let me cut to the chase for you.

"It's a mess in Costa Verde. Peralta's war kicked off on a sour note. He didn't gain enough tactical surprise and Colonel Benes' forces were on their toes. So it's dicey down there. In the meantime, Mallory wrung the confession from our runaway, Holloway."

"How'd he do that? Card him, too?"

Truman spun the rat yarn.

Foxlee whooped. "I've absolutely got to buy this Mallory character a drink. Arrange it some time, will you? But what's the deal? Is your man Burton a sell-out or what?" The President was warming to the spy stuff that always piqued his interest. He quaffed his beer.

"Don't know yet, sir. Mixed signals so far. Not Mallory's fault, of course."

"So what the hell's the crisis?"

"It's good you're sitting down, sir." Truman patted his lips with a napkin. "I think Nazis, masquerading as priests in Costa Verde, are buying control of the country. If they're not stopped right now, you're going to have a Fourth Reich on your hands, albeit a small one so far."

Foxlee carefully set his fork and knife aside and toyed with his beer bottle. "This is the most cockamamie fantasy I've ever heard, T-Square, and I've told some whoppers myself." He stared at Truman. Stare suddenly turned to glare. "Prove it, goddammit!"

Truman had been to the brink with other presidents and none ever stared him down. He wasn't about to let Foxlee succeed. "Can't prove everything yet, Mister President," he said quietly. "But here are some facts." He balled his fist close enough to Foxlee's face to remind him that he was no pushover. "*One,*" out popped his thumb, "there is nothing that's important to Costa Verde's economy that German nationals haven't bought and paid for in the last two, three years. *Two,*" he extended his forefinger, "the national cathedral is rife with German priests. At least they claim to be clergy! It's time to involve the Vatican at the diplomatic level."

Foxlee erupted. He was a Catholic, too. "What the hell do you mean, 'claim'?" He side-armed a beer cap at the wastebasket across the room. It went straight in.

Truman withdrew his fist and started over. "Mister President, this is an unprecedented situation. We now have two sources implicating the German priests at the cathedral in a scheme to fund the military governments that have ruled Costa Verde since Edwardo Peralta was toppled from power."

The President held up his hand. "Now wait a minute," he said. "You're telling me there's more than Holloway?"

"Holloway and a man we call the Jeweler." He thumb-nailed the Jeweler's contribution to the black world of secret intelligence.

"Why can't the Company get the skinny on this? And don't tell me my CIA is ignorant of the Church as a world power." The tone was sarcastic.

Truman reacted calmly. "Yes, the Vatican has nation-state status under a treaty originally cut with Mussolini's foreign minister, and in

that sense she's fair game for espionage, like any other foreign power."
He paused. His demeanor was now fully over to the presidential advisor end of the scale. "Do you want your presidential legacy to include spying on the Church?"

Foxlee bit his lip. "Hell, no. So what do we do?"

"I recommend that Secretary of State Wasserman herself make discrete inquiry of the Vatican Secretary of State, just between the two of them. He's fluent in English."

"What'll she say? The Pope's got Dirty Nazi Rats under his skirt?"

"She'll say we have some disturbing intel that the acting archbishop and members of his staff could be impostors. Ask for assurances, that's all."

"They'll think we've lost it."

"I doubt it, sir. Not if she emphasizes our motives are to protect the Church as much as our own interests."

The two fell silent as the majestic John Quincy Adams clock across the room expropriated valuable time for its clarion announcement. Three A.M.

"Excuse me, sir," Truman said, glaring at the clock. "How can you live with that damn thing?"

"You get used to it," Foxlee snorted, swigging the last of his beer. "I just let Mister Adams remind me to pause on the hour to gather perspective. Now, you were saying what?"

"Colonel Benes is a figurehead, sir."

"Right," the President interrupted, "you've told me that before." He weighed the risks in his mind. The potential for a quiet embarrassment in Rome was acceptable. A Nazi Costa Verde as part of his legacy wasn't. "All right, we'll just nip this thing in the bud. You brief Wasserman first thing. I'll see her at the Cabinet meeting at eleven and I'll stress that it's top priority. Problem is, her heavy travel schedule may be hard to rearrange."

"That's why I intruded tonight, sir. I'm hoping she'll work Rome into her Middle Eastern junket later this week."

As he headed for the elevator and the Secret Service sedan waiting to take him home, Truman wondered if anyone was capable of unraveling the imbroglio in Costa Verde.

CENTRAL AMERICA

The next day Truman slipped out of the country aboard a Navy C-20 Gulfstream based at Naval Air Facility, Washington, D.C. When they had landed at Panama's former Howard AFB, he boarded the Embassy Flight, an Air Force C-130 that hopped from one Central American capital to another, making its daily rounds like a UPS truck, picking up and depositing personnel and couriers with their diplomatic pouches.

He had boarded carrying a diplomatic passport, attaché case chained to his wrist, the very rumpled embodiment of a slightly bored State Department courier new to the Central America run. If there should be a real courier aboard assigned to the embassy in Managua, Truman might be asked what he was doing on the flight, too. To his relief, the couriers seemed to be a tight little clique who, as soon as they were airborne, concentrated on a nonstop game of hearts.

Left to himself with nothing to do but look out the window and think his own thoughts, Truman was soon asleep.

He awoke as the pilot reduced power and Lake Managua came into view, looking like a chocolate milk spill in the school cafeteria. *Ugly damn thing,* he thought. It matched his ugly mood.

He felt sick about the fact that his own reputation, built on more than thirty years' public service, rested in the hands of a snake like Holloway. His visions of picking up his Medal of Freedom at a White House Rose Garden ceremony in a couple of years and retiring happily to Maryland's Eastern Shore was slipping away like mist on a hot morning, ever since this nightmare began. He thought of Richard Nixon, who retired to the shadows all because of a silly mistake that wiped out one of the most important Presidential records of the century.

Would his own career end in bitterness like Nixon's? All because a man whom he trusted, his smiling protégé Holloway, turned rotten? Wade Holloway had screwed him, plain and simple. Truman scowled and closed his eyes.

The little sonofabitch owes his whole career to me and then, without so much as a single qualm in all likelihood, he turns and bites the hand feeding him.

He heaved a sigh as the plane banked and began its approach to the airport on the outskirts of Managua. He tightened his seat belt and continued watching out the window as details of the city came into view. As the C-130 touched down on the runway, he loosened his seat belt a little and gripped the attaché case.

He wondered what the inveterate card players would think if they knew all he was carrying was old newspapers as dunnage for a silenced Browning 9 mm automatic.

When the engines stopped, he went forward and reminded the pilots that they were to pick him up later in the day on their return leg from Honduras, El Salvador and Guatemala.

DOWNTOWN MANAGUA

Truman experienced some misgivings as he walked along the sidewalk on one of the main shopping streets. He knew he probably shouldn't be doing this kind of thing. He was too old to play the hit man. He was never trained to do it anyway. His side of the intelligence street was the sunny one where well-groomed men in business suits and hand-made ties met in paneled conference rooms, and the best of them rubbed shoulders with White House staffers and presidents. *Too late for regrets now,* he thought, as he spotted his destination and crossed the street.

The Hotel Corona was indeed as Mallory had described it—dusty, rusty, seedy, and in dire need of air freshener this morning. He entered the lobby and immediately catalogued the inhabitants: a couple of scruffy gringos trying to negotiate a lower room rate in their high school Spanish, which they had probably flunked, and a handful of

students with backpacks exchanging news of their travels to the flesh-
pots of Latin America.

Truman blended well with the scene. He wore a rumpled, light cotton seersucker suit that looked like he had slept in it, which he had, a
wrinkled white shirt with no tie, dark glasses, and a frayed Panama
fedora that looked like a prop from a nineteen-thirties movie.

When the gringos gave up negotiations and left the hotel in a huff,
Truman walked up to the front desk and inquired as to the residency
of a John Anderson. The sleepy-eyed clerk met his inquiry with a suspicious, blank stare. The stare turned into a broad smile when he
noticed a twenty-dollar bill moving his way across the counter.

"Is he in his room, number 218?" Truman asked.

The clerk nodded, after palming the bill.

"Tell him I have a package for him," Truman growled. "I'll be in
the bar."

He headed there and was pleased to note out of the corner of his
eye that the clerk immediately swung the countertop up and scurried
toward the stairs.

The bar was not at peak capacity this early in the day. A few patrons
stared into their drinks as if they were reading tea leaves while a couple of locals argued about *futbol*. Truman ordered two local beers at the
bar. When they arrived, he paid for them, picked them up, along with a
day-old copy of the local paper, and headed for a table in the far corner. He took a seat facing the door to the lobby, placed the second beer
on the opposite side of the table and unfolded the paper to its full
width, observing the door between the brim of his hat and the top of
the paper. After a swig of beer he saw Holloway appear in the doorway,
accompanied by the desk clerk, who pointed Truman's way. *Good grief,*
he thought. *Holloway's put on a lot of weight and in spite of the sunny cli-
mate his complexion looks like he lived in a cave.*

Holloway smiled vacantly as he started across the room. Truman figured the miscreant probably thought a courier had brought

another installment of his share of the money Hesse was ripping off from the Kohorte.

Holloway slid enthusiastically onto the empty chair but when Truman lowered his newspaper to the table, the man's eyes widened and his face suddenly took on a look of pure horror. That the legendary Truman had left the halls of Langley and the White House to come here and confront him was more of a shock than Holloway could quickly process.

"Well, now," Truman said, "if it isn't the elusive Mister Holloway, back from his helicopter ride. Before we get down to the business at hand, Sonny, you should know there's a silenced Company-issue Browning under the table, aimed at your belly button or thereabouts."

Holloway's pasty face lost its remaining color.

"I recall," Truman said, "from the medical records in your file that it's what we kids used to call an 'outie.' If you so much as stir in that chair, it will immediately become an 'innie' the size of a baseball."

Holloway squirmed in his seat and started to speak.

Truman smiled. "The *pffft* that you might hear for a split second," he said, "would not exactly be the shot heard around the world, not with all the charming rock and roll emanating from that rickety speaker that's about to fall off the wall behind us. Besides," Truman continued, "from the looks of the people in this place, I don't think anyone would really give a shit what happens to you. I know I wouldn't, after all the grief you've caused me."

The color hadn't returned to Holloway's face.

"So you will keep both of your greedy hands on the table," Truman advised, "while you tell me what I want to know in a businesslike manner." Truman kept his right hand under the table and noticed that Holloway noticed.

"I've even bought you a beer to calm your fragile nerves. Do we understand the rules?"

Holloway nodded and gulped half his beer.

With his left hand, Truman took a thin microrecorder from his shirt pocket, switched it on, and slid it under the newspaper with the microphone facing Holloway.

"The man I sent to find you reported the details of your ingenious defection, your skimming operation, and the untimely demise of your pet rodent. That was prologue, understand?

"I am here," Truman said, "to get to the real business between you and me . . . you no-good, lying, treacherous son-of-a-bitch!"

As Holloway looked up from the table, Truman's angry eyes tore through what little remained of his composure. Although he wore a short-sleeved shirt, he managed to wipe his runny eyes on his sleeve. Truman wondered how a crackerjack agent could tumble so far, and assumed drugs were involved.

"Stop whimpering, you damn fool," he said, "and tell me who else is in on this caper? Burton? Franck? Who?"

Holloway gulped the rest of the beer. Using his left hand again, Truman pushed his nearly full beer toward him. "Here, take this, too," he said, as Holloway blew his nose and seemed to have resigned himself to the situation.

"No, Burton and Franck didn't know anything. This was my personal retirement plan."

Truman tapped the butt of the Browning on the seat of his wooden chair, loud enough for Holloway to hear it above the sound of the scratchy music.

"Bullshit!" Truman spat. "They're not stupid. It's their job to know what the people up and down the line from them do with their spare time. How could they not have known something, anything, of your activities?"

"Okay, okay," Holloway said, "maybe they had an inkling, maybe not."

"Go on."

"Okay. Franck knew that I was moving in on Hesse. Not that I had found out anything yet. Just that I suspected Hesse of not being simply an independent businessman, but of being a link between the G-Mo and the Kraut orchestra."

"And Burton?" Truman demanded, watching Holloway's eyes intently. Holloway averted his eyes.

Shit! Truman thought. *He isn't clearing Burton. He's going to damn him with faint praise. He's going to say Burton wasn't there, he was in Mexico City and—*

"Burton was in Mexico City, for crying out loud," Holloway protested. "How the hell could he have known what I was setting up with Hesse?"

Truman reached over under the table and pressed the business end of the silencer against Holloway's kneecap.

"Look me in the eye and say that," he demanded.

"I stand by what I said," Holloway said.

Truman waited. A long moment passed with Holloway looking down at the table. He hadn't looked him in the eye.

"Okay," Truman said, "tell me about the Krauts now."

"Oh, hell, they're into everything," Holloway said, brightening. "They own Aero Verde, most of the banks, and controlling interests in a dozen major enterprises."

Holloway had some names of the German business people, and spieled them off to Truman and the recorder.

Truman studied Holloway for a moment. *This is like dentistry,* he thought. *You accomplish what you can in one sitting, then schedule the next appointment.*

"All right," he said. "One last thing before I let you up, for now. What is the current disposition of all those arms shipments to Nicaragua from the former East Germany? You were supposed to be finalizing a comprehensive report on that when you disappeared, or have you forgotten?"

"You know that's a long story," Holloway said.

Truman nodded. "So tell me about it."

Holloway rambled on about the immense cache of arms from East Germany, much of which he thought was hidden in secret depots near the border with Costa Verde. Truman repeatedly interrupted to demand specificity, names of Nicaraguan officials, and places. Holloway wasn't sure of the locations but he knew the names of a clique of Nicaraguan officials who served more than one employer.

"It would have been nice," Truman said, "if, as a trusted employee of the Central Intelligence Agency, you had conveyed this information to Langley."

Holloway shrugged his shoulders.

"But, of course," Truman said, "that might have tipped me off to your exciting new career as a double agent."

Holloway was silent as he finished Truman's beer—just as she burst through the door.

She was attractive in a sloppy sort of way, with ample hips struggling within the confines of a cheap silk dress, but with shiny, raven black hair, dark flashing eyes, and an attitude worthy of the most jealous wife.

"*¡Juan! Yo he estado esperando por una hora!*" she yelled, wagging her finger at Holloway.

So she's been waiting for an hour, Truman thought. *She can wait some more. All I need right now is his Nicaraguan honey right in the thick of things.*

Holloway's face was mobile as he contemplated the possibilities of diversion.

"Don't even think about it," Truman said, brushing Holloway's knee with the gun. "Don't move, don't get up. Just tell her to get the hell right out of here. And don't forget, my Spanish is as good as yours."

Holloway turned slightly as she hovered above the table. "*¡Vayase, Consuelo! ¡Inmediatamente!*"

Consuelo seemed to wilt on the spot.

"*Pero Juan . . .*"

Holloway pointed toward the door to the lobby.

"*¡Ahora mismo, Consuelo!*"

320

Consuelo slowly turned and headed back to the lobby.

"You certainly have a way with the ladies," Truman said, with a forced smile.

Holloway stared down at the table again.

"Continue your report," Truman said.

"I think you know everything else," Holloway said.

"That's it?"

"Yeah."

Truman leaned forward and studied Holloway's newly baggy eyes. *Is he telling all? Of course not.* Once he made the basic choice to cooperate, albeit at gunpoint, bits and pieces of information became his bargaining chips and he would try to spend them carefully. Truman nodded as Holloway gazed back at him, calmer now but without the presence of a man in control of anything. Truman had learned as much as he could in one session, but he still wanted to know what happened to the airfields and state-of-the-art radar installations the Soviets built here in Nicaragua. Were they operational? If so, what use was being made of them today? More importantly, who controlled them, the legitimate Nicaraguan military or renegade commanders?

"All right," Truman said, "that'll do for your premier lounge act appearance. But this ain't Vegas, kid, and you damn well better work some quality new material into your next performance or this particular critic could be filing some rather nasty reviews about your act!"

"Understood," Holloway said with a smile, pretending to display his old confidence but failing the attempt.

"Then get your ass into gear," Truman told him, "and find out everything there is to know these days about those radar sites. I assume you remember the importance of the radar sites? They paint the whole damn region down here. Or are you having a lapse of memory due to the excitement of seeing your Uncle T-Square again?"

"Yeah, I remember them."

Truman used his left hand to reach under the newspaper on the table, find the recorder, and unload the tape of their conversation. He dropped it into his jacket pocket, and handed Holloway a small parcel wrapped in brown paper. "Here's more batteries and tape for the recorder. I recommend you use it. Religiously. I want chapter and verse on the remaining East German arms, the radar sites in particular. Just mail the tapes to the address in the packet and I'll get them."

He slid the package across the table. Holloway looked at it, but did not attempt to pick it up.

"Your marching orders are as before," Truman continued. "You say nothing. You do nothing. You keep playing the game with Hesse as if nothing has changed. If the info you've given me checks out and I get the straight scoop on the arms and the radars—and you continue to cooperate—you'll get to retire in Argentina or wherever as planned. Not with quite as much money as you wanted, but with an amount you'll consider a godsend under the circumstances."

Holloway gazed at him with a sour look on his face. "You must think you've made me an offer I can't refuse."

He grimaced in pain as Truman raked the Browning across his shins just as hard as he could.

"It's not so bad," Truman said, "when you consider the alternative. Which . . . I believe you know the term."

"Yeah," Holloway sighed. "Termination by the Company."

Truman had had enough.

"Pick up the recorder and supplies, and put them into your pocket. We are going to get up from the table now and walk slowly," Truman paused for emphasis, "and amiably, to the lobby. Don't forget the Browning in my pocket.

"I will leave this half-star hotel and simply vanish into thin air, as is my custom. You will immediately go upstairs to your room. And when you see the charming Consuelo," Truman told him, as they passed into the lobby, "you can explain you were about to close the biggest and most important deal you ever made in your life. Perhaps she can rejoice in the fact that, due to your skilled negotiations, you may have a chance of making it."

322

FORTY-FOUR

THE VATICAN

Guilianni bear-hugged Albert, nearly lifting him off the floor, then stepped back to survey his assistant. "No, no, you must not doubt at all," the little man beamed. "The Holy Father's judgment is infallible in these matters too."

Albert was more than flustered. "Well, I think," he managed to say, smiling weakly, "it's carrying the doctrine of Papal Infallibility a little too far." He was numb inside. "Tell me again, please. I don't think I heard what you said, after that first part."

"All right, my friend. But first we shall celebrate with some of my fine port and a Cuban cigar."

Guilianni led the way to the terrace of his apartment, where the two sat under an umbrella table surrounded by Vatican buildings and the gardens below. He poured them port and produced the cigars from his cassock. "His Holiness feels strongly the next Pope should be German. That's all there is to it, Siegfried. Of course, he can't very well pick his successor but he can certainly influence the thinking. He wants a suitable candidate created a cardinal, to be available when the time comes. You're his first choice. So you are to become Archbishop of Dresden for just a few months, then you will be created Siegfried Cardinal Albert."

Guilianni beamed. "As a cardinal you will succeed me as Secretary of State right here in Rome."

Albert confronted his friend. "Did you have anything to do with this?"

"Only in the sense I'm God's humble servant."

"But what's to be your place now?" Albert asked.

"Oh, I shall remain His Holiness' principal confidant and up to my old tricks, of course, except for relations with foreign states, which shall be yours. A role, I must say, you are eminently qualified to take up. We both know you've been acting the part, lacking only the titular embell- ishment for several years now."

"That's true. But why in the world does His Holiness want a German successor? And why me of all people? I'm not even a bishop, much less an archbishop. I've never even been a parish priest."

"New times call for new solutions, Siegfried. A thorough grasp of developing international relations will be far more essential than in the past. Also, your grasp of Vatican politics," his eyes twinkled as he said 'Vatican politics,' "equals your knowledge of our State Department. This is a world, and a Church, racing headlong into untested waters. It's no time for a traditional Pope who's content to play a fatherly role. As for the choice of a German, well . . . that's simple. There's never been a German Pope. Luther didn't help the situation, of course, nor did the Kaiser or Hitler. But the years have passed, and Germany is a powerful and free country now."

"So why me?" Albert accepted a relight. He had barely smoked the Cuban while trying to cope with the startling situation. "And what about my heart? Isn't the Holy Father afraid of my dying on him unexpectedly?"

"Oh, His Holiness was briefed privately by your specialists. They all assured him your angiogram and stress–echo cardiogram results are superb, that you were merely a victim of passing stress. In fact, they assured the Holy Father that you're a better risk than someone who hasn't undergone the exhaustive testing and may have undiagnosed arterial disease." He clinked his glass against Albert's. "So, you see, it's just a simple question of age before beauty, old friend . . . your age and His Holiness'. Consideration of the Holy Father's life expectancy and yours means that you would likely be an interim Pope, serving a few vital years, giving the Church an opportunity to reorient itself to the future."

Albert chuckled. "So I'm to be a tip of the hat to Germany before the Church picks another Italian, as it almost always does?"

"You can think of it that way if you like." Guilianni put down his glass. "You will become Archbishop of Dresden early next year. Poor Archbishop Moulders isn't expected to live out the month, I'm afraid. Once installed, in a very public ceremony at Dresden Cathedral, you'll return here at once at His Holiness' request. A year or so after that you are to be created a cardinal, to remain here permanently. It's all quite simple. Of course, there's no guarantee you'll be Pope eventually. But you will be one of four or five leading candidates and the only one with His Holiness' blessing, you can be sure of that much."

Albert flushed the toilet and watched the contents of the cream of tartare bottle disappear in a milky swirl. As he undressed for bed he solemnly promised God he would do the same when Staib sent him more of the drug, and he prayed for strength to keep off the stuff. Afterward he managed to complete his private devotions for the first time in weeks, but he found he couldn't sleep. "God, what are you thinking of?" he muttered as he tossed in bed. "You are always in control. You see everything, don't you? You are the One who puts down one man and raises up another.

"How could I, serving both good and evil at the same time, become heir to Saint Peter? Or is there another possibility, a horrible, more terrifying possibility? You told your disciples that they were clean, but not all of them, for you knew that Judas was betraying you. . . .

"Am I heir to Judas? Dear Christ, please give me some kind of a sign, and deliver me. In your mercy, rescue me from the eternal damnation I deserve."

FORTY-FIVE

ARTURO'S APARTMENT

Arturo broke eggs into a skillet and was about to scramble them when he lifted the pan from the stove and turned to face Mallory, who was seated at the dinette table. "Hey, it just hit me! It'll be a piece of cake!"

Mallory frowned. "There's no free lunch and there's no piece of cake. What's going to be a piece of cake?"

"Planting the bugs, of course. Look, I've got a friend from the university. Guillermo. He can he trusted. His old man owns *Fumigacion Superior.* That's the largest pest control company in the city. They do all the big buildings. I'm betting they service the cathedral since I know his mom's a heavy-duty Catholic lay leader."

"Okay," Mallory said, "what the hell, go for it. Find out if they do the cathedral, but don't tell your friend what we're up to. I'll want to meet this Guillermo guy."

The three of them met at a cantina around the corner from Arturo's apartment. Guillermo was short and heavy set, and Mallory liked what he saw in the young man's eyes.

"Arturo told me you're a close friend of the Peraltas, *Señor* Mallory," Guillermo said. "That's good enough for me. What can I do for you?"

Mallory questioned him about his background and made the decision to tell him about the plan.

"Hey, I can definitely plant your devices," Guillermo said. "I did the Archbishop's Palace myself once."

Mallory was tempted by the offer. He took a sip of his beer. "No," he said, "I want to get in there myself."

Guillermo thought for a moment and drew a simple floor plan on a paper place mat, showing the quarters and offices of the priests. "Most of the living quarters are on the first floor," he said. "That's what you call the second story in the States. All the rooms open onto a porch overlooking the garden. The archbishop's quarters are in the corner of the building. It's actually a whole wing of the palace." He paused and looked up from the floor plan. "My mother attends mass at the cathedral every morning," he said. "She says that old Father Juan and the other parish priests attached to the cathedral don't like the archbishop and his staff, but since they no longer have any real authority they keep pretty much to themselves these days."

Arturo shrugged as Mallory nodded.

"Anyway," Guillermo continued, "I found out that we did the parish priests' quarters last month. You can say you'll only be doing the archbishop's wing this time. Mention that the company will call to schedule the cathedral itself for next month." He pointed to the floor plan again. "The service entrance to the Palace is here. We just drive up and ring the bell and someone, usually the butler, lets us in. You should start in the basement but you won't want to plant any bugs there. Just kill a few minutes there, then come up to the first floor and take this hallway, here, to the quarters of the archbishop and his staff."

Mallory traced the route with his finger.

"I'll take you there in a company truck but I don't think I should wait for you. I'll need to get the truck back before anyone misses it. Arturo can pick you up on his new Honda when you're finished."

Guillermo looked worried all of a sudden.

"You don't have to do this, you know," Mallory said.

"No," he said, "I want to. It's just that the company will hear of this eventually, and I'll have to know nothing about it. I don't like lying."

"Hey," Arturo said, "if we return the sprayer soon enough it'll just remain a mystery."

"I need to learn enough about the work so I can answer some basic questions," Mallory said, "in case I'm stopped and asked what I'm doing."

"Right," Guillermo said, "but it's really pretty simple." He described the operation of the sprayer and jotted down the names of the various pests Mallory would be spraying for and the particular chemical to be used. "For jobs like this," he said, "we spray around the baseboard and in the corners of the rooms. This chemical isn't very noticeable, unless it gets in your mucus membranes where it's dangerous as hell, so the rooms don't have to be vacated. Although we usually carry the sprayer in one hand and spray with the other, you'll want to use the back straps so you'll have a hand free to plant the bugs."

———————

When the diplomatic pouch arrived with the bugs, a young Marine from the embassy brought them to Arturo's apartment. The kid, about twenty, wore civvies and obviously didn't know what the package contained or who the recipient was. Mallory was pleased to find five thousand dollars in fifties and twenties and the promised Glenlivet.

The instructions for the bugging equipment were a masterpiece of clear technical writing and he had no difficulty understanding them at first reading. The receiver and recorder had two channels, so separate conversations could be recorded simultaneously. He felt he should be able to plant the things easily, if he found a suitable place. If he wasn't recognized. If his cover as a spider man wasn't blown. If everything went as planned. Which he knew was never the case.

THE CATHEDRAL

Mallory adjusted the coveralls over his street clothes while Guillermo drove him to the cathedral. They were a bit on the baggy side, which was good, allowing room for his sat-phone and the Browning. The name patch over the left pocket read Ricardo and the back featured Fumigacion Superior's logo. He had to assume that whoever ordered him tailed must have a photograph of him and he hoped that his ball cap and drugstore glasses would change his appearance. Exiting the van, he slung the sprayer onto his back and waited in the driveway as a chauffeur pulled the archbishop's pristine Grand Mercedes limousine past him and on into the garage. *Some wheels!* Mallory thought, taking note of the lavender-colored metallic paint job and the church pennants drooping from their staffs on the front fenders.

He stepped to the service entrance of the Archbishop's Palace and rang the bell. The door was opened by a heavy-set man in a dark suit who peered at him suspiciously.

"Good morning," Mallory said. "I'm from Fumigacion Superior, here to spray the archbishop's quarters."

Viktor, Tolt's butler and head of security, grunted. "We didn't call for any spraying." His Spanish carried a thick German accent.

"Yes, but this year we are experiencing unusually virulent infestations of phidippus variegatus and mygalomorphae spiders. It's part of our contract to take care of this before you need to call us."

"Very well," Viktor growled, opening the door.

"We always start in the basement," Mallory said.

Viktor seemed satisfied. "I don't remember you," he said, eyeing the "Ricardo" applique on Mallory's coveralls. "Where's the usual man today?"

"Out sick," Mallory answered, hoping his explanation would be accepted. "I'm new to the service here at the cathedral but my supervisor explained everything."

Viktor nodded and led Mallory to the door to the basement. "I'll wait up here," he said. "It's musty down there." He reached into the stairwell and turned on the lights for Mallory.

Mallory pulled the paper mask dangling around his neck up over his nose. The dimly lit basement was musty as described. Racks of files lined the walls: births, deaths, baptisms, and other records important to the Catholic community. He smiled as a rat peered from a file box. He made a few token sprays as he walked slowly around the cavernous place and judged enough time had passed. He climbed the stairs to find the butler, frozen like a hallway statue, near the door. Obviously, Viktor trusted no one. "I should do the archbishop's quarters next," Mallory said as he pulled down the paper mask. Viktor grunted and they took the stairs indicated on Guillermo's plan. Viktor opened the door to the first office and followed Mallory into the room. The furnishings were Spartan: a cot, a desk, file cabinets, and a small kneeling bench. A crucifix and a painting of Jesus adorned the wall. The desk showed little sign of activity and the cot little sign of use. As Viktor watched his every move, Mallory sprayed in the corners and around the baseboard. The next room showed signs of occupancy. Someone obviously used it on a regular basis. There was paperwork strewn on the desk but no clue as to whose office it was. And no chance to plant a bug. Viktor's laser stare followed him as he sprayed. Mallory motioned toward the door, indicating they should move on.

The room across the hall was definitely not Spartan in appearance. Several European art works hung on the walls, a respectable Persian rug covered the floor, and there was an eclectic mix of expensive artifacts that seemed out of place in a priest's quarters. Mallory did the first corner of the room, sprayed under a table and chairs, and was headed for the huge desk, when he saw it. On the desk, next to the lamp and a jar of pencils, lay a gold Minox spy camera! As he moved closer, he could see it was not just any Minox but exactly like the one taken when his home was broken into. Leaning over to spray under the desk, and getting a closer look at the Minox, he thought his heart would explode. There on the tiny camera's body was the crease-like dent in its side, where Luisa had inadvertently caught it when closing the pencil drawer of her desk.

MY GOD! Luisa's Minox!

This was the place for a bug if he could remain calm enough. He turned to Viktor and asked him to open the window for a little ventilation. Viktor hesitated but shrugged, moved to the window and began cranking it out.

Mallory quickly brushed the Minox onto the carpet at his feet. He stuck one of the bugs under the desk and palmed the camera as Viktor turned to face him.

"I'm finished in here," he said.

Trying his best to compose himself, with his mind and heart still racing from his discovery, he stepped out into the hallway. He loosened the mask and let it dangle around his neck so he could breathe more freely.

"This way," Viktor growled. They moved down the hall, passing over a silk Tabriz runner and through double doors separating the archbishop's apartment from the others.

"His Grace may be conducting a meeting. If so, you will wait or come back later."

Mallory stood at the entrance to the archbishop's quarters, as Viktor knocked first, opened the door and announced the man from the fumigation company was here to spray for spiders.

Tolt was pacing the floor behind his desk, speaking rapid-fire Spanish to a pair of priests, who sat with their backs to Mallory.

"Later," he growled, obviously irritated at Viktor. "Have him come back tomorrow."

Tolt stared past Viktor at Mallory, who felt a cold chill as he found himself looking into the demonic eyes of the man responsible for Luisa's death. He was momentarily paralyzed, then enraged, and he suppressed an urge to lunge and kill the monster with his bare hands. Viktor grabbed his arm and directed him back into the hallway. "You heard the archbishop," he said. "You will do the library next."

Tolt cocked his head to one side in thought. "Quick, get me that photo of Commander Mallory," he ordered. Staib rushed to an armoire in the corner of the room, pulled it open, shuffled through files, and produced the photo.

Tolt stared at it as a look of shock spread across his face. He reached for a walkie-talkie on the desk, keyed the microphone and shouted into the instrument.

"Viktor, stop that man!"

Mallory heard the receiver unit on Viktor's belt.

Viktor slowly reached inside his suit coat as he turned to face him. Mallory had no time to go for his own weapon but he swung the edge of his right hand as hard as he could, aiming for the adam's apple. Viktor went down with a gurgling sound as Mallory raced down the hallway to what he hoped would be a door leading to the porch above the garden. He found the door and once through he looked around to get his bearings. He saw a wrought-iron bench nearby and quickly used it to block the door, hoping for a few second's delay when Viktor got to his feet. He raced toward stairs leading down to the gardens. Reaching the ground, an intricate maze of narrow paths presented itself, so he ran toward a clump of bushes that might provide temporary concealment and a chance to find an exit to the street.

He heard Viktor pushing the door against the iron bench and then his footsteps clattering across the marble terrace to the stairs. He knew he had but moments to spare, as he searched in vain for some sign of an exit.

He raced along a path until he faced a ten-foot wall.

He heard the distinctive sound of Arturo's Honda motorcycle passing in the street outside, orbiting the cathedral grounds waiting to pick him up. The sound diminished down-doppler as Arturo left on another lap.

Mallory turned and raced down a path parallel to the wall. He was beginning to run out of breath as he crashed through a hedge where the path turned, with Viktor in full pursuit. He suddenly realized he still had the sprayer strapped to his back. He stopped to pull it off just as Viktor burst into the hedge with a Walther PPK automatic in his hand.

Mallory froze. *I've got to take this bastard out before he kills me,* he thought, but he realized the Browning was under the coveralls where he would never reach it in time. Viktor exploded into the clearing virtually on top of him. Panting, out of breath, the bull-necked oaf raised his weapon. Mallory aimed the sprayer at his face and squeezed the trigger again and again as hard as he could.

"*Verdammt scheisse!*" Viktor screamed, dropping the gun to clamp his hands to his eyes. Mallory kicked him as hard as he could and grabbed the gun. The giant tumbled to the dirt path, writhing and screaming for help.

"Shut up, you son of a bitch! You're spider-free now." He pulled off the coveralls and his ball cap and patted his pants pocket to make sure the Minox was there. He had to get out of the garden before others showed up, and he could hear their shouts now. *Thank God for this maze of paths.* Running further he spotted an iron gate and ran for it but it was locked. He could hear the sounds of commotion rolling toward him in the garden, and he might have panicked if he hadn't spotted a tree against the wall.

He climbed up and swung through the branches like a madman until he found himself down on the sidewalk outside, face-to-face with an elderly lady who was obviously wondering if he were an apparition. She stared at him wide-eyed with shock and solemnly crossed herself.

Arturo braked at the curb and Mallory leapt aboard and grabbed the black leather seat strap.

"Hang on!" Arturo said. "We're out of here."

Mallory glanced back at the woman, who still stood on the spot, frozen but grasping her heart. If he hadn't done so he wouldn't have seen a man and woman roaring from the cathedral driveway on a big black motorcycle, giving chase. He yelled in Arturo's ear. "We've got company. My two friends!"

Arturo punched the big Honda as Mallory tried desperately to hang on. Two blocks later they made a sharp right at an intersection, then a left at the next block. For a moment it appeared they had shaken them but the impression was short-lived. The black bike reappeared behind them about a half a block away and accelerating.

Mallory considered using the Browning to try for a shot at the pursuers but realized that turning completely around on the seat of the weaving motorcycle was impossible. A fusillade of bullets sprayed a parked car just ahead of them, blowing out its back window.

Oh shit! They've got an Uzi.

Narrow alleys bisected the short blocks of the commercial district they were racing through. He shouted in Arturo's ear. "Get as far ahead as you can. Then left, and left again, into the first alley you see. Stop there. I'll try and take them out with my sidearm."

Arturo cut in front of a truck and then another, gaining a little distance in spite of near misses with cross traffic. Mallory leaned into the turn with Arturo as the Honda hung a left and then another sharp left. Sure enough, there was a narrow alley in the middle of the block. They pulled in and skidded to a stop. The pair on the black bike were close enough to see their first turns but not close enough to see them dart into the alley.

Mallory jumped off and pulled the Browning from his belt, with the silencer still attached. Positioning himself against the brick wall of the adjoining building, he waited. As the pursuers turned into the street he raised the weapon, calculated the lead and squeezed off four rounds.

The driver's bloody head slumped forward, leaving a trail of red stripes down the side of the motorcycle as it careened out of control at about seventy miles per hour and slammed into the block wall of a building across the street. The woman passenger went into the wall head first as her Uzi flew across the street in a trail of sparks.

Arturo raced out and grabbed the Uzi, as a crowd began to form. "Let's get out of here," he said, as they hopped onto the Honda.

"How far to Nacho's command post?" Mallory asked, when they stopped at a traffic light a few blocks later.

"Three, four hours."

"I think it's the only place I can go now."

"No problem. I've made the trip plenty of times. Hang on, we're out of here for sure this time," Arturo said, as they sped away from the intersection.

Mallory hung on as best he could for what he hoped would be an uneventful ride to Peralta's base. All of a sudden he felt too limp to be clinging to a speeding motorcycle. As he tightened his muscles and tried to grip the machine, his mind went essentially blank—except for the awareness of Luisa's camera in his pocket.

FORTY-SIX

OXFORD, MARYLAND

Gretchen suddenly felt at peace, with her mind clear for the first time in weeks. The comfortable chairs on the lawn at the rambling old Victorian house afforded a broad vista of the untroubled waters of the Chesapeake here in the quaint little town on Maryland's Eastern Shore. The late afternoon air was soft, the verdant lawn was dotted with huge old trees and sloped gracefully to the water's edge, and the view in all directions was of peaceful outdoor beauty. This spot always held her in thrall, that and the incomparable crabcakes in the dining room of the Robert Morris Inn, of which the house was part. She had lost count of the many weekends she had squeezed in here in the past few years.

She watched with her mind a blank as a small sloop ghosted along parallel to the near shore, apparently seeking one of the docks up the beach. It bore an elderly couple enjoying their cocktails as the sun neared the Western horizon. She smiled as she recalled her meeting with a Realtor today. Yes, buy now before the market rises, he advised, after she had told him that she was thinking of retiring here in a couple of years. She hadn't minded his gentle pitch and described a couple of little houses that drew her attention. She had even made a date to see some listings the following weekend. She'd miss the Company. It had been her life since her late twenties. But she wouldn't miss the ugly intrigues like Burton's treachery.

Her mood darkened as she recalled how Mallory's confrontation with Holloway had let the air out of her case against Burton. The image of Burton's florid, hail-fellow-well-met face came to mind. It made her feel more sunk than ever. She bit her lip, remonstrating with herself.

Nothing to do now, girl, but just admit you were mistaken about Billy . . . apologize for your mistake and let go of your disliking of the man . . . Your distaste for Billy's personality got you into this witch hunt. . . . That's why Holloway was able to play you like a violin, telling you things he knew your itching ears wanted to hear, and you fell for it. . . . Just live and let live now. . . . And the hell with being embarrassed about it. . . .

She gathered her sunglasses and the novel she was reading and strolled across the lawn toward her room. As she reached for the screen door, suddenly a fact she had overlooked snapped back into place in her mind. According to the Jeweler's initial report, the Generalissimo, not Holloway, had funded Burton's Zurich account! Somehow that had gotten obscured by the dramatic news of Holloway's being alive and confessing that he set Burton up. That and the Jeweler's recent denial that there had ever been such a thing as a Kohorte.

Maybe Holloway didn't come clean after all, she thought. *No reason to believe he did. Maybe he really was in cahoots with Billy and one or both of them were in cahoots with the Kohorte . . . which at the start of this mess was reportedly the source of the G-mo's wherewithal and Benes' funding. And Burton,* she recalled, *had been with Benes against orders! Maybe the Jeweler is a Kohorte tool!* She smiled as she sat down in a chair, talking softly to herself and pulling off her shoes. *Just maybe, girl, your case against Billy isn't in the ash can at all. Well now, let's see,* she thought, *the missing key has got to be Herr Hesse, the Kohorte's go-between with the G-Mo and Benes. All right then, ask the Jeweler to reconfirm the initial information he supplied about who funded Billy's account, see what that jackal will say about it now.*

She reached for her sat-phone, pressed a number stored in memory, and left a message for the Jeweler to return her call. With luck, she would have something by the time she walked into Truman's office in the morning.

MEXICO CITY

Gerhardt Hesse drained his coffee and consulted the expensive watch on his fat wrist. 8:40 A.M. He looked out over Mexico City's Paseo De La Reforma from the balcony of his apartment in Tolt's Grand Hotel Ritz and decided it was time to leave for the bank to be there when it opened at nine. There he would meet with Dr. Alvarado, the bank's operations manager. Alvarado knew Hesse as an employee of the reclusive multibillionaire tycoon who occupied the penthouse atop the hotel, a short walk on the Reforma from the bank's main branch.

Leaving his apartment, Hesse nodded to the uniformed doorman and ambled like a bear toward the intersection of Avenida La Rampa and the Reforma, a rather obese picture of success dressed in a gray business suit and conservative tie. The broad sidewalk was flowing with humanity. He blended with the well-dressed tourists from the fine hotels, the shoppers, and businessmen hurrying to appointments in the financial center, which operated at a New York pace.

Rarely did Hesse's self-occupied mind notice trees in bloom, flowers in shop windows—or chicly attired women like the one dashing across the sidewalk to hail a taxi—but he did this morning. He felt just a bit detached, with a vague ache at the base of his neck, like someone observing the bustling scene from out of body. *Maybe it's stress,* he thought. With his surreptitious cut of the transactions with Dr. Alvarado this morning, he would meet his target—never mind about Holloway this time—and disappear on the evening plane to Sri Lanka. Staib wouldn't in a million years think of looking for him there, he believed. Euphoria touched him like a zephyr, as he remembered beautiful, magical Sri Lanka where he'd spend his life lolling at his beachfront mansion overlooking the bay, surrounded by his golden-skinned Ceylonese servants, who always sensed his mood and supplied his needs.

Screw stress, he decided, *it's too much coffee lately,* and he made a mental note to take mineral water when offered something at the meeting. He quickened his pace. *There it is, Avenida La Rampa with the imposing modernistic bank building rising opposite the intersection.* Wedging his way into the crowd waiting for the light to turn, he balanced himself on the curb and glanced left to keep track of the traffic. The morning smog was heavy, and an acrid combination of air pollution and diesel fumes from the trucks and buses attacked his eyes and throat. He daubed at his eyes with a handkerchief.

In a moment I'll be inside the bank, where the air conditioning is filtered. The signal changed. He didn't see the speeding taxi beating the light, as his heavy body was lifted from the pavement. The blow to his hip, the pavement spinning toward him, screeching brakes, the blue of burning rubber in the air—a second impact with the pavement—all merged with muted shouts and screams of bystanders, and the feeling of distant severe pain. Then nothing. No pain. No awareness.

The ambulance rocketed along toward its destination with siren wailing, bucking up and down at intersections on the poorly maintained side streets. Gradually, Hesse opened his eyes and was dimly aware of a woman sitting at his side, holding his right hand between hers, and a male attendant in medical whites bending over to brace him against the jouncing. He was aware of being cold though covered with a blanket, unable to prevent his body from squirming as waves of shivering coursed through it. He felt no pain.

Shock. I'm in shock, he realized.

The woman leaned close and spoke to him softly, saying words of comfort.

A nun? Yes, he realized, she's a nun.

Maybe I'm going to die, he thought, as he drifted into unconsciousness.

LANGLEY

Gretchen was a picture of gray-haired elegance in her burgundy knit designer suit, as Truman read her memorandum recommending surveillance of Gerhardt Hesse. The Jeweler had reconfirmed that the deposits made to Burton's Zurich account came from the sleazy Mexican citizen of German origin, who officed in both Mexico City and San Marcos, and once handled the Generalissimo's bank accounts but now managed Benes' money.

The Jeweler omitted mentioning the Kohorte this time.

"Yeah," Truman agreed. "Good analysis, but I already asked Bill to develop a full report on Hesse."

"But Billy can't be trusted!" she snapped. She was edging toward a snit when he calmed her with a soft answer.

"It's all right," he said. "I'm running a parallel investigation of Hesse as well. Don't you think it will be interesting comparing Bill's report with another look-see?"

"Well, that's good then, Terry."

She should have realized he'd be a step ahead of her. She no longer cared who got credit as long as they got the goods on Holloway and Burton. She withdrew her elbows from his desk when one of his phones rang and rolled her eyes upward when he selected the Mexico City instrument and took Burton's call.

"Speak of the devil," she muttered, and rose to leave. Truman gestured for her to sit and punched the speaker button. "Gretchen is here with me, Bill. Say that again so she can hear it too."

"Hi, Doll." Burton's mellifluous voice sounded like he was in the next room, not five thousand miles away.

"Hello, Bill," she said evenly, aware of Truman's admonition about her distaste interfering with business.

"I was just about to fill T-Square in," Burton continued, "on the results of the tail I put on our fat friend, Herr Hesse. In a word, we got instant results. But some background first. All we know is this bird runs a distribution company, with hole-in-the-wall offices here and in San

Marcos. It looks like his only customer is the Benes government, and the G-mo's before the coup. He provides heavy equipment and construction materials needed on government projects. And he's somehow involved with this Tolt guy, who we think heads the Kohorte, who was living in Mexico City himself until he disappeared a couple of years back. Plus Hesse seems to coffee-klatch sometimes with Costa Verde's acting archbishop, Schmehr, which seems like a funny relationship for an uncouth clod like him to maintain.

"Okay, so I decide, starting this a.m., I'll have a street team follow him twenty-four hours a day, until I can write the book on him. I spent all last week assembling a team and briefing them. I mean, we have to assume this Hesse guy is from the Dark Side and can spot an ordinary tail, so I figure better safe than sorry, and I go for the full enchilada. The team consists of men and women, young, old, and middle-aged. There're nine in all. No one is to follow him for more than a minute or two, before the next one takes up the tail. Most of the team is in radio-equipped cars racing ahead like crazy, trying to figure out where he's going so they can always get there first. You know the drill, Terry. It's the one we used in London years ago when my tag-team followed Kutsev on his daily rounds and we rolled up his network."

Gretchen sighed. Truman shushed her.

"Okay, you ready for this?" Burton bubbled, relishing the telling. "My first guy follows him for one block, after Hesse leaves his apartment on foot this morning. Then another, this time a young girl, trails along for a minute or so to an intersection where Hesse waits for the light to change. Only he never sees this speeding taxi that's running the light and it clobbers him when he steps off the curb. Now, here's the good part—"

"Kill him?" Truman asked.

"Naw, but almost. It's real serious. His pelvis is broken and there's internal damage. The prognosis is not so bad, though. But, hey, this is way ahead of the story."

"So, what's the good part?" Gretchen asked.

"Okay, my next agent is waiting there to take up the tail. She's right across the street, a gal in my office here. Alice Ramos, from Los Angeles. She's disguised as a nun, see. Before anybody can even think, Alice dashes to where Hesse landed in the street and pulls out her rosary. Glues herself to him until the ambulance comes."

"Was he conscious?" Truman asked.

"Not then but Alice forced her way into the ambulance and rode to the hospital with him. I mean, nobody's gonna deny such a determined nun, right?

"Then at *Sangre De Cristo* Hospital she pushed her way right into the E.R. I mean right into where the doctors are trying to figure out how to save Fatso's life, and she refused to leave. When they cut off his clothes she stuck out her hands and they gave them to her.

"Next thing she's in the john, in a stall, recording the contents of his pockets and wallet, even the labels in his clothes, with her digital camera. Finally, she cruised back into the E.R. and returned the clothes and effects. She even called later to inquire about his condition."

"That's one cool lady you've got there!" Truman said.

"You bet she is, Terry. Ought to get a medal, really.

"There wasn't much to photograph, though, I'm afraid. But there are some leads we'll be checking out down here. Like Mexican and German passports with entrance and exit stamps showing he's been to Costa Verde regularly and Nicaragua a few times. There's a couple thousand dollars in various currencies. Oh, and there're a couple of series of numbers we think might be bank account numbers. They were inked on a tiny paper about the size of a fortune cookie message and tucked into a pocket in his wallet. Maybe the Jeweler can decipher them. You ready to copy?"

"Ready," Gretchen said, and wrote down the numbers.

"So what do you make of all this, Bill?" Truman asked.

"Hell," Burton offered, "chalk it up as a lucky break, no pun intended, for the good guys, that's all. I mean, what are the odds of a creep like Hesse stepping in front of a taxi right after I put a tail on him? Kinda renews your faith in the Man Upstairs nailing the bad guys sooner or later, doesn't it?"

"Okay," Truman said. "Keep me posted."

"Where did you get the nun idea, Bill?" Gretchen asked, rising to leave.

"Alice's own idea, 'cause her sister's a nun. She figures most people, even good Catholics, avert their eyes when they bump into a nun and don't really give them the old once over. Why, hell, I'll bet we could put a dozen nuns in a line-up and half our field agents couldn't identify the one they shook hands with two minutes ago."

Truman hung up and folded his hands behind his head, leaning back in his swivel chair, staring at the ceiling. Gretchen knew to wait until he was finished thinking. Presently, he swung his chair around to face her.

"I doubt Bill put the hit on him," he said. "How could anyone be sure of hitting the right pedestrian in a crowd like that? Look," he said, "try to remember we're all on the same team—you and me and Bill."

"I'd like to believe it, Terry. But this hasn't changed my mind. We both know that disinformation," she waived her note pad with the numbers, "is the *sine qua non,* when diverting suspicion from one's own guilty ass."

She gathered up her papers. "I want to check these numbers out myself."

"Sure, but don't make a career of it."

———

Gretchen brooded in her office. *Was it an accident?* she wondered. *Probably, but who knows for sure? If Burton put the hit on Hesse what would he be covering up? Well, she mused, it hardly requires an epiphany: Bill discovered Holloway milking Hesse, so he cut himself in!*

She tried to put it all out of her mind for a while. For a few minutes she tried doing some work but she couldn't concentrate. She got up and went to the window where she leaned her elbows on the sill, staring down at the parking lot, pondering the news from Mexico City.

Look, girl, it's not really very complicated. Forget the recent developments. Stick to the original facts but make a couple of assumptions. Say Hesse works for the Kohorte. Say the Generalissimo was a Kohorte tool. . . . Holloway and my Jeweler agreed on that once. Say Bill was on the junta's payroll. Or say he discovered Holloway milking Hesse and cut himself in on Holloway's action. Either way, he damn well better cover up his connection with Hesse. And what better way than to put the hit on him?

She glanced at the notepad laying on her desk. Was the slip of paper really found in Hesse's wallet? Or was it planted by Billy's efficient little nun?

The hellish part, she knew, was that even if the Jeweler made sense of the numbers and they tended to substantiate Burton's innocence, the question about the origin of that little paper slip would dangle forever, like an eternally misplaced participle.

And that's why Burton was such an effective nemesis.

FORTY-SEVEN

THE COUNTRYSIDE EAST OF SAN MARCOS

It was impossible to think and hang on at the same time, so Mallory clung to the big bike with his mind in neutral. To the good, it was clear they had no pursuers. The people in the few cars and trucks they passed paid no attention to them. After more than an hour they pulled into a roadside gas station. While Arturo refueled, Mallory found what passed for the men's room and put it to immediate use. The last two hours on the big Honda added a butt-busting rationale for his never being attracted to motorcycles. His tailbone cried out for relief from the hammering it took, his guts felt like he had undergone surgery without benefit of anesthesia, and he wouldn't be surprised if he required a chiropractor the rest of his life. A helmet would have eased the engine's mega-decibel assault on his eardrums but Arturo apparently didn't believe in helmets. He did give Mallory an extra set of goggles, which mercifully shielded his eyes from the insects and road grit, but he imagined the rest of his face and exposed skin resembled a mummy from a prehistoric bog.

He bought two bottles of cold beer, gave one to Arturo, and sat down on a tree stump to call Truman.

"Okay, T-Square," he said, "I've planted one of the bugs, and nearly got myself killed." He related the highlights of his career as a pest exterminator. "I'll give Arturo the other bug," he reported. "He thinks he can plant it in the archbishop's limo while it's at a gas station."

"Hey! Excellent!"

"Listen, those priest sons-of-bitches are a bunch of gangsters. I can tell you right now you don't need any more proof for the Vatican."

"Well, Captain, we do need hard evidence that—"

"Okay," Mallory shot back, "I've got it right here." He took a deep breath, drained his beer, and tossed the bottle in a nearby trash can. "I found Luisa's Minox sitting on a desk in their quarters just like a goddamn trophy. The same camera she used to snap their picture when she was down here only days before she was murdered."

Truman's voice was matter of fact. "How do you know it's hers? Minox turned those things out like popcorn."

"Because it was the gold plated commemorative edition and she dented it when she shut it in a drawer." Mallory pulled the camera from his pocket. "There's a little diagonal crease. Proof doesn't get any more conclusive."

"Can you see a serial number?" Truman asked.

Mallory opened the camera and read it to him.

"I'll have that checked out right away."

"Okay. We're headed to Peralta's base. The rescue's still on, isn't it?"

"You bet it is."

"I hope Peralta can somehow get me the hell out of here. I'm already late for work in Washington."

"I'll get you out if he can't," Truman said.

———

Arturo stayed on a smooth highway for the next leg of the trip and in spite of his angry bones Mallory thought the ride seemed downright peaceful compared to earlier. Arturo never once consulted a map, but it was obvious he knew exactly where he was going. Mallory felt confident he would get them there, but he found himself instinctively scanning the sky for aircraft. He reasoned the search for them may have expanded, and he kept track of everything that flew. Half an hour later a speck in the sky caught his attention as it grew larger. Arturo had turned off the paved road and they were leaving a trail of dust behind them on a dirt road now, an easy thing to spot from the air. The speck soon took on the recognizable profile of a North American T-28D as the plane banked and headed their way. T-28Ds were counterinsurgency aircraft carrying rockets on six hardpoints and four .50-caliber machine guns. They were ubiquitous in Latin America to keep insurgents in line.

Peralta's got a T-28, Mallory thought. *Maybe it's his.*

It wasn't. As it drew closer he could see the markings of the Costa Verde Air Force. He tapped Arturo on the shoulder and pointed. With the plane reducing power and beginning to drop down in altitude, Arturo quickly pulled off the road near a grove of trees. As they slid to a stop he pointed to a thick clump of shrubbery among the trees.

"If they're looking for us they're looking for two guys. Hide in there. I'll take care of this. You already had your target practice today. This dude is mine."

Mallory jumped from the bike and entered the shrubbery. Arturo quickly reached back to the small trunk on the rear of the bike and removed the Uzi he recovered from their would-be assassins. He pulled his right arm from his jacket sleeve, slung the Uzi over his shoulder with the muzzle pointing downward and the stock up under his armpit, and pulled the jacket loosely up over his shoulder again. He grinned at Mallory, remounted the bike, and returned to the roadside in full view of the now circling aircraft.

The T-28 dropped its flaps and slowed for a low pass and a better look. Arturo casually walked a few feet from the bike, where he appeared to be relieving himself by the side of the road, with the Uzi hidden from view.

Mallory watched the unfolding drama from his place in the bushes, shaking his head in silent admiration of the gutsy performance. He hoped the pilot wouldn't realize that no one could take so long emptying his bladder.

The aircraft pulled into in a tight turn and made another pass with its wings level, in perfect firing position. Mallory's heart leapt. He pulled the Browning from his belt and removed the silencer for greater power.

Arturo just stood there smiling and, with his free hand, he waved to the pilot. The pilot waved back, added power and pulled up and headed away in the general direction of San Marcos. Apparently, a peeing biker wasn't any great threat to the regime.

Zipping up his jeans, Arturo unslung the Uzi, broke it down and returned it to the trunk. Mallory emerged from his hiding place and, without a word between them, they mounted up for the rest of the trip to Campo Alto.

After a few minutes of off-road travel, Mallory shouted in Arturo's ear. "Wouldn't a road be easier?"

Arturo shook his head. "Short cut," he shouted. "I bought this particular bike with off-road work in mind, and I've covered this ground lots of times."

As the terrain rose higher and higher, a cloud layer obscuring the mountaintops loomed before them. Mallory realized they were headed for what Elena called the cloud forest. Moist air from the ocean, rising over the savannas toward the mountains, ultimately condensed to a point of saturation and hung as a permanent halo on the mountaintops. The cloud forest was a land of perpetual damp where myriad air plants—bromeliads, orchids, and ferns—grew on tree branches without benefit of soil.

"We going up there?" Mallory yelled, pointing toward the cloud cover. "Into that?"

"Almost," Arturo yelled, as they plunged into a ravine, picked up the barest suggestion of a path for a while, and then went off-road again, plowing tall grass this time.

They climbed a narrow trail for a couple of miles and finally bounced onto a fairly straight portion of dirt road. Arturo stopped the bike at the end of the road where it seemed to disappear into the grayness of the cloud forest. The engine idled in neutral as he produced a small whistle and blew a sequence of blasts—one short, two long, and one short. Mallory recognized Morse Code for the letter P.

PERALTA'S CAMPO ALTO

They had waited for what seemed like minutes when the vine-covered foliage suddenly parted and slowly opened like a giant clam shell, revealing a wider and smoother continuation of the road deeper into the forest. As Arturo put the bike in gear and proceeded more slowly, Mallory looked overhead and saw a high canopy of foliage held together by netting. Shafts of gray misty light penetrated the improvised camouflage as puffs of clouds passed through it. A minute later Arturo stopped in front of the largest of several trailers.

Mallory dismounted stiffly and surveyed the foliated cover of what was obviously a small airport. He could see a couple of Bearcats parked within a large building under the camouflage and some trucks and Jeeps nearby.

He stood still a moment, unsure of his ability to walk, until he was satisfied his bones hadn't turned to rubber. Then his heart leapt when he spotted her. "Hey, what's a nice girl doing in a place like this?" he called.

"Deke!" Elena squealed, as she dashed from one of the trailers. She wrapped him in a viselike hug, kissing him on the cheek several times.

"I needed that," he said softy, as they disengaged.

"So did I."

She laughed, but quickly turned serious. "It's no time for levity," she said. "We've got serious problems." She turned to Arturo. "Where did you find him?"

Arturo shrugged. "He was doing penance at the cathedral, and I just happened to be in the neighborhood. We decided to field-test the Honda."

Elena stared at both of them.

"It's a long story," Mallory said, "but we're definitely ready for a liquid debriefing. Where's Nacho?"

Elena led the way to a large trailer where they found Peralta hunched in a chair with his left foot in a splint, resting it on a box. Diego, with one of Nacho's pilots, whom she introduced only as Smith, watched as a radio operator repaired his equipment in a corner of the room.

"You're the last guy I ever expected to see here," Peralta said. "I'd get up to greet you, but nurse Elena says to keep this elevated."

"Well, Nacho," Mallory said, "I see you finally fell off a bar stool."

"If only I had. I took some ground fire hits on my last sortie."

"How the hell did it get your foot without going through the fuel tank under the cockpit?" Mallory asked, as he surveyed the makeshift splint.

"We caught some F-80s on the ground before they could scramble to come after us, after we bombed the tank depot at the Armored Corps base adjoining their field. I was in a steep left turn with the wings almost vertical as I pulled up and away from the target."

"Yeah," Smith snarled, "we really kicked ass. All that armor's burnt toast now."

"And so are the F-80s," Peralta said. "The agility of the Bearcats, coupled with the element of surprise, has really worked out well for us." He shifted his weight in the chair. "And you, my friend? Bring me up to date on your mysterious activities, including," he flashed the old playboy grin, "what brings you here of all places?"

With glasses of Peralta's *Reserva Especial* in their hands, Mallory and Arturo summarized their adventure. Mallory held nothing back this time.

"I thought the principal maxim of American military service was never to volunteer for anything," Peralta said.

"Who said anything about volunteering, Nacho?"

Peralta eyed Mallory's disheveled appearance. "For God's sake, use the bathroom in there to freshen up. At least we have some of the amenities of civilization here. Not many, but some. You'll find some clean clothes in the other room."

Mallory stood. "Elena, you said there were big problems?"

"Yes," she said, "but take your shower. We'll discuss it all later, after you're deloused."

Mallory removed his jacket and Peralta noticed the silenced Browning in his belt.

"Well," he said, "I see you're armed and dangerous. A silenced weapon, no less. Looks like you dumped your navy for the CIA."

"Well, I suppose I did in a manner of speaking."

———

Mallory emerged from the bathroom and collapsed in a chair in the corner of the room. Smith was lounging on the couch with a dog-eared *Playboy,* as Peralta and the others huddled at the radio.

Smith looked up from his magazine and scowled. "My, my," he prattled. "So you won the big Kewpie doll at the shooting gallery. You actually offed a woman, did you? Well, goody, goody for you, tiger."

Mallory was too tired to respond and simply glared at him. Smith spoiled his mood, which wasn't all good to begin with, but that wasn't what bothered him. All of a sudden he was uneasy with the atmosphere he found here at Campo Alto. He not only felt trapped, but he knew he was trapped by his own decision to come here. *What's gone wrong that Nacho and Elena are so reluctant to talk about?* he wondered.

He stepped outside to collect his thoughts and walked down the path toward the hangar area. As Arturo quickly joined him, Mallory knew he was about to say something to lighten the mood. He held up his hand before Arturo could speak, drew a deep breath and nodded toward the trailer.

"I've never seen Nacho so down in the mouth," he confided, "or Elena so preoccupied. The tide must have gone against them."

Arturo's eyes turned serious after an embarrassed pause. "I don't know everything they know, but I think you're right." He fixed Mallory with his gaze. "What I do know is that they need the strength they draw from your friendship and whatever wisdom you can offer them now."

Mallory regarded him thoughtfully. There was something truly decent about this brash, yet strangely humble young man who seemed so guileless and yet so tough inside. He had never met anyone with such contrasting good qualities.

"You're a good man, Arturo," he said. "I hope it always goes well with you."

Arturo's eyes softened, then he shrugged and stuffed his hands into his hip pockets.

Mallory looked up to see Elena come out of the trailer and beckon to them. As they started back, Mallory took Arturo's arm and stopped.

"Where's this Enrique Maldonado I was told about, the Argentine Nacho's so proud of having aboard?"

Arturo seemed to hesitate before speaking. "He stays in the hangar all the time, out of Smith's way, won't even eat or drink with him."

"Won't he fly with him?" Mallory asked.

"He's still willing to go into action, but not with Smith. In a word, Maldonado hates his guts."

Mallory's heart sank as he grasped more of the situation. Dissention, added to losses, he realized, undercut Nacho's command of his pitiful little squadron. "Any particular reason Maldonado hates him?"

"With Smith, who needs a particular reason?"

FORTY-EIGHT

CAMPO ALTO

Peralta swung along on crutches, as he and Mallory took the path to the hangar at Campo Alto. "You should see what's left of my squadron while you're here. Although there's not much to see anymore."

"I gather you've suffered heavy losses," Mallory said.

Peralta paused to shift his weight on his crutches. "There were four of us last week at this time," he said, "two two-plane sections, like I planned. Smith, whom you've met; a Frenchman named La Porte; the Argentinean I think you've heard about, named Maldonado; and me."

Peralta rested on his crutches, obviously in pain.

"You okay, Nacho?"

"My foot throbs like hell," he said. "It helps to rest for a moment when it does." He slowly moved on toward the hangar. "La Porte was my wingman. He bought it the day before yesterday from ground fire. He tried to belly-in to save whatever could be salvaged of the airplane but the terrain didn't cooperate." Peralta sighed. "He was a good man, Le Porte was. Funny, he was the black sheep of a wealthy Marseilles family and joined me pretty much just for the hell of it. He picked up a Bearcat a few years ago from the Royal Thai Air Force and flew it in air shows in Europe until he pranged it doing an exhibition at the Paris Air Show the year before last. I heard about him and sought him out." Peralta shook his head. "Now I'm responsible for his death, I guess."

"No, you're not. He knew the risks. And he must have had some sense he was flying for a good cause."

"Well, I hope so," Peralta said. "He was loyal to me and he had guts."

They continued along the path in silence.

"What about Smith?" Mallory asked.

"He's a former Marine pilot who was cashiered from the Corps," Peralta said. "Later he flew for the CIA's Air America operation. There's not much more to say. He showed up at the finca one day looking for work, and he turned out to be a good mechanic and a superlative pilot. He seemed like a natural and I had to assemble the squadron."

Mallory rubbed his jaw and was silent.

"Well," Peralta said, "he does have a pugilistic mentality and a black belt in bad manners. I'm not complaining, though. He's good at what he does."

Mallory could see Smith was going to be a problem, and he sensed that Peralta was careful not to admit even to himself that things could easily spin out of control.

"And where did you find the Argentinean, Maldonado?"

"I got real lucky. I found Enrique in Buenos Aires," Peralta said. "In the bar at the Park Tower Hotel. He was in the Argentine Navy, said he was tired of military service and wanted some action that didn't involve saluting. He's had recent carrier experience so he isn't spooked by short field landings. He flew A-4s in the Falklands War and can handle a Bearcat exceptionally well, even though he'd never flown one before."

The two Bearcats remaining at Campo Alto had been rolled out under the jungle canopy where they were being rearmed and fueled. Peralta stopped in front of one and swept his hand around as workmen changed hydraulic fluid and checked systems.

"When we flew our practice flights in these—never more than two planes in the air at once—it gave the appearance of testing my racing planes. They were all painted white then, with racing stripes. I put it about I entered two planes at Reno this year." He pointed to a piece of equipment under the aircraft's wing.

Mallory stooped to inspect the equipment.

"That's a loudspeaker," Peralta told him, "designed by an acoustical engineer at the university. It emits low-frequency recorded panther growls that are audible above the engine noise, heralding La Pantera's vengeance, of course. It's purely psychological, but maybe it helps galvanize our supporters and disorient the government troops."

A young man with an Uzi slouched by the hangar door. He straightened as they approached.

"There's state-of-the-art security here at Campo Alto," Peralta said, "even though we're as remote as a Shangri-La. Nothing gets close to this place undetected. Even the local jaguars have lost their natural curiosity after one of them triggered the system."

The guard stepped forward to swing open the metal hangar door. Mallory saw what he thought looked like leftovers from a small aviation museum. In addition to airplane parts, a North American T-28D was parked to the rear of the hangar, together with a gray camouflage airplane that he thought looked something like an oversized, very ugly Piper Cub.

"And what's this contraption?" Mallory asked, walking over to stand in front of the ungainly appearing aircraft.

"That is no contraption. It's a Fiesler 156 Storch. "Storch" means stork in German. Look at the STOL configuration of its wings. It can take off and land on a city street, in a backyard, in fact. With a strong enough wind it can take off in its own length. The Germans used them in World War Two to get in and out of cramped places where nothing else could operate. It came in handy when I was setting up my bases."

Lunch was a moody affair graced only by the absence of Smith, who retired to his trailer with a bottle. Nacho, Elena, Mallory, and Arturo ate in silence as the meal was picked at and nibbled. It seemed to be topped with a heavy glaze of tension and stress, with Peralta and Elena reeling from the first days of war and Mallory on the edge of frustration awaiting David's rescue.

Elena was especially quiet, punctuating her meal with glances at Mallory as Peralta explained the unique features of his three camouflaged air strips. Mallory was impressed with his explanation of the logistics of supplying them with bombs, rockets, 20 mm ammo, food, water, and other supplies for the crude living quarters. Communications were maintained by discrete radio frequencies, changed daily for security, he learned. Elena, Peralta told him proudly, was recording new radio messages every day, which they sent by courier to her mobile broadcasting units, collectively known as *Radio Pantera*. The transmitters were always moved to new locations between broadcasts.

Mallory broke a short silence. "I heard your first broadcast driving down from Nicaragua. The one on the Emergency Broadcast Network."

She brightened. "That was a real bonus," she said. "It was the only time I could expect to use the government stations until we win this thing." She didn't seem to want to say more as they continued to pick at their plates.

As the tension at the table tightened, Mallory pushed his plate away and took the plunge. "Well, don't you want to talk about it?" he asked. "I gather the war isn't going very well? Or am I wrong?"

Nacho laid down his knife and fork and patted his lips with his napkin. "Maybe it's going as well as we could have expected, realistically," he said. "One section of Bearcats is out of the action with Le Porte's death and my foot. The other section is split with Smith here and Maldonado leaving for Campo Medio at dawn. Don't worry, it's planned that way, so we don't lose them both in one air raid."

Mallory wondered.

"What about Carlos? How's he doing?"

Nacho seemed to brighten. "Better than expected, actually. His brigades have locked up the countryside to the north and west, where the fighting is, and have the army penned up in defensive positions at their garrisons."

"The problem," Elena interjected, "is that Carlos is low on ammunition and fuel, and he has only light trucks for transport. He's badly in need of resupply. He may have to withdraw to the jungle for protection." She looked sad, Mallory thought.

"And the peasants and townsfolk? How are they doing?"

Peralta spoke. "An embarrassment of riches. Carlos has seven thousand new volunteers who rallied just this week from everywhere, even from San Marcos and the other cities. But he hasn't enough weapons or time for training them. So he sends them to the jungle camps where they're out of danger until we rectify the situation."

"Didn't you foresee this happening, Nacho?"

"Of course, but what we didn't foresee was the full might of the enemy falling on our supply dumps the first day of the war. It was just dumb luck, or maybe we had a traitor, but our supposedly secret supply depots, near the villages of Guetsera and Malacon, were immediately overrun and the supplies taken or destroyed." Peralta shrugged. "The fortunes of war can be unpredictable, like a fluke in the Falklands War Maldonado told me about. The British lost all but one of their helicopters on the first day of hostilities." He turned his palms up in a gesture of helplessness. "A single Argentine A-4 fired a single Exocet missile at a British cruiser, which responded with chaff to confuse the missile. The missile then found and sank the ship with all the helicopters, just as the first chopper was becoming airborne. So the Brits had to fight the whole war with just that one helo. Who could have predicted that?"

"Got any other problems?" Mallory asked, half in jest.

"No," Peralta said. "Just losing half our Bearcat strength and half our means of carrying on the land war."

"What are you doing about it?"

"Praying," Elena said, "that Carlos sustains the offensive until we bring in more supplies. In fact, that's what all those volunteers are doing. They're manning supply trails and waiting for the shipments to arrive from Caribbean ports and trickle down the Pan American Highway. It takes time, you know."

Mallory turned to Peralta. "What are you doing about replacing your planes and pilots?"

"I've got the T-28D you saw in the hangar and two more are being modified in Miami. They should be here within a week. As for pilots, Maldonado has a friend coming from Argentina who wants the bonus I'm offering."

"That's it?"

Peralta nodded.

Mallory pulled the sat-phone from his pocket. "I can use this," he said, "to contact Washington at the highest level. Make a priority list of what you need immediately and I'll relay your request for aid."

Nacho and Elena seemed stunned.

"Frankly, I wouldn't get your hopes up too much," Mallory cautioned. "But it can't hurt to ask."

"Who will you talk to?" Elena asked.

Mallory thought of mentioning Foxlee but he didn't.

"A man who has President Foxlee's ear," he said.

Peralta beamed Mallory a smile and excused himself, saying the list would be ready in a few minutes.

Mallory rose slowly from his seat as did Elena. They stood facing each other for a moment and then slowly embraced, holding each other tightly. Mallory released her after a few seconds and spoke.

"I don't know what to say. I . . . I just can't seem to express what I feel right now. Except, I'll miss you when I go. And worry about never seeing you again."

"We will see each other again," Elena said brightly. "La Pantera decrees it!"

Arturo spoke up. "I think your security expert should get back to San Marcos now. There may be some conversations on the tapes." He held out his hand to Mallory. "Let me have that other bug. I'll plant it in the cathedral limo or my name ain't James Bond or whatever."

Mallory handed it over. "Thanks for the shuttle service, Arturo. You really saved my ass."

He went to the door and watched as Arturo fired up the Honda and rode away into the dank mists of the cloud forest.

"I don't know what we'd do without Arturo," Elena said. "He picks up the payroll from one of the few banks that's still loyal to us and delivers it to all three of Nacho's secret bases, and that's just an example of the tasks Nacho has assigned to him."

"You're very fortunate to have him," Mallory said.

"He's got a bright future," she said, "after all this is over. He could be president of the university one day."

Mallory didn't doubt it, as they turned to go inside, as the sound of the motorcycle died out.

FORTY-NINE

SAN MARCOS

Arturo dragged himself up the stairs to his apartment. The weariness he felt from the recent days' events numbed all sense of time, and the bone-jarring ride he had just finished left him without any reserves of physical energy. He paused on the top stair to catch his breath. All he could think of now was a cold beer, a hot shower, and a night's uninterrupted sleep. He found the door to his apartment, fumbled in his pocket for his key, and after two near misses he managed to insert it in the lock. Night was falling fast as he entered the dimly lit apartment and crossed the small room to turn on the lamp on his desk.

As he reached for the switch he sensed an alien presence in the room. Turning around, he could see someone sitting in the chair in the far corner, almost hidden in shadow. Twilight was fading fast, but he could make out the unmistakable shape of a priest's hat on the man's head.

"Why don't you turn on the light?" Staib said, in his heavily accented Spanish. "So you can properly greet your guest." Arturo thought the voice sounded familiar but he couldn't place it at first.

"Father Martin?" he gasped, as the light suddenly illuminated the room. "What brings you here?" he stammered.

Staib's face slowly took on a satanic smile as he produced a silenced Walther PPK pistol from the folds of his cassock. "I find your reports most interesting," he snarled, "but their content is nothing but lies."

Arturo somehow summoned the strength to attempt to cover the sheer horror he felt as he realized that his duplicity was unmasked.

"I have no idea what you mean, Father," he said after regaining his breath.

"You have betrayed the trust I placed in you," Staib snarled, "and wasted a lot of my money."

"No, you misunderstand, really," Arturo said, as he began to calculate the odds of escape through the window or the door. The door seemed to offer the best odds even though he would have to wrest the gun from Staib to make it. "Look, Father Martin," he said, as warmly as he could manage, slowly edging toward the door, "you certainly must understand it's not easy to motivate students for protests of the kind we discussed. First, they have to be educated in the importance of the cause."

"Yes," Staib said, as he rose from the chair. "You should have done just that, but now you are the one who is about to be educated."

If there is to be a time it's now, Arturo thought. He suddenly threw his shoulder into Staib's midsection, grabbing for the gun and spinning away toward the door.

It was a mistake to try to neutralize the weapon and get to the door all in the same motion.

Staib reacted in a split second and delivered a powerful blow to Arturo's stomach that knocked him to the floor where he lay doubled up like a fetus, gasping for breath. Staib reached down with his free hand and grabbed Arturo by the arm, yanking him onto the sofa.

"You might as well stretch out," he said, "and enjoy a relative sense of comfort as your education continues." Arturo lay still, holding his stomach.

"Sit up, you swine," Staib demanded. "If you are thinking of shouting for help, I don't think you would be heard above the traffic noise outside."

Arturo slowly rose to a seated position and leaned back on the sofa. *There may be noise outside in the street,* he thought, *but there are neighbors right down the hall.* "*¡Ayudame!*" he screamed. "*¡Ayudame!*"

Staib delivered a blow with the butt of the pistol that almost knocked him off the sofa.

Stunned, Arturo slumped back on the couch as Staib reached for a large black canvas bag and withdrew a roll of duct tape. He quickly taped Arturo's mouth shut, his hands behind his back, and his feet together.

"Calling for help will do you no good," the assassin said, leaning down and looking into Arturo's eyes. "Oh," he continued, "I see in your eyes that you are wondering who I really am."

Arturo nodded.

"Well now," Staib said, pulling up a wooden chair just beyond range of Arturo's feet, "I see nothing wrong with our having a little chat." He leered at his prey. "First of all, I'm sure you've already guessed that my name isn't really Father Martin," he continued with a laugh. "It's Staib, Ludwig Staib. SS-Kohorte Lieutenant Colonel Ludwig Staib, in fact, at your service." He bowed mockingly. "You may regard me as a professional angel of death. I kill people who stand in the way of the Kohorte which, by the way, owns your country now for all practical purposes. And if I may say so," he said, softly, "I am quite good at my profession—any time, any place," he stroked his chin and smiled, "and any way I choose."

Arturo's eyes widened as a look of sheer terror contorted his face.

The sound of a commotion outside in the hall was followed by rapping at the door. Staib slowly walked to the door, opened it just wide enough to step outside, and pulled the door almost closed behind him.

He faced an excited elderly couple.

"What is happening, Father?" the man said. "We heard Arturo call for help."

"Yes, he did," Staib said, in his best priestly manner. "It's such a shame," he continued. "I was called here to hear his confession and, as we talked, it has become obvious he is suicidal, overcome with the enormity of his sins. What you heard was his calling for God's help and forgiveness in this, his darkest hour."

"But *Señor* Arturo seems such a fine young man," the woman said. "He has done so many nice things for us."

Staib held up his hand and shook his head. "We can never really know a person, you know, by just what we see. Unfortunately, demons live within us all, *Señora*."

Her eyes widened and she backed away from the priest.

"Please don't be disturbed by what you may hear," he advised. "I have done exorcisms many times," he smiled. "I can assure you he will soon be at one with his God."

The couple solemnly crossed themselves.

"And now, if you will excuse me," Staib said with a slight bow, "I shall continue my priestly duties."

He returned to the room and closed the door behind him. "I'm sure you heard our conversation in the hall," he told Arturo. "How fortunate you are to have such fine neighbors who are so concerned about your circumstances."

Arturo snorted on the sofa.

Staib furrowed his brow. "What a stupid plan you and that foolish Commander Mallory devised!" he chided.

Arturo's eyes widened as he realized they must have discovered the bug under the desk.

"There could have been only one or two reasons for your friend Mallory to play the pest exterminator. Either to observe our activities or to plant a listening device. It didn't take long to find it under my desk." He produced the small receiver Arturo kept in his apartment and held it in front of him. "I took the liberty of searching before you arrived and quickly located this," he said. "Don't worry, I'm going to leave it here and let it continue to record the activities in my office." He stifled an outburst of maniacal laughter. "The tapes should be engrossing, you'll agree, with their endless details of administrative trivia, boring discussions of the catechism and, of course, my heartfelt prayers for the souls entrusted to my care."

Arturo closed his eyes. *Perhaps he's praying,* Staib thought. The eyes popped open again and he glared at Staib.

Staib smiled. "This equipment can be remotely accessed, you know, like when you call a telephone answering machine, so I have no doubt the CIA is thoroughly frustrated by now with what they hear."

Arturo had stopped struggling on the sofa and was having increased trouble breathing.

Staib reached into the duffel bag and pulled out the pest control coveralls from *Fumigacion Superior.*

"Your accomplice left these in the Cathedral gardens," Staib said, holding them in front of Arturo and then dropping them on the floor. He reached into the bag again and produced the chemical canister and spray wand and waved them in front of Arturo too.

"This is very effective with regard to spiders and bugs and especially so with humans. For instance," Staib hissed, "Viktor, our former Security Chief, is no longer with us due to his having died shortly after getting a snout full of this from your accomplice.

"Your friend Guillermo won't be needing these things anymore. Instead of spraying for spiders in the cathedral, he is being eaten alive by them in the jungle."

Arturo struggled against the tape.

"My predecessors were careless when you were lucky enough to gun them down in the alley." Staib stood and smiled down at Arturo. "Rest assured there will be no careless mistakes this evening." He walked to the window, opened it and looked down at the street below, as the lights of the city began to come on. "Yes, it is dark enough now, I think," he said, and returned to face Arturo on the sofa. "Your neighbors crossed themselves when they heard of your suicidal tendencies. Good Catholics, I'm sure. I'm sure you would want to do the same in preparation for the next part of your solemn rite. Of course, that won't be possible under the circumstances so, as your priest, I will do it for you." Reaching into the duffel bag, Staib brought out the mask and placed it over his nose. He set the canister upright on the floor and pointed the wand at Arturo's face. He smiled as he saw his victim's facial muscles contort and his eyes widen in sheer terror.

Staib slowly made the sign of the cross with the wand. "In the name of the Fuhrer," he said, and squirted a blast of pesticide into Arturo's eyes.

Arturo frantically blinked and writhed in pain, as his eyes burned and their lids puffed and began to swell.

"The Reichsfuhrer"—another blast, this time directly into Arturo's nostrils.

"And the Obersturmbannfuhrer. That's me"—another blast directly up the nose.

A final blast to the nose. "Amen!"

Arturo's chest began to heave in an involuntary effort to rid his lungs of the deadly chemical. With his mouth taped shut, he seemed to be choking on expectorated fluid, which began oozing from his nostrils.

Staib moved his chair in front of the open window and sat down as he watched Arturo continue to twitch and foam at the nose. After a few minutes all struggling stopped and he slumped over on the sofa.

Staib remained seated, took off the mask, and lit a cigarette. He smiled as he observed the final twitches of the dying man. He remained seated as he finished his cigarette, then rose and put it out on a plate on the desk. Returning to the sofa, he felt for a pulse. Finding none, he removed the duct tape bindings and put them in the duffel bag along with the mask, leaving the coveralls, the canister and the wand on the floor. He was not concerned about any forensic detective work on the part of the police, as those on the force in the Kohorte's pay would see to it this was ruled a suicide.

Staib carefully surveyed the room. Satisfied it was as he wished it to appear, he let himself out the door. As he passed the couple's apartment, the lady peered out furtively from the doorway.

"Ah!" Staib told her, "your friend Arturo went through his private hell this evening but, thanks to the exercise of my sacerdotal duties, he's at peace now." He glanced back at Arturo's door. "The young man needs to remain alone, so please see to it he isn't disturbed," he said softly.

The woman clasped prayerful hands under her chin.

"Oh, bless you," she said. "And thank you, Father."

FIFTY

ABOARD AIR FORCE ONE

"Cleveland Center, this is Air Force One," the copilot reported, "leaving your airspace now, at three-niner thousand. Good day and thank you, sir."

Air Force One is the radio call sign of whatever Air Force plane is carrying the President—usually one of two modified Boeing 747-200 jets.

"Roger that, Air Force One. Contact Chicago Center on one-two-seven-point-four, and good day."

Truman rode in a jump seat behind the pilots, listening to them and watching the vast expanse of snow-covered land, as small cities and the cold gray surface of Lake Erie slowly unfolded below. He could see Toledo ahead and Detroit in the distance off to their right. He wore running shoes and gray athletic warm-ups with the Air Force Academy's eagle logo on the pants and AIR FORCE emblazoned in block letters on the sweatshirt. It was the perfect dress to allow him to roam the aircraft without drawing attention from the forty-something reporters sprinkled through the center and aft sections of the plane. Just some retired general hitching a ride, they would think.

He stood and stretched, declined more coffee, and decided to stroll the length of the aircraft for exercise. President Foxlee would beep him when he was ready, but the President was a known night owl and late sleeper and was probably resting after leaving the White House in the early hours in order to board the plane at six in the morning. Maybe the Fox was working on the speech he would deliver to a packed house of fat cats at the Century Plaza Hotel in Los Angeles this evening.

Truman saw that the door to the Presidential Suite was still closed as he ducked around the railing of the stairwell leading from the Boeing's upper deck to the main cabin below. He checked the beeper in his pocket to make sure it was working and descended the stairs.

Some of the journalists were dozing in their chairs, while others chatted over coffee or tapped at their laptops. This was first-class travel, with every passenger seat in the center and rear sections first-class size, six lavatories, eighty-five telephones and two kitchens that could serve a hundred people. The plane was full today with journalists taking up whatever space wasn't occupied by senior White House staff, Secret Service agents, and guests. The latter were mainly California legislators hitching a prestige ride home to their districts, where they would regale constituents with details of the plane and bask in reflected glory as assumed confidants of the President.

The door to the medical compartment was open, and Truman looked in as a young doctor and his attendant checked the lighting above the operating table. Cupboards held what he assumed were medical supplies. A small X-ray machine was evident as was some oxygen equipment.

"Ever had to use this place?" Truman asked, curious.

"Sure, sir," the doctor replied. "One of the media people suffered a heart attack last month and we stabilized him while we diverted to Denver, where he was met by an ambulance. Maybe we saved his life, I don't know."

Truman nodded. "Then I'm glad you're aboard, son."

"Thank you, General," the younger man said.

Truman smiled and was about to continue aft when the beeper sounded and he headed forward again past fax machines, copiers, and computers, and through the main cabin, where breakfast was now being served. He took the stairs, knocked softly at the President's suite, and entered.

Foxlee was in his dressing room, having just emerged from his lavatory and shower. He poked his head out and motioned for Truman to go to the dining room. He did so, passing the President's office and conference room with their leather seating and wood grain paneling.

Somewhat to his surprise, he found the table set for only two. Apparently, Foxlee had dismissed the ubiquitous staffers, his acidic Chief of Staff included. The fact this President liked playing at spymaster and detective had its good points, Truman had learned, and having a President all to your self now and again was one of them.

He sat down at the polished table to wait. Through the window he could see the snow-covered southern suburbs of Chicago passing under the leading edge of the right wing. He thought about the fact this was definitely a world apart, where they could use the port in the nose for refueling in flight to stay aloft indefinitely or at least until the three-week supply of food and booze ran out.

Foxlee came in and plopped down opposite Truman. The President wore exercise togs, too.

"So you've had a conversation with Peralta?" he asked.

"No, Mister President," Truman said. "Captain Mallory relayed Peralta's request to me. Peralta's irregulars are doing well. They've got the army penned up in their garrisons, and recruits are flocking to join Peralta's cause. His tiny air force has already taken out about half of Benes' air force."

"So what's the problem, then?" Foxlee asked, munching toast and offering marmalade to Truman.

"Supply, sir," Truman told him. "Peralta is desperately short of everything. The one thing that Benes did right was to capture half of Peralta's supplies the very first day of hostilities. That was just last week."

373

"What else did the captain have to say?" Foxlee asked.

"He relayed Peralta's short list of top priority needs. They're very low on all kinds of ammo, fuel for his vehicles and planes, and field radio communications. And Peralta would like some more shoulder-fired Stingers for use against Benes' helicopters."

Foxlee waited as a steward served eggs and bacon and refilled their coffee, left, and closed the door.

"Do this," the President said. "Check with the Joint Chiefs, then poll the National Security Council by phone. You can do it from the plane even after we land in Los Angeles. Then we can meet in my suite at the Century Plaza tonight. I should be able to finish up in the ballroom downstairs and get back to my suite by about ten o'clock. Based on what you report then, I'll make a decision."

"It would be helpful, sir," Truman said, "if I could give the NSC members some idea of your leaning."

"Hell, tell them I think Peralta is doing a job we'd have to do ourselves sooner or later. We should at least lend him the garden hose he needs to put out the fire down there." Foxlee grinned, proud of his paraphrase of FDR's Lend-Lease analogy.

"Here, finish this bacon," he said, pushing the platter toward Truman. "Now, tell me," he asked, leaning forward with interest, "what's Captain . . . what's his name? . . . Mallory been up to down there in Costa Verde since you last briefed me?"

Truman summarized his own follow-on encounter at the Hotel Corona, mentioned the bug Mallory planted in the archbishop's palace, and described the aftermath leading to Mallory's being at Peralta's Campo Alto.

"Well, then," Foxlee said, patting his lips with a napkin, "you've certainly taken care of any questions about your man Burton's loyalty, haven't you?"

Truman was glad that here was a president he could share his unspoken concerns with. He hadn't had the luxury since Nixon died.

374

"Not really, sir," he told him. "This is one of those cases where it comes down to trusting someone or not."

"How so?" Foxlee asked.

"Burton has been spotted visiting the archbishop's quarters at the cathedral, and I personally know him to be a little too cozy with Colonel Benes. Holloway claims the priests at the cathedral are funding Benes, having bankrolled the Generalissimo before him. Then there's Burton's allegation that Gretchen Reece controls the Jeweler, who's the source of the money transfer information, but the Jeweler has now recanted about nearly everything. And, for a cherry on top, there's a never-to-be-resolved question of whether Burton had some exculpatory evidence planted on Gerhardt Hesse."

Foxlee puffed out his cheeks and exhaled through his teeth. "Jeez. You still got a real can of worms there, all right. My advice is to keep your powder dry and find out everything you can about those priests."

"That's why I asked you to have the Secretary of State go straight to the top at the Vatican, sir."

"Yeah," Foxlee said, pouring them more coffee. "So what's the status there?"

Truman shrugged. "Secretary Wasserman made the request of the Vatican State Department, which is as high as you can go, given the fact the Pope can hardly be expected to know the answer to this sort of question."

"And?"

"She called on their secretary of state, Cardinal Guilianni, on her way to the Middle East. She told him we had reason to question the identities of Monsignor Schmehr and three of his staff at the cathedral in Costa Verde."

"That must have gone over like a lead balloon."

"Hard to tell. She said he was most cooperative and promised to look into the matter. He requested time to check with the German authorities among other things."

"Well, that seems fairly promising then," Foxlee said.

"Right. At least he didn't toss her out on her ear."

Truman remained aboard Air Force One for several hours after they landed in Los Angeles. By late afternoon, he had managed to speak with the Chairman of the Joint Chiefs of Staff and all fifteen members of the National Security Council. All but a few NSC members unhesitatingly endorsed the idea of limited covert aid to Peralta. Three or four, though, worried that military aid, however insignificant, would lead to the slippery slope of greater involvement in another country's civil war. "Shades of Viet Nam," a naysayer commented. Truman was glad the NSC was advisory to the President and he didn't need unanimity.

That evening Truman arrived in a hired limo at the Century Plaza Hotel on the west side of Los Angeles, wearing a tux and carrying a raincoat. It rained earlier in the evening and threatened to do so again. At the door he flashed the credential of a contributor who had bought a seat at the dinner and he soon blended into the crowd of six hundred guests who were pushing against the open bars that had been set up in the carpeted foyer of the giant ballroom where Foxlee would be the dinner speaker. Truman remembered this as the site of Reagan's 1980 Victory Speech and appearances by every President since Richard Nixon.

As ushers went about with quiet gongs, drawing the guests to their tables, he found his way to Table 73 where, he was pleased to note, none of the people looked familiar. He introduced himself as Terence and was pleased to note that they apparently thought it was his last name. He waited until after the main course of thousand-dollar-a-plate chicken, excused himself while dessert was being served, and went upstairs to the nineteenth-floor Presidential Suite, where he watched the President's talk on closed-circuit TV with some of the Secret Service detail. It was vintage Foxlee, a version of the basic stump speech from his recent campaign. Truman noted one addition in particular, however. During the foreign policy portion of his remarks, Foxlee said, "Americans are a caring people by nature, who care about the well-being of their neighbors right here in this hemisphere . . . for we are all members of the same human family." Then he had looked directly into the camera and continued, "Make no mistake, this Administration will not tolerate a neighboring government mistreating its own citizens!"

Mild applause.

Interesting, Truman thought. *Peralta should be in good shape now for getting the material he wants.*

"Get any flack about Peralta?" Foxlee asked, when they were finally alone in his hotel suite after the speech.

"Not really," Truman told him, recounting what the naysayers said. "The Joint Chiefs have no problem with covertly supplying Peralta's insurgents what they asked for, providing it can be done without putting our military advisors on the ground there."

"That's super, T-Square," the President said. "Get right on implementing it, will you?"

Foxlee sank onto the sofa.

"I already did, sir. I would need to be making some urgent calls had you said no. The aid's on its way."

"Then pour us a couple of scotches, will you? My throat's dry as hell from entertaining my fans."

As Truman found the ice and poured them drinks, Foxlee kicked off his shoes and put his feet on the coffee table.

"Say, what's the status of Mallory's son?" he asked.

Truman explained the plan for freeing the prisoners. "This operation needs your approval, Mister President."

"Sounds dangerous as hell," Foxlee said, as a shadow of concern seemed to fall across his face.

"I pray to God we pull it off without any casualties among our SOF people . . . or the prisoners," he said, nursing his drink. "It's a go as far as I'm concerned.

"Say, where's Mallory now?"

"Cooling his heels at one of Peralta's supposedly secret bases," Truman said, "until we airlift him. But he just won't leave while his son is still captive."

"That's hard on a man of action, like he seems to be," Foxlee said, shaking his head. "I'll bet he wishes he could be doing something to contribute to rescuing his boy."

FIFTY-ONE

PACIFICO PROVENCE, COSTA VERDE

Peralta's ungainly appearing Fiesler Storch glided along above the savanna in near silence, as Maldonado throttled back to search the ground in the dim moonlight. Now and again light danced off a stream or marsh among the trees as he looked for the road leading to the remote monastery where Bishop Subueso had arranged a rendezvous with them. It was a bad night for flying, with windstorms mercilessly ripping the lonely grasslands passing beneath them and buffeting the airplane. A careful pilot wouldn't dream of flying on such a night, but time was running out for the Peraltistas and they hadn't the luxury of choice.

Elena thought the commanding view from the Plexiglas-enclosed cockpit was like sitting atop an amusement park ride, as she watched from the tandem seat directly behind Maldonado's. The reason for their dangerous sortie wasn't amusing, she knew. Carlos' forces were nearly out of ammunition and there was little hope, they were told, of getting more from the United States for at least two weeks. Nacho's aircraft had been thinned out by attrition, and without air support there was no prospect of Carlos taking the offensive. The additional T-28s Nacho's contractor was rebuilding in Miami wouldn't be combat-ready for at least a month. And now, underscoring their plight, a Pacific hurricane was bearing down on Costa Verde's west coast, with prospects of doing far greater damage to the rural territory Carlos controlled than the cities where the Benes forces had withdrawn to their fortified garrisons. The word that leapt to her mind was "quagmire," quagmire in every sense.

She looked down at the dark sea of wind-torn trees dancing below, contemplating the evening's mission. They had flown from Campo Alto at altitudes of no more than thirty feet above terrain to avoid any radar that might be in the area and the ride had been hair-raising, with the buffeting winds tossing the light plane helter-skelter.

Startled by the engine quitting, she instinctively grasped at the small crucifix on her necklace until she saw Maldonado reach up to a lever above his head and switch fuel tanks. The engine soon caught and began running smoothly.

An off-hand remark of Carlos' had given her the idea. "I guess this is how the British felt during the siege of Malta," he had quipped, "before air reinforcements arrived."

"And how was that?" she had asked.

"The Germans kept up relentless air raids on the little island fortress. Malta's air defense was finally reduced to where it couldn't withstand many more attacks, like the position we're in today with few of our planes left."

"What did they do?" she had implored him.

"Reinforcement Spitfires were loaded aboard the U.S. aircraft carrier *Wasp* in England, as many as could be crowded onto the flight deck and still allow room for take-off. The *Wasp* sailed through the Strait of Gibraltar to launch the Spitfires within range of Malta. Actually, they did it twice," Carlos had continued. "The siege was broken and Malta survived. `Who says a wasp can't sting twice?' Churchill was quoted as saying."

"That's interesting history," she had said, "but I don't think the United States Navy is going to send an aircraft carrier to deliver our new T-28s from Miami."

Nevertheless, the vignette got her to thinking about military strategy, and she had had a revelation. She had realized that although their own resources were being drained by the struggle, Benes' apparently weren't. *What's the source of his strength?* she had asked herself. Then in a flash of inspiration she had seen it all very clearly. If the fake archbishop had the awesome power to manipulate the Vatican, it stood to reason he must be the power behind Benes. The Vatican was the jugular, she had realized, and therein was her opportunity as well. Sever the connection at the Vatican and the Hydra would stop growing new heads; heads like the Generalissimo and Colonel Benes and the Russian MiG 29s rumored to be on the way from a Ukrainian arms dealer. Even though Nacho thought she was overdoing feminine intuition, he hadn't dissuaded her. Elena was sure it had been the Lord's prompting. Returning to the present, she braced herself as they spotted a dirt road and Maldonado dropped even lower, following it toward an isolated cluster of single-story buildings in the distance.

Bishop Subueso thought he caught the faint muttering of a light plane's engine in the eastern sky, but he couldn't see anything yet in the faint glow of the early dawn. The sound grew a little louder until the plane appeared just above the tree tops. It made a circle of the monastery buildings before lining up to touch down on the road where he and the monks waited by the front gate.

The aircraft looked like none he had seen, with its long spindly legs and strange wing flaps on both the leading and trailing edges. He watched as its rudder flopped back and forth and the awkward-looking craft gyrated, pitched, and yawed. There was an insectlike quality to the Storch's appearance anyway, but it was heightened in frontal view by the cockpit windows that bulged outward sideways, bug-eyed for added visibility. The Storch was quite close now and seemed to hesitate like a gull hovering in a stiff wind to consider a morsel of food on the ground. Suddenly, the plane flared out as Maldonado forced it down onto its wheels. The landing gear spread out as the struts expanded to absorb the weight of the landing. Subueso thought it looked like his cat reacting to being dropped from his arms. Maldonado cut the engine, the propeller stopped, and the Storch rolled to within a few feet of where the bishop waited. Maldonado got out and assisted Elena to the ground.

"Welcome, child," Subueso called, with a concerned look on his face. "I was perplexed to receive the message that you were risking coming here like this," he continued, as they met in an *abrazo*.

The energetic Subueso led the way to the chapel as Maldonado and the gawking monks pushed the Storch around so he could take off from the road as soon as Elena was ready.

"I've got to be brief," Elena said. "We must return before the air force comes looking."

She dropped onto a wooden bench near the altar in the musty, primitive chapel. Her eyes searched the bishop's as he sat down next to her. "You are our last remaining hope of surviving and prevailing," she said, relating the precarious state of their military situation.

When she had finished he frowned and turned his palms up in a gesture of futility. "What could a humble bishop do, my child, that would make any difference in your military affairs? I don't even have very much power within the Church itself," he said. "Why, being from lowly Pacifico Province, I've always been considered to be just a country priest."

Elena smiled. "But you're a country priest with fire in his belly," she said, gripping his arm. "Like a Saint Peter or even a Martin Luther. And Luther was right about abuses in the Church, wasn't he?" she said.

"Yes, he was," Subueso admitted. "But he shouldn't have torn the Church apart. And besides, what's that got to do with whatever it is you want from me?"

"Far from tearing it apart," she said, squeezing his arm more tightly, "the Church has got a boil on its head, and needs you to lance it," she said. "This money," she continued, pressing a large envelope into his hands, "should be enough for your trip to Rome."

"Rome?" he asked, puzzled.

Elena nodded. "Yes, Rome," she said, squaring her shoulders. "You must see the Holy Father and tell him about the goings-on at the cathedral," she continued, as her eyes blazed with emotion. "Tell him about the missing priests who dared to question the acting archbishop. Tell him about Captain Mallory's finding his wife's camera in the acting archbishop's quarters. Tell him that the fiend tried to poison me at the communion rail. You must tell the Pope everything. Everything!"

The bishop seemed agitated and perplexed. She suddenly remembered that she hadn't spoken to him since the christening and quickly told him what happened that day. His wide-eyed response indicated that he would go to Rome.

Maldonado poked his head into the chapel and tapped his watch. "Let's go," he said.

"Wars are not won merely by killing people," she said, as she rose to leave. "They are won by denying the enemy's means of support . . . and I am certain that the clique at the cathedral is Colonel Benes' main means of support."

Maldonado primed the engine and pushed the starter button. The engine coughed to life immediately and was soon running smoothly. He set the trim and flaps and glanced about, returning waves from the bishop and the monks who stood by looking on. The dirt road they had landed on led into the rising sun, which was just now peeking above the foothills to the east. He lined up in the center of the road, pushed the throttle forward, and they were quickly aloft and out of sight of those on the ground.

Strapped in the second seat, Elena crossed herself, and prayed for safe travel for the bishop, and themselves, as Maldonado picked their way between scattered clumps of trees, hedgehopping the grassy savanna toward the foothills leading up to Campo Alto.

Bishop Subueso entered the chapel and sank onto the bench where their conversation took place, trying to think. *She's right,* he thought, *there seems to be a kind of evil power behind Monsignor Schmehr and the men around him.* It had been clear to Subueso for some time that the country's clergy were plain afraid of them. At least five priests that he knew of had disappeared after they had raised questions or spoken out against perceived irregularities and the obvious lack of piety at the cathedral. He shook his head, got to his feet, went to kneel before the altar.

"Forgive me, Father," he prayed, crossing himself. "I should have realized that things were this bad, and I should have tried to do something about it."

———————

Elena felt peace settling over her as Maldonado climbed above the foothills, heading toward Campo Alto in the mountains. She settled back in the seat and smiled, picturing the jolting impact the fiery little bishop would have bounding into the Vatican demanding to see the Pope.

FIFTY-TWO

THE PRESIDENTIAL PALACE

"I said, Paco," Benes repeated, addressing his young aide, "the captives at Prison Number Five are to be killed . . . terminated if your sensitivity requires a euphemism." In the Roman times the order to slay the prisoners was a dreaded one. To the foot soldier it meant the situation was dire and a gaggle of prisoners was weighing the army down. To the prisoners it meant they would fall to the sword here and now and not survive as slaves.

Major Paco Martinez stiffened. The ancient world may have been cruel, he knew, but this was San Marcos, with cars and people streaming by in the sunlight outside.

"Sir, this is a monstrous act. I cannot carry out such a bestial order. It would be murder. Multiple murders."

Benes stood with his back to him, looking out the window of his third-floor office in the Presidential Palace toward the twin towers of the cathedral across the *Plaza Catedral*. He had just returned from one of his increasingly frequent sessions with the Reichsfuhrer. The maximum leader's words had stung him. They rang in his ears yet.

"But Reichsfuhrer," he had cautioned, "are you forgetting that there are four Americans with the others at Prison Number Five? The American government will certainly take measures against us."

"I am not forgetting anything! The Americans are two doctors, an archaeologist, and the son of the meddlesome Mallory."

"Reichsfuhrer, the very fact of an American military family is all the more reason their government will act."

"It is you who are forgetting, Reich Marshal Benes. Mallory killed my Viktor, so it is fitting to repay him with the death of his son. As for his government, I'm not worried in the slightest. If they do not yet know about Prison Five, we must assume they will find out soon enough. That is all the more reason to liquidate the prisoners now." Tolt had sneered, and continued his lecture.

"You see, Reich Marshal, the Americans are quick to mount rescue attempts but they are loath to respond to a *fait accompli*—especially one that is packaged properly. The prisoners succumbing to tropical disease, let us say."

"Since when was a hail of bullets a tropical disease?"

"Since I gave you the order just now.

"You are dismissed, Reich Marshal Benes!"

As Benes' mind returned to the present, he turned around to face the major.

"Very well, Paco, you have made your point now."

He drew his sidearm and leveled it at his aide.

"Carry out my order, Major Martinez!

Martinez drew himself to attention. "As a professional soldier, I will not murder unarmed prisoners!"

Benes shot him dead and reached for the phone.

"Capitan!" he shouted, "dispatch a Death Squad to Prison Number Five! All the prisoners are to be killed before sundown. . . . Yes, yes . . . and if the prison guards resist, kill them all too!"

FIFTY-THREE

THE VATICAN

Monsignor Albert entered Guilianni's penthouse with a stack of files under his arm. The heavy drapes were drawn against the noonday sun but he could hear through the French doors standing open behind the drapes that the cardinal and his guests were having lunch outside on the terrace. The American Ambassador to Costa Verde, a Frederick Cathcart, was here to receive the reply to his government's inquiry about Tolt and the others.

Ambassador Cathcart probably knows them by sight, Albert thought, *may even have a speaking acquaintance with Tolt. It's probably why he's here in place of their Secretary of State Wasserman who lodged the matter with us.* He paused and tried to pray but it was no use. He slipped into the cardinal's bathroom to compose himself for the pivotal interview. *Good God!* he whimpered, peering in the mirror and pawing the colorless folds of flesh under his chin. *I look so old and tired.* He had read somewhere that men appear ten years younger to themselves than to others. *If so,* he decided, *these damn overhead fluorescents are the cure. They jerk you into the stark reality.*

Instinctively, he pressed both hands to his chest, aware of his beating heart. The recovery from his episode was uneventful, and the doctors had assured him that with beta-blockers as precautionary medication a reoccurrence was unlikely. Albert knew better. He was convinced that the stress of his double life would one day cause his heart to stop. He was sure that the conflict festering within him took its toll physically. *Well, nothing's to be done about the way I look.* He switched on the mirror's ring of incandescent bulbs and they made him feel a little better.

What the devil am I doing primping like a schoolgirl? I belong outside with the others before Guilianni sends someone to fetch me.

Pausing behind the drapery, he straightened his cassock and adjusted its sash. *How long can the great deception continue?* he asked himself for the thousandth time since craven fear had tumbled him into Staib's orbit. His tepid faith seemed so impotent recently. He got hold of himself and mentally rehearsed the story-line he had advised Guilianni to tell the American. It was simple and straightforward and he felt comfortable with it. Although the sovereignty of the Vatican state could be asserted to preserve confidentiality of its records, Albert had made copies of everything for his file and would give the originals to the Americans as a gesture of good faith, which he hoped would resolve the matter speedily. Moreover, the bona fides of Monsignor Schmehr and his staff were further substantiated by documents obtained from the German government, or so Albert had convinced Guilianni. In fact, these were sketchy and not helpful. But Albert had salted the file liberally with the Stasi dossiers Staib provided in the beginning. There was also a new ace-in-the-hole, thanks to Karpf's professionalism. The old spymaster had provided stacks of memoranda questioning the defectors' loyalty to the communist regime. These would pass muster, being authentic Stasi documents prepared while Karpf was running state security in East Germany. Everything and more was there in the file under his arm to prove Tolt's, Kreeber's, Kaalten's and Staib's authenticity as priests of the Church.

Why am I so nervous? he wondered. *Why do I cower from a meeting I can so easily control? Indecision, that's it!* He clenched his teeth. *I must and damn well will preserve my deception.* He had rationalized his failure to make a clean breast of things on the basis that his close association with Guilianni would destroy the cardinal's brilliant career. Men caught up in sin grasp whatever rationalization they can, and this rationale made sense to him. He straightened his cassock again and smoothed his thinning hair. *Oh, God,* he prayed, *if this is to be the end of my road, give me grace to accept it. Help me to finesse this meeting. Preserve my soul.*

It didn't occur to him that he had just asked God to bless a fraud on the Church.

Cocking his ear to the conversation to pick the moment for his entrance he could hear the voices of a couple of preteen girls and Guilianni's voluble banter. He smiled, buoyed by the cardinal's infectious light heart.

"Yes, Misses Cathcart, that's right," he heard him chirp. "You're very observant. That one indeed is the little chimney where puffs of white smoke signal the election of a new Pope."

A bubbly female voice, the Ambassador's wife's of course, rose above the clatter of dishes being cleared. "Oh, Frederick!" she gushed. "Isn't this simply wonderful. I'm so glad we saw the movie—what was it? Oh, dear! Now I've forgotten. You know, with Anthony Quinn—"

"The Shoes of the Fisherman," Guilianni bubbled. "Yes, I quite enjoyed it myself."

"You know, Cardinal," she confided, "we're just Episcopalians ourselves, but I've always felt so very, you know . . . Catholic—"

"Dear," Cathcart now, "I'm sure the cardinal's time is very limited and—"

"Not in the least," Guilianni protested. "It's been wonderful to share the hour with you, Mister Ambassador, and your lovely family. But," he paused, probably consulting his watch, "it's time for the little tour I promised Misses Cathcart and your lovely daughters, while you and I,

389

Ambassador, must attend to the important business which has brought you to us today."

Now! Albert told himself, stepping onto the terrace, where he waited by the door as Mrs. Cathcart and the girls were escorted away. The images he had formed from the table talk were on target. Mrs. Cathcart, a very pretty woman, was wearing too much jewelry and her daughters, ages about ten and thirteen, were attractive and well-mannered. And Ambassador Cathcart seemed the archetypal upper-crust political appointee, firm of jaw, exuding the obligatory, vaguely superior manner of his class. He thought it unprofessional that Cathcart brought his wife and children to such an important, hastily arranged, high-level meeting. A career diplomat wouldn't do such a thing.

"Ah," Guilianni announced, beckoning, "and here's the monsignor now." Turning to face Cathcart, the cardinal offered a broad smile. "It's such a beautiful day, Mister Ambassador," he suggested, "I wonder if you wouldn't like to remain right here in the shade of my awning and enjoy a Cuban cigar with some more of this humble red wine from my native village in Tuscany?"

"Yes, splendid," Cathcart intoned, glancing at Albert and the stack of papers he placed on the table. "This is such a wonderful setting," the American breathed, gesturing toward the acres of tile roofs and formal gardens below.

"Well then, let us begin," Guilianni proposed, signaling for cigars and reaching for the wine. "As you no doubt know, Mister Ambassador, when your Secretary of State, Miss Wasserman, was in Rome last week and took the time to come to see me about this business personally, I begged a few days to inquire of the civil authorities in Germany.

"You see," the little cardinal continued, clipping the end of his cigar, "our files are complete, except in one respect and the deficiency has now been rectified. Just the day before yesterday we received . . .

"Monsignor," he motioned to Albert, "won't you please explain it all to the ambassador? By the way, Ambassador, you will be interested to know that Monsignor Albert is about to become Archbishop of

Dresden in his native Germany. It's a most unusual thing to be elevated from monsignor to archbishop in what you Americans call one jump and signals His Holiness' high regard for him."

Cathcart beamed. "That indeed is an honor, Monsignor." He looked to Guilianni. "When will this occur, if it's appropriate to ask?"

"Early next month, in a public installation at Dresden Cathedral."

"My heartiest congratulations, Monsignor Albert. Now, before we go any farther," Cathcart continued, accepting a light from Guilianni, "I want to say I have never experienced such rapid response to an inquiry as yours. My government and I are deeply appreciative."

Guilianni smiled. "It is not often the American Secretary of State visits us personally, but in truth it was no bother to pull all this information together for you."

"Very well, Eminence," Albert said, turning to face Cathcart and sliding the papers across the table to him. "What his Eminence was saying is that when the four souls in question defected from behind the Wall, we had no confirmation of the stories they told. Well, we could hardly ask East Germany's secret police to substantiate—"

"Yes," Cathcart said, "right you are, there. I know something about the Stasi, actually, from my reading."

"In that case, Mister Ambassador," Albert told him, "these documents from the German Foreign Ministry in Berlin will interest you. Unfortunately, I haven't had time to translate them yet—"

Cathcart's face lit up as his moment arrived. "Well, of course, I do read German," he said, nasally. "Yes, quite well enough, I should think."

Albert reached across the table and with his finger tapped a sheaf of papers on the stack in front of Cathcart, who quickly thumbed through them and selected one to read.

"Well, this is dated 5 January 1988," he announced, holding the page in both hands with the cigar between his teeth. "State Security," he translated—"read Stasi for State Security"—he told them, peering over half-rim reading glasses at Albert, then Guilianni, and enjoying the opportunity to showcase his expertise, "has determined that Josef

Schmehr, Priest, is to be considered an Enemy of the State, under Day Order No. Five-Three-Seven-Seven. . . ."

"If I may, Ambassador," Albert offered, "what you have there are the actual dossiers that Stasi maintained concerning each of these poor servants of God."

Cathcart raised an eyebrow and seemed impressed. "Communist East Germany," Albert continued, "was closed to us since the Church wasn't favored by that regime. And, frankly, Mister Ambassador," he leaned closer as if to confide, "we hadn't the need of probing the matter further; that is, not until Secretary Wasserman's inquiry.

"Not many documents escaped the wholesale destruction at Stasi headquarters, as they anticipated German Reunification. Very fortunately, these were found when the Bonn government took over. When you examine it all very carefully," Albert suggested, "you'll see that Father Martin was also classified an enemy of the state, while the others were under observation for suspected anti-communist activities. It was only a matter of time until—"

"Well, I certainly do see," Cathcart said, enjoying his cigar as Guilianni topped off his wine. "Little wonder these people sought asylum in the West."

Albert nodded gravely. "You are welcome to take all these files with you, Mister Ambassador," he said. "And please do note the dates of birth," he advised, "when you have opportunity read everything carefully. You'll notice, for example," he continued, "that the oldest of these priests, that would be Monsignor Schmehr, was only sixteen in 1945 when the war ended. So, of course, they couldn't be Nazi war criminals as your government may have feared."

"Oh, not war criminals, exactly," Cathcart said, fondling a cuff link. "I believe our concern, rather, was they might have ties to the neo-Nazi-leaning government of the current strongman of Costa Verde, a Colonel Benes. But these documents certainly put things in a different light."

Guilianni slapped his knee. "Yes!" he interjected. "And, you see, I myself sponsored them for Vatican citizenship," he said with pride. "I can give the utmost personal assurances they are simple men of God, albeit perhaps unsuited, culturally, to service in Costa Verde. But you would know more about the society there, Ambassador. Perhaps," the Little Pope acknowledged with upturned palms, as a pout formed on his lips, "the fault is mine for assigning German speakers to the cathedral in San Marcos."

Cathcart raised his hands in protest.

"By no means, Eminence!" he said. "Far be it from me or my government to suggest any such kind of a thing. Far from being unsuitable," he said, "they are no doubt serving the Church and the faithful wonderfully."

The skilled Guilianni seized the moment with a flourish, as he gestured expansively with his cigar and rose from the table.

"May I count on you, Ambassador, to thank Secretary Wasserman once again for stopping by to see me? When you pass through Washington, as I suppose you will on your return to Costa Verde, please reiterate my hope I may have the pleasure again, and soon. Perhaps when I travel to the United Nations in January?"

Mission accomplished! Cathcart realized. He could give Wasserman solid answers to pass along to the CIA. He beamed and extended his hand to Guilianni.

"My government's sincerest appreciation, Eminence, and my personal gratitude for your superb hospitality. My girls will never forget it."

He shook Albert's hand. "Again, Monsignor, my government's heartiest congratulations on your elevation."

———————

Albert escorted Cathcart to a driveway where his wife and daughters waited in a U.S. Embassy sedan. His monsignor's cassock rippled in the afternoon breeze as he shook Cathcart's hand and watched the ambassador enter the car with the files under his arm. Cathcart waved as the sedan rolled through the massive iron gates and disappeared into the rushing traffic beyond the wall.

Albert's emotions welled within him as he stood at the top of the driveway staring into space. His eyes were tearing for no reason he could identify.

I am aging too fast! Am I edging toward the confessional?

It had been easy to lie to Cathcart as the representative of a foreign government, and yet the encounter had taken a greater emotional toll than it should have.

What if today's visitor were a brother priest, instead? He decided not to think about that.

FIFTY-FOUR

CAMPO ALTO

Mallory awoke with a start and found himself in the trailer, wedged onto a cot by the wall. He looked at his watch and realized he had lain there fully clothed about three hours, knotted with worry about the outcome of the operation intended to rescue David and the others from Prison Number Five.

He took some comfort in knowing that America's Special Operations Forces were the best in the world and should know what the hell they're doing, but the obvious dangers kept recirculating in his brain. He tried to massage the grogginess from his head. *Will there be a shoot-out endangering the inmates? Will they kill the prisoners to prevent the rescue? Just how fanatic are their captors?* Stumbling into the main room he found the others huddled by the radio. "What news about David?" he asked. "What's been happening?"

"Good news!" Elena beamed. "American Special Ops and Carlos' column made a coordinated assault on the prison. We think the prisoners have been rescued."

"What do you mean, 'you think'? What about David?" The strain and impatience were clearly evident in his still-thick voice.

"We're not sure yet," Peralta said. "We lost radio contact. Your stealth helicopters could be airlifting the American captives to Panama by now."

"Dammit, Nacho, is David with them? What's happening?"

"We don't know," Peralta answered, as Mallory hovered over him. "We're assuming he's definitely out of the prison, but we haven't been able to confirm whether he's with your SOF people or with Carlos' column."

"When will we know?" Mallory demanded, beginning to pace the floor.

"As soon as we re-establish communication with Carlos," Peralta said, turning to the radio operator who remained glued to his equipment. "Still no luck, Pepe?"

Pepe shook his head. "I'm trying," he said, holding an earphone to his right ear. "The signal keeps fading."

Mallory grimaced and pounded his fist into his hand as thoughts of losing David as he'd lost Luisa assaulted his mind. He willed them to cease.

Protect David, protect them all, he prayed.

He tried to smile. "Sorry I'm so edgy. I guess I need something to do while we wait this one out, Nacho, so why don't you entertain me with how the hell you can operate out of this trailer park?"

Peralta struggled to his feet as Elena handed him his crutches. "It's really pretty simple," he said, relieved to change the subject. "We're just below the normal cloud level here, and there's about five hundred feet of clear road outside those big clamshell doors, which are camouflaged with jungle material." He shifted his weight on the crutches, warming to Mallory's interest. "With the doors closed we can't be seen from the air. Not even if the cloud cover moves away from the entrance a few minutes as it sometimes does. The clam shell is opened for landing and we complete our roll-out on into the sheltered area here. On takeoff, we run up in here and the Bearcats are airborne in less than 300 feet. The road is whisked down with shrubbery to cover the tire tracks after every take-off and landing. There's a sentry post a short distance down the hillside to report anyone approaching by land. So far, no one's come near us. It's a good system."

Mallory nodded. "What if the cloud layer drops below the entrance and socks you in, as it looks like it's done right now? How do you take off?"

"No problem," Peralta breezed. "It's a real clear shot straight ahead so, if you're socked in, you take off on instruments, fly straight and level for ten seconds and then drop down under the cloud cover. We've done it many times."

"And if you're socked in when you return?"

"We divert to one of the other bases. They're not far and they're all manned like Campo Alto," he swept the air with a hand, "with mechanics, armorers, fuel people, living quarters, everything. They offer great flexibility. For example, as soon as I can fly again, Maldonado and I will hit the main garrison on the coast, then lay over at *Campo Bajo* in the lowlands." He hobbled to the table and indicated the location of the other two bases on a chart. "Maldonado is now at *Campo Medio,*" he tapped a spot on the map, "here in the foothills. We don't mark the locations on our charts in case they fall into the wrong hands. On the next sortie, we'll rendezvous in the air."

"Okay," Mallory said, "you mentioned fuel supply. I doubt a tanker truck could go unnoticed driving up here."

Peralta's face broke into a satisfied smile. "That's true. So we have several smaller tankers disguised as trucks carrying produce. They carry phony bills of lading, but none has been stopped. We bring in ordnance in the same way, but there's plenty stored here already."

Mallory nodded approval. "Well, I must say again, you seem to have thought of just about everything."

"I hope so. Stuff like this has occupied my thoughts for several years."

The radio crackled as Pepe jabbed the speaker button. "Here's Carlos, Jefe!" he shouted excitedly.

Carlos sounded out of breath as he reported being pinned down under fire in a ravine not far from the prison. "We need close air support, immediately!" he shouted.

Mallory asked about David. "Don't know," Carlos gasped. "The Americans lifted some prisoners out, but most of them are with us here in the ravine."

"Stand by," Peralta told him. "Damn," he shouted, cursing his leg. "We've got to get up there with whatever we have to give them support, but I can't even climb up into a goddamn cockpit." He looked to Smith who lounged on the couch with his leg over the arm. "Smith, you'll have to get up there and go it alone. It's life or death for them. Every minute counts."

"Really?" Smith said, slowly putting down his magazine. "So far, I've flamed my share of aircraft, blown up a hell of a lot of tanks and strafed the shit out of their grunts on the ground. But right now your half-assed cause isn't going so well, and you want me to risk my life bailing out a column of gooks?" His face took on a self-satisfied smile. "I think it definitely calls for extra pay."

Peralta glared and started to move toward Smith but he stopped, racked with pain.

"Loser!" Smith leered. "So what if I just upped the ante for this mission?"

"You slimy bastard!" Peralta shouted. "You've already made more money than your last dozen jobs combined."

"Sure," Smith said, getting up and stepping toward Peralta, "and that's why you're going to break out lots of greenback dollars before I even mount up this time."

Peralta fought to control his rage. "All right. Ten thousand more. You know we don't keep money here. You'll get it when Arturo brings the payroll."

"No way," Smith spat. "Just count me the hell out."

"How can you do this," Elena pleaded, "when you know people are dying? You know Nacho's word is good."

"I don't know shit, lady." Smith waved his hand around the room. "This is the losing team if I ever saw one."

He stormed from the trailer.

Peralta turned to Pepe. "Raise Maldonado at Campo Medio. If he's fueled and ready, he could make it in time." But everyone knew that Campo Medio was at least a half hour's additional flying time from the prison.

Pepe began adjusting the dials on his set.

Elena bolted outside looking for Smith. She spotted him coming out of his trailer with a duffel bag over his shoulder, heading for his Jeep.

"Please don't leave us like this," she pleaded. "Our kids are dying out there."

"This is a dying outfit," he snarled. "I say screw it, there's money to be made elsewhere. Colonel Benes pays a bonus too, you know."

"You bastard!" she shrieked. "You came to us with nothing and made tons of filthy money, tax-free money deposited to your offshore bank."

"Get the fuck out of my way," he shouted, as he reached the Jeep. "Look, your jerks still haven't closed the gate, so I'm gonna drive right through and down to San Benito."

"No!" she screamed.

"Who's to stop me?" he laughed. "Your imaginary panther friend? Your pathetic brother with his busted foot? Captain Deke Fucking Midnight or whatever his name is?"

She lunged to beat him with her fists, but he pushed her to the ground. She tried to get to her feet. He kicked her in the stomach and yanked the Jeep's door open.

Mallory dashed out of the trailer in time to see Smith draw his sidearm. There was a loud report and Smith flopped backwards to the ground. Turning around, he saw Diego crouching for another shot should Smith so much as twitch.

"Never trusted the filthy dog," Diego spat. "I've been watching him for days."

Men appeared with drawn weapons. "Take this piece of shit and throw him in the jungle," Diego ordered, as they dragged Smith's body away. "Let the scavengers have him."

Peralta burst from the trailer and leaned against the door post. *"Santa Mierda!"* he shouted, surveying the scene.

Mallory knelt down and scooped Elena up in his arms. She clung tightly to him as he carried her into the trailer and laid her on the couch. She started to say something, but he held his finger to her lips until she relaxed.

Peralta was raging like a wounded animal. "Diego!" he shouted, "help me to my Bearcat. Pepe, get the medical kit with the novocaine and shoot my foot full of it."

All Mallory could think about was David being exposed to punishing fire in the ravine and he made his decision. He turned from his place kneeling by Elena's side to glare at Peralta. "Shut up, Nacho, you're not going anywhere in your condition." He rose to his feet with Elena's hand still entwined in his. "You know as well as I it takes strong legs to work the rudder on a Bearcat. So back off, I'm taking Smith's place," he told him. "You know Maldonado can't possibly get there fast enough. Just give me your helmet and the chart. Show me where the prison is."

"No, Deke," Peralta pleaded, "you can't afford—"

"Don't argue with me, Nacho. It's life or death for those people up there. They're desperate for close air support, right now!"

Peralta slowly pointed to his helmet atop a locker as Pepe retrieved the charts from the table. Selecting one of them, Peralta pointed to their location at Campo Alto, circled the area of the prison, which was marked by a small black square, and silently handed the chart to Mallory.

"Both flyable Cats are armed and fueled," Peralta said. "Better take Smith's. It doesn't have as many holes in it."

Mallory turned to Pepe. "Try to reach Carlos and tell him help is on the way. I'll try to get back here afterward . . . assuming I can find this place."

As he reached the door, Elena grabbed his arm and tugged him around for a kiss on the lips. She let him go, put her hand over her mouth, and turned away.

Men were securing the clamshell camouflage doors across the entrance. Mallory called for them to open it again. Smith's plane was the first in line, armed with a 250-pound bomb on each wing. There were no chocks to pull. He climbed up in the cockpit, strapped in, and plugged in the microphone mounted on the left side of the helmet.

He immediately realized this wasn't his racing plane but a war machine. The gear stripped from the racer was back where it belonged, as designed by Grumman engineers to sweep the skies of enemy aircraft: gunsight, arming switches, gun charging levers, bomb release switches—the tools of war.

Aware of the emotions and mounting alarm draining the energy from his mind and body, he paused to squeeze his eyes shut and try to forcefully compose himself. There was no way of knowing if David was safely on the way to Panama or still pinned down in a ravine with Carlos. And the fact that an active-duty Naval Officer could be court-martialed for what he was about to do would just have to take a back seat to his fear for David's life.

Satisfied that he was in charge of his faculties, he quickly checked to make sure the battery switch was OFF, put the fuel tank selector on MAIN, the prop control to FULL INCREASE RPM, and cracked the throttle about an inch. Making sure the cowl flaps were open, he turned the battery switch to ON, the generator switch and auxiliary fuel pump to ON, turned the ignition switch to BOTH, and hit the starter. His memory served him well, the engine fired, and he advanced the mixture control to full RICH.

The powerful R-2800 engine cranked, coughed, sputtered, and then belched yellow flame back past the open cockpit. He ducked his head. In his haste he forgot to close the canopy for starting. The flame turned to black exhaust as he sat upright and idled the engine at about 1000 RPM.

He moved the throttle forward, lined the Bearcat up with the entrance, and locked the tail wheel. The clamshell was open now. With no time to waste on a run-up, he continued the throttle on slowly to full military power of 58 inches of manifold pressure—on the theory if an engine took the smooth application of power, the plane would fly. He released the brakes, passed through the vine-covered entrance, and was off the deck in about 250 feet. With full right rudder to counter-act the incredible torque, he brought the gear up, re-trimmed, counting to ten as he roared through the damp, gray void outside before drop-ping into the clear. Skimming the bottom of the cloud layer, he turned to a heading he knew would take him to the area of the prison.

Please God! Don't let me be too late!

FIFTY-FIVE

ABOVE THE SAVANNA

Mallory took the Bearcat down to an altitude of less than 200 feet, hugging the tropical savanna consisting of grassland with scattered clumps of trees. He hoped that any radar that might be operating in the area wouldn't be able to paint him this low. With vivid memories of blowing his engine at Reno, he held his speed of 410. Checking his shoulder harness for the business at hand, he studied the chart as carefully as he could while flying so fast near the deck. The column was pinned down somewhere east of the prison, trying to cross a ravine running roughly north and south, with government troops probably occupying the higher ground west of the ravine. If so, he would make his runs south to north and back again to give the column time to reach the thick jungle to the east.

The savanna gradually gave way to a coastal jungle near sea level. Soon he was skimming the tops of palm trees, a sight evoking images of combat footage of Viet Nam. A split-second image of threatening SAMs triggered a spasm of terror and for a moment he was going to jink the Bearcat, when his mind returned to Costa Verde. As with most combat pilots, his own experiences were impersonal; just your aircraft against the enemy's, flown by a faceless, bloodless fighting machine without personality or identity. If you scored a victory, it was because you outflew and outfought the enemy pilot, who just happened to be strapped in a mass of metal that went down in flames. If the enemy scored a victory over you, then it was your flesh and blood in a very real, human death. Even flying close support of friendly ground troops your involvement in their fortunes was remote, though they were your people.

He shuddered as he suddenly sensed that David was under fire up ahead someplace with Carlos' column, and he realized that for the first time in his career he was personally involved with the outcome of combat.

A few miles from the target he pulled up to get a broader picture of the battlefield. In the distance he made out structures that could be the prison. To the east were the shadows of what was probably the ravine. A moment later he saw puffs of gray smoke rising in the air. Mortar fire!

Realizing the moment of truth, he searched the instrument panel for the gun-charging switches. He remembered where they were on a half-dozen Navy fighters, but he had never flown an armed Bearcat. *They would have to be on the left, operated by the throttle hand . . . yes, here they are to the left of the gunsight. Okay, master armament and gun switches ON.* The charging levers for the 20 mm cannons should be below. There they were, above the rudder pedals at the base of the instrument panel. He reached down and turned the levers to the UP position and pushed the handles in. The guns charged and the handles sprung back out. He fired a short burst for confirmation.

The cannon-fire brought home the harsh reality of his situation: an active-duty Navy captain, supposedly vacationing in Costa Verde, working undercover for the CIA, was about to attack the military of a sovereign nation—a court-martial offense if there ever was one. He bit his lip, contemplating the gravity of it, but then smiled as he recalled this wasn't the first time he had violated rules of engagement.

"All right," he muttered, "so I'm doing it again! But it's different this time with David down there someplace."

If he had a clear picture of the deployment of the government troops, he would use the two bombs on the first run or two, then strafe with 20 mm. He found the bomb selector switches where he expected, to the right of the gunsight on the top of the instrument panel, and turned the port switch to ON.

THE PRESIDENTIAL PALACE

Colonel Benes was livid with rage as his new aide reported the breaching of the prison and the freeing of the prisoners. "How could they do that?" Benes bellowed.

"Their assault," Captain Santanna told him, "was preceded by unmarked, black helicopters carrying commandos. They're the ones who breached our security."

Benes pounded his fist on his desk. "Peralta doesn't have helicopters. They're *Norte Americanos!*"

"Yes, sir. But the Peraltistas are still in the area."

"Get me *Mesa del Norte*," Benes shouted. "I'll launch my COINs and F-80s and napalm the bastards."

"The COINs are there already, sir. But after the recent attack, we have only one operational F-80."

"Then launch it, goddammit," Benes screamed. "Launch the F-80 NOW!"

ABOVE THE JUNGLE

Mallory spotted government troops concentrated in a clearing east of the prison. He swung to the left and then back to the right, aligning his bomb run to put the most troops in line for the drop. Suddenly, a glance to his left showed two Cessna A-37B Dragonflies swinging around for a run at the ravine. They apparently hadn't seen him approach low from the south and continued on into their turn. It wasn't mortar fire he'd seen, it was ordnance from these counter-insurgency aircraft. His primary target was now the A-37 Dragonflies. In addition to cannon in the nose, they could carry four 800-pound bombs, plus gun and rocket pods. They were a masterpiece of destructive firepower, and they were again about to do exactly what they were designed for. He didn't want the burden of bombs in a dogfight but he didn't want to waste them by dumping them either, so he decided to go for the brass ring. He would try to take out one of the A-37s and bomb the troops during the same run. He flipped the second bomb selector switch to ON.

He swung the Bearcat in behind the trailing A-37 as it was lining up for its own bomb run. Even though his target was a twin engine jet, he knew he could easily match its speed and rate of climb and he could out-turn it. He had no trouble easing up on the adversary's tail. With the unsuspecting aircraft securely in his gunsight, he squeezed the trigger, sending a burst of 20 mm up its tailpipes, then walking the fire back and forth with the rudder to ensure maximum damage to both engines. The Dragonfly exploded in an orange ball of fire, and he pulled up sharply to avoid the flaming debris. He nosed over for a bomb run at the troops on the ground, hoping to do major damage with both bombs before the lead Dragonfly figured out what had happened to his wingman.

The troops ran for cover as he released the bombs. Meanwhile the second Dragonfly had completed a half circle to the left and was now rolling into a firing run on him. No surprise left in the game! It was *mano-a-mano* with this guy, and he would find out if his adversary was any good. Mallory firewalled everything on the throttle quadrant—full rich mixture, full RPM, and the throttle to military power, and tried to recall in a split second what he knew about the A-37. All he had time to consider was that it wasn't designed as a fighter whereas his plane was. As he wrapped the Bearcat into a steep vertical bank to the right, he heard his own voice in his earphones.

"Okay, hot shot, let's see what you've got!"

The imprint of 10,000 hours of fighter time deposited in the bank of his memory kicked in. The Dragonfly was off to his left, coming in on his six. Even though he could out-turn it, he knew he might not be able to pull enough lead to get into firing position himself if he stayed in the horizontal plane, but he could try. He tightened his turn and strained as hard as he could to tighten his abdominal muscles. Without a G-Suit it was his only defense against the vascular narcotic of G forces that drained blood from your brain, tunneled your vision, and clouded it with little black dots. He was almost on the Dragonfly's six now. There! He was in the saddle for a shot. But as the A-37's image swung back and forth like a pendulum in the concentric circles of his gunsight, he realized he wasn't pulling quite enough lead to fire his cannon.

Better try something else.

The increased power of jet fighters during Viet Nam had taken the classic dogfight into the vertical dimension, with "yo-yo" and "scissors" maneuvers. The Bearcat had the power to do that, too, and he instinctively added full power and pulled up into a high yo-yo. As he came over the top with his wings almost vertical, he slid back down inside the Dragonfly's turn and positioned himself well for a deflection shot of about 20 degrees. He calculated the necessary lead and fired a long burst, just as the Dragonfly reversed direction. As it disappeared from his gunsight he thought he had scored hits but he wasn't sure. He snapped into a high barrel roll to the left, hoping to come out near the Dragonfly's tail but as he came out the A-37 wasn't there. Frantically, he swiveled his neck, realizing that the A-37 was out there somewhere and about to pounce on him.

He didn't have to wait long. The A-37 pilot had recovered skillfully and was now chewing on Mallory's tail. He could see yellow flashes coming from its cannons and quickly pulled into the vertical, knowing that for these few seconds the Bearcat could outfly the Dragonfly. *The guy's better than I gave him credit for,* he thought, as he looped into the inverted and craned his neck to keep the COIN in sight. *Okay, there he is. Good.* Pulling out of the looping dive, he slid into the saddle for a dead astern shot. Pouring a massive burst of 20 mm at the A-37, he had so much excess speed he shot past in an overshoot, again not knowing if he had scored hits. Swinging around to the right he saw his target heading south, trailing smoke.

His adversary was out of the game.

He whipped the Bearcat back to the north and lined up for a strafing run at the ground troops. Carlos' column with the prisoners was nowhere in sight, apparently having advanced in the gathering darkness to the relative safety of the jungle to the east. Pulling up from the run, he eased back on power and swung around to see if there was any additional threat to their retreat. As he approached a clearing in the jungle, he could see Carlos' men emerging from the shelter of the trees and waving to him. As he scanned for David they suddenly retreated to cover like rabbits running from a hawk's shadow.

He looked up to see a Lockheed F-80 jet fighter, with yellow flashes surrounding the six .50-caliber guns in its nose. Breaking into a hard left bank he realized he was in the worst possible situation, low and slow at near treetop level—a fighter pilot's worst nightmare! The Bearcat could accelerate rapidly in a climb, but the F-80 pilot need only trade a little speed for more altitude to be in an ideal firing position on the climbing Bearcat.

He quickly searched the sky for the F-80's wingman, fully expecting hits on his plane any second. Fortunately, the F-80 appeared to be alone and his mind raced with the tactics available to him under this most miserable of circumstances. There weren't any!

He was a sitting duck, and as soon as the F-80 pilot gained some altitude, he would be in a position to pounce at will. Although the F-80 jock had the tactical advantage, Mallory knew he had the advantage of years of combat experience, including a few hours in F-80s which the Navy called TVs—if he could get into a position to use it.

Mercifully, the F-80's stream of lead missed again.

As the F-80 leveled off in preparation for his next run, Mallory scanned the cockpit in a frantic search for advantage. Peralta had reinstalled the emergency water injection system. *Where is it? It has to be on the left. Yes!* There it was on the canopy rail above the throttle quadrant.

He quickly flipped it to ON, hoping he had a full tank of water. From what he could remember, it gave about five minutes of emergency power by injecting water to cool the intake from the supercharger so the engine could take the increased power. He looked up at the higher-flying F-80 and heard himself addressing the enemy pilot aloud. "Okay, buster, you've just enrolled in my personal TOPGUN fighter combat school. So pay attention."

He watched the F-80 begin to roll into another run at him and imagined the smug grin on the pilot's face. He coolly waited until the adversary was almost in firing position and—with a quick prayer for an operational system and a full tank of water—he jammed the throttle past the wired detent. The engine screamed to combat power and the Bearcat shuddered as it accelerated in a climb, just as the F-80 fired. Its stream of lead again fell short, and the F-80 flew past and pulled up for another pass. Mallory remained in combat power as he leveled the Bearcat momentarily, then quickly barrel-rolled left, which put him right on the F-80's tail. He eased the throttle and swung in dead astern. As he closed to effective firing range, he instinctively sensed a slowing of the F-80, then saw its dive brakes coming out beneath the fuselage. It was an old trick: you jam on your brakes, your pursuer doesn't and shoots right on past you. Presto! now you're on his six!

No way! I won't be suckered into an overshoot.

He instinctively moved his thumb down the throttle for the speed brake control that would have been on an F-18, but realized instantly the Bearcat didn't have any. But it did have dive recovery flaps to be used at high speeds to avoid compressibility. He pulled off power, reached for the console to the left of the throttle and activated the lever. The little flaps on the underside of the fuselage just inboard of the wheel wells came out. As he pushed forward on the stick to compensate for the change in trim, he could feel the deceleration as the Bearcat closed slightly but remained in the saddle for the shot at the F-80. He squeezed off a burst but realized that, in the time spent figuring out how to activate the dive recovery flaps, he'd lost concentration and his aim.

The jet retracted its brakes and accelerated in a slight dive, obviously hoping to outrun the Bearcat with its superior speed and then reposition itself for another run. Mallory pulled in the dive recovery brakes, pushed the throttle back to combat power, and maneuvered for a dead astern tailpipe shot. The F-80 pilot, confident of his jet's comfortable speed advantage and unaware of the capabilities of a water-injected Bearcat to overtake him, maintained a straight course with no evasive action.

"Bad career move!" Mallory shouted, triggering the 20 mm cannons. "You flunked my course!"

If the adversary had a last thought it was probably one of total surprise, as his aircraft exploded in an orange fireball. The water injection had done its job. Mallory backed the throttle out of combat power, hoping the engine had been sufficiently cooled to prevent any damage.

A quick check of the battle area revealed no other aircraft in the air and no further evidence of government troops. Fervently hoping that his impromptu mission had pulled David from harm's way, he leaned the mixture and set the power for a fast cruise back to base. He was suddenly aware of the dismal fact that if Campo Alto was still socked in, he would never find it. In his haste he hadn't confirmed a radio frequency for contact with the base.

His attention soon focused elsewhere. He was becoming critically low on fuel. He must have taken a hit in a fuel line from ground fire. He remembered Nacho showing him the other bases on the chart, but the fuel gauge said NO. As his mind raced with preparations for a forced landing in the relatively flat savanna, if he could get there, he recalled Arturo mentioning an abandoned CIA air strip near here, once used to supply covert aid to the Nicaraguan Contras. Arturo thought the land once belonged to U.S. officials close to the White House. He glanced at the chart, but the strip wasn't there of course. Arturo said it was at the base of a prominent peak at the bend of a river. According to the topo lines and terrain colors on the chart, there was a peak in the area, and it was near a bend in the river.

A glance at the fuel gauge—lower than before and sinking—left no choice. He headed for where his chart showed the peak. After a minute or two he could make out what appeared to be the top of a mountain protruding from the jungle carpet. Passing over a small meandering river, he dropped down and circled for a closer look. There was no open spot in view where he could land, and the savanna to the west was now well out of range, given his fuel condition. He was committed to the unknown.

———————

He followed the little river toward the mountain peak rising from the jungle. If this wasn't the mountain Arturo described—or the fuel gave out before he got there—he would plow into the dense jungle stretching everywhere as far as the eye could see. He redirected his mind and dropped down to about two hundred feet as the river faded in the gathering darkness below. Another glance at the fuel showed the needle bouncing off the empty peg as what remained sloshed in the tank with the plane's movement. A glance at the river showed no place straight enough for a ditching. A glance at the nearing peak was reassuring, only in that there wasn't another in the area.

The strip has to be here!

He could see a large bend in the river now. Passing overhead, his heart leapt as he thought he saw a narrow portion of dirt road passing under his left wing. Something was down there. He made a 270-degree turn, dropping lower, trying to check it out in the remaining light.

Yes! There it is!

What had looked like a road was the CIA's old abandoned landing strip. But it wasn't abandoned by the jungle, which had engulfed it from both sides and reduced it to maybe half its original width. Even so, he thought he could make it.

All right, Hot Shot, the first order of business is to get down onto the deck, while there's still some fuel in the tank. There was no evidence of wind in any direction, so he chose to land with the setting sun at his back. He

411

quickly set up for an upwind leg to the west and, passing his intended point of landing, broke to the left, dropping his gear and, at the 180-degree point, his flaps. He imagined the narrow strip as a carrier deck, and set up an easy descent on base leg, but soon found he would have to sideslip on final to increase his rate of descent once past the trees. Coming up on the tree line at the end of the strip, he crossed-controlled with right rudder and left aileron, dropping rapidly. Straightening out, he applied a short burst of power, corrected his alignment with rudder, and plopped the Bearcat down about mid-field. Taxiing to the far end of the strip, he swung the plane around as close to the edge of the jungle as possible and shut down.

Thank you, God, that my fuel held out!

THE ABANDONED CIA LANDING STRIP

Mallory unstrapped but didn't have the energy to climb out of the cockpit. Taking off Peralta's helmet and putting it between his legs, he sat slumped in the seat staring at the gunsight. The last time this happened, he was in the cockpit of a sea-blue Bearcat with his old squadron's markings, listening to the siren of an approaching fire truck in the desert near Stead Field, Nevada. This time the Bearcat wore jungle cammies and the sounds were of the myriad jungle creatures great and small surveying him from the ground, the trees, and the air.

He slid the canopy open and immediately closed it in defense of flesh-hungry insects. After what seemed like hours but was probably only minutes, he realized he still had the sat-phone and he dialed the number Truman gave him for direct communication. Busy.

Peralta also had a sat-phone, but Mallory was never given the number, only a list of Peralta's patriot friends to call if he ever needed help. He pulled the list from his shirt pocket but he could barely see the numbers in the fading light, so he dialed the first one on the list, which appeared to be a San Marcos number for a Juan Carillo, whoever Carillo was. After several rings, a man answered.

"*Señor* Juan Carillo?"

"Sí."

"Viva Pantera!" Mallory said. *"Yo soy Quetzal."*

After a brief pause the man replied in Spanish, "I'm sorry, *señor.* You must have the wrong number. There is no one here by that name."

"But you don't understand, I am Quetzal."

"I don't know any such person." The man hung up and Mallory sat staring at the phone. *My God! Have they breached Peralta's security?* He visualized Benes' agents in the room holding a gun to Carillo's head.

He tried Truman's number again and got through.

"Good news, Deke! David and the other Americans are safe and sound at a SOF base in Panama. They're all in pretty good shape. They should be leaving right about now for check-ups and a debriefing at Walter Reed Army Medical Center here in Washington."

Mallory collapsed with relief and stared at the floor of the cockpit, expecting to see a puddle of tension there, draining from his body. The black humor of imagining what a puddle of tension would look like drained even more as bursts of laughter blended with his choked sobs of relief.

"You all right, Deke?"

"Yeah. I was just having an out-of-body experience."

"Where the hell are you?"

Mallory explained his unexpected involvement in the operation and his predicament.

"So you wound up in the middle of the holy war after all," Truman said. "Two A-37s and an F-80! Counting that Syrian MiG 21 you flamed, you, sir, are just a victory short of being an ace. Admiral Frazier will be proud of you. Unofficially, of course."

"Oh, come on now, T-Square, I wasn't even in the neighborhood today. This never happened."

"Right," Truman said with a laugh. "It must have been one of those mercenary pilots of Peralta's."

"Must have been," Mallory said. "Peralta's planes all look alike. But how do I get the hell out of here before the Benes forces track me down? After flaming three of his bozos, I'm sure to be on his Most Wanted list."

"No doubt you are," Truman said. "I remember that strip you're sitting on real well from the Contra days. The CIA built it, you know. Look, I'll have a Special Forces chopper there at first light. Meantime, I'll get through to Peralta somehow and report your location. Try to get some sleep. Considering the way Peralta usually does things, there may be a mint on a pillow in the cockpit."

"I'll check with the concierge," Mallory said. "I could use sleep but it won't be easy." He slid the canopy open and held the phone outside.

"Holy shit! It sounds like the Washington Zoo at feeding time," Truman said. "Just hang in there a few more hours, Deke. You'll be out of there in the morning and on your way back here to the States and David."

Darkness fell quickly as it does in the jungle, like someone had dimmed and turned off the lights. The Bearcat was parked as close to the surrounding jungle as possible. If he had a machete, he would chop some foliage to hide the aircraft but he was as woefully lacking in survival gear as he was in energy. At least the Bearcat wore jungle camouflage paint, which would make it difficult to spot from the air and, God willing, he'd be rescued in the morning. Recovering the plane would be Peralta's problem.

He wished for the usual survival gear—radio, knife, flashlight, and some rations in the survival vest. It had been a long time since he had anything to eat, and the tasteless MRE rations, "Meals Ready To Eat," would be as welcome as they were in survival school where combat pilots were trained to stay alive until they could be rescued. Curiosity led him to search the cockpit. He found the cockpit light switch on the panel, toggled it, and poked around. Reaching down into the map case on the left, he came up with several airline miniatures of rum and scotch. He remembered this was Smith's plane, who had obviously stocked his own bar. The liquor relaxed him as he listened to the now cacophonous sounds of the surrounding jungle, with the canopy partially open after darkness fell.

He had read William Henry Hudson's *Green Mansions* in college, an exotic romance set in the tropics of South America, and he speculated that the sounds he heard were those of the bell bird that made the sound like a hammer on an anvil, blending with the maniacal screech of the laughing falcon, whose call sounded like the recorded demonic laughter at a carnival "fun house." He also knew from survival training that the jungle was home to poisonous snakes like the nine-foot-long fer-de-lance, the bushmaster, and their arboreal neighbor, the boa constrictor. In the jungle, mosquitos feasted on any exposed patch of skin, inch-long ants could incapacitate a man in minutes, and ferocious chigger mites devoured one's blood, leaving large, itchy lumps in their wake. If he left the safety of the cramped cockpit, he would be on the menu as their MREs tonight. Uncomfortable as he was, he managed to urinate in a plastic water bottle and toss it into the jungle. Twisting the cap from one of the miniatures led to another, and another, as he celebrated David's rescue and the end of his own participation in the Bearcat War.

The third or fourth little bottle brought welcome sleep to his weary body.

Leaning against the broken fuselage of what was left of his downed F8 Crusader, he rummaged in the pockets of his survival vest for the insect repellent. Better get some on before I'm eaten alive by Viet Cong insects. He splashed generous amounts on his face and, to his surprise, he noticed it smelled like his favorite after shave, St. John's Bay Rum. He licked his lips. Tasted good, too. He drank it down. Looking up, he saw something black emerging from the jungle, coming toward him. A VC in black pajamas? No! It was a panther! The panther came close and licked his broken ankle. The panther smiled and its face became Elena's face. She whispered into his ear, "La Pantera Vive" and kissed him warmly on the lips. As it was about to disappear into the jungle the pan-

ther turned and looked at him again—this time with the smiling face of Luisa—and was gone.

He could hear the approaching Jolly Green Giants, backed up with A-1 Skyraider Sandies and Cessna Dragonflies to cover his rescue.

His survival radio came alive. "Quetzal, this is David in Sandy One. How do you read, Dad?"

Mallory keyed the mike on his survival radio. "David, you're supposed to be in school."

"They gave me time off, and three units of credit for Rescue One-A. What's your position?"

"I'm right under a big blue and green bird, the one with the red breast and the long tail, sitting in this tree by the river."

"Roger that, Quetzal. The VC are closing in on you and I'm commencing my run. The Dragonflies are right behind me, but they're ours this time. Hang in there, Dad. We'll nail the bastards for you."

The roar of the A-1 Skyraider as it passed overhead and the exploding of its bombs on the encircling VC was deafening.

"I'm sorry, Mister President," he said. "I can't quite hear you amidst all this racket."

"That's okay," Nixon said. "Say, you weren't involved in that Tailhook thing, were you?"

"No way, sir."

"Good. You know, I called that lady lieutenant commander who blew the lid to tell her she did the right thing."

"That was nice of you, Mister President."

"Well, I want you to know I'm proud of you too, Captain, for what you did today."

Mallory watched the A-1 Skyraider make another low pass, inverted this time, wagging its wings at him and drowning out Nixon."

"Captain, are you still there? This is President Foxlee. Can you hear me?"

"Yes, sir. I appreciate your calling, Mister President."

The predawn din of the howler monkeys woke him from his dream and blended with the screech of a thousand birds and the likely growl of a jaguar. The faintest suggestion of dawn could be seen through the trees masking the eastern sky, as he rubbed his eyes and stretched as best he could in his cramped space. He tried to clarify the details of his dream but mostly what came to his mind's eye was the image of the panther tending his wound—Elena's nurturing presence, Luisa's approving smile. He recalled reading somewhere that Nixon actually called the lady officer about Tailhook, so that was the source of that. But Foxlee? That part of the dream seemed different, like maybe he really had called. He decided not to try to figure it out.

Spending the night in the cockpit had not been on the itinerary for his luxury vacation, and he hoped Truman's choppers showed up soon. He climbed down from the cockpit, slid off the wing and stretched. A dip in Peralta's pool would be nice right about now. Surveying his surroundings, he suddenly thought he heard the sound of a large outboard motor, perhaps two, coming from the direction of the river. He hadn't seen any settlement from the air or any sign of river traffic. As the now obvious engine sounds drew nearer, he assumed the Benes forces had tracked him down.

Before he could react with a plan to hide he heard another sound coming from the opposite direction, the quiet puttering of a light airplane's engine, throttled back, gliding along above the roof of the jungle. Looking down the length of the runway, he could see something in the sky now. It was bobbing up and down and coming his way. With the Browning in hand he scanned the jungle, assessing where to slip into it. The agony of indecision was punctuated by the sudden appearance of the airplane as it crossed the tree line. He crept to the Bearcat's vertical stabilizer and peered around it, just as Peralta's Storch settled to the runway nearby and rolled to a stop with the engine running.

"Good morning, Captain Mallory," Diego called. "I've been looking for you."

417

Mallory waved the Browning toward the river. "So is someone else," he said.

"Government patrol boats," Diego called, shifting his weight on the seat to open the canopy for Mallory. "They go in pairs. It will take them a while to find us if they decide to leave the safety of the river and come looking."

"There's supposed to be an SOF helicopter here for me at dawn," Mallory said, as he climbed into the Storch.

"Better come with me, Captain Mallory. You're sure to be at the top of Colonel Benes' shit list by now. Let's get you out of here before his Air Force comes looking for you."

Diego turned the plane around, gunned the engine and they were flying immediately. Peralta was right, the thing could take off in its own length. As Mallory hunched behind him in the tandem seating arrangement, Diego reached over his shoulder to hand him a sandwich and thermos of coffee.

"Do keep a lookout for enemy aircraft, Captain Mallory. Spotting them first is our best defense."

Mallory thought about this strange airplane he had called a contraption at first meeting.

"You mean . . . it's our only defense!"

Diego shrugged.

FIFTY-SIX

CAMPO ALTO

Mallory opened his eyes and gradually focused on the rusty window sill of the trailer. A light rain beat a faint tattoo on the metal roof. He closed his eyes again and as he rolled onto his back he was suddenly bombarded by a replay of dream elements parading back and forth in his mind: dodging SAMs, ground fire, and MiGs, flaming an A-37 and an F-80 in the Bearcat, David being taken to the Hanoi Hilton in a bamboo tiger cage, pulling Gs on the freeway escaping from the skinheads who shot Luisa, and chasing them through the streets of La Jolla on a motorcycle.

The smell of coffee wasn't part of the dream, it was right under his nose. He rolled onto his right side and slowly opened his eyes.

"Welcome to the land of the living," Elena said, setting a carafe on the bedside table. She touched his shoulder. He took her hand and pressed it to his lips.

"How long have I been asleep?" he asked, holding her hand against his cheek.

"About fifteen hours." She poured a cup of coffee and handed it to him as he swung his legs from the bunk. He knuckled his eyes and took a deep whiff of the brew.

Suddenly his heart leapt. "What about David? We've got to have heard by now!" Then he remembered calling Truman from T-Square International Airport and learning David was on his way to Walter Reed in Washington. "My God," he grinned, "I guess I'm still a basket case."

"Woven rather tightly I would say," she laughed. "Do you remember trying to reach Mister Truman on your sat-phone when Diego brought you in yesterday?"

"Yeah, now I do. He didn't answer, wasn't available."

"Nacho and I think it's the new Middle East oil crisis. Saddam Hussein's air force bombed the Saudi's main pipeline while you were asleep, and the U.S. is racing to put together yet another coalition to go after him."

Mallory's shoulders sagged. "I guess I understand, but why does it have to be right now when all I want is to be airlifted out of here so I can see David?"

He reached for the sat-phone and tried Truman's number. Still no answer.

He shrugged and sipped his coffee. "Maybe Nacho could call the SOF base in Panama," he muttered.

She smiled and brushed his stubble with the back of her hand. "I understand about David, but I wish you weren't in such a hurry to leave. Anyway," she told him, "the SOF people have changed the frequencies they used with Carlos, and your government doesn't list its strike teams in the yellow pages."

She kissed his forehead. "God is good, Deke, isn't he? David is safe now in the States."

He closed his eyes and nodded. His eyes popped open a moment later. "Fifteen hours. Good grief," he said, sniffing the steaming brew again. "I've had my share of combat exhaustion, but never like this."

"You had some busy days."

He massaged his jaw. "I guess. Some backbreaking motorcycle rides with the Evel Kneivel of Costa Verde, a firefight with the hit team, aerial combat against the Colonel's jet jockeys, and spending the night in

Mister Smith's Bearcat listening to carnivorous critters arguing about who was going to have me for breakfast."

She reached out and took his hand and slowly kissed his fingers. "Oh, Deke. You're safe. And Carlos now controls everything this side of that river you followed to the old air strip. You absolutely leveled the playing field by taking out three of Benes' dwindling aircraft inventory."

She closed her eyes and shook her head. "I'm at a loss for words to express what this means to our cause."

"I hope you're not at a loss for something to eat. I'm totally starved."

"I was coming to that. Since you didn't leave your breakfast order on the doorknob, I ordered for you. Breakfast for two—*al fresco,* of course—in Campo Alto's Five Star Jungle Room."

"We don't have any medals for you," Elena smiled, "so you may consider this your Distinguished Flying Breakfast."

"With Oak Leaf Cluster," Mallory said, removing a leaf that drifted from the jungle canopy overhead onto his plate. "Hey, I've never had eggs flavored quite like this before. They're great."

"Neither has anyone until we ran out of the usual condiments and found a spicy root here at Campo Alto."

Mallory grinned. "Well, I'm calling it Eggs Pantera. When this is all over you'll be a whole lot more famous than those Benedict sisters."

Elena frowned. "That's debatable right now. We're just holding on as best we can until the aircraft and supplies arrive."

"Where's Arturo?"

"He was due the day before yesterday. Obviously, something's detained him."

"Deke!" Peralta shouted, as he hobbled into the clearing. "My Top Gun is operational again!" He took a seat on the bench, propped his crutch against the table and reached for the pitcher of orange juice, pouring a glass and adding a shot of rum. "To you, sir," he raised his glass, "for bringing death and destruction to the enemy. In fact, you're one kill short of being an ace!"

Mallory grinned. "I'm sticking with the single MiG in my log book. Yesterday never happened. Besides, I'm too old for your brand of aerial Special Olympics."

Peralta shook his head. "No way! After what you did."

Mallory glanced at Elena and back at Peralta. "Okay. Now tell me the whole truth. How goes the war?"

Peralta swigged his juice. "Until we build up our air strength with new planes and pilots, we're limited to small-unit ground actions. Carlos keeps hitting as many different sectors as possible to mislead the enemy about his actual strength. He's got plenty of manpower, but the shortages continue plaguing him. Meantime, I've got the T-28Ds being prepared in Miami, and my broker got lucky yesterday and picked up two pretty elderly A-1 Skyraiders at Chino, of all places. Skyraiders did a hell of a job in Viet Nam. They're perfectly suited for our missions."

"Perfect indeed," Mallory agreed.

"We're desperate for supplies and the A-37s Truman promised, but we have no idea when that will be. Meanwhile, my people in Miami are recruiting pilots with the right kind of combat experience."

WALTER REED ARMY MEDICAL CENTER
WASHINGTON, D.C.

David Mallory rubbed the sleep from his eyes and answered the door of his sparsely furnished hospital room.

"Hello. I'm Terry Truman, a friend of your father's." He extended his hand. "I brought you some things."

David tightened his maroon U.S. Army Medical Corps bathrobe and accepted a shopping bag, inviting Truman inside. "Were you one of Dad's shipmates?" he asked, peering into the bag.

"No, I'm in finance with the CIA. I met your dad through Admiral Frazier. I heard about the rescue and figured you needed some duds."

David pulled polo shirts, khaki pants, shorts, socks, and casual shoes from the bag. "Gee, thanks," he said, puzzled. "How did you know my size?"

"Phoned your nurse. Your measurements are part of the medical file."

David grinned. "Well, at least something positive has come of all the tests they've run on me."

"If you picked up anything in that prison, a rare parasite, say, they'll find it here at Walter Reed."

The other Americans from Prison Five were at Walter Reed for observation, too; but their families surrounded them and Truman knew that David was alone. Truman pulled out his sat-phone and pressed a sequence of buttons.

"Here," he said, handing David the phone. "If a man answers, don't hang up."

"T-Square?" Mallory answered.

"Dad! I'm at Walter Reed with Mister Truman."

Truman stepped into the hallway and closed the door behind him while they talked.

"My dad wants to say hello," David said, with a big smile on his face, opening the door and motioning Truman back to the room.

"That's a damn nice thing you did," Mallory told him.

"Well, I was in the neighborhood. You'd do the same. How's Peralta's foot or whatever's wrong?"

"A doctor friend of Elena's came here to the camp and checked him out. He thought he'll be fine even though he'll probably have a slight limp from the bones not being set soon enough. But Nacho's perfectly delighted. He thinks the merest suggestion of a limp should enhance his war-hero image with the ladies. Anyway, T-Square, when are you going to pluck me out of here?"

"Not for another day or two. There's a hell of a tropical storm ravaging Panama. I can't risk our SOF guys as long as you're safe with Peralta. They'll pick you up as soon as weather permits."

"Understood." Mallory gave Truman the coordinates for Campo Alto. "Tell them to set down on the road where it looks like it disappears into the jungle. Say, how did the Minox check out?"

Truman's spirits fell for the first time in days. He excused himself from David and stepped into the hallway again to speak privately.

"It didn't check out," he said. "The serial number was a dead end. The factory reported they shipped your Minox to their distributor in Paris. How it got to Hong Kong where you purchased it is a mystery. The French distributor was defunct years ago, and there's no way of tracing anything through the dozens of shops in Kowloon's Nathan Road. They've all changed hands more than a few times in the twenty years since you bought the camera."

"Yeah, I know," Mallory said, with a sigh. "I know it's Luisa's camera but guess I'll never be able to prove it with documentary evidence.

"Okay," he continued, "what happened with the mission to the Vatican? Did we unmask the bastards?"

"You better sit down," Truman told him. "The Vatican Secretary of State, the number-two guy behind the Pope himself, vouches for them. And he supplied unimpeachable documentary proof, I'm afraid. Monsignor Schmehr and the others are the good priests they've purported to be all along. The bug you planted hasn't picked up anything unusual either, just normal conversation and a couple of small group discussions of theological topics. We'll keep listening as long as the battery holds out, but I'm no longer optimistic on that front."

The silence on Mallory's end was longer than Truman expected. "You there?" he asked.

"Yeah, I'm still here," Mallory snapped. "I guess I just don't understand why we can't act on the truth as we know it and take out those murdering bastards. Look, I've still got the Browning, Goddammit! Do I have to go back there and off the sons-of-bitches myself?"

"Listen, Captain, President Foxlee and I have a problem you're not considering. The Vatican is a sovereign nation state. It has granted these people its citizenship and it's vouching for them after we made direct inquiry at the highest level. Now, how the hell can we just brush all that aside and send in the Marines?"

"Well, we sure as hell differ, don't we?" Mallory snapped, with the edge still in his voice. "As you know damn well . . ." He paused and reconsidered his words. "Oh, hell, T-Square," he said, "let's not spoil a friendship over it. I really appreciate your seeing David and letting us talk just now."

"You take care, Deke," Truman said. "And thanks for everything you've done for me and the President."

Truman reentered David's room and handed him the phone. "Here," he said. "Talk to your Dad some more."

───────────

"Take me straight on home," Truman told his driver as he got into the government Cadillac parked in the brick circular driveway at Walter Reed. No point returning to Langley this late in the day with no crisis awaiting him. The Saddam Hussein threat had been temporarily averted by the dictator's agreement to submit the pipeline dispute to mediation at the World Court, with smiling assurances he wouldn't attack the Saudis again. Truman grimaced at the thought of trusting the sociopath's word, but the need for direct military action was past for the time being.

As he closed the division window separating him from the chauffeur, his mind returned to the Costa Verde situation that Mallory would be extracted from after the storm in Panama fizzled out. Not many things had distilled-out down there. *Why, hell, he groused, it's just a damn Mexican standoff with Benes hanging onto San Marcos and Puerto Quintana and Carlos controlling the boonies and Bahia Pajaros.* Time would tell if covert aid to the Peraltistas would tip the balance in their favor.

He let out a sigh and pulled off his tie. *One thing's sure,* he thought. *Shanghaiing Mallory was the best damned idea since Repeal of Prohibition.*

425

His mind returned to the Burton question. It was still unanswerable and the focus kept shifting. Although Holloway's accusing finger was amputated by Mallory's mission to the Hotel Corona, the Swiss account gambit had been supplanted by new doubts arising from Burton's subsequent behavior. Complicating matters was the news that Gerhardt Hesse had died of an infection he contracted in the hospital, without regaining consciousness. With the Hesse hit, if that's what it was, still hanging in the air, and as if it weren't enough, Burton had capped things off with another of his gratuitous visits to the cathedral to meet with Schmehr personally. *Disturbing as hell!* Truman thought. Bill laughed it off, of course, in his usual way, as a natural enough thing for a good Irish Catholic boy like himself. Besides, he had parried, "You gotta to know the territory and the guy's definitely in my territory."

If Burton had learned anything important from his encounters with the acting archbishop he wasn't saying. All he would say was that Monsignor Schmehr was a real stern old sour-puss type of priest.

Gretchen, of course, had gleefully switched horses and was now riding the Schmehr visits with the kind of enthusiasm she had once shown for Holloway's fairy tales.

All told, though, Truman concluded, there was reason to feel somewhat better about things. Lifting a heavy load from his shoulders was his own decision to trust Burton for the time being. And with Costa Verde and Burton in holding patterns he was free to turn his attention elsewhere, a most refreshing change since nothing else on the horizon carried the same potential to destroy his reputation.

He triggered the CD player and settled back against the headrest, letting one of Telemann's baroque suites massage his weary mind, as the Cadillac crept slowly along the Beltway in late afternoon traffic.

FIFTY-SEVEN

THE PAPAL PALACE AT THE VATICAN

The shouting erupted at the entrance to the room where the Pontiff was scheduled to receive his weekly world affairs briefing. "For the love of God, man! I must have action this very minute!" The staccato boomed like gunshots in the marble hallway. "I will NOT be put off!"

Just then Albert rounded a corner on his way to the briefing and took in the scene. Someone was furiously berating a tall young priest, whose misfortune was to be manning a red velvet rope controlling admittance to the briefing room. The aggressor, a rotund, volcanic little man, wore the purple sash of a bishop and spewed Italian with a Spanish accent. The flustered gatekeeper's lips moved wordlessly, as the bishop and his party crowded him.

The aggressor jammed a finger under the young man's nose. "A catastrophe has befallen the Holy Father in Costa Verde! I tell you I must see his Holiness NOW!"

Albert recognized the end game the moment he saw it; even so, he realized he mustn't proceed on a mere assumption. He had to make sure of what this was all about, so he approached, as onlookers fell back in stunned disbelief.

"May I be of some assistance?" he asked in an overloud voice, with a Teutonic air of command. The question was directed to any who might answer.

The explosive little bishop answered, "Monsignor!" he blurted, face red and shiny with perspiration, "a horrible fraud has been perpetrated on his Holiness. At our national cathedral! We are here to—"

"The Holy Father's favor," Albert told him, in a level voice, "will not be curried by you disrupting the dignity of his palace in this way. I am Monsignor Albert, administrative assistant to Antonio Cardinal Guilianni."

The bishop's eyes widened, as did those of the men with him. "The Little Pope?" one of them asked.

Albert let it hang in the air, feeling the pleasure of his post for what he knew was the last time. He consulted his watch, gaining a moment to think.

"If you will please appear at the Secretary of State's office at four o'clock this afternoon, I can guarantee you he will be willing to see you and hear you out in your complaint, whatever it might be."

The bishop eyed him suspiciously as his companions stood mute, anxiously awaiting their leader's decision.

"Monsignor Albert," the young man recovered and told them, "is known to speak for Cardinal Guilianni. And he has given you his assurance that the cardinal himself will see you this very day."

The Pope entered the lobby behind the roped-off area, walking slowly, surrounded by his usual entourage of half a dozen clergy and a distinguished visitor or two. This time it was a cardinal and an archbishop who followed, with some of the papal secretaries. They went into the assembly room where His Holiness would be briefed for half an hour on everything from world affairs to the state of various departments within the Vatican.

The little bishop's moment to strike was lost. Albert could see the disappointment on his face.

"I am Ernesto Subueso," he told Albert, "Bishop of Pacifico Provence, in Costa Verde. I accept your invitation," he jabbed a finger at Albert, "and I and my companions will be there at 4 o'clock today. *En Punto!*"

He mopped his brow. "Thank you, Monsignor Albert," he exhaled, as an afterthought.

The young attendant looked at Albert with relief in his eyes, hooked the rope to its stanchion and ducked into the briefing hall just as the door closed.

Albert was gone before the Costa Verde contingent could react. He took the stairs to the ground floor, where he entered a rest room, aching with an actual physical pain centered near his solar plexus.

Suicide leapt to mind. *No!* Antonio Guilianni, his dear friend, a true man of God, deserved to hear the truth. *All of it, right now and from me.*

He strode purposefully to Guilianni's office suite where he found the cardinal finishing a meeting with a Papal Nuncio who was leaving for China to plead for religious tolerance and pave the way for a trip by the Pontiff. But for this exigency, Guilianni would have attended the morning Papal briefing himself and Albert wouldn't have been there as his eyes and ears—which is to say, he couldn't have short-stopped the problem the way he did.

Through the open door to Guilianni's office Albert could see him embrace the other and dismiss him. The nuncio greeted Albert warmly as he passed through the reception area on his way out.

"Cancel all appointments for the rest of the day," Albert instructed Guilianni's secretary, an elderly Italian priest who looked a little surprised but was used to Albert holding sway. He wasn't called "The Hammer" without reason. "See to it we are not disturbed," he told him, as he stepped into the cardinal's office while Guilianni walked to his desk.

"Eminence," he said, "I have cleared your schedule to accommodate an important meeting I just arranged for you at four this afternoon."

429

"What's wrong?" Guilianni asked, genuinely puzzled. "You don't look at all well, old friend."

"Prepare yourself, please," Albert told him. "My health pales compared to what I am about to relate. Pray, Eminence, for the gift of special wisdom so you will know how to handle this and properly advise the Holy Father."

The cardinal dropped into the chair behind his desk with a worried expression on his face.

Albert's face crumpled as he slumped into a chair opposite. When his tearful sobbing ran its course, he straightened himself and looked Guilianni in the eye.

"I am a traitor!" he said.

FIFTY-EIGHT

CAMPO ALTO

The heavy rain stopped as abruptly as it had started. Peralta found his crutches and headed with Mallory for the hangar, where a tall man wearing a flight suit approached. He sported a dapper pencil-thin mustache. Mallory could see he was upset about something.

"Diego called," the man said. "He can't get back until the day after tomorrow."

"Diego went to San Marcos to check on Arturo's whereabouts," Peralta told Mallory. "What's happened?" Peralta asked.

The tall man set his jaw. "Arturo was murdered."

The news hit Mallory like a thunderbolt to his heart. He was speechless.

"What?" Peralta demanded.

"Diego wants you to break the news to Elena."

"Who would want to kill Arturo?" Peralta cried.

Maldonado shook his head. "Diego spoke with the neighbors and pieced it together. He is sure one of the phony priests, Father Martin, is the killer."

"How does he know that?" Mallory demanded.

Maldonado's face crumpled as he related Arturo's end. Mallory experienced rage and guilt and the desire to cut loose and weep, all at once. Instead, his facial muscles tightened as he remembered he still had a full box of shells for the Browning, more than enough to clean out the cathedral.

Peralta spoke. "I'll tell her," he said. He turned to Mallory and back to the man in the flight suit. "Deke, this is Enrique Maldonado, my Argentine compatriot."

Mallory extended his hand. "Sorry we meet this way. I know Nacho is lucky to have you as his wingman."

"It's an honor to meet you, Captain Mallory. Congratulations on yesterday's victories."

Maldonado turned to Peralta. "Diego says there's a new security cordon around the city and he'll have to find some chinks to slip through."

Peralta blew out his breath. "Damn!" he said. "He was going to take the Storch and ferry Enrique out to pick up the Bearcat you left in the jungle. We're down to one Bearcat and the T-28, if we lose Smith's plane."

Mallory was about to defend himself when Peralta put a hand on his shoulder. "Oh, I don't mean it that way, Deke. It's not your fault. But that bird is too important to abandon for the bad guys to find. I've already sent my best mechanics there along with a gang carrying fuel cans."

"Gang?" Mallory asked.

"Thirty men have been hacking their way through the jungle since yesterday, carrying five gallon cans of av-gas. It's over sixty miles," he looked at his watch, "but they should be getting there in a couple of hours."

He swung away on his crutches.

Maldonado called after him. "*Señor* Peralta, wait. Perhaps the captain could fly me out to the strip. It's a short hop over secure territory that Carlos controls now."

Mallory stared at Maldonado. "My tour with the Panther Squadron is over and done with."

432

Peralta stopped and turned around. "Deke's right," he said. "He's risked enough for us. Diego will be back and then we can recover the Bearcat."

"I apologize, Captain," Maldonado said. "You should check out the Storch sometime, though. I can't imagine your not being absolutely fascinated with it."

Torrential rain again beat on the metal roof of the main trailer as Mallory and Peralta waited for Elena. Mallory turned to face his friend. "It's my fault," he agonized. "I'm fully responsible for Arturo's death. I'm going straight back to San Marcos, track down his killer, and personally shoot the evil psychopath."

Peralta poured two Reserva Especials. "Look, Deke, Arturo knew exactly what he was doing." His voice softened. "He was a true patriot who died for his country. You and I . . . well, it was a privilege to know such a man." He handed Mallory the drink and raised his own. "To our dear friend Arturo."

Mallory nodded and raised his glass. "I feel just like I've lost a son," he said.

Elena burst into the trailer soaking wet from the rain with her raven hair plastered about her face but a look of absolute delight dancing in her eyes. She struggled to close the door against the driving wind before spinning around to face Mallory and Peralta.

"Wonderful, wonderful news!" she cried. "Bishop Subueso has absolutely scored at the Vatican! He's got a Papal mandate to throw those fiends out of the Cathedral!" She twirled about with her arms in the air. "If that murderous bunch is even half smart, they'll clear out right now before he arrives with the Vatican delegation!"

With Arturo on his mind Peralta was caught off guard. "What? How do you know?" he managed to say.

"The bishop left a message on my machine at the beach house as we had agreed he would. I just called and played my messages."

Mallory stood. "We've some very bad news, Elena."

Peralta offered her his drink. "No," she said, looking back and forth between them. "It's about Arturo, isn't it?"

"Yes, he's dead," Peralta said, as Mallory's arms gently enfolded her.

"It's called the Nazi Grasshopper," Maldonado said, as they walked to the far end of the hangar. "As you can see, it looks like a giant insect, and with a head wind of twelve to fifteen knots it can take off in about three fuselage lengths. They were used extensively by the Luftwaffe during World War II as staff transports and light observation planes. The ones the Allies captured they put to immediate use, too. This plane can get in and out of tight spots like city streets. A Storch even snatched Mussolini from a mountain ledge to avoid his capture by the Allies."

Mallory ran his hand over the doped fabric surfaces and inspected the tubular steel construction. "This thing could take a ton of bullets and keep flying," he said, "unless they hit the engine or fuel system." He studied the folded wings. "And this is the same principle Grumman used with the Hellcat and the Avenger, with the wings pivoting and folding backwards along the fuselage."

"Climb in and check her out, " Maldonado said. "It's a pretty unusual cockpit."

Mallory grabbed the plane's built-in boarding ladder and reached for the cockpit, stretching for the first rung which was almost waist high. "Good grief," he said. "It takes an acrobat just to get into the damn thing." He settled into the front seat and studied the controls and instruments. "Fantastic visibility," he said, looking downward through the bay windows on each side.

Maldonado climbed the ladder part way and pointed to the airspeed indicator. "The gauges are in German but they're marked in the usual white, green and yellow arcs for operational limits." He leaned closer and lowered his voice. "I can tell Nacho is worried sick about

Smith's Bearcat." His eyes met Mallory's. "If you could see your way to fly me there, well, it would make a huge difference." He lowered his eyes. "Arturo would definitely approve."

Mallory continued his silent inspection of the instrument panel. He lightly fingered the ignition switch and was immediately rewarded with an inner prompting. *This would be a dumb-ass mission—of the just one-too-many variety—where you end up buying the farm. I'm old enough to know better,* he told himself. *It's a miracle I'm still alive after what I've been through. And, thank God, David is alive too and safe in the States.*

From now on, he resolved, *knowing better is going to be "Mallory's Rule."* He slowly shook his head.

"Very well, Captain," Maldonado said softly, "but it's only a matter of time before the bad guys capture that Bearcat out there."

FIFTY-NINE

THE ARCHBISHOP'S QUARTERS

"Treachery!" Tolt screamed. "Treachery! Treachery!"

Staib was used to his sporadic fulminations, had seen and weathered them before, but this was the worst ever. Tolt was pacing the room like a whirlwind, waving Kreeber's intel reports in the and air spewing expletives in German. He was no longer even keeping up pretenses by speaking Spanish. Contrasting with his outrageous behavior was his almost Papal appearance. He had just donned the most ornate vestments yet to arrive from Rome, trying them for size and comfort.

"You failed to liquidate that vermin when I ordered his death last year!" he bellowed.

Staib stood mute. The reverse was true. When he was preparing to kill Monsignor Albert it was Tolt who prevented it, claiming a continuing need of influence at the Vatican.

"Someone got to him and turned him against me," Tolt yelled, as he smashed a lamp against the wall.

"Peralta!" Kreeber hissed, playing to his rage.

"No!" Tolt shouted, "that's a stupid conclusion. Peralta is too busy running his pitiful revolution. He has his intelligence resources, but they couldn't reach all the way inside the Vatican. No," he growled, "it's someone much smarter than Ignacio Peralta."

Staib knew better than to offer suggestions.

"It's got to be the CIA!" Tolt screeched maniacally. He banged his fist on top of the desk, breaking the protective plate glass covering it. "Mister Truman has been snooping around here for months now. A man with Truman's resources and experience would go far afield to get answers, even tracing us back to those priests you, Staib, liquidated in East Germany. He must have come across some clue you left in Europe!"

"Perhaps you are correct," Kreeber offered.

Staib glared at him.

"Of course I'm correct," Tolt barked, just as the phone rang. He picked it up and the others could hear the frantic, rapid Spanish of Colonel Benes spewing from the earpiece. Tolt's face slowly took on an even harsher edge as the cascading stream of words continued.

"When was that?" Tolt shouted. "Are you certain?" he demanded. "How much time is there?" He slammed the phone back onto its cradle.

"The Vatican Secretary of State just landed at the airport," he told them, "with that rancid little Bishop Subueso and a whole host of experts and lawyers from Rome. They've declared us frauds! Benes is sending an unmarked car and driver to pick us up."

The veins in Tolt's neck bulged as he waxed apoplectic. "Corporal Albert has betrayed me!" he screamed again.

Staib didn't move a muscle except to furrow his brow and purse his lips in what he thought an appropriate display of concern. Kreeber unconsciously fondled his crucifix. Kaalten burst into expletives and began blubbering about the turn of events.

"Shut up!" Tolt yelled, and sank into his desk chair to catch his breath. "Benes," he blurted, "has one of his cigarette boats waiting at Puerto Quintana. We'll dash to one of the small ports on the Caribbean coast of Nicaragua and make our way back to Mexico City from there."

"Cigarette boat?" Kaalten asked.

"What they call a go-fast-boat," Staib told him. "A drug-running boat. They can outrun anything afloat."

Now Tolt's face took on a kind of a glow the others had seen only once or twice before. He rose to pace the floor again, seeming to have drawn new energy from some deep well within himself. His eyes danced about and he tossed his shoulders and lantern face this way and that as if he were performing in front of a mirror. All of a sudden he seemed completely oblivious to the others' presence as he lunged into planning a new chapter in Kohorte history, with Mexico City again their base of operations.

They exchanged furtive glances as he expounded about seeing in the oyster of his defeat the priceless pearl of a greater victory than could ever have been won in Costa Verde, even had everything gone flawlessly from the beginning. "My unshakable will . . . ," he bellowed, as he raised a fist while brushing his forelock with the other hand in perfect imitation of Hitler haranguing the Reichstag, "is irresistible . . . the timetable for the conquest of all Central America is now accelerated!"

He suddenly stopped and turned to face them, and his entire body took on a more relaxed, somewhat nonchalant appearance. "Yes," he told them, "I do think it quite prudent to leave now. It's not possible to bluff our way out of this. And the good part," he rubbed his hands together, "is that Corporal Albert doesn't know I control the government here. He thinks we merely own some corporations, so he can't possibly have told Truman about Case Green. Ha!" he snorted, bending over to slap his knee. "We needn't remain here. We'll continue to run Colonel Benes from Mexico City now."

"But what about all our money in Banco Central?" Kreeber asked. "I have moved most of our money here from Mexico. Without resources, we're powerless."

The others looked at each other with raised eyebrows.

Tolt's mouth formed a crooked smile. "Only a portion of our wealth is in Banco Central," he said slowly. "I didn't anticipate this particular scenario but I did have foresight and arranged for a very substantial amount to be transferred to Uruguay, should we be faced with

439

a bad turn of events. I also have more than adequate funds in offshore banks," he continued, as he went to a wall safe and began to twirl the dial. "We will hardly be begging in the streets," he laughed, leering over his shoulder at them.

He opened the door and withdrew several packets of American currency. He tossed two each to the others and stuffed the rest in his vestments.

That was the very moment the dam of their hoax broke.

Tolt began grabbing belongings to take with him. Staib put only the tools of his trade into a small black leather satchel. Having fewer valuables to pack than the others he sat quietly observing as Tolt removed a small jewelry box from one of the drawers of his desk. The Reichsfuhrer took out his Iron Cross with Swords and Diamonds and carefully draped it around his neck, then stuffed it out of sight inside his robe. He patted it reverently as the phone on his desk rang again and he quickly picked it up. Benes' excited voice announced his personal driver would meet them behind the building.

"Destroy the files of the Kohorte!" Tolt shouted. "Everything's there," he told them, pointing to built-in filing cabinets behind his desk. "There's no time for shredding. Burn everything in the fireplace," he ordered.

Staib and Kreeber rushed to the files and started throwing papers into the huge fireplace, which soon became an inferno. "Take only what is important from your quarters and get back here," Tolt shouted as he yanked open the drawers of his desk. Kaalten and Kreeber darted down the hall as Tolt shoved more papers into the fire. The rest he threw onto the hearth. The fire spread to the papers on the hearth by the time Staib and Kreeber returned. Seeing the flames, they grabbed fireplace tools to contain them, as Staib looked on, calculating his own plans.

"Let it burn!" Tolt ordered. "We don't give a damn what catches fire. The staff will be too busy putting out the flames to pay attention to our escape."

Kaalten and Kreeber carried small duffel bags and Staib, who suddenly returned from his own world, zipped his satchel closed. Tolt knew the bag contained handguns with silencers, an assortment of knives for cutting and puncturing, and the assassin's pharmacopoeia of poisons.

"Very good, Ludwig," Tolt said, as he reached in a desk drawer and withdrew his own gold-plated Walther PPK.

The phone rang again and Tolt quickly picked it up. Benes' driver was at the rear service entrance.

"Excellent, we're coming right down."

The four left the room as smoke poured into the hallway. Staib locked the door and they hurried down the hall to the back stairs just as a pair of priests from the cathedral were throwing open the huge double doors to the Archbishop's Palace, and a throng of excited clerics burst through downstairs. Staib caught a glimpse of them over the banister. He spotted a cardinal, a bishop or two, and half a dozen he couldn't identify—and Subueso doing most of the shouting and gesticulating.

"By God, justice will be done!" he was yelling.

Benes' unmarked Lincoln Town Car was waiting in the rear with the motor running. As they emerged from the building, the Archbishop's driver stepped forward.

"Where will you be going, Excellency?" he inquired.

Tolt paused to address the driver. "An unexpected emergency has come up and we must go with Colonel Benes' driver. But I have a special assignment for you," he instructed. "I am expecting a man who will be arriving at the airport. You will fetch him here to the cathedral."

"Of course, Excellency, but how will I know him?"

"You won't have to. Everyone knows the cathedral's lavender Grand Mercedes."

Staib caught Tolt's ear and whispered. "Send him and the Benes car to the airport and take the cathedral limo. Every little village knows it by sight, so we'll have no trouble making our way to Puerto Quintana."

"Nothing can go wrong now!" Tolt crowed, climbing into the Grand Mercedes, still robed in his latest High Mass regalia. Kreeber and Kaalten piled in the back with him. "We're on our way to a new chapter in the Kohorte's illustrious history!" Tolt told them. He lowered the division window as Staib took the wheel, alone in the front compartment. "As much as I revere the Fuhrer," Tolt continued, "I could never accept his final solution for himself. For the Jews, yes, but not for himself. Suicide is cowardly. He should have fought to the end, whatever the consequences." Staib nodded as the heavy car accelerated smoothly. He knew better than to comment on such an opinion of the Reichsfuhrer.

"Yes," Tolt chattered, enthusiastically slapping his knee as they made a left turn onto the road to Puerto Quintana. Staib thought he heard him mumble, "After all these years everything was within my grasp and it shall not elude me now. Yes! I shall fight on with the Valkyries at my side." He adjusted his robes. "Naturally," he boasted, repeating himself, "I had foresight to secret working capital in the Cayman Islands, Montevideo and—"

The sound of his voice was lost as he lowered his window and poked his head out, waving to people lining the curb to cheer their archbishop.

Staib, alone with his thoughts, made a selection on the CD player and raised the volume, filling the Grand Mercedes with maniacal Wagnerian soprano highs.

THE HIGHWAY FROM SAN MARCOS TO PUERTO QUINTANA

Alone at the wheel of the Grand Mercedes, Staib was struck by the historicity of the hour and likened it in his mind to Hitler's last hours in the *Fuhrerbunker*, only played on a different stage with maybe a different ending.

"Reichsfuhrer," he called, "you must close the division window between us. It's a matter of appearances," he advised. Tolt did so without comment.

The assassin was driven to capture his impressions of the day in real time as they unfurled. He pulled a micro-recorder from his shirt pocket, flicked it on and returned it to his pocket. He lowered the volume of the CD player, which was still blaring Wagner. A glance in the mirror showed Tolt occupying Kreeber and Kaalten with a monologue.

Staib spoke in a quiet, clear voice.

". . . I, Ludwig Staib, dictate this to my micro-recorder for my enjoyment and for the official Kohorte historian after I finish my career. . . . We are on our way to Puerto Quintana and freedom in this huge lavender car belonging to the archbishop and flying his pennants on the front fenders . . . yet I have a sense of an historic occasion . . . a decisive turning point in Kohorte history, that for Tolt may represent the ultimate disaster; though he is bristling with renewed optimism as we dash to escape in one of the Colonel's drug-running boats. . . . I will make a last-minute decision whether to accompany them. . . . My psychological needs, to state it delicately, are more vivid than the others, even including Tolt's, and I am not sure I can live my predatory life to the fullest starting over in Mexico City. . . . If I decide to remain behind I will find a way to stop the car along our route and disappear. . . . Tolt just banged on the window and shouted instructions, as if there's more than one road to the coast . . . but he's like that, always in charge whether he needs to be or not. . . . With Tolt, you never know if his brain is going to be on macro or micro about something. . . . I am wearing my simple black priest's business suit. . . . As it happens I'm properly dressed for chauffeuring . . . and for disappearing. . . . Tolt made a good point this morning when he told us victory in battle belongs to him who will not accept the idea of defeat but sees every adversity as his opportunity to catch the adversary off balance when he least expects it. . . . Hitler, according to those who were present at the end, Speer, for example, was resigned to his defeat, let go the controls to an extent and seemed to stay on his course only because of the inertia stored within him. . . . Tolt isn't like that. . . . I suppose he knows he must keep going forward toward his destiny or he'll de-construct. . . . There's a hollowness about Tolt, like there's nothing inside, only the strength of his hard monocoque exterior shell. . . . I often wondered if he's actually who he claims to be, and I suspect there's something he has never revealed to us . . . Like him, I occasionally depart so-called reality but in my case it's a conscious choice to enjoy the narcotic of the hunter-killer. . . . In Tolt's case, I think it's involuntary. . . . I have to pass a truck up ahead. . . . There, I can get around him now. . . . I will say this about Tolt. . . . He isn't taking leave of reality now. . . . He's attacking it with his hypnotic voice and laser eyes. . . . How many in this predicament would wax enthusiastic, as if fleeing like rats were really a good thing? . . . He may see through me, if I plead urgent tasks awaiting me here . . . though on balance I think he would consent to my staying behind to have me as a counterweight to Benes. . . . On the other hand, should I go with them the advantage is that Tolt soon will reach the age where a successor arises. . . . There's a Texaco station. . . . I think there's another a few miles further on, just this side of the hills we must go over to reach Puerto Quintana. . . . Yes, that's where I'll leave them . . . if I decide to slip away. . . . I intend to be that successor . . . Whether to stay close to Tolt to seize, or precipitate, the moment is the question I must decide in a matter of minutes now. . . . As for me, Ludwig Staib, I, too, had foresight and stashed adequate working capital in off-shore banks, and Switzerland of course. . . . There's the last Texaco this side of the mountain coming into view a mile up ahead, so I'm switching this recorder off now. . . . I must make my decision. . . ."

SIXTY

CAMPO ALTO

The Storch leapt into the air almost immediately as its leading edge slats and the *Rollflugel* flaps did their work. Forward movement was almost imperceptible as it seemed to climb straight up like a helicopter.

"Careful now. You don't need forward stick," Maldonado coached from the rear seat, anticipating Mallory's instincts. "She won't stall."

"I can see why Nacho couldn't fly this with his busted foot," Mallory said, as he struggled to work the snowshoe-size rudder pedals to offset engine torque during the climb.

"Let's keep down on the deck," Maldonado shouted, "in case someone's watching. With the camouflage scheme we're pretty hard to see against the jungle. When we get to the savanna stay over as much foliage as possible."

Mallory shook his head. "I guess the Germans had their own way of doing things. The mixture control is backwards, and this stick's about twice the normal size."

Maldonado cupped his hands and shouted. "More leverage is needed because the control surfaces are larger than usual."

Mallory nosed over and leveled off at a hundred feet above the jungle. Reaching down from the throttle with his left hand, he trimmed for level flight and adjusted the throttle and mixture for fast cruise.

"I'm glad you changed your mind, Captain."

"Well, the sooner I get back to Campo Alto the better I'll feel. I must be a real sucker for dumb-ass adventure." The truth was that he was touched by the courage of the thirty men who had hacked through the jungle carrying heavy cans of aviation gas, and he was still boiling mad about Arturo's death.

"You're right about this plane, though. It's like a carnival ride."

"Now you're the only United States Naval Aviator with Storch time in your logbook."

"I'll pass on the logbook entry," Mallory called.

They flew in silence for forty minutes.

"There it is," Maldonado shouted, tapping Mallory's shoulder and pointing.

"I don't see the Bearcat," Mallory shouted, as he set up for a downwind leg.

"I should hope not," Maldonado called. "They damn well better have it concealed from view."

Mallory bled the airspeed down to fifty-five miles per hour and set the flaps for landing.

"Shoot for about forty-five over the threshold," Maldonado called, "and bleed off your speed from there. It'll stall just above thirty. Stay on those rudders for directional control."

The Storch's landing gear struts spread out to cushion the landing as men emerged from the jungle waving to them. Taxiing forward, Mallory could see the Bearcat under cover of cut foliage. He pulled up as close to it as he could and shut down. Maldonado jumped down and trotted over to confer with the mechanics, nodding repeatedly as they described their ministrations to the stricken warplane.

Watching from the cockpit, Mallory experienced a little pang of fear as he recalled Mallory's Rule, his now day-old vow to know better than to ever get caught up in a dumb-ass mission again. He dismissed a fleeting thought that he had exhausted his allotment of luck but he suddenly wished he were the hell away from here and safely back at Campo Alto.

Maldonado returned to the Storch. "It's fueled and ready," he said. "They had to patch up a severed fuel line, but there were no other problems. There's even some 20 mm left."

Mallory scanned the sky through the Plexiglas cockpit cover. "Then I'm getting the hell out of here," he said.

"Right. Thanks for the lift, Captain. If you get pounced on the way back call me on the discrete frequency *du jour.*" He pointed at a strip of adhesive tape on the instrument panel with the frequency penned on it. "I'll launch in a few minutes so I can cover you. If we try to stay together with you making only eighty knots, it'll drive us both nuts."

"There weren't supposed to be any surprises. You said Carlos controls the area between here and Campo Alto."

"Sure, but we don't have air superiority. You better be monitoring the frequencies the Benes air and ground forces use. They're printed on that other tape above the radio. Unlike us, they always use the same ones."

"Then I'll be all ears today," Mallory agreed.

He taxied the Storch to the center of the strip and set the flaps and trim for takeoff. With full throttle the plane leaped into the air and rose almost vertically above the jungle canopy. Looking back through the side window he saw Maldonado climb into the Bearcat as men removed the foliage cover.

Mallory flew for about fifteen minutes on a heading to Camp Alto, constantly monitoring the frequencies used by the Benes forces. Aside from an outpost reporting in, some problem at a motor pool and a routine air patrol returning to San Benito AFB, there wasn't much radio traffic.

SAN BENITO AIR FORCE BASE

A young *teniente* burst into the mess hall where Benes and his staff were having afternoon coffee. "Colonel, sir," he stammered, "a Jeep patrol in Sector Eight just reported spotting Señor Peralta's German aircraft, his Fiesler Storch, sir."

Benes exploded with joy, excitedly pounding his fist into his palm. "This is the break I've waited for! How could he be so stupid as to go flying in that old kite? We haven't seen it since the war began, and now he presents himself to us like a sitting duck!" He pounded a location on the wall map. "Scramble the T-28s on standby alert immediately. He paced the floor, rubbing his hands together. "I want Peralta in flames. NOW!"

Captain Gustavo Romero grinned as he looked over at his wingman as their two planes waited at the end of the runway for the signal to take off. He keyed the mike. "I'll never complain about standby duty again, Ricardo. This is the opportunity of a lifetime. I am going to shoot down the notorious Nacho Peralta in that silly observation plane of his. We can be sure of a decoration and maybe a promotion for this mission. Remember, when we approach the target we'll spread out twice as far as usual to cover any way he could try to turn to avoid us.

"Arm your guns!"

ALOFT IN THE STORCH

Mallory overheard the Costa Verde pilot telling his wingman to arm his guns. *Holy shit!* he thought, scanning the sky for dots that could be fast-approaching aircraft.

He glanced quickly at the chart, estimating the distance to San Benito and the time remaining before they bounced him. It didn't matter whether they were jets or T-28s, the crawling Storch was a paper kite in comparison.

He switched to the tac frequency.

"Enrique, I'm spotted and they've scrambled two aircraft. They think I'm Peralta. They're crowing about rewards for shooting Nacho down. Get the hell up here!"

He gave Maldonado the map coordinates.

Maldonado sounded confident. "On my way, Captain."

Mallory gripped the oversized stick in anger at himself. "Dammit!" he fumed. "I knew I should have passed on this mission!" He quickly controlled his emotions and began to evaluate his predicament. He was unarmed, flying an ungainly insect designed and built for slow flight. At eighty knots top speed he was on the wrong end of an almost literal turkey shoot. He couldn't land in the thick jungle below. Even if he tried and somehow succeeded, Peralta wouldn't be able to find him and get him out of there again. An isolated bank of cumulus clouds came into view. Maybe he could make it there and hide until help arrived.

A minute later Maldonado checked in loud and clear.

"I just flamed one of them, Captain," he called, "but I'm out of ammo. Maybe I could bluff this other guy and keep him off your six a while but I've barely got enough fuel to return to base."

"Return to base," Mallory told him. "Just pray I make it home in this flying snail."

He could see a T-28 approaching at high speed from the right, at his own altitude. He tried to push the throttle forward but realized it was already at the stop.

A minute later, fully expecting to be ripped with machine gun fire any second, he plunged into the cloud bank. There, alone in the frigid white-out, he adjusted quickly to the world of basic instruments: needle/ball, turn and bank indicator, airspeed indicator, altimeter, and vertical speed indicator. His next move would be simple: stay here as long as possible, even at the risk of a mid-air with the T-28.

He no sooner made the decision to circle in the clouds when he broke out into a picture book clear blue sky. He scanned for the T-28 but couldn't see it. He was way off course for Campo Alto now, not that he should head there and risk disclosing the location of Peralta's base. He decided it was too dangerous to turn around and try to find cover again in the one and only cloud formation which was now miles behind. He would have to outguess his adversary instead. He began talking to himself.

"There in the distance on the left I can just make out Puerto Quintana and, yes, there's the winding road from the port city through the mountain pass to San Marcos. Careful now, that's Benes-controlled territory, but it's not near any of the fighting. There probably isn't much military presence over there either.

"I doubt Benes has a decent communications system to put the whole country on alert looking for Peralta's funny airplane. No, right now, that highway over there in Benes' territory is the last place anybody would think of searching for Nacho Peralta.

"If I can just get there, I could improvise. Worst case, I plop this thing down in San Marcos and try to make it to the embassy. Best case, I overfly San Marcos and continue all the way to Carlos Country near Bahia Pajaros.

"Let's see now, yeah, plenty of gas in the tanks. With luck, I might even catch a commercial flight to another country, maybe even to Miami."

He decided to take his chances and head that way. He would overfly the outskirts of Puerto Quintana and then follow the road west through the pass toward San Marcos. He frantically scanned the sky again for the T-28 but found he was alone. So far so good.

Flying into the afternoon sun two hundred feet above the westbound ribbon of the Puerto Quintana-San Marcos divided highway, Mallory was beginning to feel a little like the police traffic patrol. He negotiated the mountain pass and dropped down on the western side, following the terrain. The rolling plains on the San Marcos side were spreading out into the distance ahead, when he noticed a lavender limousine weaving in and out of oncoming traffic in the eastbound lanes.

The cathedral's Grand Mercedes!

There can't be two like that in this little country, he thought, remembering the car he saw at the Archbishop's Palace when he sprayed for spiders.

Maybe the rats are fleeing before Subueso exposes them, just like Elena said.

He rolled into a tight 180 turn and dropped even lower for a closer look. The archbishop's pennants were streaming from their staffs on the front fenders as the big car cut in and out of traffic.

He pulled alongside, about twenty feet above and to the right, and slowed slightly to match the car's speed. He could see the impostor archbishop wearing ornate robes and looking up at the Storch.

"That's the son-of-a-bitch!" he shouted, pulling the Minox from his pocket and frantically waving it outside the cockpit for his quarry to see.

"You killed Luisa!" he screamed, but his words were swept away in the slipstream.

I can't let the bastard get away! he thought. A blowout, he realized, might send them off the edge of the road into a ravine to the left.

The trailing traffic, horrified at the sight of a plane attacking the archbishop's car, had slowed and was following at a distance. He wrestled the Browning from a pocket of his flight suit, took it in his left hand, not his best, and loosed several rounds at the tires. The limo immediately accelerated and he was forced to return his left hand to the throttle in order to keep pace. *Try again,* he thought, as he lined up the Storch for another firing run. *To hell with the tires this time . . . maybe I can take out that Nazi bastard or the driver.* He fired into the limo and kept firing until he emptied the magazine.

No hits as far as he could tell as he wrestled the plane's big, heavy foot and hand controls, staying as close to the car as he could while looking for ways to force the driver into a fatal mistake.

Someone in the front passenger seat returned his fire with an automatic pistol.

Pulling quickly up and over the limo he was out of their line of fire for the moment. With his left hand back securely on the throttle, he felt he still had positive control of the Storch in spite of some small rips he could see in the fabric underside of the left wing. Flying even with the limo on either side was too risky. As he kept pace directly over the speeding car—*thank God,* he thought, *it hasn't a sunroof*—he recalled a quick-thinking F4U Corsair pilot running out of ammunition but still downing a Japanese Zero by chopping its tail off with the Corsair's huge propeller. *That's my move!* he thought, knowing the Storch was fitted with a huge two-blade steel prop.

We'll see if the driver has nerves of steel, he thought, as he dropped down near the rear of the limo.

Nosing over slightly, he managed to put the tips of the prop on the trunk of the swerving car and rake across it. The Storch shuddered horribly until he raised off. The vibration and noise inside the car should be horrendous, but the driver was still maintaining control.

Angered, Mallory eased down and forward again and pushed the tips of the prop through the rear window this time. As safety glass exploded in the faces of the terrified occupants in the rear seat, the limo swerved to the right, plowed across the shoulder of the road in a cloud of flying dirt, sideswiped the rock face of the sheer cut on the mountain side of the road, then careened back to the left, where it tore through the guard rail and flew off over the side and down the steep ravine below.

Pulling up to the left, Mallory looked down to see the limo hit several times going down the canyon wall before bursting into flames on the rocky-dry riverbed below. As he watched the flames consume the limo and its occupants, he realized he was holding his breath. He expelled the pent-up air in his lungs and slumped in the cockpit, marveling at how the Storch was still flying after its steel-on-steel encounter. He figured he must have lost a chunk or two out of the prop because there was a new, seemingly asymmetrical vibration that wasn't there before. It didn't seem too bad, though, at least for now.

A feeling of incredible release swept through him.

The dumb-ass mission had threatened to take his life, but he was still alive. He was rid of the demons who killed Luisa. Monitoring the adversary frequencies again, he was pleased to hear the search for his aircraft was now concentrated a hundred miles to the north.

Five minutes later, over the westbound highway once again, with the terrain below now covered in lengthening shadows, the Storch suddenly staggered and seemed to stand still as a hail of .50-caliber ripped through the fuselage and Plexiglas canopy behind Mallory. In his weary euphoria, he hadn't monitored the radio or kept a good lookout for other aircraft. His head swiveled about until he located the speck of a government T-28 pulling up from its firing run and rolling into a left turn for another pass at him.

Shit! I've bought it now!

I'm-shit-out-of-luck, he thought, scanning forward to where the road threaded its way through the jagged spine of Central America's central plateau that rises to 5,000 feet. The pass was riddled with deep ravines, gorges, and box canyons. Carlos' territory and freedom lay to the west well beyond the pass and San Marcos.

No place to go, no place to hide.

His only chance was to stay low over the road through the pass. He pounded his knee in anger. This would be his second trip east to west after reversing course and chasing the limo most of the way back to Puerto Quintana.

"Okay, you bastard," he shouted, "we're going to have a go at it down there," and he rolled into a turn and headed for the deck. His only advantage was the Storch's maneuverability and incredible ability to almost hover like a helicopter. He could see the T-28 dropping down in pursuit and was relieved as it overshot and pulled back up without firing.

"Mistake One, Ace. You should have used your flaps."

He plunged into the narrow vee in the cliffs where the highway climbed toward the pass. There was little vehicular traffic so he dropped down to about thirty feet above the surface of the highway. He looked over his shoulder to keep track of the T-28. It was circling above while the pilot figured out his next move.

Mallory's face lit up with a devilish smile as he quickly tuned to the Costa Verde Air Force frequency and keyed the mike. "Hey, Stupid," he said in Spanish, "if you ever get your shit together, come on down here and show me what you've got." That should get his adrenaline flowing, he figured, and possibly screw up his judgment.

A string of Spanish expletives exploded into his headset as the T-28 banked for another pass. Suddenly, a myriad of voices filled Mallory's ear as a dozen or more Benes units monitoring the frequency chimed in, shouting questions, demanding to know what was happening.

Mallory's attacker didn't enlighten them. He obviously wanted this kill for himself. *Good!* Mallory thought.

He could see a grove of trees in the shadows ahead where he hoped the camouflaged Storch would blend with the background and make it harder for the adversary to define him as a target.

The T-28 opened fire just as Mallory turned sharp left, alongside and below the tops of the trees. His tormentor pulled up and barely missed the trees. The sound of the T-28's engine was deafening through the shattered Plexiglas behind Mallory. He thought he felt strikes on the right wing and hoped they went clean through without damaging any control surfaces.

The angry Spanish of the Costa Verdean pilot crackled in his headset, loud and clear. "Peralta . . . you . . . rich . . . bastard . . . this time I'm going to kill you!"

Mallory thought better of replying. Let the guy seethe until his judgment's gone. Gaining some altitude, he flew parallel to the right canyon wall and waited for the T-28's next run. Watching it line up for attack he suddenly turned the Storch at a 45-degree angle toward the canyon wall. Then at the instant he figured the adversary pilot was in the saddle for a shot, he turned even more sharply toward the cliff, now only a couple of hundred feet away.

As the T-28 fired, Mallory leveled his wings and deployed full flaps and leading edge wings slats. The Storch seemed to hover in mid-air a split second, then quickly levitated almost straight up.

The other pilot overshot—and flew straight into the canyon wall, the T-28 exploding in a huge yellow fireball.

"There you go again, Stupid. Chalk up another one to Target Fixation."

The night swallowed the Storch as Mallory overflew the northern fringes of San Marcos and continued on westward toward Bahia Pajaros under a thick cloud cover that blocked out the moon. The lights of a few scattered farmhouses were his only beacons. He was showing no lights himself, so that any planes still searching for him would have a needle-in-the-haystack problem.

He found the instrument panel rheostat and fully illuminated the basic instruments. Wings level, whatever else, he cautioned himself, keeping an eye glued to the artificial horizon. The altimeter read a little over 200 feet, the compass 245, west toward Bahia Pajaros and the freedom of Carlos' territory—if he could just get there.

Then it happened. The engine quit over the darkest of places with none of the comforting lights below. A glance at the fuel gauge showed him why. He had already drained the wing tanks into the main, so that was that.

Am I over hills? Fields? Trees? No time to locate the switch for the landing lights, Ace. Should have thought of that before.

The Storch was nose-heavy now as she slowed and the weight of the engine tipped her forward toward the ground that had to be there in the dark. He applied backward pressure on the oversized stick, instinctively trying to stretch flight as far as possible. As the airstream whistled through the ruptured Plexiglas behind him, the fear of death gripped him.

Suddenly the dark tops of large trees flew past below to the right. He veered left to avoid them, and thought he saw a clearing up ahead. Less than a hundred feet of altitude now and dropping.

No choices now. I'm going down here and now.

He tightened the harness and braced himself for crashing into whatever was there on the ground.

Please, God . . . don't let me die here!

The nearly flat soil of what he would call a truck farm in his native Southern California rose swiftly to meet him. The Storch kissed down on the soft earth with its usual grace and rolled to a stop just a few feet from a disinterested cow. The animal slowly swung its tail and turned its head away.

He collapsed against the instrument panel, breathing deeply and wondering if he made it as far as friendly territory. A moment later men were calling to one another and shouting military orders in Spanish. They surrounded the airplane. Mallory froze in the cockpit as he was caught in the beam of a high-powered flashlight. He blinked, trying to see his captors in the glare. A soldier mounted the ladder and poked an M-16 in his face.

"Quien es?" he demanded.

He was a pimply faced kid of maybe eighteen. Mallory could see a half dozen other assault rifles pointed at him from the ground.

"I am Decatur Mallory, Captain, United States Navy, serial number 6325574," he said in Spanish.

"Como?"

"I am an American Naval officer—"

The boy lowered the rifle a little, enabling Mallory to glimpse the black panther logo on his cammies. Mallory's body crumpled involuntarily in relief. "This airplane is *Señor* Peralta's personal transport," he managed to say.

When the boy repeated it for the others the cockpit was suddenly illuminated with muzzle flashes as they cut loose with bursts of gunfire to the sky amid hearty shouts of *"La Pantera Vive!"* The kid extended his hand. *"Bienvenido, Capitan!"*

Mallory climbed from the cockpit and stretched. "Got any gasoline?" he asked.

"I think we could spare you fifty *galones.*"

SIXTY-ONE

CAMPO ALTO

"It's time to go!" Peralta shouted, poking his head into the trailer. "This weather's getting worse by the minute, not better."

Mallory shoved the sat-phone into the leg pocket of the flight suit the Special Operations Forces had given him.

"Be right there," he said, as he instinctively scanned the room for belongings. He quickly remembered he hadn't brought any, save the Minox, which was zipped into a pocket on his sleeve.

Elena and Peralta waited outside where the rain was coming through the overhead camouflage with enough force to telegraph that there was a downpour out on the road, where an Air Force Special Operations Command MH-53 Pave Low helicopter was waiting. The helo was about 300 feet away but Mallory could tell at a glance that its strangely silent rotors were whirring at near take-off speed, as the pilots went through their checklist.

The three headed for the aircraft, walking slowly, with Peralta still on crutches. Elena slipped her arm through Mallory's and pulled close to him.

"It's hard to find the right words," Peralta said, with emotion. "We're all eternally grateful for what you've done for us." He smiled as he pulled a crutch out of a watery hole in the now muddy runway. "I've always known you're one hell of a pilot, but you outdid yourself for us."

Mallory shrugged. "You know the TOPGUN motto, Nacho. I fought as I was trained, and I was trained to out-think the adversary pilot."

"Well, you certainly did," Peralta said. "Maybe even more important, I think the prison raid and your take-out of those evil bastards in the limo is going to have a first-crack-in-the-wall effect on the morale of the government forces the way the Doolittle raid destroyed the myth of Tokyo's invulnerability."

"I hope you're right," he said, eyeing Peralta's leg.

"Don't worry about me," Peralta laughed. "Your flight surgeon said to dispense with the cast and crutches in a week or ten days. I'll be back in the saddle again."

"It'll be interesting," Mallory observed, "to see how well Benes holds up without funding from the cathedral."

"I still can't believe they actually tricked the Vatican," Elena said, "but God always vindicates his people." The statement left no doubt as to her faith.

Mallory hugged her against his side as they passed through the open clamshell doors of Campo Alto into the full force of the cold, driving downpour. He returned the salute of a Peraltista guarding the entrance with an automatic rifle. *The kid can't be more than sixteen,* he thought.

As they approached the waiting helo he could see that the crew and flight surgeon were already aboard. He stopped in the ankle-deep mud a few feet from the whirring rotors of the highly modified Sikorsky SH-60. Pulling the Browning from his flight suit, he slowly handed it to Peralta, who accepted it without a word and jammed it into his belt. A crew member leaning from the open door gestured for Mallory to hurry up.

Elena pressed her hot, tear-streaked face against Mallory's. "I think I love you, Deke."

458

Mallory wrapped his arms tightly around her. "I think I love you, too," he said. He pressed his lips to her ear and whispered. "I know you're the invincible Pantera, but please stay safe. I can't lose you, too."

He turned to Peralta and they gripped each other in a fierce *abrazo,* as the heavy rain suddenly increased to torrential. "You watch your six, Nacho."

"God be with you, Deke. Thanks for joining my war you tried so hard to avoid."

Mallory ducked toward the helicopter and climbed aboard, turning to wave at them from the door as the rotors spooled to takeoff speed.

Without even thinking, he heard himself shouting "I'll be back!" above the noise of the levitating machine.

Rising from a swirling column of muddy spray, the ungainly black aircraft turned to the east and skimmed the roof of the jungle. As it gathered speed and disappeared over the tops of the trees, Elena ran to where it had stood moments before. With her face to the sky, and the rain pelting her drenched form, she waved until all she could hear was the sound of the downpour.

SIXTY-TWO

The air bubbles popping in the sand swept by the receding surf were of considerable interest to the sandpipers running after them like little wind-up toys, as Mallory and David walked along the shoreline. The salt air, the sound of the waves, the cry of gulls, and the chance to walk barefoot in their bathing suits provided a welcome tonic after the frantic pace of testing the Lockheed Martin X-35 JSF prototypes in final preparation for sea trails.

Mallory had spent the last several days at NAS Patuxent River, Maryland, solving glitches in the engine vectoring nozzle. The X-35 was finally declared ready for deployment and Mallory had flown one of them to the Naval Air Warfare Center Weapons Division Station at Point Mugu, a few miles north of here. Test pilots and tech reps from Lockheed, Northrop Grumman and other contractors had assembled there for final preparation before sea trials. Soon Mallory and his Navy pilots would polish their field carrier landing skills prior to receiving the prototype aboard USS *Ronald Reagan,* CVN-76, off the California coast.

He stopped to ponder his son, who was now at UCLA Law School and would be driving him back to Magu tonight. "It's good to feel this very sand in my toes again," he said. "I left a lot of footprints here when I was at UCLA myself. My officer's jacket says I'm a senior naval officer, but I'm just a sandy-footed surf bum at heart."

David laughed. "I come here as often as I can for hydrotherapy when the work load at school gets me down. The energy of these curlers can drain off lots of angst."

"That's why we're here, isn't it, Son?"

"Dad, I just can't believe you did what you did in Costa Verde. Tracking down the rogue agent and terminating his rat, your Spiderman gig, offing the hit team after the chase, and taking out half the enemy air force. You must be the toast of every O-Club."

"Not really. You realize, don't you, that none of this ever happened?"

"Right. Mister Truman and all that stuff."

They walked in silence for a while, scattering strolling gulls that retreated to higher ground.

David stopped. "I'm glad you told me you flew the Bearcat over the prison. Mister Truman was vague about that part, but I figured it out. Nacho may be a real good pilot, but he couldn't be that good. It had to be you."

Mallory shrugged. "I guess you were bound to realize it, sooner or later."

David turned to face his father. "There's one thing I haven't figured out," he said. "The real truth about Mom, well, it still eludes me."

Mallory realized the moment had arrived.

"I wasn't the only bullshit prisoner in that stinking hole. They were political prisoners, not criminals. They fervently believed their country was controlled by some kind of German Mafia. I guess they were right on, too."

"That information is in the need-to-know category and you're not in that loop."

"I understand that, but there's a common thread to what little I do know."

"Oh?" Mallory tried to give it the light touch.

"Think about it, Dad!" David's eyes flashed. "*One,* Mom comes back from visiting in Costa Verde and gets shot by skinheads on the freeway. Skinheads! Dad. *Two,* we show up down there and they bust me for a bullshit reason and I wind up incarcerated with some very solid citizens who got in the way of city hall. One guy was head of a bank taken over by an offer they shouldn't refuse, á la *The Godfather. Three,* you wind up with a hit team on your six. What's missing in this picture, Dad?"

Mallory felt his jaw tighten.

"There has to be a common denominator. Mom's death was *not* coincidental." He fixed his father with a laser stare. "There's more to the story, isn't there?"

They walked in silence before Mallory found the right words. "You'll make a fine lawyer," he said, as he sat down on a high bank of sand a few feet from the water line. "Yes there's more to it and, yes, I think you should know. Your mother's death—" He shook his head. "She . . . she was targeted for death."

David sank onto the sand beside Mallory. "But the police report and the papers? They said just another road-rage shooting."

"That's what I thought until I found out otherwise at the cathedral."

"You mean Mom was intentionally murdered?" David mumbled softly.

"Yes, she was."

David bristled. "What did you find out?"

"Mom's camera. The little gold Minox they took when our house was broken into. It was on one of the impostor's desk. Elena told me that Mom had snapped their picture at the airport in Bahia Pajaros like she was always doing for her paintings. Maybe they thought it would blow their cover, I don't know. How they managed to track us down and orchestrate her death, I don't know that either. Skinheads are

Nazi-oriented, but I can't take it any further than that. There's a lot I don't know."

David tensed, hunched over with his head on his knees, and dug his feet into the sand.

Mallory continued. "After the spider thing, I was next on the hit parade. They even tried to assassinate Elena." Mallory let out a huge sigh and caught his breath. "I began to hate their filthy Nazi guts and anyone connected with them. I guess I had a lot of rage in the cockpit that day above the prison. And that last time too."

"What last time?"

Mallory waited until he had his emotions under control before he spoke. "There's no need for you ever to think about revenge, son. The account is balanced now. I ran the cathedral car straight off a cliff. At least three or four of them died in the crash, including the ringleader." He returned David's gaze and then looked out to sea. "They were evil men and I'm glad they're dead. I guess I have no real feelings about killing them, either. No more than shooting the rat in what's-his-name's hotel room. No more than I suppose your namesake felt when he killed Goliath and cut off his head."

David sat clenching fistfuls of sand and then he suddenly leapt to his feet, dashed into the surf, and dove over an incoming wave.

Mallory, too, needed the energy of the waves for closure. He plunged into the surf and followed David through the breakers, stroking hard for the blue-green curl of what he hoped was the power-packed ninth wave of the set.

EPILOGUE

WASHINGTON, D.C.

Mallory shed the blouse of his dress blues and draped it over his favorite wingback chair. Stripping off his tie and unbuttoning his collar, he walked to the sliding glass door, slid it open and stepped outside to the spacious brick terrace of his Georgetown condo. He stood at the balustrade inhaling the fresh fall air and taking in the effect of the setting sun on the vibrant pallet of fall colors and the silver-gray Potomac unfurling to the west, with Georgetown University to the right, the span of the Francis Scott Key Bridge in the foreground, and Arlington in the distance across the river. He tried to forget the lousy day up on Capitol Hill where Connie Frazier and he got a thorough blistering from angry Senators who were tooling up for election year by pouncing on alleged cost overruns and poor performance of the Navy's portion of the JSF Program.

Nothing was farther from the truth. Military officers hauled on the carpet can hardly cut loose and straighten out their legislative tormentors. Besides, ever since Tailhook the Navy had been the service target of choice on Capitol Hill. So he and Frazier had been spotlighted in a shallow hearing-room pit, well below the high-backed, leather-covered seats of the mighty—schoolboys sent to the principal's office, trying to make sense out of endless questions being put in the form of self-congratulatory ramblings that always seemed to end up with a "when-did-you-stop-beating-your-wife?" zinger. Mallory wondered if the subcommittee's Senators really gave a damn about anything but themselves.

With the end of the week-long hearings an hour ago, he could forget it all now, get a night's sleep and return to the USS *Ronald Reagan*, now at Norfolk but scheduled to put to sea in a few days. He could hardly wait to take to the air again and put this bullshit behind him.

He watched the smooth strokes of the George Washington University crew practicing on the river as the sun neared the overcast hugging the Western horizon. As their racing shells slid along like water bugs, he realized how much he had come to enjoy Washington. As a third-generation Californian, he looked forward to retiring in La Jolla, but Luisa's death changed that. When he traded California stucco for the red brick of Georgetown, it seemed to fit. He began to appreciate the old tree-lined streets here and the sights of official Washington. When in town he found he was an inveterate visitor to the Smithsonian, the National Gallery, the Library of Congress, the Archives, and other magnets of history and culture. Wherever the future might take him, he would hang onto this condo and maintain his connection with the nation's capital. The only remnants of earlier periods of his life, other than family photographs and a wall of Navy memories, were the antiques Luisa had skillfully assembled over the years and some of her paintings, including his favorite seascape of the mica-flecked beach at La Jolla Shores.

He turned away from the peaceful scene as the setting sun glinted from the golden dome of the old Riggs National Bank at N Street and Wisconsin a couple of blocks east and was headed to the bar when the doorbell rang.

Now, who the hell is that? Can't I just have a peaceful evening with a couple of drinks and my fire?

He opened the door to a polka-dot bow tie, capped with the smiling face of Terry Truman.

"Sarah's out of town," Truman said. "After that contentious Senate hearing today, I figured you could use a medicinal scotch," he held up a paper bag, "to heal the fulminations of Senator Follett, who sure as hell pushed the limits of rationality with you and Connie today." Oregon Senator Barbara Follett was the subcommittee's chairman.

Mallory quickly recovered from his tentative foul state of mind. "You've come to the right place," he declared, ushering Truman in and closing the door.

"Well, the Senator does seem to combine the Wicked Witch of the West's charm with a Flower Child's grasp of national defense issues." He took the Glenlivet and reached for two glasses from the bar. "Come on out on the terrace. We'll splice-the-main-brace."

————————

The orange sun squashed itself onto the horizon as Truman relaxed in his deck chair, enjoying the view and the prospects of a lingering twilight.

"What do you hear from Peralta?" he asked.

Mallory shook his head. "Not much, with the war dragging on. You must know more than I do."

Truman didn't seem to want to talk about the progress of the war. He was gathering sheaves, not planting seeds.

"What did you think of Carlos?" he asked. "I only know him by phone, but he seems like a heads-up guy."

"You probably know him better than I by this time," Mallory said. "I think he's the second coming of Vinegar Joe Stillwell. If any field commander can win in those jungles, he can. You should back him to the hilt."

Truman changed the subject. "Tell me about you and Elena. Any romance here?"

Mallory brightened. "She's more beautiful than ever and one hell of a woman." He seemed to be transported as he gazed out at the view.

467

He rose from his chair and went to the colonial secretary just inside the door. When he returned he handed Truman a small velvet-covered box. Truman opened the lid and inspected the diamond solitaire in its Tiffany setting. He handed it back with a smile.

"Terrific!" he said, clinking his glass with Mallory's.

"My problem now is waiting for the war to end so I can go back there and give it to her."

He freshened their drinks as Truman closed his eyes and shook his head. "It was terrible what happened to your friend with the motor-cycle."

"It hurt like hell when I heard about it."

Mallory told about Arturo facing down the T-28 pilot, while the United States Navy watched from the bushes.

"Must have been a hell of a guy," Truman said.

"I just can't believe I was involved in all that."

Truman laughed. "Well," he said, "as keeper of our nation's dark secrets, I can assure you that you're the only ace in aviation history who claims but one of his five kills. The other four don't exist."

Mallory shrugged.

"You did what had to be done in the circumstances," Truman continued. "Don't worry, I'm the only one who knows all about these things. Well," he said with a shrug, "the Fox knows but if it ever comes out it will be long after we're all dead and buried."

"You're sure?"

Truman smiled and held up three fingers of his right hand. "Scout's honor. And what about David? Has he recovered from being there at the wrong time?"

"He's together. He finished his first year near the top of his law school class but after what he's experienced, and being bilingual, I doubt he'll be content with the law. Hell, T-Square, he could want your job some day."

Truman grinned. "He'll make his mark for sure."

"I think the grill's hot enough now. How do you like your steak?"

468

"The rarer the better."

"I'll double that order," Mallory said, inspecting two filets and placing them on the grill.

They ate slowly, savoring the meal, the soft night air, and recalling the strange events that brought their lives together.

"What about the Kohorte?" Mallory asked. "They must have been a pretty extensive operation."

Truman cut his last slice of steak. "That's right," he said. "We're finding out more every day. Right now our main objective is identifying the leaders who've stepped in to fill the vacuum created by Tolt's death."

Mallory stiffened at hearing the Kohorte was still functioning.

Truman looked at him with raised eyebrows. "We know that Tolt made a mad dash for Puerto Quintana," he said, "just as a Vatican posse closed in on the cathedral. He never made it. According to witnesses, an airplane forced the cathedral limo off a cliff." He looked up at Mallory. "Now, you wouldn't know anything about that, would you?"

Mallory carefully set his wine glass down. "I know he damn well got what he deserved," he said, softly.

Truman smiled slightly. "A couple of his immediate staff were in that car too."

Mallory's jaw tightened. "Which ones?" He felt his adrenaline pumping. "What about the one with Luisa's camera on his desk? He probably ordered her death."

"If he wasn't in the car, he's still at large. There are unconfirmed reports of one of them fleeing to Montevideo. There are professional Nazi hunters already on the trail, along with one of my guys."

"I hope to hell they all roasted," Mallory said.

They sat in silence, watching the Key Bridge.

Mallory turned to face Truman. "How could they pull off the charade? I mean the Vatican runs a taut ship, don't they? Unless it was an inside job."

Truman nodded. "Yes, it was an inside job. A mole Tolt had planted decades before rose to a high post. He arranged for them to assume the identities of some priests they murdered under the protection of the head of the Communist East German secret police. Everything else flowed from that. When confronted by Peralta's emissary to the Vatican, Monsignor Mole confessed everything and supplied some information about the Kohorte. But the Kohorte's a compartmentalized operation, so I don't think he really knew all that much. He's been confined at a monastery in Northern Italy. Their Secretary of State's embarrassed as hell about the whole thing, of course."

Mallory nodded. "Was Burton a traitor?"

"Despite everything, I still felt I could trust him. He retired last month, so it's not as important anymore.

"Holloway was the real culprit. He finally disappeared, like he planned, but without as much cash as he dreamed about before you scared shit out of him with your theatrical hit on his pet rat. He finally got to work and put together a white paper the Administration may use to suggest a plan for scrapping the remaining armaments Nicaragua received from the Soviets. Some Nicaraguan officers have been jailed for complicity in a Kohorte-sponsored theft ring that amassed tanks and artillery pieces at a jungle depot near the Costa Verde border. Apparently, Tolt was going to deploy the stuff eventually to threaten his neighbors."

"It's scary how close we came," Mallory observed, "to having a Nazi country right in our own backyard."

"Right, but don't forget that Colonel Benes is a neo-Nazi himself. Yet the Fox is having to work around much the same problem that faced the Reagan Administration in supporting the Contras against the Sandinistas in Nicaragua."

Mallory nodded. "Yeah, I know," he said. "I guess the general public is still phobic about the possibility of getting into another Viet Nam."

Truman shrugged. "That's why, except for keeping the key leaders of Congress on both sides of the aisle informed, we're keeping pretty quiet about our aide to Peralta."

Mallory walked to the balustrade and turned to face Truman. "There's something I want to know about Luisa's death. I can see how a photo might identify them, but they already had new identities, so why would a tourist's snapshot bother them? I can't see why they killed her."

"I can," Truman said, after a moment. "I didn't want to open old wounds, but since you asked I'll tell you what we found out. As I'm sure you know, there are whacko militia and skinhead groups here, in South America, and in the UK and Europe. There're more than a thousand Nazi-leaning hate groups you can contact on the Internet right here in this country alone. One in particular started in California and now claims to have about five thousand members nationwide. This group doesn't have a given turf like most gangs. They're rovers, Deke, and their sideline is being on call when the Kohorte puts out a contract in the States. We learned via a defector that they were activated to target your wife. She was under surveillance upon returning from Costa Verde, and the hit was planned to look like a road-rage thing. We don't know the actual perps, only that it was the work of this gang, as was the break-in for the camera."

Mallory shook his head in silence. "But I still don't see why they thought the simple act of a lady snapping their picture would endanger them. Hell, they were already posing as priests and getting away with it big-time."

"Don't forget that it was early in the great charade. Once they established themselves at the cathedral it shouldn't have made a difference. But they were only just arriving in Costa Verde when Luisa spotted them, so they probably overreacted.

"When you figure out the Nazi mind," Truman continued with a sigh, "let me know. I've been trying for years."

Mallory shook his head again. "You don't seem to think we've seen the last. How long can Nazism keep going?"

"Just about as long as there are two kinds of people left in the world," Truman said, leaning his backside against the balustrade. "The ignorant who think that Nazism died with Hitler and the malevolent who become Nazis for the classic reason."

"Classic reason?"

"The low barrier to membership, of course. Nazism has the lowest barrier to membership of any group in the world. All you have to do is say you're a Nazi and, *ipso facto,* you are one, with full right and privilege to lay claim to all the Wagnerian secret society bullshit you could ever imagine, and the license to hate whoever you want to hate—which, when you think of it, is the easiest thing to do in the first place."

"What do you think keeps Nazism going?"

"Evil, of course, a spiritual force. There's evil in the world, you know. I've seen it in my own experience.

"I've said all this before," Truman continued, pointing over his shoulder in the direction of the Capitol and the White House. "Many times, to members of Congress, to the Cabinet, and to presidents in the privacy of the Oval Office. Some listened pretty well. Oddly enough, the Fox takes me more seriously than any of the others. Some didn't listen at all, thought I was a paranoid old spook living in the past, who doesn't understand the realities of today's world." He shrugged and turned around to lean over the balustrade. "The old Nazis are dying off but there are young people out there who think they're the true heirs to Hitler's malignant dream of a Thousand-Year Reich—disaffected, tattooed, leather-clad gangs, gathering strength and seeking any vacuums that provide breeding grounds for their virulent credo. We didn't kill the beast in 1945, Deke, like we thought we did. We just wounded it."

Mallory's jaw tightened. "Yes, but the War on Terrorism has our attention now, as it damn well should. It's like Nazism's gone into remission somehow."

Truman smiled thinly. "Remission? Don't forget that remission is the temporary abatement of a disease. No, Nazism's still out there tonight, like the wounded monster in a creepy sci-fi movie, waiting to slip into the creases, where we least expect it. Skinheads in Germany have begun showing up at rallies wearing their jeans, jackboots, and leather topped, of all things, with Palestinian headdress! You can bet we're keeping tabs on that one, given the Neo-Nazi's and Islamic extremists' shared hatred of the U.S."

Mallory walked back to the table and poured the remains of the Glenlivet into their glasses. When he returned they both leaned over the balustrade. Slowly nodding his head, Mallory raised his glass. Truman raised his and they both stared silently out over the Potomac.

Their thoughts were unspoken as they finished their drinks. No words were necessary.

ABOUT THE AUTHORS

HOWARD LAWSON is a former carrier based Navy fighter pilot qualified in over 30 types of military and civilian aircraft, including the Bearcat. With two previous books in print, he has been a contributing editor of local newspapers and magazines in California and Washington, writing on aviation, adventure and travel. He is a member of Tailhook and the Association of Naval Aviation. He lives in Elk Grove, California.

RON SPEERS is an attorney admitted to practice in both California and the District of Columbia. For more than twenty years he was Top Secret Cleared for the black world of the intelligence community as a director of Logicon, a principal supplier of highly classified services to the Navy, Army, Air Force, Marines and the CIA. He is an associate member of Tailhook and a member of the U.S. Naval Institute, and lives in Newport Beach, California.

ACKNOWLEDGMENTS

THE AUTHORS ARE INDEBTED TO THE FOLLOWING FOR THEIR VALUABLE ASSISTANCE IN THE WRITING OF THIS NOVEL:

RADM Robert McClinton, USN (Ret), for his advice regarding Navy regulations;

CAPT Steve Millikin, USN (Ret) and CDR Doug Siegfried, USN (Ret), Editor and Contributing Editor, respectively, of *The Hook, The Journal of Naval Aviation*, for their generous contribution to cover design;

LCDR Matthew Paradise, USN, Air Wing Landing Signal Office in USS *Kitty Hawk*, (CV-63), for his careful reading of the F/A-18 Hornet chapters;

LCDR Tom Popp, USN, NAS Patuxent River, and his wife, Ruth (USNA 1989) for their encouragement;

Roger Seybel, of the Northrup Grumman Corporation History Center, for details of the operating systems of the F8F Bearcat;

Ken Snyder, of the Naval Aviation Museum, Pensacola, Florida, for his personal recollection of the flight characteristics of the Bearcat;

The Naval Aviators of VFA-125, Naval Air Station Lemoore, California, for their advice regarding the operational envelope of the F/A-18 Hornet;

Captain Mark Bjorklund, for his extensive knowledge of Central America and the Caribbean;

Anna Jimenez Lawson, for her familiarity with Latin American society and culture;

Ann Foreman, for her judicious attention to editorial detail;

Gina Speers for her cover design; and

Ken Sadlock of Digital ReTouching, for enhancing the cover photograph.

AN HISTORICAL NOTE

REGARDING THE LEGENDARY GRUMMAN F8F BEARCAT:

With twice the climb rate and roll rate of the Grumman F6F Hellcat, the workhorse of the carrier Navy during World War II, the Grumman F8F Bearcat was designed for quick response to attack and could climb from a carrier deck to 10,000 feet in 90 seconds. It first flew in August 1944 and was deployed with VF-19 aboard USS *Langley* (CVL-27) in 1945, but the war came to an end while the squadron was enroute to the Pacific theater. Returning to NAAS Santa Rosa, California, the squadron continued their training in the new fighter, and soon became known for embarrassing Army pilots on the West Coast. When the squadron's skipper was challenged by the CO of a nearby P-38 squadron, serious money was bet on whether, following a section take-off, the Bearcat could gain enough altitude for an overhead gunnery run on the Lightning before the P-38 could raise its wheels. LCDR Joe Smith actually completed a second pass before the Army pilot got his gear up. One contributing factor to this remarkable performance was the fact the Bearcat could be airborne in less than 200 feet.

The later F8F-2, armed with 20 mm cannons, could reach 455 mph, and highly modified Bearcats still compete in the National Air Races at speeds in excess of 500 mph. The Navy's Blue Angels flew Bearcats from 1946 to 1948, when they were replaced by Grumman F9F Panther jets.